MW01625109

DEAD
AFTER DARK

DEAD AFTER DARK

SHERRILYN KENYON

J.R. WARD

SUSAN SQUIRES

DIANNA LOVE

This is a work of fiction. All of the characters, organizations, and events portrayed in this novel are either products of the author's imagination or are used fictitiously.

DEAD AFTER DARK

For information address St. Martin's Press, 175 Fifth Avenue, New York, NY 10010.

ISBN: 978-1-60751-409-1

Printed in the United States of America

St. Martin's Paperbacks are published by St. Martin's Press, 175 Fifth Avenue, New York, NY 10010.

CONTENTS

SHADOW OF THE MOON

by

Sherrilyn Kenyon

1

New Orleans

Fury Kattalakis was about to walk straight into the dragon's lair. Well, not exactly. There *was* a dragon in the attic of the building he was headed toward, but that dragon wasn't nearly as dangerous to Fury as the bear guarding the door.

That nasty sonofabitch hated his guts.

Not that he cared. Most people and animals hated his guts which was fine by him. He didn't have much use for the world anyway.

"The things you do for family," Fury said under his breath. Though to be honest, this whole family concept was still new to him. He was more used to being screwed over by everyone around him. It wasn't until his brother Vane had taken him in during the summer of '04 that he'd realized not everyone in the universe was out to kill him.

The bear, however, still was . . .

Dev Peltier tensed as soon as he saw Fury step out of the shadows near the door of Sanctuary—a rough biker bar and dance club that stood at 688 Ursulines. Like that address hadn't been chosen intentionally by the bear clan who owned it. They were nothing if not ironic.

Dressed in a black Sanctuary staff t-shirt and jeans, the bear looked human at present, complete with long curly blond hair, black biker boots, and a pair of sharp eyes that missed no detail or weakness, not that Fury had a weakness. But for all of Dev's human appearance, to those lycanthropes such as Fury, Dev's alternate form was like a thrumming beacon that warned all otherworldly types that Dev was ferocious.

Then again, so was Fury. What he lacked in magick abilities, he more than made up for in sheer strength . . .

And FU attitude and anger.

No one got the better of him. Ever.

"What are *you* doing here?" Dev growled.

Fury shrugged nonchalantly and decided that a fight wouldn't get him inside—which was what he'd promised to do. Him . . . keeping a promise to someone other than himself . . . yeah. Right. Hell was freezing over. He still wasn't really sure how he'd allowed his brother Fang to talk him into this act of blatant suicide.

The bastard owed him.

Big Time.

"Peace, brother." Fury held his hands up in mock surrender. "I'm just here to see Sasha."

Dev bared his teeth threateningly as he raked a glare over Fury's body that normally would have caused Fury to slug him for the insult. Damn, his brother Vane was rubbing off on him. "The Kattalakis patria isn't welcome here and you know it."

Fury arched a brow as he looked up at the sign over Dev's head. Flat black with electric blue and brown, it held a motorcycle on a hill that was silhouetted by a full moon. It also proclaimed Sanctuary to be the home of the Howlers, the house band. To the unobservant, it looked like any other club sign. But to those born cursed, like them, the shadows in the moon formed the outline of a dragon rising—a hidden symbol to the preternatural beings the world over.

This club wasn't just named Sanctuary, it was one. And all paranormal entities were allowed inside where no one could harm them. At least so long as they obeyed the first rule of a limani: No spill blood.

Fury tsked at Dev. "You know the laws of our people. You can't pick and choose who enters. All are welcomed equally."

"Fuck you," Dev snarled.

Fury shook his head as he bit back his natural caustic retort. Instead, he decided to handle it with biting sarcasm. "Thank you so much for the offer, but while you do have a certain feminine quality in your demeanor and a remarkable head of hair that any woman would envy, you're far too hairy for my tastes. No offense."

Dev curled his lip. "Since when does a dog care about what it humps?"

Fury sucked his breath in sharply. "I could go so low with that that even the gutter would envy us, but . . . I know what you're trying to do. You're trying to provoke a fight with me so that you can legally turn me away."

He clenched his fists, and he made a show of struggling with what he wanted to do and what he'd promised to do. "I really, really want to give you that fight, too, but I have to see Sasha and it can't wait. Sorry. We'll have to hump and fight later."

Dev growled threateningly, a pure grizzly sound. "You're on thin ice, Wolf."

Fury sobered and narrowed his gaze to that of his wolf form. When he spoke, his voice was low and feral and filled with the promise of whup-ass that was waiting if Dev wanted to continue this game. "Shut up, sod off, and let me in."

Dev took a step toward him.

Faster than Fury could even tense in expectation of the

hit Dev was about to deliver, Colt was there. A head taller than both of them, Colt had short, jet-black hair and lethal eyes. He put one large paw of a tattooed hand on Dev's chest and held him back.

"Don't do it, Dev," Colt said in a low, even tone. "He's not worth it."

Fury should probably have been insulted, but the truth had never bothered him. "He's right. I'm a worthless bastard fathered by a bastard even more worthless than I am. You definitely don't want to have your sanctuary license pulled over the likes of me."

Dev shrugged away Colt's touch, which caused the sleeve of his shirt to pull up and expose the double bow and arrow tattoo on his arm. "Whatever. But we're watching you, Wolf."

Fury gave him a one-finger salute. "Then I'll try not to piss on the floor or hump the furniture . . ." He glanced down at Dev's black, silver-studded boot. "Your leg, though, might be another matter."

Dev growled again while Colt laughed and tightened his hold.

Colt indicated the door with a jerk of his chin. "Get your ass inside, Fury, before I decide to feed you to him."

"I'm seriously not worth the indigestion." With an antagonistic wink at Dev, Fury sauntered past them to enter the bar where the music was loud and pumping, something that made the wolf in him want to whine in protest as it assaulted his heightened hearing.

Since Colt was one of the Howlers, they weren't on stage yet. But there was already a good-sized crowd gathered. Tourists and regulars were dancing or milling about on the first level of the three-story bar. No doubt it was just as crowded on the second floor, too. The third floor, however, was reserved for their kind only.

Fury tucked his hands into his back pockets as he moved

through the people. It was easy to spot the bikers from the others since many of them were old school and covered in leather. The younger, hipper crowd wore nylon or Aerostitch suits like his while the tourists and college kids wore everything from short skirts to khaki pants to jeans.

As Fury passed the tables where customers could sit down and eat, he caught the gaze of the beautiful blond waitress who just happened to be the sister of the asshole outside.

Aimee Peltier.

Like her brother Dev, her long hair was blond, and she was tall and thin. Lithe. All in all, very attractive except for the fact that when she went to bed at night, she turned into a bear. He shuddered at the thought. His brother's taste in women left a lot to be desired.

Aimee froze the moment she saw him.

He subtly indicated the bar with his eyes to let her know he had a message for her. She was the real reason he was here, but if any of her numerous brothers found that out, they'd both be dead.

So he continued on his way to the bar where three bartenders were making drinks. Since Dev was one of a set of identical quads, Fury felt like he was seeing double as another werebear came over to him. The only reason he could pick out Dev from his other three identical brothers was from the tattoo on his arm. With the other three, well, he really didn't give a rat's ass about who it was.

The quad narrowed his eyes threateningly. "What you want, Wolf?"

Nonchalant, Fury sat down. "Tell Sasha I need to see him."

"Why you need to see him?"

Fury gave him a droll stare. "Wolf business, and the last time I sniffed, which I'm trying real hard not to do 'cause the stench of you assholes is rough on my heightened sense of smell, you're a bear. Grab his hide and send it over."

"Do you have to piss off everyone you meet?" That soft voice went down his spine like a caress.

He turned to find Margarite Neely standing beside him. Tiny and human, Margery had one of the finest posteriors he'd ever seen on a woman. But therein was the problem. She was human, and he had a hard time relating to that breed, or any breed for that matter. Social skills were so not his forte. Like Margery had pointed out, he tended to piss off anyone dumb enough to come near him. Even when he didn't mean to.

"It's a congenital habit that serves me well most days."

Laughing, she held a bottle of beer out toward him.

Fury shook his head, declining the offer. That stuff on his tastebuds . . . nasty. He frowned at her. "I'm surprised to see you down here." She was the nurse for the Peltiers, and he normally only saw her when he was injured and in need of care. As a rule, she avoided the bar area and stayed in the hidden hospital that was attached to it.

She took a swig of beer. "Yeah, but there's some bad mojo going down. I had to have a drink to steady my nerves."

Since he'd never known her to drink, that intrigued him. "What kind of bad mojo?"

Sasha joined them and answered for her. "There's a Litarian in Carson's office."

Fury scowled at Sasha, whose face was pale. If he didn't know better, he'd think the wolf was shaken. "Yeah, so? There's a lot of shit in his office most days." Carson was the resident doctor and veterinarian that all the Were-Hunters in New Orleans went to when they were in need of medical services. The fact that he had a lion in his hospital shouldn't even cause an eyebrow to raise.

Margery shook her head at him. "Not like this, Fury. He can't turn human or use his magick."

Now *that* was shocking. "What did you say?"

"The Arcadians hit him with something," she said in a

low tone as if afraid of being overheard. "We don't know what. But it drained his powers instantly. He can't even project his thoughts to his mate."

Fury couldn't breathe at the thought of that happening. Even though his base and primary form was that of a wolf and he lacked a lot of magick control, he still couldn't imagine what it would be like to live entirely as an animal. "And you're sure he's not a regular lion?" It was a stupid question, but one that had to be stated.

They both gave him a "duh" stare.

Fury held his hands up in surrender. "Just checking. You guys could have had an aneurysm or something."

Margery took a deep draught of her beer. "It's been a bad day."

"Yeah," Sasha agreed, taking the bottle from her and duplicating the gesture. "We're all rattled by it. Imagine minding your own business and having a tessera come out of nowhere, pop your ass with something we can't identify, and then losing yourself forever."

Fury let out a long breath. "I saw that movie once. It sucked."

Sasha bowed his head sheepishly as he remembered Fury's past. "Sorry, man. I didn't mean anything by it."

No one ever did. Yet it stung regardless of intent.

"You needed to see me?" Sasha asked, changing the subject.

Fury checked his peripheral vision to make sure none of the bear clan were nearby. Then he gave a pointed look at Margery. "We have a bit of Wolf business, if you don't mind."

"It's all right. I need to get back upstairs anyway. The Litarian's mate had to be tranqed earlier and she should be coming out of it any moment." She stepped past him to slap the bar to get the Bear's attention. "Remi, give me one more bottle and I'm back to work."

Fury choked at her words. "Glad I'm not the patient."

Margery gave him a chiding glare. "It's for Carson."

He snorted. "And I repeat what I said. Just what I need, a bunch of drunk fucks working on me." He met Sasha's amused expression. "Remind me not to do anything stupid tonight. Oh wait, I'm here. Too late for that warning, huh?"

Sasha ignored that question as he crossed his arms over his chest and shifted his weight to one leg. "What do you need, Fury? We're not exactly friendly."

Fury led him a few feet away from where Remi was handing off another bottle of beer to Margery. "I know, but you're the only wolf the Peltiers aren't suspicious of and the only one I could trust to get this to Aimee." He palmed the small note into Sasha's hand. "Make sure you wipe your ass with it or something to get the stench of Fang off it. I did what I could, but he's pretty fragrant."

Sasha looked less than pleased by the request. "You know the last time I involved myself in subterfuge, I was mortally wounded and branded, and saw my entire clan put down over it. Take my advice and don't let your brother drag you down with him."

"Yeah, but I'm not stepping in between two gods." Which was what had almost gotten Sasha killed. "I'm just doing a favor for my brother."

"That's what I told myself, too. But the problem with family, they get you into shit and then abandon you to it. Or worse, get themselves killed off."

It was true, and he knew it. But he owed Vane and Fang for welcoming him in when no one else ever had.

For his brothers alone, he was willing to die.

"So will you give her the note?"

Sasha ground his teeth. "I'll do it. But you owe me."

Actually Fang owed him, but . . . they were brothers, and for the first time in his life, he understood what that meant. "I know and I really appreciate it."

Sasha slid the paper into his back pocket. "You know what really kills me over this is that I've never seen two animals act more human. What kind of Romeo-Juliet bullshit are they playing anyway?"

Fury shrugged. "Hell if I know. He says she's the only one who understands him. Given the girly way he's been acting lately, I actually agree with that 'cause I definitely don't get any of it. If he starts wearing lipstick and pink, I vote we take him out and shoot him. Put his whiny ass out of *my* misery."

The corner of Sasha's lips curled up as if he were trying not to smile.

"What are *you* doing here?"

Fury tensed at the sound of Nicolette "Mama" Peltier's deep French accent. Since his brother was making time with Mama's only daughter, Aimee, he more than understood her hostility toward their entire clan, but it didn't mean that he appreciated the tone.

He started to tell her what she could do with it, but before he could draw breath to answer, Sasha spoke up. "I asked him to come. I wanted to warn him about what happened to the Litarian."

Mama relaxed a degree, but her expression was still deeply troubled. "That's bad business there." She cast her gaze around the room as if looking for someone suspicious. "May the gods take mercy on us all if we don't stop the ones behind this. I shudder at the thought of what else they might be capable of."

So did Fury. "Are the bears doing anything to find out who's responsible?"

She shook her head. "*Non*, the laws of sanctuary prohibit it."

"Then I'll do some digging."

Sasha snorted. "You just can't help this kamikaze streak you have, can you?"

Fury grinned. "Not really. I find it easiest if I just go with it rather than fight it. Besides, if someone is screwing with us, I want to know who and how. Most of all, I want their throat for it."

Respect glowed in Nicolette's eyes. She looked at Sasha. "Take him upstairs before too many scents contaminate the lion so that he can track the ones who did this."

Sasha inclined his head to Nicolette before he motioned for Fury to follow after him.

Fury didn't speak as they left the bar and headed through the kitchen and into Peltier House. Once they were out of sight of any humans, Sasha used his powers to vanish and pop into the doctor's office on the second floor. Fury was a little more cautious.

Because no one had mentored him on how to use his magick when he hit puberty, his control of it was less than desirable. More to the point, he refused to let anyone know just how little control he had. No one knew his shortcomings and lived to tell them.

So he walked up the stairs to the rooms that were set aside for medical aid.

As soon as he entered the small office area, he saw Margery, Carson, and Sasha waiting for him.

"Why didn't you follow me?" Sasha snapped.

"I did."

"Yeah but—"

Fury interrupted him. "I'm not leaving a power trail for one of you assholes to use against me. Walking works for me. So where's this lion?"

Carson stepped to the back of the office where another door led into the hospital area. "I have him in here."

Fury followed him. As soon as he entered the sterile room, he froze. There was a woman leaning over the lion on the gurney, weeping. She had one hand buried deep in his mane while the other was lying palm-up on the table. In the center of her palm was the elaborate design that marked her as someone's mate. The affection she showed toward the lion made it a safe bet that he was hers.

"Anita?" Carson said gently. "This is Fury Kattalakis. He's here to help find the ones who did this."

Sniffing, she lifted her head to give him a look that said she wasn't impressed with his offer. "My pride is after the ones who caused it."

"Yeah," Carson said gently, "but the more trackers we have, the more chances to find them and hopefully get a cure."

"We are lions—"

"And I'm a wolf," Fury said, cutting her off. "If I need raw brutality and force, I'll call you. But if you're looking for someone who did you wrong, nothing tracks better than one of us."

Carson put his hand on the woman's arm. "He's right, Anita. Let him see if he can help us find the culprits before they prey on someone else."

She tightened her hand in the lion's mane before she got up and stepped away.

Fury approached the table slowly. "Is he fully animal or does he retain any human rationale?"

Carson sighed. "We're not sure."

Those words wrung a deep sob from the woman.

Fury ignored her and approached the table. The lion growled low as Fury neared him. It was an animal warning. The wolf inside Fury rose to the forefront, but he tamped it down. While the wolf might want to fight, the man knew a lion would tear him up. Sometimes it was good to have human abilities, even if those sometimes went to war with his wolf's heart.

"Easy," he said in a level tone as he balled his hand into a fist to protect his fingers. If there was nothing inside the lion but animal, it would respond to any hostile or fear pheromones it smelled. He held his hand out slowly so the lion could catch his scent and intent.

The lion swatted at him but didn't hurt him. Good. Fury put his hand on the lion's back. Leaning closer, he felt the muscles shifting, but they weren't bunching to attack. He breathed in and smelled the scent of Carson, Margery, the female lion, and others. But it was the lightest smell that sent him reeling . . .

A wolfswan.

Fury looked at the lioness. "Have you been around any other Lykos?"

Anita indicated the wolf by Carson. "Sasha."

"No," Fury said slowly. "Female."

Anita scoffed. "We don't mix with other breeds. We are purists."

Maybe . . . but there were other scents he picked up on, too. Jackal, panther, and wolf. "When were you around a jackal?"

"Never!" she spat, indignant at the mere suggestion. The jackals weren't exactly anyone's favorite breed. In the land of outcasts, they were the omega animals. The ones everyone avoided and picked on.

Sasha moved closer. "I smell it, too."

Carson exchanged a worried look with Margery. "Anita, tell us everything you can remember about the ones who attacked your mate."

"I didn't see them. Jake was out with his brother, in natural form, just running to run. They were harming no one. His brother said that a tessera of Arcadians flashed in and came at them. They fought, and the Arcadians shot Jake with something, and he went down hard. Peter ran for help."

"Where's Peter now?" Fury asked.

A tear slid from the corner of her eye. "Dead. Whatever

they shot hit him in the head. He only lived long enough to tell us what happened."

Carson handed her off to Margery before he led Sasha and Fury out of the room. "I've dug through Peter's head and couldn't find anything. There's no entry wound, no exit wound, no blood. Nothing. I don't know what killed him."

That didn't bode well. "Magick?" Fury asked.

Carson shook his head. "But what would be that powerful?"

Sasha shifted his weight. "The gods."

Fury disagreed with that. "I didn't smell a god. I smelled us."

Sasha let out a long sigh. "You know how many Lykos patrias exist?"

"Since I'm the Regis for the Katagaria, yeah, I do. There are thousands of us and that's just in this time period." What he didn't tell them was that the scent was one he was more than familiar with. One from a past he'd done his damnedest to forget. "I'm going to do some digging around and see what I can come up with."

"Thank you," Carson said.

Fury disregarded his gratitude. "No offense, I'm not doing this for you. I'm worried about my people. We need to know what's causing him to hold onto his form."

"And if it's reversible," Sasha added.

Fury nodded. "I'll be in touch."

"Hey, Fury?"

He turned to Sasha who hit his chest three times with his fist, then swept his hand down. A silent gesture to let him know Sasha wouldn't forget to give the letter to Aimee. He inclined his head respectfully before he left the room and headed downstairs.

But with every step he took, his long-buried memories burned through him. He went back in time to a woman who had once been his entire world. Not his lover or relative, she'd been his best friend.

Angelia.

And in one heartbeat, when his brother had told his clan what he really was, she'd not only betrayed her sacred promise to him, she'd tried to kill him. He could still feel the bite of her knife as she drove it in to the hilt—the scar was still jagged on his chest just inches from his heart. The truth was, she hadn't really missed that organ. Her words to him had done more damage than any weapon ever could.

If she was behind this, he'd make sure it was the last mistake that bitch ever made.

2

Angelia hesitated inside the infamous Sanctuary bar. They'd popped into the third level of the limani—the area that had been designated for those teleporting in so that no one would see them—and were now trying to get the lay of the foreign landscape. Dimly lit, the club's ceiling was painted black, and the walls were made of dark red brick. Black railings and trim added to the cave-like feeling of the place.

She'd spent most of her life in medieval England, preferring the open countryside and untainted air to the chaos of twenty-first-century life. Now she knew why. Buildings like this were claustrophobic. She was used to thirty-foot arched ceilings. The flat one above her head couldn't be more than ten feet, if that.

Skittish, she eyed the electric lights around her. As a Were-Hunter, she was susceptible to electrical currents. One tiny jolt and she could lose control of not only her magick, but her human appearance as well.

How did her people live in these horribly crowded and overly electrified places? She'd never understand the appeal. Not to mention the clothes . . .

She wore a pair of blue coarse pants and a white top that, while it was soft, was very strange.

"Are you sure this is a good idea?" she whispered to her companion Dare.

He stood a full head and shoulders above her. At first glance his hair looked dark brown, but in reality it was made up of all colors: ash, auburn, brown, black, mahogany, even some blond. Long and wavy, that hair was more beautiful than any male's should be. She, herself, would kill for it. Yet he thought nothing about it or the fact he was unbelievably sexy and hot. Not that she'd ever sleep with him. He was practically Katagaria with the way he went through women, and as an Arcadian female, she found that animalistic behavior repugnant.

Still, he was one of the fiercest wolfswains in her patria, and the women of her clan had been fighting over him for centuries.

Tonight he was out for blood.

Luckily it wasn't hers.

He turned those smug hazel-green eyes on her. "If you're scared, little girl, go home."

She barely stamped down the urge to shove him in anger. His arrogance had always rubbed her the wrong way. "I fear nothing."

"Then follow and remain silent."

She made an obscene gesture behind his back as he headed for the stairs. That was the one drawback to living in the past. Male egos. Here she was, an Aristos, one of the most powerful of their breed, and he still treated her like she was his inferior waste.

Gods, how she wanted to beat him down.

But he was the grandson of their former leader and the

head of her tessera, so she was honor-bound to follow him. Even if she wanted to kill him.

Remember your duty, she reminded herself. She and Dare were born of the Arcadian branch of Were-Hunters. Humans who had the ability to shift into animals. Their job was to police the Katagaria. The Were-Hunters who were animals able to shift into humans. Just because the Katagaria sometimes wore the skin of mankind didn't make the beasts one of them. They had no understanding of human rationale, complex emotions, or decorum. At the end of the day, the Katagaria were still animals. Primal. Brutal. Unpredictable. Dangerous.

They preyed on people and each other like the animals they were. None could be trusted. Ever.

Yet how ironic that it was a group of Katagaria who owned this bar and who maintained its laws of peace. In theory no one here could harm anyone else.

Yeah, right. She didn't believe that for a minute. They were probably just better at hiding the bodies.

Or eating them.

Harsh and judgmental, perhaps, but there was a sixth sense inside her that said they should leave before they finished their mission.

That feeling worsened as they descended past the second level where a bear bared his teeth at them in warning as he looked up from the card game he was playing against a group of humans. Frowning, she waited for Dare to react, but he merely continued on his way to the bottom floor. She assumed he must have missed the bear's reaction, though that wasn't like the man who normally caught every nuance of hostility around him.

Suddenly a loud electrical shriek pierced the air, making her flinch as it assaulted her wolf's hearing. She covered one ear with her hand as she prayed it wasn't bleeding. "What is that?"

Dare pointed to the stage where a group of Weres were tuning instruments. A loud guitar wailed before they started a song and the crowd cheered them.

She grimaced at the sight and sounds. "What terrible music," she groused, wishing they were back home and not in the midst of this dive.

Once they were on the ground floor, Dare was only able to take two steps before he was surrounded by five of the meanest-looking werebears she'd ever seen. The eldest of them, who looked to be their father since he bore an uncanny resemblance to the younger ones, stood over seven feet tall. He looked down at Dare as if he were about to tear him into pieces.

"What the fuck are you doing here, Wolf?"

Dare's nostrils flared, but he knew the same thing she did. They were outnumbered and in hostile territory, surrounded by animals.

Angelia cleared her throat before she spoke to the eldest bear. "Isn't this Sanctuary?"

One of the younger blond bears shoved at Dare. "Not for him, it's not. It's more like cemetery."

Dare caught himself and held the look of hell wrath on his face. Luckily, he held his temper and didn't fight back.

Yet.

A tall blond woman, who resembled the men closely enough to be another relative, stopped beside them. She gave Dare an insulting once-over before she raked the werebears with a scathing glare.

The bearswan laughed at them. "He's not Fang, guys. Congratulations, you're about to skin an innocent wolf." Tucking her tray under her arm, she stepped away only to have the eldest bear stop her.

"He looks and smells like Fang."

She snorted. "Trust me, Papa, he's nothing like Fang. I

know my wolf when I see him and that boy there is seriously lacking."

The youngest bear in the group snatched at Dare's hair. "He has the mark of a Kattalakis."

The waitress rolled her eyes. "Fine, Serre. Kill the bastard. Not like I care one way or another." She walked off without looking back.

Serre let go of Dare's hair and made a sound of disgust. "Who the hell are you?"

"Dare Kattalakis."

Angelia froze at the deep, resonant voice that went over her like ice. It was a voice she hadn't heard in centuries, and it was one that belonged to someone she'd assumed was long dead.

Fury Kattalakis.

Her heart pounding, she watched as the bears parted to let him approach. Tall and lean, Fury held the kind of toned body that most men had to work out for. But not him. Even in his younger years, he'd possessed defined muscles that had made the other males in their patria green with jealousy and the women swoon with heat.

If anything, these past centuries had honed him even more. Gone was the insecurity of his youth. The wolf before her was sharp and lethal. One who knew exactly what he was capable of.

Merciless bloodshed.

The last time she'd seen him, his blond hair had been long. It was much shorter now, falling just to his collar. But his eyes were still that unique color that was one shade darker than turquoise.

And the hatred in them sent a chill over her.

His black leather Aerostitch-styled jacket had red and yellow flames on the sleeves and on the back, was a white skull and crossbones that peeked out threateningly from behind the flames. Unzipped in the front, it showed off a plain black t-shirt underneath. The Kevlar padding on the jacket added to the width of his already wide shoulders. Black Aerostitch pants were tucked into a pair of black biker boots that held silver buckles up the sides.

She swallowed at the incredibly sexy sight he made as he stood there, ready to take them all on. And against her will, her heartbeat sped up. Whereas Dare was hot, Fury was incredible.

Mesmerizing.

And that werewolf had a butt so tight and fine, it had to be illegal even in this day and age. It was all she could do not to stare at it. Or more to the point, stare at him.

Ignoring her obvious ogling, Fury glared at Dare. "Long time no see, brother."

"Not long enough," Dare said between his clenched teeth.

"You know him?" the father bear asked.

Fury shrugged. "I used to. But if you guys want to chop him up and make hamburgers out of him, I wouldn't mind in the least. Hell, I'll even go get the grinder."

Dare moved toward him.

Serre grabbed him and held him back. "Hitting him here would be a very big mistake on your part. Even if we don't like him."

Fury winked sarcastically at the bear. "Love you, too, Serre. You guys always make me feel so welcome here. Appreciate it."

"Our pleasure." Serre let go of Dare.

The father bear sighed. "Since it appears we've made a mistake, let's leave the wolves to their business." He cast a warning look to Dare. "Remember. No spill blood."

None of them spoke until the bears were completely out of earshot.

Fury watched the two before him warily. Dare and he, along with Vane, Fang, and their two sisters, Anya and Star, were litter mates. All born at the same time to their Arcadian mother. Their mother had kept him, Dare, and Star, and then sent the others to live with their Katagari father.

That was when they'd assumed Fury had been human. Yeah. And the moment his family had found out he wasn't human, they'd turned on him and tried to kill him.

So much for human compassion.

As for Angelia . . . he hated her even more than he hated his brother. At least Dare he understood. The punk had always been jealous of him. From the earliest memory of his childhood, Dare had been there, trying to push him out their mother's affections.

But Lia had been his best friend. Closer than siblings or even lovers. She'd blood-promised to stand at his back for eternity.

Then the very moment Dare had exposed his secret, she had turned on him, too. For that alone he could kill her.

Even so, he had to admit she still dazzled him. Her long black hair was shiny and soft. The kind of hair that begged a man to brush his hand through and bury his face in until he was drunk from her feminine scent. Her large dark eyes held a sleepy quality to them that was as seductive as it was pretty. And her lips . . .

Large and plump, they begged for kisses. They were also the kind of lips a man couldn't help but imagine wrapped around a part of his anatomy while she looked up at him with those dark bedroom eyes.

Damn, the very thought made him hot and hard.

Clenching his teeth, he narrowed his eyes at the scrolling marks that covered half her face. Those marked her as the worst sort of sanctimonious Arcadian.

A Sentinel.

They were the ones who thought themselves so much better than the Katagaria. Even worse, they were sworn to hunt them down and cage them like the animals the Arcadians accused them of being.

It was hard to believe he'd ever thought he cared about her. He must have been insane.

"I saw your work on the Litarian," Fury said, his tone guttural. "Want to tell me how you did it?"

Dare, whose eyes looked so much like Vane's that it was spooky as hell, glared at him. "I don't know what you're talking about."

Fury sneered at him. "Yeah, right. And I assume the two of you are here for drinks because those kind of screwed-up coincidences happen all the time." He sniffed the air. "Oh wait, what is that? Bullshit? Yes, I smell lots of bullshit."

"As if," Dare spat. "You can't smell shite in this cesspit of cheap alcohol, oversprayed perfume, and animal stench."

"Oh see, there you're wrong. I live in this cesspit. Picking out the scent of shit is my specialty, and, Brother, you reek of it. So if I were you, I'd tell me what you did, or I'm going to turn you in to the Peltier bears."

Dare scoffed. "What are they going to do? They have to maintain the laws of No Spill Blood."

"True, but there are three Omegrion reps under this roof and two more live just a howl away. We call a vote and . . . Basically, Brother, you're fucked."

"No, *Brother*," Dare mocked the word. "You are."

Before Fury could blink, Dare lifted a gun and aimed it at Fury's head. Fury caught Dare's wrist at the same instant it fired. Docking and twisting, he fell to his knees, pulling Dare's arm with him.

Screams rang out around them.

"Gun!" someone shouted, causing the human patrons to panic as they ran for the door.

Angelia caught Fury by his throat.

"Hold him down!" Dare snapped, as he tried to wring his hand out of Fury's.

Fury refused to let go of Dare's hand. If he did, the bastard would shoot him with whatever he'd used on the lions.

Angelia wrapped her arm around his throat, choking him. "Let him go, Fury."

Before he could answer, all three of them were thrown apart. Fury tried to get up, but someone had them pinned down with one hell of a forcefield. Growling, he struck out with his powers in anger. Instead of breaking the hold, it turned him into a wolf.

He barked at Mama Peltier, who moved to stand between them. But he knew from experience that it wasn't her powers he felt. The trouble was, he didn't know who they belonged to.

"No one comes into my house and does this," she snarled. "All three of you are banned from here, and if I ever catch you inside Sanctuary again, you won't live long enough to regret it."

"He attacked us," Dare said. "Why should we be banned?"

Dev hauled him up from the floor. "Anyone who participates in a fight is thrown out. Those are the laws."

Colt was far more gentle picking Angelia up.

"There was no bloodshed," Angelia argued.

Mama curled her lip. "Doesn't matter. You almost exposed us to the humans. Lucky for you, they evacuated quickly. Now get out."

Fury tried to turn human again to tell them what was going on, but his magick wasn't cooperating. Not even his mental powers were working. It most likely had to do with the fact that someone else's powers were holding him down.

Damn it!

Dare glared at him and made a gesture to let him know it wasn't over. Then, he and Angelia left.

"That means you, too, Wolf," Dev growled. "Max, let him go."

The forcefield dropped.

Finally he was able to turn back into a human. Though he could have done without the public nudity. Unlike other Were-Hunters, he couldn't manifest clothes at the same time as he shapeshifted. *I really hate my powers . . .*

As he reached to scoop up his clothes, they were put on his body. Confused, he looked around and caught Aimee's gaze. She inclined her head to let him know that she was the one who'd helped him. No doubt Fang had told her about his weakness.

Dev stepped forward.

"I'm going," Fury said. "But before I do, let me congratulate all of you on your stupidity. Those two assholes who just left were the ones who screwed the lions upstairs. I was trying to get the information out of them."

Dev cursed. "Why didn't you tell us?"

"I was trying. Next time you forcefield someone to the ground, you might not want to stifle their ability to talk, too."

The dragon, Max, shook his head. "I thought you were just going to insult me for holding you down. It's what you normally do whenever you speak to me."

"I probably would have had I not had something more important to tell you."

Dev cleared his throat to get their attention. "Are they from this time period?"

"No."

Mama nodded. "Then they have to be in town somewhere. There's no full moon for them to use to time jump."

Fury wished, but there was another truth about his old friend. "The woman was Aristos. She's not bound by the moon. They could be anywhere, in any time."

Dev sighed. "Well, at least we got the humans out before they saw anything unnatural happen."

"Bully that." Fury zipped his jacket up. "Now if you'll excuse me—"

"Hey."

He looked at Dev.

"You're still banned from here."

"Like I care." He'd been banned from much nicer places than this, and at least there he'd had people who'd actually cared for him . . . at least for a few years.

Without a backward glance, he left them and headed back to Ursulines. The street was strangely quiet, especially given the fact that a large number of humans had gone screaming into the night only a few minutes before. The threat of violence must have really gotten under their skin.

But that didn't change the fact that he still had a wolf to track. Two of them to be precise. Common sense told him to return to his pack and tell Vane what was happening.

Fury scoffed. "Lived my whole life without any sense. Why should I start having some now?"

As he reached his bike, a strange fissure of power went down his spine.

He turned in expectation of a fight, but before he could even move, he was hit with a fierce shock. Cursing, he hit the ground hard. Pain exploded through him as he changed into his wolf form, then human, then wolf again. He was completely immobilized as his body struggled to hold onto one form and was incapable of it.

Dare walked up to him slowly, then kicked him hard in the ribs. "You should have died, Fury. Now you're going to wish you had."

Fury lunged at him, but his muscles wouldn't cooperate. If he could lay hand or paw on the bastard, he'd rip his throat out.

He looked up at Angelia to see sympathy on her face an instant before Dare shot him again. Unbelievable pain ripped through him as he struggled to stay conscious.

It was a losing battle. In one heartbeat, everything went black.

"What are you doing?" Angelia asked Dare.

"We need to know what he knows about our experiment. More to the point, we need to know who he's been talking to. We can't afford for our secret to get out."

She cringed as she watched Fury's body continue to shift from human to white wolf and back again. At least until Dare wrapped the collar around his throat that kept him as human. Since Fury's natural form was a wolf, keeping him as a human, especially in daylight, would weaken him.

And it would hurt.

She shook her head at his actions. "You know he's not going to tell us anything."

"I wouldn't be so sure."

The Fury she remembered would never tell secrets. He'd die before he did, and he could take a lot of pain. Even as a child, he'd been stronger than any other. "How can you bc so certain?"

"Because I'm going to turn him over to our Jackal."

Angelia sucked her breath in sharply at the threat. Oscar was a jackal whose heart was so black, he was more animal than man. "He's your brother, Dare."

"I have no brother. You know what the Katagaria did to my family. To *our* patria."

It was true. She'd been there the night Dare's Katagari father had led the attack on their Arcadian camp. Just a child, she'd been hidden as the attacks began. Her mother had smeared her with earth to mask her scent before she'd placed her in the cellar.

Even now, she could see the wolves as they attacked her mother and killed her while she'd watched in horror through the slats in the floor.

Dare was right. They had to protect their people. The

animals needed to be stripped of their powers and put down like the rabid creatures they were.

Even Fury.

"Are you with me?" he asked.

She nodded. "I won't see another child suffer my fate. We have to protect ourselves. Whatever it takes."

3

Angelia paced the small camp they'd made as she listened to Fury insulting Oscar while he and Dare tortured Fury for information. Honestly, shc didn't have the stomach for it. She never had.

Maybe Dare was right. Maybe she shouldn't be on a tessera after all.

Then again, she was a warrior of unparalleled skill. In battle, she didn't hesitate to kill or to wound. It was just the idea of beating someone who couldn't fight back that sickened her.

He's an animal.

No doubt he'd kill her in a heartbeat. She knew that with every part of herself and yet . . .

She cringed as Fury howled in pain.

An instant later, Oscar came outside toward her and the fire they'd made. Without a word, he walked past her and manifested an iron pole.

Frowning, she watched as he placed it in the fire. "What are you doing?"

"I thought a little branding might loosen his tongue."

A wave of nausea went through her.

Dare came outside the tent with the same look of disgust on his face. "I say you should ram it up his ass until he talks."

Oscar laughed.

Horrified, she didn't move until they started back with the poker in hand. "No!" she said sternly.

Oscar angled it at her. "Get out of the way."

"No," she repeated. "This is wrong. You're acting like one of *them*."

Dare's expression was stern and cruel. "We're protecting our people."

But this wasn't protection. This was all-out cruelty. Unable to bear it, she tried another tactic. "Let me question him."

Dare frowned. "Why? Like you said, he won't say anything."

She gestured toward the tent as she tried to keep her anger under control. "You've been beating on him for hours, and it's gotten us nowhere. Let me try another approach. What will it hurt?"

Oscar put the poker back into the fire. "I need to eat anyway. You have until I finish, and then I'm going to try my way again."

Repulsed by them both, Angelia turned around and headed into the tent. The sight of Fury on the floor stopped her dead in her tracks. Still in human form, he was naked with his hands tied at an awkward angle behind his back. Another rope held his legs tied together. He was covered with bruises and cuts to the point that she could barely recognize him.

The fact that he was this wounded and in human form had to be excruciating for him. Anytime they were wounded, they reverted to their natural form. For her it was human. For Fury . . .

He was a wolf.

Trying to keep that in mind, she knelt by his side.

He growled threateningly until he looked up and met her gaze. The pain and torment in those dark turquoise eyes made her wince. And as she dropped her gaze, she saw the scar on his chest. The wound where she'd stabbed him.

Guilt tore through her over what she should never have done.

"Why don't you just finish the job," he said, his tone hostile and deadly.

"We don't want to hurt you."

He laughed bitterly. "My wounds and the glee they had in their eyes when they gave them to me tells me a different story."

She brushed the hair back from his forehead to see a vicious cut that ran along his brow. Blood poured from his nose and lips. "I'm sorry."

"We're all sorry for something. Why don't you be an animal for once and just kill me?" He glared at her. "You might as well. I'm not going to tell you shit."

"We need to know what happened to the lion."

"Go to hell."

"Fury—"

"Don't you fucking dare use my name. I'm nothing but an animal to all of you. Believe me, all of you made it more than clear to me four hundred years ago when you beat me close to death and then dumped me out to die."

"Fury—"

He barked at her like a wolf.

"Would you stop?"

He continued making wolf noises.

Sighing, Angelia shook her head. "No wonder they beat you."

Baring his teeth in true canine fashion, he growled, then

woofed. There was nothing human in the sound or his demeanor.

Angelia stepped back.

The moment she was away from him, Fury slumped on the ground and stopped making any sounds at all. He lay completely still.

Was he dead?

No, his chest was still moving. She could also hear his faint breathing. As she watched him, her thoughts turned to the past. To the young man she'd once been friends with. Even though he was younger than her by four years, there had been something about him that had touched her.

Where Dare had always been arrogant and bossy, Fury had held a vulnerability that had made her protective of him. More than that, he'd never treated her as inferior. He'd seen her as a partner and confidant.

"I'll be your family, Lia." Those words haunted her. It had been Fury's vow to her once he'd learned that her family had been killed by the Katagaria—by his own father's pack. *"I won't ever let the wolves hurt you. I swear it."*

Yet she'd stood by this morning while they'd tortured him relentlessly.

It's nothing compared to what you did the last time you saw him.

It was true. She hadn't stood by him then either, and he'd been beaten a lot worse than this.

"Fury," she tried again. "Tell me what we need to know, and I promise you this will stop."

He lifted his head up to pin her with a furious glare. "I don't betray *my* friends."

"Don't you dare say that to me. I was protecting my people when I attacked you."

He let out a disbelieving snort. "From *me*? They were my people, too."

She shook her head in denial. "You don't have people. You're an animal."

He twisted his lips into a vicious snarl. "Baby, you untie me, and I'll show you just how much of an animal the man in me really is. Trust me. He's a lot crueler than the wolf is."

"Told you," Oscar said as he joined them in the tent. He angled the red-hot poker toward the flap. "You should leave. The stench of burning flesh is going to be hard on your nose."

She saw the panic in Fury's eyes as he tried to scoot away from them.

Oscar grabbed him by the hair and rolled him over. Fury kicked at him, but there wasn't much he could do given how tied up he was. Still he fought with a courage that was admirable.

"Get out," Dare said as he entered the tent.

As she started for the flap, Fury let out a howl so fierce and pain-filled that it shattered her soul. Turning, she saw that Oscar had dropped the poker across his left hip where it burned in a foul stench.

Right or wrong, she couldn't let them do this to him anymore.

She shoved Dare out of her way, then kicked Oscar back from Fury. Before they could recover themselves, she knelt by Fury's side and placed her hand on his shoulder. Using her powers, she took them out of the tent and moved them farther into the marsh where they'd been camped. Since she didn't know the area all that well, it was the safest place she could take him.

When he met her gaze, there was no gratitude there. Only rage and a hatred so sharp it was piercing. "What are you going to do now? Leave me here for the gators to eat?"

"I should." Instead, she manifested a knife to cut through the ropes that held his hands.

Fury was stunned by her actions. "Why are you helping me?"

"I don't know. Apparently I'm having a moment of extreme stupidity."

He wiped at the blood on his face as she cut the ropes on his feet. "I wish your stupidity had kicked in sooner."

She paused at the sight of the raw blister on his hip where the jackal had laid the poker. It had to be killing him. "I'm so sorry."

Fury snatched at the collar on his throat and jerked it free.

Angelia gasped at the action. No one should be able to remove their collar.

No one.

"How did you do that?"

He curled his lip at her. "I can do a lot of things when I'm not being shocked."

She started to leave, but before she could, he snapped the collar around her throat. Shrieking, she tried to use her powers to either attack him or remove it.

It was useless.

"I saved you!"

"Fuck you," he snarled. "I wouldn't have been there had the two of you not jumped me last night. You're lucky I don't return the favor you did for me."

Raw panic tore through her as she realized he could do anything to her and she'd be powerless to stop him. "What are you going to do?"

There was no mercy in his expression. No reprieve. "I ought to rip your throat out. But lucky for you, I'm just a dumb animal and killing for revenge isn't in my nature." He tightened his grip on her arm. "Killing to protect myself and those in my pack is another story. You'd do well to remember that."

As she opened her mouth to respond, Fury flashed them out of the marsh and into his brother Vane's large Victorian house.

Vane's mate was in the living room, standing by the couch where their son was napping. Tall and curvaceous with short, dark auburn hair, Bride was one of the few people Fury actually trusted. She let out an almost wolf-sounding yelp before she spun about and gave them her back. "Good grief, Fury, warn me if you're going to jump in here naked."

"Sorry, Bride," he said, trying to keep his focus. But it was getting hard given his wounds.

"What happened to you?"

He looked over his shoulder to find Vane standing in the doorway. He wanted to answer, but the drain on his powers combined with the wounds was more than he could take. His ears were buzzing. The next thing he knew, he was a wolf again and exhaustion was overtaking him.

"Don't let her escape and don't take that collar off," he projected to Vane before he let the darkness take him under again.

Angelia jumped away from Fury in his wolf form. Realizing he was unconscious, she started for the door only to find a man there who bore a scary resemblance to Dare. This guy, however, was a lot more intimidating and even more handsome. "I need to leave."

He looked past her to the woman by the couch. "Bride, take the baby and get upstairs." Though his tone was commanding, it was also gentle and protective.

She heard the woman leave without questioning him.

As soon as she was gone, he narrowed those eerie hazel eyes on her that were more wolf than human. "What are you doing here and what happened to my brother?"

She tilted her head at his question. His scent . . . it was unmistakable. "You're Arcadian. A Sentinel like me." But unlike her, he chose to hide the marks on his face that designated him as one of their rare and sacred breed.

He curled his lips. "I'm nothing like you. My allegiance is to the Katagaria and it's to my brother. He told me to keep you here and so I shall."

Anger ripped through her. She had no intention of staying here. "I have to get back to my patria."

He shook his head, his face set by determination. "You're part of my mother's patria which makes you my mortal enemy. You're not leaving here until Fury allows it." He stepped past her to where Fury lay on the floor.

She was aghast at his actions. "You're kidnapping me?"

Effortlessly, he picked Fury up from the floor. No small feat given the size of the wolf. "My mother kidnapped my mate and took her back to medieval England where the male members of your patria then attempted to rape her. Be grateful I don't return that favor to you."

Those words were so eerily similar to Fury's that it sent a chill over her. "I just want to go home."

"You're safe here. No one's going to hurt you . . . unless you try to leave." He turned and carried Fury up the same stairs the woman had taken just a few minutes before.

Angelia watched him until he was out of sight. Then she ran for the front door. She'd only made it three steps before four wolves appeared in front of her. Baring their teeth and snapping, they blocked her way.

Katagaria.

She could tell from the smell of them. That scent of wolf mingled with human and magick. It was daylight which meant it was hard for them to appear human. Not impossible, but difficult, especially if they were young or inexperienced.

She tried to press forward, but the animals prevented it.

"Do what Vane told you."

She turned and froze in shock. In human form, this

werewolf looked similar enough to Dare to be his twin. "Who are you?"

"Fang Kattalakis, and you better pray to whatever god you worship that nothing happens to Fury. My brother dies and I will have your throat." He looked at the wolves around her. "Keep her guarded." Then he returned to a wolf's form and ran up the stairs.

Angelia backed slowly into the living room. Catching the sight of another door to the outside, she started for it only to find more wolves in front of her.

Fear sliced through her as she remembered being a helpless child as the wolves ravaged her mother. Over and over she heard the screams and relived the nightmare of them tearing her parents into shreds. She tried to blast the wolves before her, but the collar rendered all her powers useless.

She was at their mercy.

"Get back," she snarled, throwing a lamp at one of them.

The others snarled and woofed, circling her.

She couldn't breathe, as panic set in. They were going to kill her!

Vane wanted blood as he saw the deep wounds on Fury's body.

"What happened?"

He turned to find Fang standing in the doorway. "It looks like the Arcadians grabbed him and had some fun with him."

Fang's nostrils flared. "I saw one of their bitches downstairs. Want me to kill her?"

No.

Vane frowned as he heard Fury's voice in his head. Fury opened his eyes to look at him.

Where is she?

"Downstairs. I have the pack guarding her."

Fury turned human instantly. "You can't do that."

"Why?"

"Her parents were killed by our pack. Ripped apart in front of her when she was only three years old. She'll be terrified."

Before Vane could respond, Fury vanished.

Angelia kept swinging at the wolves with her broken lamp as they closed in on her. Terrified, she wanted to scream, but the sound was lodged in her throat. All she could really see was blood, and feel the same horror she'd had the night her parents' screams had echoed in her head.

She couldn't breathe or think.

The next thing she knew, someone was grabbing her from behind.

She turned, trying to hit her new attacker, then froze as she saw Fury there in human form.

His touch gentle, he took the lamp from her hand and set it on the floor. His expression stoic, his eyes were every bit as blank. "I won't let them hurt you," he said, his tone soothing. "I haven't forgotten my promise."

A sob came out from deep inside her as he pulled her against him.

Fury cursed at the way she trembled in his arms. He'd never seen anyone more shaken and it pissed him off. "Back off," he barked at the others. "You're acting like fucking humans." Angry at their cruelty, he led her toward the stairs.

"I didn't need your help," she snarled at him.

But he noticed that she didn't pull away. "Believe me, I'm well acquainted with your willingness to stab and kill in cold blood."

Angelia stumbled at those cold words that were tinged with a well-deserved hostility. It was true. He'd been unarmed when they attacked him and she'd left him to his family and their brutality.

Shame and horror filled her. "Why did you save me just now?"

"I'm a dog, remember? We're loyal even when it's stupid."

She shook her head in contradiction. "You're a wolf."

"Same difference to most people." He stopped before a door and knocked.

A gentle voice told them to enter.

Fury pushed it open and nudged her inside. "It's me, Bride. I'm still naked so I'm hanging out here. This is Angelia. She's not real fond of wolves so I thought she might want to stay with you . . . if that's okay with you?"

Bride rose from her rocking chair as she cuddled a sleeping toddler in her arms. "Are you all right, Fury?"

Angelia saw the fatigue on his face and could only imagine how much he must be hurting. Still, he'd come for her . . .

It was amazing.

"Yeah," he said in a strained tone, "but I really need to lie down and rest for awhile."

"Go sleep, sweetie."

Fury paused and met Angelia's gaze with a feral hostility so potent, it chilled her all the way to her soul. "You hurt her, you even give her a bad look that hurts her feelings and so help me, I will slaughter you like yesterday's meal and no power, yours or otherwise, will save you. Do you understand me?"

She nodded.

"I'm not kidding," he warned again.

"I know you're not."

He inclined his head to her before he shut the door.

Angelia turned to find Bride closing the distance on her. Without a word and still holding the toddler, Bride stepped past her and opened the door. Fury was back in wolf form, lying in the hallway where he must have collapsed as soon as he closed the door.

Her expression sympathetic, Bride knelt on the floor and sank one hand in his white fur. "Vane?"

He manifested in the hallway beside her. "What the hell's he doing here? I was looking for him downstairs."

"He wanted me to watch Angelia."

Vane looked at Angelia and gave her a nasty glare. "Why?"

"He said she was scared and wanted me to stay with her. What's going on?"

Vane's face softened as he looked at his mate. The love he felt for her was more than obvious and it touched Angelia's heart. No man had ever looked at her with that kind of tenderness.

He brushed a strand of hair back from her face before he dropped his hand down to the dark hair of the sleeping toddler. "I'm not sure myself, baby. Fury always talks more to you than he does me." He returned his gaze to Angelia and it turned lethal and cold. "I warn you now. Anything happens to my mate or my son, we will hunt you down and rip you into so many pieces they'll never find all of you."

Angelia stiffened. "I'm not an animal. I don't prey on people's families to get back at them."

Vane scoffed. "Oh, girl, trust me. Animals don't revenge-kill or -attack. That's *purely* human. So in this case, you better act like an animal and guard her with your life. 'Cause that's what I'm going to take if she so much as gets a paper cut in your presence."

Angelia returned his lethal stare with one of her own. If he thought to attack her, he was going to learn that she wasn't a weakling. She was a trained warrior and she wouldn't go down without a brutal fight. "You know, I'm really getting tired of being threatened by everyone."

"No threats. Just a stated hard-core fact."

Angelia glared at him, wanting to go for his throat. If only she wasn't wearing her collar.

"All right, people," Bride said. "Enough. You," she said to Vane, "get Fury in bed and take care of him." She stood up and walked to Angelia. "You, follow me and I promise I won't threaten you unless you do something to deserve it."

Vane laughed low in his throat. "And keep in mind that even though she's human, she took out my mother and caged her. Don't let her humanity fool you. She can be as vicious as they come."

Bride made an air kiss at him while she cradled her son's head with one hand. "Only when I'm protecting you and Baby Boo, sweetie. Now get Fuzzhead in bed. We'll be fine."

Angelia stepped back to allow Bride to lead the way back into the nursery. The walls were a pale baby blue decorated with teddy bears and stars. She put the toddler in his matching white-and-blue crib before she lifted the side into place.

Feeling awkward, Angelia folded her arms across her chest. "How old's your son?"

"Two years. I know I should take him out of the crib, but he's a kinetic sleeper and I'm not ready for him to accidentally fall out of bed yet. Silly, huh?"

She bit back a smile at Bride's concern. "Protecting your family is never silly."

"No, it isn't." Bride sighed as she brushed a hand through the baby's dark hair. Turning, she faced Angelia. "So you want to tell me what's going on?"

Angelia debated on the sanity of that. Telling her that she'd helped kidnap Fury and then stood back while two of her tessera ruthlessly tortured him didn't seem like an award-winning act of intelligence.

More like suicide given the nature of these "people."

"I'm not sure how to answer that."

Bride's gaze narrowed. "Then you must be one of the ones who hurt him."

"No," she said indignantly. "I didn't torture him. I wouldn't do that to anyone."

Bride cocked her head suspiciously. "But you let it happen."

She was smarter than Angelia wanted. "I *did* stop them."

"After how long? Fury was in pretty bad shape and I know how much damage he can take and still stand and fight. To pass out like he did . . . someone beat him for a while."

Angelia looked away, ashamed. It actually hurt her on a deeper level than she would have thought possible that she hadn't intervened sooner. What kind of person stood by while someone was brutalized? Especially someone she'd once called friend.

Yet twice now in her life, she'd allowed Fury to almost be killed and done nothing to protect him.

She wasn't any better than the animals she hated, and that part of herself she despised even more.

"I'm not proud of it, all right. I should have done something sooner and I know it. But I did keep them from doing anything more to him."

"You're rationalizing your cruelty."

Angelia clenched her teeth. "I'm not rationalizing anything. Honestly, I just want to go home. I don't like this time period and I don't like being here with my enemies."

Bride gave her no reprieve. "And I don't like what was done to Fury, but until I know more about it, we're not enemies. The hostility at this point is only coming from you. I told Fury I'd keep you company and that's what I'm doing. No enmity here."

Angelia cut a vicious glare toward the woman and her patronizing tone. "You have no idea what this feels like."

"Oh wait . . ." Bride said with a sarcastic laugh. "I was minding my own business when Bryani sent in a demon to kidnap me here in my time period and take me to her village in medieval England—this back when I didn't even know such things were possible. Once there, everyone I came into contact with threatened me when I'd done absolutely nothing to any of them, ever. And that included Dare Kattalakis. Then the males of their patria tried to rape me for no other reason than I was mated to Vane . . . Oh, wait, what am I saying? We hadn't gone through the mating ritual yet. They were willing to attack me for nothing more than bearing his mark. So, I think I do have a little clue about what you're feeling here. And in our defense, you're not being manhandled."

Angelia put more distance between them. What Bride described had been four years ago. And though she hadn't participated in it, she knew from the others how much damage they'd intended to do to the woman before her, and that sickened her, too. "I wasn't there when they did that to you. I was out on patrol. I only heard about it afterward."

"Well, bully for you. It was still extremely traumatic for me. And unlike *your* people, I can assure you that not a single wolf in this house will attack you unless you provoke it by something *you* do against them."

Angelia scoffed at her arrogance and naivete. "You're human. How can you entrust your life to animals? Don't you understand how savage they are?"

Bride shrugged. "My father's a veterinarian. I was raised around all kinds of animals, wild and tame, feathered, furred, scaled, and other. And honestly, I find them much more predictable than any human. They don't backstab and they don't lie or betray. In all my life, I've never had an animal hurt my feelings or make me cry because of something they did."

"Count yourself lucky," Angelia sneered. "I watched my entire family as they were eaten alive by the very pack of animals you have downstairs in your house with your child. The blood of my parents flowed from their bodies through the floorboards and drenched me while I lay in terror of being torn apart by them."

She looked to the crib where Bride's son slumbered, peacefully unaware of how much danger he was in because of his mother's stupidity. "I was only a year older than your child when it happened. My parents gave their lives for mine and I watched as they gave them. So you'll have to excuse me if I have a hard time thinking good of any animal except those who are dead or caged."

"It really makes you wonder what the animals did to be provoked, doesn't it?"

Angelia turned at the sound of the low, deep voice that rumbled like thunder and sent chills over her. Standing head and shoulders above her, this man had a bad attitude so fierce it bled from every pore of his skin.

Dressed all in black, he wore jeans, Harley biker boots, and a short-sleeved t-shirt that showed off a perfect male body. He had a long silver sword earring in his left lobe with a hilt made of a skull and crossbones.

As he scanned her body, his lips were twisted into a sneer made even more ominous by his black goatee. Straight black hair that reached to his shoulders was brushed back from a pair of startlingly blue eyes.

His demeanor tough and lethal, he reminded her of a cold-blooded killer. And when he looked at her she had the feeling he was measuring her for a coffin.

Her heart pounding, she glanced down to his left hand. Each finger, including his thumb, was covered with a long, articulated silver claw and tipped with a point so sharp that it was obviously his weapon of choice. This man liked to get down and dirty with his kills.

To call him psychotic would be a step up for him.

Instinctively, she took three steps back.

Bride laughed a happy sound as she saw him and disregarded the fact that he obviously wasn't right in the head and that he was most likely an even bigger threat to them than the wolves downstairs. "Z . . . what on earth are you doing here?"

He cut those cold eyes away from her and focused on Bride. "Astrid wanted me to check on Sasha. Apparently something bad went down at Sanctuary last night and she's worried about his safety."

Bride's eyes widened. "So what do you know?"

He cut a suspicious glance toward Angelia that made her blood run cold. "Some Arcadians have found a way to trap Katagaria in their animal forms and strip out their magick. Sasha said the ones responsible attacked Fury and no one had seen him since. Hence my unannounced presence here without Trace's playmate. If Sasha's threatened, Astrid's upset. If Astrid's upset, I'm going to kill whatever's upsetting her until she's happy again. So where's Fury?"

From any other man, that would have come across as a joke, but Angelia didn't doubt for one instant that Z fully intended to carry out his threat. Especially not the way he was flexing those claws on his hand.

"Wow, Zarek," Bride said slowly, her eyes shining with amusement. "I think that may be the most words you've ever spoken to me during any single visit. Maybe even all of them combined. I'm impressed. As for Fury, I think I should state that he's not the one who upset Sasha, so please don't kill him. I'd miss him if he was gone. He was badly wounded and passed out as soon as he got home."

He let out an expletive so foul, Angelia actually blushed from it.

Zarek narrowed his gaze in her direction. "What about her? Does she know anything?" The tone of it wasn't a question. It was an undeniable threat.

Angelia straightened and tensed, ready to fight if need be. "I'm an Aristos. I don't think you want to tangle with me."

He scoffed at her bravado. "Like I give a shit. I'm a god,

baby, so in the grand scheme of things, if I wanted to rip your head off and use it for a bowling ball, there's not many who could stop me and most of those who could would be too afraid of me to even try."

She had a feeling he wasn't boasting.

"Zarek," Bride said in a chiding tone. "I don't think torturing her will get you the information you want."

A slow, sinister smile curved his handsome lips. "Yeah, but it could be fun. I say let's try it and see." He stepped forward.

Bride planted herself in front of him. "I know you want to please your wife, and I can seriously appreciate that. But I told Fury that she'd be safe. Please don't make me a liar, Z."

He growled deep in his throat and for the first time Angelia respected Bride, who didn't flinch under his cutthroat scrutiny.

"Fine, Bride. But I want to know what's going on, and if I have to stay here without my wife and child for too long . . . let's just say it won't go well for any of you. Where's Vane?"

"With Fury. First door on your right."

He flexed his claws before he turned and left. He started to slam the door, then glanced back at the sleeping toddler and changed his mind.

He closed it quietly.

"Thank you," Angelia said as soon as they were alone.

"You're welcome."

She rubbed her hands up and down her arms in an effort to dispel the chills his presence had left behind. "Is he always like that?"

Bride covered her baby with a small blue blanket. "Actually, I'm told he's a lot mellower now than he used to be. When Vane first met him, he really was suicidal and psychotic."

"And you think that's changed . . . how?"

Bride smiled. "Good point, but believe it or not, when he

brings his son over to play with mine, he's actually very gentle with the two of them."

That she would pay money to see. She couldn't imagine someone that insane being paternal or tender.

Pushing Zarek out of her thoughts, Angelia walked to the window to look out on the street below. It was so unlike her home. But she knew that Dare and Oscar would be looking for her. Dare was one of the best trackers in their patria. He shouldn't have any trouble finding her and bringing help.

May the gods have mercy on this pack when they arrived . . .

"So . . ." Bride said, letting her voice trail off a bit. "Care to tell me what this weapon is that you guys have invented?"

Angelia didn't speak. The weapon was ingenious, and it was one they would die to protect. With it, they had proven that mankind was at the top of the food chain. None of the animals in the Katagaria would have ever been able to design it.

It was the one thing that could protect her people from them forever.

"It really makes you wonder what the animals did to be provoked, doesn't it?" Z's words haunted her. Honestly, she'd never really thought about that before. All she'd ever heard was that the attack had been unprovoked and undeserved.

She had no reason to doubt that.

But what if it hadn't been?

"Why did Bryani attack you?" she asked Bride.

"She claimed she was trying to save me from being mated to her monster of a son. Personally, I think she was just a little whacko."

That was an undisputed fact. Bryani had been the daughter of their leader. As such, her story was known by everyone. It was a story the mothers in their patria used to frighten misbehaving children. Given what the Katagaria had done to the poor woman, it was amazing she had what little sanity she did. "They kept her in their den and repeatedly raped her. Did you know that?"

Bride's expression turned sad and sympathetic. It was obvious the tragedy of that event wasn't lost on her. "Only Vane's father did that, but yes. Vane has told me everything about his family."

"And did he ever say why they attacked us that night?"

Bride frowned. "Don't you know?"

"We have theories. Everything from the wolves must have been hungry and smelled our food to they were rabid Slayers bent on drinking our blood. But no, no one knows why we were attacked."

Bride looked stunned by her words. Her expression turned from disbelief to disgust. "Oh, they know exactly what they did. They just don't want anyone else to know. Those lying dogs . . ."

Now it was Angelia's turn to be baffled. "What are you talking about?"

When Bride answered, her tone was rife with anger and disdain. "Not *one* male in your pack has ever confessed to what they did?"

"We were innocent victims."

"Yeah, and I'm the tooth fairy. Trust me. The attack was provoked." Bride shook her head. "You know, I will say this, the Katagaria at least admit what they do. They don't lie to cover it up."

"Well, if you know so much, then please enlighten me about what happened."

"Fine. The Katagaria had a group of females who were pregnant and unable to travel." That was common to both the Arcadian and Katagaria. Once a female was pregnant, she couldn't shapeshift or use her power to teleport until after the children or pups were born.

Bride folded her arms over her chest. "Since they were in

medieval England at the time the females conceived, the males took their females deep into the woods away from any people or their villages to make their den in safety. They'd been there for several weeks with no problems. Then one night, the males went out to hunt for food. They found deer and were chasing them when two of the wolves ended up in snares.

"Vane's father, Markus, turned human to free the two who were trapped and while he was at it, he was approached by a group of Arcadian males—the ones who'd set those traps. Markus tried to explain that they meant no harm to them, but before he could, the Arcadians executed the two wolves in the traps, then shot arrows at the others. Outnumbered, the pack returned to their den where they found most of their women and children missing."

Angelia swallowed as a bad premonition went through her.

"The wolves tracked their scent back to Bryani's camp, where they found the remains of most of their women. They'd been butchered and their hides strung up to tan. There were a handful of pups still alive, but caged. So the wolves waited until nightfall . . . At dusk, a group of the Katagaria led the Arcadian males out of camp so that the others could go in and free their remaining women and children. Bryani's father and others attacked them and the brutal fighting you remember happened."

Angelia shook her head in denial. "You lie! They attacked us unprovoked. There was no reason for what they did. None."

"Sweetie," Bride said in a gentle tone, "you don't know the real truth any more than I do. I can only tell you what Vane's pack has told me about that event. Honestly, I believe them for several reasons. One, they don't have any females that old. Something happened to kill them off. And now every male over four hundred years old in their pack is insanely protective of any female brought in. I've been with the wolves for the last four years and not once have I seen them be aggressive to anyone unless they or their pack was threatened. Nor have I ever known one of them to lie. If anything, they're honest to the point of brutality."

Angelia still refused to believe it. "My people wouldn't have attacked women and children."

"They tried to attack me."

"In retaliation!"

"For what? Vane hadn't hurt them and I most certainly hadn't. Not one male in your entire patria, including your leader, Vane's own grandfather, would come to my defense. None. But I tell you what. If anyone or anything came into this house and threatened me, there's not a wolf downstairs who wouldn't give his life to keep me safe. And that goes for any female in their pack, too."

The baby woke up and started crying for his mother.

Bride left her to pick him up. "It's okay, Trace. Mommy's here."

He laid his head on her shoulder and rubbed his eyes. "Where's Daddy?"

"He's with Uncle Fury and Uncle Z."

The boy perked up instantly. "Bob play with Trace?"

She smiled indulgently. "No, honey. Bob didn't come with Uncle Z this time. Sorry."

He pouted until he saw Angelia. Then he turned bashful and buried his head against Bride's shoulder.

Bride kissed his cheek. "This is Angelia, Trace. Can you say hi?"

He waved at her without looking up.

In spite of it, Angelia was strangely charmed by the small boy. She'd always loved children and had hoped to one day have a litter of her own. "Hi, Trace."

He peeped at her over the safety of his mother's shoulder. Then he whispered in Bride's ear while his mother rubbed his back affectionately.

In that moment, a repressed memory came flooding back to her. It was something she hadn't thought about in centuries. Fury and several boys had been injured while climbing a tree. The boys who'd skinned their hands and knees had run to their mothers for comfort. Fury had broken his arm. Crying, he'd gone to his mother, too. Only when he reached Bryani, she'd angrily shoved him away.

Angelia's uncle had started to comfort Fury.

Bryani had stopped him with a sharp growl. "Don't you dare comfort that boy."

"He's hurt."

"Life *is* pain and there is no comfort for it. The sooner Fury accepts that, the better off he'll be. Let him know early on that the only one he can depend on is himself. He broke his arm by being stupid. He must tend to it."

Her uncle had been aghast. "He's just a child."

"No. He's my vengeance and one day I'm going to unleash him on his own father."

Angelia flinched at that memory. How could she have forgotten it? Then again, Bryani had never been an overly doting parent, so why should it stand out in her memory any more than all the other times Bryani had failed to comfort her sons? It was why Dare was so cold to everyone around him. He'd spent his entire life trying to earn his mother's acceptance.

And it was the last thing she'd ever give her children.

"Does it feel good to be hugged?"

She could still hear Fury's baffled tone as he'd asked her that. It'd been her fourteenth birthday and her uncle had hugged her before he allowed her to go outside and play with Fury. "You've been hugged, Fury."

He'd shaken his head. "No, I haven't. At least not that I remember."

She'd tried to think of a time when someone had held him, but true to his words, she couldn't recall a single time. Heartbroken, she'd put her arms around him and given him his very first hug.

Instead of hugging her back, he'd stood there with his arms at his side. Stiff. Unmoving. Not even breathing. It'd been as if he was afraid to move for fear of her hurting or abandoning him.

"Well?" she'd asked after she released him.

"You smell nice."

She'd smiled. "But did you like the hug?"

He'd walked into her then, rubbing his head against her shoulder in a very wolflike manner until she'd wrapped her arms around him again. Only then did he stop moving. "I like your hugs, Lia." Then he'd run away and hidden from her for three days.

He'd never allowed her to hug or touch him again.

Even with all the secrets they'd shared. Even when she cried. He'd never touched her. He would merely hand her a cloth to wipe her eyes with and listen until she felt better. But never had he come close to touching her again.

Until today, when he'd gone to protect her from the other wolves.

Why would he have done that?

It made no sense. He was an animal. Disgusting. Brutal. Violent. There was nothing redeeming about them. And yet she couldn't shake the images of her past. The times when Fury, an animal, had been closer to her than anyone else.

"I'm a Sentinel, Fury!" She'd awakened to find her marks and had snuck out of their cottage at dawn to find Fury by the stream where he'd gone to sleep. It'd been a strange custom that she hadn't understood at the time. Only later would she learn that he slept there because he was a wolf and he'd been afraid of his family learning that secret.

He'd smiled an honest smile. Unlike the other males of

their patria who'd been jealous when they learned she'd been chosen, Fury had been genuinely happy for her. "Have you told your uncle?"

"Not yet. I wanted you to be the first to know." She'd tilted her head to show him the faint markings that had yet to be fully formed. "Do you think I'll be pretty once the lines fill in?"

"You're the most beautiful wolfswan here. How could your marks ever make you anything else?"

She'd gone to hug him, but he'd run off before she could.

Even though she'd told herself he was nothing but an animal, the truth was, she'd loved him. And she'd missed him horribly.

Now he was back.

And nothing had changed. He was still an animal, and she was here to kill or maim him so that he would never be able to hurt another human being again.

4

Fury came awake slowly, his body aching. For a moment, he thought he was still trapped in human form. But as he blinked his eyes open, he breathed a sigh of relief. He was a wolf and he was home.

He rubbed his snout against the lilac-scented sheets. Bride always sprayed them with her spring water stuff whenever she made the bed. Normally he hated the smell. But today it was heaven.

"How you feeling?"

He lifted his head to find Vane propped against the wall, watching him. Flashing into human form, he was grateful Vane had put him under the covers. "I'm okay."

"You look like shit."

"Yeah, well, I wouldn't date you either, asshole."

Vane gave a short laugh. "You must be feeling better. You're back to you usual surliness. And speaking of surly, Zarek was here. He wants to talk to you when you're up and about."

Why would an ex–Dark-Hunter-turned-god want to talk to him? "What does he want?"

"He filled me in on what's been happening at Sanctuary. They cancelled their celebration and have the whole place locked down until they get to the bottom of this new attack. No one can come or go."

"Good. Where's Angelia?"

"She's in the nursery and refuses to come out. I think she's hoping her patria can track her here and release her from us animals."

Fury snorted at the idea. "Nah, she's probably plotting my dismemberment." Sitting up, he took a breath before he stood and went to pull his clothes out of the chest of drawers.

"You know I can dress you."

Fury scoffed at his brother's offer. "I don't need your help."

"Then on that note, I'm going downstairs to eat dinner."

Fury's ears perked up at that. "What did Bride make?"

"Leftover turkey and ham."

"Mashed potatoes?"

"Of course. She knows how much you love them."

That made his stomach rumble greedily. Fury debated on whether he should eat or see Angelia.

He was really hungry . . .

But . . .

"Save me some."

Vane inclined his head to him. "Wouldn't think otherwise. Oh, and Fang has been dying to know if Aimee got his note."

He pulled on his pants. "I gave it to Sasha to hand to her. So I assume she has it by now unless Dare happened to eat Sasha before he could complete his mission."

"Doubtful. Z would have been a lot surlier had that happened. I'll let him know." Vane exited the room.

Fury finished dressing, then left to see Angelia. He knocked on the door before he pushed it open to find her sitting in the rocker with her back against the wall. She jerked up as if she'd been napping.

Damn, she was the sexiest thing he'd ever seen. Especially the way her lips were swollen from sleep.

She almost smiled until her face froze as if she remembered that she wasn't supposed to be nice to him. "What do you want?"

"I wanted to make sure you were all right."

She tightened her grip on the chair's arms. "No, I'm not all right. I'm stuck here with animals whom we both know I hate. How can I be all right with that?"

He gave her a droll stare. "Yeah, well, no one's beating on you. From where I stand that looks pretty damn good."

Angelia looked away from that gimlet stare of his and tried not to focus on how handsome he was. On how beautiful those turquoise eyes could be . . .

But the longer he stood there, the harder it was to remember he was nothing but an animal just like the ones who'd threatened her downstairs.

He stepped into the room.

She shot to her feet to keep distance between them. "Stay away."

"I'm not going to hurt . . ." His voice trailed off as his eyes dilated dangerously.

Angelia swallowed as she recognized her worst fear had manifested.

He'd caught her scent. Terrified, she backed into the wall and prepared to fight him until one of them was dead.

Fury couldn't move as raw lust burned through him. His body instantly hard, it was all he could do not to attack her. No wonder she'd blockaded herself in this room. "You're in heat."

She picked up Trace's brass piggy bank as if she was about to throw it at him. "Stay away from me."

That was a lot easier said than done since every male

particle of him was attuned to her in a way that was virtually irresistible. The wolf in him salivated at the scent of her and it wanted nothing more than to throw her down and mount her.

Lucky for her, he wasn't the animal she thought him to be.

He approached her slowly. "I'm not going to touch you."

She threw the bank at his head.

He caught it in one hand before he returned it to its spot on the dresser.

"I'm not kidding, Fury," she growled at him.

"And neither am I. I told you I wouldn't hurt you and I have no intention of going back on my word."

Her gaze dropped down to the bulge in his pants. "I won't mate with you willingly. Ever."

Those words cut him more than they should have. "Trust me, baby, you wouldn't be worth the scratches. Unlike the Arcadian bastards you're used to, I don't have to force a woman into my bed. Sit up here and rot for all I care." He walked out and slammed the door behind him.

Angelia didn't move for several fearful heartbeats as she waited for his return.

He was gone and she was safe again . . . she hoped.

Over and over, she heard the stories in her head about how the Katagaria treated their females when they were in heat. If unmated, the woman was handed off to the unmated males of the pack, who passed her around until they'd had their fill of her. The female had no say whatsoever.

"You're all animals," she snarled, cursing the fact that it was her fertile time of the month and she was trapped here with them. "Where are you, Dare?"

As if in answer, a flash startled her.

She tensed as she realized it wasn't Dare coming to her rescue.

It was Fury. His eyes brittle with anger, he stalked toward her. A true predator bent on the gods only knew what.

"Don't touch me!" She struck out at him.

He caught her hand in his and held it. "You know what? I'm going to teach you a valuable lesson."

Before she could ask him what it was, he teleported them out of the nursery and into a dining room.

Angelia panicked as she realized the room was filled with eight male wolves in human form. By their scents, she knew they were as unmated as Fury was.

Her heart hammering, she tried to run, but Fury wouldn't let her. Blocking her escape, he quickly pulled his clothes on.

"You will sit and you will eat," he growled low in his throat. "Like a civil human," he spat the word as if it were the lowest thing imaginable.

How she wished she had her powers to blast him and make him pay for this. No doubt she'd be the first course and he'd probably hold her down while the others raped her.

Fury walked her toward the table, to the right hand of Bride where a young, handsome wolfswain sat. His eyes darkened as he caught a whiff of her scent.

Angelia braced herself for his attack.

His eyes black and dilated, he stood up slowly. This was it . . .

He was going to throw her down for all of them.

Just as she was sure he would, he inclined his head respectfully to Fury, picked up his plate and glass and moved away to sit at the other end of the table.

Fury sat her in the vacated chair.

Bride, who'd been watching curiously, let out a sigh. "I take it the two of you will be joining us."

Fury nodded. "We will."

A younger wolfswain who was sitting across the table

from her stood up immediately, making Angelia flinch. "I'll get plates for them."

Bride smiled kindly. "Thank you, Keegan."

Thin and blond, he practically ran into the other room only to return with china and silverware. He handed one setting to Fury, then turned to Angelia. "Would you like me to serve you?"

"Sit, Keegan," Fury barked.

He immediately put the place setting in front of her and returned to his seat.

There was so much tension in the room that Angelia could almost taste it. Ignoring it, Fury put food on their plates and then set one in front of her.

"Uncle Furry!"

She looked up to see Trace entering the room with Fang. He ran from Fang to Fury, who scooped him up into a tight hug.

"Hey, whelp." He squeezed him even harder while the boy laughed in happiness.

"Trace hit his target!"

Fury laughed, his face softening to the expression she'd known so well in their younger years . . . before they were enemies. "Glad I wasn't here for the potty training. Good job, Fang."

Trace squirmed out of Fury's arms to run to his mom. "Trace hit three ducks, Mommy."

"That's wonderful, baby. Good job." She pulled him up to sit in her lap.

Fang's eyes widened as he neared them and he, too, caught her scent. He sucked his breath in sharply, before he sat down on the other side of Fury. "Sorry you missed Thanksgiving this afternoon."

Fury put more mashed potatoes on his plate. "Yeah, me, too."

Angelia didn't understand why that would make him sad. "Thanksgiving?"

Fury looked at her as he cut a piece of turkey on his plate. "It's an American holiday. Every year they come together with their families to give thanks for their lives and company."

"It's why all the wolves are here," Bride said. "The mated ones went home with their wives earlier. Traditionally, the unmated males stay here for dinner and marathon gaming tournaments."

Again, she had no idea what they were talking about. "Gaming tournaments?"

"Video games," Keegan said.

Fury scoffed at the young wolf's eagerness. "She's from medieval England, whelp. She has no idea what you're talking about."

"I can show you."

Fang rolled his eyes. "Down, boy. Arcadian females equate being with us to bestiality."

His face stricken, Keegan returned to his food and didn't bother to look at her anymore.

One of the older males at the table pushed his plate back. "I've lost my appetite. Thank you, Bride, for the food." He looked at Vane. "You need me to stay and help protect your house?"

"I'd appreciate it if you would. We still don't know how many are able to wield whatever took down the lion."

He inclined his head before he headed toward the living room.

Two of the others joined him.

Fang handed a bowl of bread to Fury. "So, Keeg, you been practicing Soul Calibur?"

Keegan grinned. "I'm going to pwn you so bad, buddy. No ring-outs this time."

Vane laughed. "Careful, Keegan, he's setting you up. Fang knows all the special moves for half the characters."

That set up a whole conversation about a subject Angelia had no understanding of. But as they chatted and joked with each other, she relaxed.

Strange how they didn't seem so animalistic like this . . .

They seemed almost human.

Trace slowly moved from his mother's lap around the table to all the men who took turns holding him for a bit. When he got to Fury, he stood on his legs and reached over to her.

"You got drawing face like my daddy sometimes."

Her cheeks heated up as that brought her back to the full scrutiny of the wolves.

The wolf on the other side of Keegan sighed heavily. "Damn, woman, stop panicking every time we look at you. We're not going to throw you down and . . ." He stopped as he looked at Trace. "Do what you think we're going to do. Yes, we know what's going on with you. And no, we don't do that to women."

Bride took Trace back from Fury. She handed him a roll to eat while she directed her attention to Angelia. "I know you don't know Katagaria customs. When a woman is . . ." She paused and looked at the baby before she continued, "in *your* condition, she selects the male she wants. If she can't decide, they fight and she usually picks the winner, and if he doesn't satisfy her, she picks another. But it's always the woman's choice. The males give their lives and their loyalty to their women. Since their survival hinges on their ability to procreate, that is hardwired into their beings."

As Bride started to rise, Keegan took Trace from her arms to hold. "Do you need something?" he asked her.

"Just going to the restroom, sweetie." She patted him on his arm as she walked past him.

Angelia looked at Fury as he ignored her presence.

Was that why he'd never touched her? Thinking back, she remembered how he'd always been more respectful to his mother, sister and her than Dare had been. Always worried about them and their well-being. If they'd ever needed anything, he'd been there for them.

"Why did you bring me here?" she asked him.

He swallowed his food before he answered. "I want to know what that weapon is."

Everyone's attention focused on her and every hair on her body stood on full alert. They were poised to attack and she had a hard time controlling her panic.

"We've already had this discussion," she said between clenched teeth. "You can torture me all you want, but I will tell you nothing."

Vane laughed. "Katagaria don't torture . . . they kill."

Two of the older wolves stood up. "So we kill her?" they asked in unison without even a hint of emotion in their voices.

"No," Fury said. "I've given her my protection."

"Oh." The younger one who'd spoken picked up his plate and carried it into the kitchen.

Bride returned to the table and retook her chair.

One by one, all the men left except for Vane, Fury, Fang, and Trace.

"What happened to Zarek?" Fury asked.

Fang swirled his wine in his glass, something that struck her as very human. "He and Sasha are hunting down Dare."

"I hope they don't kill him before I do."

"He's your brother," Angelia reminded him.

Fury cut a harsh glare at her. "Let me explain something to you, babe. When Fang and Anya found out Vane was human, they protected him from our father. If he was wounded or sleeping, they'd take turns guarding his human form to make sure no one learned his secret. The instant Dare found out I was a wolf, he called out the patria to kill me. I think I should return that favor to him tenfold. At least he's a grown man, not an adolescent who had no real way to protect himself from the stronger, older warriors."

"He also has an unfair weapon. I think we should take it and . . ." Fang paused as he looked at Trace. "Put it someplace really uncomfortable."

Fury's gaze didn't leave hers. "I'd like to put it in the same place he wanted to drive that hot poker."

Angelia shook her head at his brutality. "All of you do realize that holding me here is an act of war."

Fury arched one brow. "How so?"

"You are wolves holding a patria member."

Vane snorted. "And I'm the Regis of your patria. Absent, true, but I am the head of the Kattalakis Arcadian Lykos. As such, you fall under my governance. To declare war on Fury and his Katagaria pack would require my edict, which I'd never give."

"So you condone his behavior?"

"For the first time in our relationship, and as scary as that thought is . . . yes. And as the Regis, I want to know what that weapon is that you used on the lion. Failure to give it to me will result in a trial and I think you know what the Katagaria council members will demand as punishment."

Her life. But not before she was brutalized. Whenever a Regis, especially one who ruled your particular patria requested something of you, you were compelled to give it.

Never had she hated that law more than at this moment. "We call it the Pulse."

Fury scowled. "What the hell is that?"

"It sends out small electrical charges. Not so much that it causes us to change back and forth, but rather it keeps us locked in our base form."

Bride sighed. "Like that collar you wear."

She nodded. "Only the pulse is permanent."

Fang shook his head. "It can't be. If it works on electrical impulses, it has to have a battery."

"It uses body chemicals to keep it charged."

Vane looked ill at the thought of it. "Can it be pulled out?"

"It's too small to be seen. There's no entry wound and no way to find it once it's inside a body."

Fang nodded. "That's what Carson said, too."

Bride grimaced in distaste. "Who would invent such a thing?"

"A Panther in the year 3062," Angelia said with a sigh. "He's now selling them to the highest bidders."

"Why?" Vane asked. "We don't need money like that."

Fury pinned him with an angry glare. "You're thinking like one of us, Vane. The Panther's Arcadian. Think human for a minute. Greed is their god."

Angelia was beginning to understand the differences herself.

Vane looked at Fury. "You should take her to the Lion at Sanctuary. Let her meet his mate who can no longer communicate with him. Or better yet, let her meet his children who will never know how much their father loves them. Never hear the sound of his voice as he tells them how proud he is. Or warns them of danger. Good job, really. I couldn't be prouder of your brutality."

Angelia refused to be intimidated by him. She knew better. "Animals don't do that."

Fury choked on his food before he pinned her with a vicious glare. "Yeah. I *never* said anything like that to you, did I?" He stood up and wiped his mouth. "You know what? I'm sick of looking at you. I remember a girl who used to be capable of caring about others. One who gave people the benefit of the doubt before she attacked them. But obviously she died. I want you out of here before you finish destroying what few good memories I have of that girl." He jerked the collar off her neck, then left the room.

Stunned, Angelia sat there, unable to believe what had just happened.

She was free . . .

"Uncle Furry?" Trace looked up at his mother. "Why is Furry mad, Mommy?"

"His feelings were hurt, baby. He'll be all right."

Vane met Angelia's baffled gaze. "You're free to leave. And I should warn you, the lions are out for blood. The guy you nailed . . . his brother is Paris Sabastienne, and you killed their youngest brother. While as a rule animals aren't big on vengeance, they are big on protecting their family. You've attacked them without provocation and they intend to slaughter all of you when they find you to keep you from doing this to any more members of their pride. You are their prey. Good luck."

Angelia swallowed in panic. "But I didn't shoot him."

Fang shrugged nonchalantly. "They're animals. They don't care who pulled the trigger. They're hunting by scent, and yours was all over Jake. Have a good life, cupcake, at least for the next few hours."

Angelia drew a shaky breath at his morbid forecast. As much as she hated it, she knew he was right. She wouldn't get far and there really was nothing she could do. She'd been a part of this. Willingly.

There was no way to change the past. Any more than she could keep the lions from killing her. They wouldn't listen to reason and honestly, if that had been done to someone she loved, she wouldn't be forgiving, either.

This was what she deserved for her part in Dare's brilliant plan. She would fight, but she wouldn't run. It wasn't in her. If this was her fate, then she would meet it with dignity.

Yet she didn't want to die without at least saying she was sorry to one person.

Excusing herself, she flashed from the table, up to Fury's room.

What she found there stunned her most of all.

Fury stood in front of the dresser holding the small medallion she'd given him when he'd reached puberty at twenty-seven.

"What's this for?" he'd asked her when she'd handed it over to him.

"You're a man now, Fury. You should have something to mark the occasion."

It hadn't been expensive or even particularly nice. Just a small circle with an X on it. Yet he'd kept it all these centuries.

Even after she'd betrayed him.

Balling it in his fist, he looked at her. "Why are you here?"

She wasn't sure really. No, that wasn't true, she knew exactly why she'd come. "I couldn't leave without telling you something."

He rolled off his retort in a dry, brittle tone. "You hate me. I suck. I'm an animal unfit to breathe the same air." He dropped the necklace back into the top drawer and closed it. "I know the tirade. I've heard it my entire life. So go away."

"No," she said, her voice cracking from the weight of her fear and guilt. "That's not what I wanted to tell you." Uncertain of her reception, she approached him slowly, like she would any wounded animal. She placed her hand over the one he had balled into a fist. "I'm sorry, Fury. You gave me your friendship and loyalty, and when I should have treasured it, I turned on you. I have no excuse for it. I could say I was afraid, but I shouldn't have been afraid of you."

Fury stared at her hand on his. All his life he'd been rejected. After he'd left his mother's patria, he hadn't reached out to anyone for fear of being hurt again. Because of his untrained powers, he'd always felt awkward around everyone.

The only person who'd ever made him feel like the man he wanted to be was . . .

Her.

"You stabbed me."

"No," she said, tightening her grip on his hand. "I stabbed at a painful memory. You know me, Fury, but what you don't know is that I have never in my life turned into a wolf. Even though it's part of me, it's a part that I have never been able to accept. I've lived my entire life trying to silence a nightmare that has never relented. We were friends, you and I. And not once since you left have I ever found anyone who made me feel like you did. In your eyes, I was always beautiful."

He met her gaze and the pain inside him scorched her. "And in your eyes, I'm a monster."

"A monster named Furry?"

He snatched his hand away from hers. "He can't pronounce my name yet."

"No, but you answer to it and you protected a woman who twice wounded you."

"So what? I'm a stupid asshole."

She reached up and touched his face. "You were never stupid."

He turned his face away. "Don't touch me. It's hard enough to fight your scent. After all, I'm just an animal and you're in heat."

Yes, she was, and the closer she was to him, the more that basic part of herself wanted to be with him. Every hormone in her body was on fire and it was weakening her will.

Or was she just using that as an excuse? The truth was, even without this she'd spent hours at night remembering him. Remembering his scent and his kindness. Wondering what it would have been like had he been Arcadian and still with her.

In all these centuries, he'd been her only real friend and she'd missed him terribly.

Swallowing her fear, she forced herself to say what she really wanted to. "Sate me, Fury."

He blinked at her words. "What?"

"I want you."

He shook his head and cast her a scathing glare. "That's your hormones talking. You don't want me. You just need to get laid."

"There's a house full of men downstairs I could pick from. Or I could go home and find one. But I don't want them."

He moved away from her.

She followed him and wrapped her arms around his waist. "Your brother told me that the lions are hunting us. I have no doubt they'll find me and kill me. But before I die, I want to do the one thing that I used to dream about."

"And that is?"

"Be with you. Why do you think while you were in the patria that I never chose a male to sleep with after I reached my prime?"

"I figured you thought they were limp."

She smiled at his insult. It was so classic Fury. "No. I was waiting for you. I wanted you to be my first." She trailed her hand down to cup him in her hand.

Fury sucked his breath in sharply. It was so hard to think while she fondled him. Hard to remember why he wanted her to leave.

"Be with me this one time." She nipped at his earlobe.

Chills ran the length of his body as the wolf in him howled in pleasure. In all honesty, he'd never taken many lovers. Mostly because of the woman whose hand was squeezing his cock through his jeans. How could he trust another one after the way she'd betrayed him?

He'd always held himself back from the other wolfswans. When they'd been in heat, he'd withdrawn until the woman had claimed another wolf.

It was easier that way. He didn't like human emotions,

and he didn't like any kind of intimacy. It left him too vulnerable. Left him open to hurt, and he didn't like being hurt.

He should shove her away and forget how good it felt to be held. He was just about to do that very thing when she wrapped her arms around him and gave him the one thing he hadn't had from anyone other than his nephew.

A hug.

"Do you have anyone who holds you?"

That one question shattered his last resistance. "No."

She walked around him and lifted herself up on her toes to reach his lips. Fury hesitated. Wolves didn't kiss when they mated. It was a human action and it was one he'd never experienced.

But as her lips touched his, he realized why it meant so much to the humans. The tenderness of her breath tickling his skin. Of their breathing mingling while her tongue parted his lips to taste him. That was something the wolf in him understood.

Growling, he pulled her into his arms, tasted her fully.

Angelia moaned at the gentle ferocity of his kiss. He cupped her face in his hands as he explored every inch of her mouth. Part of her couldn't believe she was touching a wolf.

But it's Fury . . .

Her Fury.

Even though they didn't pick their mates, he was the one man she'd given her heart to, even when she'd only been a child. *"You'll always be my best friend, Fury, and one day when we're grown we'll be warriors together. You protect my back and I'll protect yours."* How innocent that promise had been.

And how hard to keep.

Fury pulled back from the kiss to look down at her with those eyes that seared her with his pain and uncertainty. She was afraid. He could smell it. He just didn't know what she was afraid of. "You know that I am, Lia. You're about to den down with an animal. Are you ready for that?"

Den down . . . it was Katagaria slang and repugnant to the Arcadians.

Angelia traced the outline his lips. "If this is my last night to live, I want it to be with you, Fury. Had the Fates not been cruel to us and turned you into an animal when you hit puberty, we would have done this centuries ago. I know exactly what you are and I love you in spite of it." She smoothed the angry frown on his brow. "Most of all, I love you because of what you are."

Fury couldn't breathe as he heard words he'd never thought to hear from anyone's lips.

Love.

But did she mean it?

"Would you die for me, Lia?"

It was her turn to scowl. "Why do you ask me that?"

"Because I would die to keep you safe. That to me is what love is. I want to make sure that this time we both understand the terms. 'Cause if love to you is stabbing me and leaving me to die, then you can keep it."

She choked on a sob at his heartfelt words. "No, baby. That wasn't love. That was me being stupid, and I swear to you if I could go back and change that moment, I would stand there and fight for you . . . like I promised you I would."

Closing his eyes, he nuzzled his face against her cheek, stroking her skin with his whiskers. Angelia smiled at the purely wolf action. He was marking her as his. Mingling their scents together.

And honestly, she wanted his scent on her skin. It was warm and masculine. Pure Fury.

He stepped back and pulled her shirt over her head. His eyes flashing, he ran his hands over her bra, gently massaging her. She smiled at his hesitancy. "They won't bite you."

A slow smile curled his lips. "No, but their owner might."

Laughing, she nipped at his chin as she reached around to unfasten her bra.

Fury sucked his breath in sharply as she dropped the bra to the floor. On the small side, her breasts were still the most beautiful things he'd ever seen. His blood thrumming in his ears, he dipped his head down to taste her.

Angelia shuddered at the way his tongue teased her nipple. He nuzzled and suckled her in such a way that she actually came from it a few moments later. Crying out, she felt her knees give way from the ferocity of her orgasm.

Fury scooped her up in his arms and held her close as he carried her to the bed.

"How did you do that?" she asked breathlessly. "I didn't even know that could cause that."

He made a rumbling sound deep in his throat that was purely animalistic as he laid her back on the mattress. He bent his head down to sweep his hair against her breasts while he unfastened her jeans. "I'm a wolf, Lia. Licking and tasting is our foreplay." He slid her pants and panties down her legs before he removed them and her shoes.

Her heart hammering, she waited for him to return to her.

He jerked his shirt off over his head, showing her a body that was perfect in spite of the scars and bruises that marred the deep tawny skin. Cocking his head, he watched her. "Why are you hesitating?"

"I'm not hesitating."

"Yes, you are. I might be a wolf, but I know what Arcadian wolfswans do when they take a lover for the first time. Are you rejecting me?"

"Never," she said emphatically.

"Then why aren't you welcoming me?"

"I was afraid it would insult you. I don't know what Kataria do. Should I turn over?"

Anger darkened his eyes. "Do you want to be screwed by an animal, or loved by a man?"

She sighed in frustration. No matter what she did, she made him angry. "I want to be with Fury as *his* lover."

Fury savored those words. "Then show me like you would any lover."

Her smile warmed him completely as she spread her legs wide. Her gaze never wavered from his as she reached down to carefully spread the folds of her body and hold herself open to him so that he could see exactly how wet she was for him. How ready and willing she was.

Arcadian custom dictated that he enter her while she was like that. They would mate face-to-face with very little tasting.

But that wasn't what he wanted. Removing his pants, he crawled up the bed between her legs.

Angelia trembled, waiting for him to enter her with one forceful thrust. Instead, he nipped her fingers, licking her moisture from them. His gaze on hers, he held her hand in his before he took her into his mouth.

Arching her back, she groaned at how good he felt there. His tongue swirled around her, delving deep inside her body. Her head swam from the intense pleasure that kept increasing more and more until she feared she'd explode from it. Unable to stand it, she buried her hand in his hair while he continued to please her.

And when she came again, he stayed there, wringing every single spasm out of her until she thought she would weep from the sweet ecstasy.

Fury was panting from the pain in his cock as he ached to take her. Among his kind, the female must be fully sated. If not, she'd take another lover after him. It was a mark of shame to have a female call for another male to satisfy her, and though he hadn't taken many lovers, he'd never had one call in for a second.

There was no way he was going to allow Angelia to be his first.

Sitting back on his haunches, he held his hand out to her.

She took it and frowned. "Is something wrong?"

He pulled her up slowly until she was sitting on the bed. "No. You wanted to know how a wolf takes his woman . . ." He moved her to the foot of the bed where he put her hands on the brass poles.

Angelia wasn't sure about this. "What are you doing?"

He kissed her passionately before he indicated the dresser with a tilt of his head. "Look in the mirror."

She did and watched as he moved around to her back. The moment he was there, he lifted her up so that they were kneeling on the bed with his chest pressed against her back. He brushed the hair away from her neck so that he could nip her skin. Wrapping her in his arms, he nuzzled her and breathed in her ear.

His muscles flexed around her as he cupped her breasts in his hands. He nudged her legs wider apart, then dipped his hand down to tease the tender folds.

Angelia watched his play, entranced by it. How could someone so fierce and dangerous be so gentle?

When she was wet and aching again, he lifted his head to meet her gaze in the mirror. With their gazes locked, he slid himself deep inside her.

She gasped at the girth and length of him there. Biting his lip, he thrust against her hips, sinking in even deeper while his hand continued to tease her. She felt her powers surging. Sex had always made her kind more powerful. Stronger. But never had she felt like this.

It was as if he were feeding her from a primal power source.

Fury buried his face against her nape as his senses swirled over how good she felt. There was nothing sweeter than the feel of her body around his. If she were a wolf, she'd be clawing at him by now, demanding he ride her harder and faster.

Instead, she let him take his time and savor her softness. Savor the beauty of intimacy. This was a side of himself that he'd seldom shared with any female.

And deep in his heart he knew why that was.

Because they'd never been his Lia. How many times had he closed his eyes and pretended it was Lia he held? Pretended it was her he smelled.

Now there was no pretending. She was here and she was his.

"Say my name, Lia," he whispered in her ear.

She frowned at him. "What?"

He thrust deep inside her and paused to look at her in the mirror. "I want to hear my name on your lips while I'm inside you. Look at me like this and tell me again that you love me."

Angelia cried out in pleasure as he thrust against her again. "I love you, Fury."

She could feel him growing larger inside her. It was something all the males of their species did. The more pleasure they felt, the more they expanded. The thick fullness caused her powers to soar even more. Arching her back, she reached over her head to cup his cheek.

He quickened his strokes while his hand continued to tease her cleft. There was a ferocity to his strokes now. One that was both commanding and possessive. She'd always heard the term of being taken by a lover, but this was the first time she'd experienced it.

And this time when she came, she actually howled from the sheer ecstasy of it.

Fury ground his teeth at the sound of her orgasm. At the sensation of her body spasming against his. It ignited his powers, arcing them until they caused the lamp on the nightstand to shatter. Still he pleased her, wanting to wring every last sigh and murmur from her.

It was only after she collapsed back against him that he allowed himself to come, too. He growled at the sudden burst as his release exploded and he finally felt his own relief.

Angelia smiled at the sight of Fury in the mirror as he buried his head against her shoulder and shuddered. His panting mixed with hers while he held her in his arms and kept her there. Unlike regular humans, they would be locked together like this until his orgasm finished—which would take several minutes. Normally, an Arcadian male would fall against her and wait for it to end.

Instead, Fury took the brunt of her weight while he nuzzled her neck and held her tight.

"Did I hurt you?" he asked.

"No."

He laid his cheek against hers and rocked her gently. Angelia smiled, placing her hand to his cheek. In all her life she'd never experienced a more tender moment.

And to think it was in the arms of an animal that she'd found it. It was inconceivable.

They stayed there like that until he finally was soft enough to pull out without hurting her. Angelia fell back on the bed.

Fury lay down beside her so that he could stare at her naked body. "You are so beautiful." He traced the Sentinel markings on her face.

"I'll bet you never thought you'd mate with an Arcadian."

"I did until I turned out to be a wolf."

She looked away at his blunt truth. "Why did you keep that secret from me?"

He laughed bitterly. "Oh gee, I can't imagine. Maybe because I was afraid you'd freak out and hate me. What a ridiculous thought that was, huh?"

Blushing, she looked away, ashamed of the fact that he'd been right about her and he shouldn't have been. "I'm sorry for that."

"It's all right. You weren't the only one who tried to kill me."

No, his entire patria, including his mother, siblings and grandfather had tried to kill him. And still he'd managed to survive.

"Did your father welcome you in?"

"I never gave him the chance to reject me. I found his pack and when I saw how little respect he had for Vane and Fang, I decided to lay low and not tell him I was his son. I figured one near-death experience at the hands of a parent was enough for anyone." He traced circles around her breasts. "You've really never shapeshifted?"

"Why would I?"

He stopped to stare at her. "I think you should."

"Why?"

"It's part of who and what you are."

So what? "It's a part I don't have to accept or like."

"Yes, you do."

She tensed at his tone. "What are you saying?"

"I'm saying either you shift into a wolf, or I'm going to shock you and make you."

She gasped at his threat. "You wouldn't dare."

"Try me."

Horrified, she sat up. "This isn't funny, Fury. I don't want to be a wolf."

His turquoise eyes were relentless. "For one minute, humor me. You need to know what it is you hunt, and what it is you hate."

"Why?"

"Because it's what I am and I want you to understand me."

She wanted to tell him to shove that. She did understand him, but before she could say that, she stopped.

He was right. How could she understand what he was when she'd never experienced it herself? If it was important to him, then she would do this.

"Then for you only, and only for one minute."

He inclined his head and waited.

And waited.

When a full three minutes had gone by and she was still human, he arched a brow at her. "Well?"

"Okay. I'm doing it." Glaring at him, she flashed into her wolf's form.

Fury smiled at the sight of her on his bed. Dark brown with black and red, she was as beautiful in this form as she was in her human one. He ran his hand through her fur. "See, it's not so bad, is it?"

Can you understand me?

"Of course I can. Just like you can understand me. Now look around the room. See how different things look. How much sharper sounds and scents are."

She looked up at him.

"You're still human, Lia. Even as a wolf. You retain all of yourself in this form."

She flashed back to herself. "Do you—"

"Yes. What we are in one form, we are in the other. Nothing changes."

Angelia sat there thinking that over. She'd assumed as a wolf that they became animals with no rational thought at all . . . but that hadn't been true. She'd kept all her cognizance. The only difference had been heightened senses.

Gratitude swept through her, and as she went to kiss him, a searing pain tore through her hand. Gasping, she sat back, shaking it to help alleviate the pain.

Fury cursed before he lifted his hand and blew air across it. As he did so, the geometric pattern of his pack appeared on his palm.

It was identical to the one on hers.

Holy shit . . .

"We're mates?" Angelia gasped.

Fury looked at her in disbelief. "How?"

She continued staring at her palm. In their world, the Fates determined who they would mate with at their births. The only way to find the mate was to sleep with them and if it was meant to be, they would have matching marks.

Those marks would only appear for three weeks, and if the woman failed to accept her mate within that time, she would be free to live out her life free of him. But she would never be able to have children with anyone else.

The male was left celibate until the day she died. Once mated, he could only sleep with his wife. He would never be able to have an erection for anyone else.

"We were chosen." She placed her palm to his and smiled. "You are my mate."

Fury was having a hard time with this. He'd always wondered what it would feel like to be mated. The Dark-Hunter Acheron had told him that he'd already met his mate, but he hadn't really believed him.

To have it be the one woman he'd always loved . . .

It just didn't happen like this.

He looked at Angelia, his heart pounding. "Will you accept me?"

She rolled her eyes. "No. I'm here naked with you because all my clothes fell off by accident and I can't find them."

"You're a sarcastic little critter, aren't you?"

"I learned it from you."

Laughing, Fury leaned forward to kiss her, but before he could make contact with her lips, a bright flash exploded. He pulled back and scowled as four lions appeared in his room.

Their expressions were furious as they threw something at him.

He caught it and then grimaced before he dropped the jackal's gruesome head to the floor. "What the hell is this?"

"I'm Paris Sabastienne," the tallest lion said, "and I'm here to kill the bitch who killed and ruined my brothers."

5

Angelia used her powers to clothe them as she braced herself for Fury to hand her over to the Litarians for their dinner.

Instead, he rose from the bed with an aura so deadly it gave her chills. "I don't know what you think you're doing here, tree-humper, but you don't come into my brother's house with that attitude and tone." He looked down to the severed head on the floor. "And you damn sure don't bring filth into the presence of my mate."

"We've tracked her scent here."

Fury gave him a sinister smirk. "And do you smell it in my room?"

One of the lions moved to grab Fury. Faster than she could blink, he twirled away from the lion and then pinned him against the wall. Hard.

"You really don't want to test me," Fury snarled, banging his head into the wall. "I'm not a gazelle on the savannah, punk. I'll have your throat faster than you took the jackal's head."

Paris took a step forward. "There are four of us and one of you."

"Two of us," Angelia corrected, cutting him off from Fury. "And the only thing deadlier than a wolf is his mate when he's threatened."

Paris approached her. He sniffed the air around her as he eyed her warily.

"Is it her?" one of the other lions asked him.

"No," he said disgustedly. "We've lost the scent." He turned toward Fury. This isn't over, Wolf. We won't stop until we're satisfied. If I find the bitch responsible, I will feast on her entrails."

Fury shoved the lion he held at Paris. "You're not welcome here. Really. Get out."

Paris made a feral growl before they vanished.

"And take your nasty trophy head with you," Fury snarled as he slung it into the portal with them so that it went wherever it was they were going.

Angelia let out a slow breath in relief. "What just happened? How did they not smell me?"

Fury shrugged. "The one power I did develop was the ability to mask my scent. Since it's now part of yours, I was able to mask yours, too."

"That's why you don't smell like a Katagari!"

He inclined his head to her in a sarcastic salute.

But that raised another question in her mind. "So how is it Dare found out about your base form if he couldn't smell it?"

Fury looked away as pain swept through him. To this day, the betrayal of it shredded his soul.

Angelia placed her hand on his cheek where he had his teeth clenched tight. "Tell me."

He didn't know why he confided in her when it went against his nature. But before he could stop himself, the truth came pouring out. "We were attacked by a group of outlaw humans in the forest. They shot an arrow. Dare didn't see it, but I did. I shoved him out of the way and took it for him."

She winced as she understood what had happened. "The pain made you change forms."

Fury nodded. "He knew as soon as I fell down. I tried to stop him before he reached the village, but by the time I got there, my mother had already been told."

The rest she remembered with crystal clarity. She'd heard the shouting and had gone to the main hall where they'd all gathered. Fury had been bleeding, but he was still in human form.

Dare had shoved him at their mother. "He's a fucking Wolf, Mum. I saw it."

Bryani had grabbed Fury by the hair. "Tell me the truth. Are you a Katagari?"

Fury's gaze had gone to Angelia's. Pain, shame and torment had shone deep in his eyes. But it was the pleading look there that had taken her breath. He'd silently begged her to stand with him.

"Answer me!" His mother had demanded.

"I'm a wolf."

They'd set on him with a vengeance so fierce that she found it hard to believe that she'd ever taken part in it. But there, in that moment . . .

She was such a fool.

"Will you ever trust me again?" she asked him.

He took her marked palm into his hand. "Do I have a choice?"

"Yes, you do. This only means I can bear your children. It has nothing to do with our hearts."

Fury sighed. No, it didn't. His parents hated one another. Even now all they did was plot each other's murders.

"If you can lay aside your hatred of my kind, I'm willing to forget the past."

Angelia looked around the room. "I will have to live here in your time, won't I?"

"Do you really think you can go home wearing the mark of a Katagari?"

He was right. They'd destroy her.

Fury stepped away from her. "You have three weeks to decide if you can live with me."

"I don't need three weeks, Fury. I agreed to den down with you, and so I have. I will even bond with you."

Anger sparked in his eyes at her suggestion. "No, you won't. I have too many enemies who want me dead. I won't bond your life force to mine. It's too dangerous."

She laughed. "*You* have enemies? What was that lion tessera that just left? Who were they after?" She cupped his face in her hands. "You and I should have had a lifetime together already. I allowed my stupidity to rob us of four hundred years. I don't want to lose another minute of being with you."

"You didn't feel that way twenty-four hours ago."

"You're right. But you've opened my eyes. What Dare is trying to do is wrong. I can't believe I've ruined that poor lion's life. God, how I wish I could go back and shove Dare when he fired the gun so that he'd miss."

Fury's face went stark white. "Dare killed an unarmed lion?"

"No, that was the jackal. Dare shot the one who lived."

"And your part in all this?"

"Stupid onlooker who thought she was going to make the world safe for other little girls so that they wouldn't have to watch their family get eaten. I didn't realize that I was fighting for the monsters and not against them."

Fury sighed. "Dare's not a monster. He's just an insecure asshole who wanted his mother to love him."

"And what about you?"

"I was an insecure asshole who knew he could never get too close to his mother for fear she'd smell the wolf on him and kill him."

She pulled him into her arms to kiss his lips. “Mate with me, Fury.”

“You’re a bossy thing, aren’t you?”

“Only when there’s something I want.” She looked at the bed. “Shouldn’t we get naked?”

He put his hands on her arms and held her back. “We have to settle this first. I want to make sure that you’re mating with me out of choice and not out of fear.”

“Don’t you think I’m smart enough to know the difference?”

“I’m the one who has to be sure of your motivation.”

Because he still didn’t trust her. The sad thing was, she couldn’t blame him. “Very well then. How do we end this?”

“I think I have an idea.”

Angelia sat downstairs with Fang sniffing at her hand.

“No wonder he was acting so weird. The bastard’s mated.”

“Fang!” Bride snapped at him. “Leave the poor woman alone, or at least congratulate her.”

“On what? Being mated to Fury seems like a nightmare to me.”

There was a time Angelia would have agreed. Strange how she no longer did. “Your brother is a wonderful wolf.”

Bride smiled approvingly.

“So where is lover-wolf, anyway?”

“He said he was going to see a friend about getting the lions off my trail.”

Fang’s face blanched.

“What?” Angelia asked, immediately scared by his reaction.

“Fury doesn’t have any friends.”

Why would he have lied to her? Dear gods, what was he doing? “Then where is he?”

The question had barely left her lips before Vane appeared.

He glared at her before he turned to Fang. "I need you at the Omegrion. Now."

Fang frowned. "What's going on?"

"Fury has turned himself in as the one who maimed the lion."

Angelia shot to her feet. "What?!"

"You heard me! Stupid idiot. I've been summoned by Savitar who asked me to bring any witnesses who can testify to his innocence."

Fang cursed. "Where was he when it happened?"

"I don't know."

Fang shot to his feet. "I'm going."

They started to leave.

"Don't forget me." Angelia moved to stand in front of Vane.

Vane hesitated.

Fang gave him a stern look. "She's his mate, V. Let her come."

Nodding, he took her with them to Savitar's island and into the chamber room where the Omegrion met and decided the laws that governed all lycanthropes. All her life, Angelia had heard stories about this place. Never had she thought to see it.

Here the Regis, one representative for each branch of the Katagaria and Arcadians, met. It was amazing to her that they didn't fight. But then that was why Savitar was here.

More like a referee, Savitar held the final fate of all of them in his hands. The only problem was no one really knew what Savitar was. Or even where he came from.

"Where's Fury?" she asked Vane.

"I don't know."

"Are all the members here?"

He scanned the group. "All but Fury."

Before she could ask another question, she felt a ripple of power behind her. Turning, she found an unbelievably gorgeous man there. At least six-feet-eight, he had long dark hair and a goatee. Dressed in surf clothes, he eyed her suspiciously.

"You have your witnesses, Wolf?" he asked Vane.

"I do."

"Then let's proceed." He walked past the round table where the Omegrion members sat and took a seat on a throne that was set apart.

"Savitar?" she asked Vane.

He nodded.

Damn. He *was* scary.

Savitar let out a long, exaggerated sigh. "I know everyone here wants to be somewhere else. Trust me. So do I. But for those who haven't heard and you'd have to live under a rock . . ." He looked over to the Arcadian Hawk Regis and hesitated. "Okay, so some of you do, which is why I have to explain this. It appears some of our good Arcadians have created and now used a weapon that can take away your preternatural abilities and lock you into your base form."

Several members sucked their breaths in sharply.

Savitar nodded. "Yeah, it sucks. Two days ago, a couple of bastards decided to go hunting. I have the head of two of the four people responsible." He indicated the lions to his left. "The family of the victim wants the other two. Dead. But tortured first. I can respect that."

"Do we hunt?" Nicolette Peltier asked.

"No. It seems one of those responsible has come forward to turn himself in. He claims he killed the fourth member and doesn't want to run."

"Where is he?" Paris's brother demanded.

"Wait your turn, Lion, or I'll be wearing your eyeballs as jewelry."

The lion backed down immediately.

Savitar snapped his fingers, and Fury appeared before his throne in chains.

Angelia started for him, only to have Vane stop her.

Fury did a doubletake as he saw her. "Dammit, Vane, I told you not to—" A muzzle appeared on his face.

Savitar glared at him. "Next person or animal who interrupts me is going to get gutted."

Fury's gaze was locked on hers. *Don't speak*, he projected to her. *It's better this way. Trust me. You can go home and have your life back.*

Was he out of his mind?

That thought died as she saw Dare appear next to Fury.

Savitar eyed Dare with contempt. "We have a witness who swears he saw Fury in the act. Since that corroborates what Fury has said, I suppose your vote on his fate will be an easy one. Unless someone in the room has something more to add."

Sasha stepped forward. "Fury didn't do it. He's protecting someone. I know him. I might not like his ass, but I know he's innocent. I was there at Sanctuary when he saw the lion and he knew nothing about it."

"It's true," Nicolette Peltier said. "I, too, saw him. He told me he would find the one responsible and make them pay."

Savitar stroked his chin. "Interesting, isn't it? What do you have to say about that, Fury?"

The muzzle vanished. "They're on crack."

Savitar shook his head. "Anyone else on crack?"

Tears stung Angelia's eyes at the sacrifice Fury was willing to make. But she couldn't let him do this. Looking down, she traced his symbol in her palm.

It would have been her greatest honor to be his mate and have his children.

If only it could have been.

"Fury's innocent," she said, stepping forward. "He confessed to save—"

"Me."

Angelia froze in shock as Dare cleared his throat.

"What was that?" Savitar asked.

Dare glanced to her, then looked at Fury. "I'm the one who fired the shot that maimed the lion. The one who killed the other is already dead."

"And the others?"

"Also dead."

Fury shook his head at Dare. "Why are you doing this?"

"Because it was my wrongdoing, and I refuse to have an animal show me up by being noble. Fuck you."

"We had a bargain," Fury said under his breath.

"I'm altering it." Dare looked back at Angelia. "It's time for once that I did the right thing for the right reasons."

Savitar folded his arms over his chest. "We have another confession from Dare Kattalakis. Going once, going twice . . . are there any more confessions in the room? Anyone else want to admit to shooting a lion?" He paused. "Didn't think so."

The lions moved forward. "Then he's ours."

Savitar shook his head. "Actually, he's mine. Sorry. You've already taken the heads of two Arcadians. Be glad I don't demand justice for their families. We're going to assume they were guilty, but without a trial . . ."

The lions looked less than pleased, but no one dared to question him.

"As for this little toy they used, don't worry. I've already made sure the inventor doesn't invent anything else. I have my people tracking down the handful he sold and we should have them destroyed soon. In the meantime . . ."

Dare vanished, and Fury's shackles melted.

"Omegrion is adjourned."

The council members flashed out.

Except for the wolves and Nicolette. Fury walked over to where they were standing. He held his hand out to Sasha. "Thanks."

"No problem. And we're still not friendly."

Fury's eyes danced with humor. "Yeah, you prick, I hate your guts." He looked at Nicolette. "It was decent of you, too, to speak up."

"You are still banned from my house . . . unless you're wounded." She teleported out.

Fury shook his head, then looked at her. All humor died. "You were going to turn yourself in to save me."

"I told you, Fury. I will always stand at your back."

He took her hands into his and then kissed each one in turn. "My back isn't where I want you."

She arched a brow. "No? Where would you prefer me, then?" She expected him to say under him—it was what an Arcadian male would say.

But he didn't.

"I want you at my side. Always."

"Ugh," Fang groused. "Wolves, get a room."

Angelia smiled. "Sounds like a great idea."

The next thing she knew, they were home.

Savitar didn't move as he watched the last of the wolves clear the room. The moment it was empty, he felt a power surge next to him.

It was Zarek.

"Sasha went home, Z."

"Yeah, I know. I was checking with you about our earlier discussion."

"My demons got most of the weapons."

"But . . ."

"There are still a few out there."

Zarek cursed. "If Sasha gets nailed with one, Astrid will lose her mind."

"Believe me, Z, I know." Savitar looked out toward the clear horizon, but inside, he knew the same thing that Zarek did. There was a storm brewing. Fierce and violent.

They'd stopped this minor bout. But it was nothing compared to the one that was coming.

Fury lay in bed, naked, with Angelia on top of him. Their palms were still pressed together from their mating ritual.

"I still can't believe you would have died so that I could go home."

"I can't believe you were going to call me a liar and take my place under the guillotine. Next time I try to save you, woman, you better stay saved."

She laughed, then nipped at his chin. "I shall promise to behave, on only one condition."

"And that is?"

"That you bond your life force to mine."

He scowled at her. "Why is that so important to you?"

She swallowed against the lump in her throat. "Don't you know?"

"No."

"Because I love you, Wolf, and I don't ever want to spend another day in this life without you. Where you den, I den, and when you die, I die, too."

Fury looked up at her in disbelief. In all his life, he'd only ever wanted one thing.

And Lia had just given it to him. A woman he could love and depend on.

"For you, my lady wolf, I would do anything."

Anglia smiled as she felt him growing hard again. Kissing his hand, she knew that this time they wouldn't just have sex. This time they would be joined throughout all eternity.

THE STORY OF SON

by

J.R. Ward

For my family,
both those of blood and choice,
with all my love.

1

Claire Stroughton palmed her travel mug without looking up from the will she'd drafted and was reviewing.

"I hate when you do that."

Claire glanced across her office at her executive assistant. "Do what?"

"That heat-seeking missile routine with your coffee."

"My mug and I have a very close relationship."

Martha pushed her sleek glasses up on her nose. "Then good thing it's got a lid. You're going to be late for your five o'clock if you don't leave now."

Claire stood and pulled on her suit jacket. "How bad's the time?"

"Two twenty-nine. Drive to Caldwell is a minimum of two hours plus in this traffic and your car is waiting for you down in front. Your conference call with London is scheduled for sixteen. . . fifteen minutes from now. What kind of cleanup do you need me to do before the long weekend?"

"I've reviewed the revised merger documents for Technitron and I'm not impressed." Claire passed over a stack of paper big enough to be used as a doorstop. "Courier them down to 50 Wall now. I need a meeting with opposing counsel seven a.m. Tuesday morning. They come to us. Do I owe you anything before I go?"

"No, but you can tell me something. What kind of sadistic bore schedules a meeting with their lawyer for five o'clock on the Friday of Labor Day weekend?"

"Client's always right. And sadistic is in the eye of the beholder." Claire packed up the will in a document case then grabbed her Birkin bag. As she looked around her spacious office, she tried to think of the work she planned to do over the weekend. "What am I forgetting?"

"Pill."

"Right, right." Claire used what was left in her mug to polish off the prescription she'd been working her way through for the last ten days. As she pitched the orange bottle in the wastepaper basket, she realized she hadn't sneezed or coughed since Sunday. Stuff had worked evidently.

Damn airplanes. Germ pools with wings.

"Walk with me." Claire gave a couple more marching orders on the way to the elevator, all the while waving to some of the two hundred-odd attorneys and support staff that worked at Williams, Nance & Stroughton. Martha kept pace with her in spite of the load of paper in her arms, but then that was what was great about the woman. No matter what, she was always there.

At the bank of elevators, Claire punched the down button. "Okay, I think that's it. Hope you have a good weekend."

"You, too. Try and take a break, would you?"

Claire stepped into the mahogany-paneled lift. "Can't. We have Technitron on Tuesday. I'm going to spend most of my weekend here."

Four minutes later she was in her Mercedes inching forward in the Manhattan traffic, trying to get out of the city. Eleven minutes after that she was being patched into London.

The conference call lasted fifty-three minutes and it was a good thing she was basically in a parking lot because the virtual meeting didn't go well. Which was pretty common. Mergers and acquisitions of billion-dollar companies were never easy and not for the faint of heart. Her father had taught her that.

Still, it was a relief to hang up and just focus on driving. Caldwell, New York, was probably only a hundred miles from downtown, but Martha was right. Traffic was a bitch. Apparently everyone and their uncle was trying to peel out of the Big Apple and they were all using the same route as Claire.

Normally, she wouldn't be taking the time to drive to see a client in a private home, but Miss Leeds was a special case for a lot of reasons and it wasn't like the woman could come down to the office easily. She was what? Ninety-one now?

Christ, maybe she was even older. Claire's father had been the woman's lawyer forever and after he'd died two years ago, Claire had inherited Miss Leeds along with his equity in the family firm. When she'd taken his seat at the partners' table, she became the first female in the history of Williams, Nance & Stroughton to park it in the boardroom, but she'd earned that right, in spite of what Walter Stroughton's will said. She was a fantastic M&A lawyer. Second to very, very few.

Miss Leeds was her only trusts and estates client, which had been the same for Claire's father. The elderly woman was worth close to two hundred million dollars, thanks to her family's interests in a variety of companies, all of which were represented by WN&S. These holdings were the heart of the relationship. Miss Leeds believed in sticking with what she knew and her family had been with the firm since its inception in 1911. So there you had it. An M&A rock star doing T&E for an NHC.

Or in human speak: a mergers and acquisitions specialist doing trusts and estates work for a nursing home candidate.

Believe it or not, the interaction algebra added up. The will and the trusts in it were fairly straightforward once you got familiar with them and Miss Leeds was easygoing compared to most of Claire's corporate clients. The woman was also good for business when it came to that will of hers. She approached revisions of it the way some people got into gardening, and at $650 an hour for Claire's time, the billable hours added up. Miss Leeds was constantly reworking the charitable portion of her estate, tilling that section, trimming and replanting the philanthropies as she changed her mind. The last two alterations Claire had handled over the phone, so when Miss Leeds had asked for a personal meeting this time, there was every reason to go up for a quick visit.

Hopefully it would be quick.

Claire had only been out to the Leeds estate once before, to introduce herself after her father's death. The meeting had gone well. Miss Leeds evidently had seen pictures of Claire through her father and had approved of Claire's "ladylike deportment."

Which was a joke. Although it was true that clothes could make both the man and the woman, and Claire's wardrobe was full of conservative suits with below-the-knee skirts, that was surface gloss. She had her father's head for business and his aggressive streak, too. She might look like a lady from her chignon to her sensible pumps, but on the inside she was a killer.

Most people picked up on her true nature about two minutes after meeting her and not just because she was a brunette. But it was a good thing Miss Leeds was fooled. She was from the old school and then some—part of a generation where proper women didn't work at all, much less as high-powered attorneys in Manhattan. Frankly, Claire had been surprised Miss Leeds hadn't gone with one of the other partners, but the two of them did get along for the most part. So far, the only hiccup in the relationship had occurred during that first face-to-face when the woman had asked whether Claire was married.

Claire was most definitely not married. Never had been, not interested, no thank you. Last thing she needed was some man with opinions about how late she stayed at the firm or how hard she worked or where they would live or what they would have for dinner. Eliza Leeds, however, was clearly of the you're-defined-by-what-was-sitting-next-to-you-in-pants set. So Claire had braced herself as she'd explained that, no, she had no husband.

Miss Leeds had seemed daunted, but then she'd rallied, moving swiftly on to the boyfriend question. The answer was the same. Claire did not have and didn't want one of those and no, no pets, either. There had been a long silence. Then the woman had smiled, made a brief comment along the lines of "my, how things have changed," and that was where they'd left things. At least for the moment.

Every time Miss Leeds called the office, she asked whether Claire had found a nice man. Which was fine. Whatever. Different generation. And the woman took the *no*'s with grace—maybe because she herself had never been married. Evidently she had an unfulfilled romantic streak or something.

If Claire was honest, the whole relationship thing bored her. No, she didn't hate men. No, her parents' marriage hadn't been dysfunctional. No, in fact her father had been a very supportive male figure. There was no bad fallout from a relationship, no self-esteem issues, no pathology, no history of abuse. She was smart and she loved her work and she was grateful for the life she had. The home and hearth stuff was just made for other people. Bottom line? She totally respected women who became wives and mothers but didn't envy them their burden of caretaking. And she didn't have a hole in her heart on Christmas morning because she was alone. And she didn't need soccer games or drawings on her refrigerator or homemade gifts to feel fulfilled. And Valentine's Day and Mother's Day were just two more pages on the calendar.

What she loved was the battle in the boardroom. The negotiation. The tricky ins and outs of the law. The energizing responsibility of representing the interests of a ten-billion-dollar corporation—whether it was buying someone else or divesting assets or firing a CEO for having illicit eight-digit personal expenses.

All of that was what juiced her and, as she was at the top of her field and in her early thirties, she was in a damn good place in life. The only trouble she had was with people who didn't understand a woman like her. It was such a double standard. Men could spend their entire lives devoted to work and they were viewed as good earners, not antisocial spinster-aunts with intimacy issues. Why couldn't a woman be the same?

When Caldwell's span bridge finally appeared, Claire was ready to get the meeting over with, head back to her apartment on Park Avenue, and start prepping for the Technitron showdown on Tuesday. Hell, maybe there would be enough time to even go back to the office.

The Leeds estate consisted of ten acres of sculptured grounds, four outbuildings, and a wall that you'd need rapelling gear and the upper body strength of a personal trainer to surmount. The mansion was a huge pile of stone set on a rise, an ostentatious display of new wealth erected during the Gothic Revival period of the 1890s. To Claire, it looked like something Vincent Price would pay taxes on.

Navigating the circular drive, she parked in front of the cathedral-worthy entrance and set her cell phone to vibrate. Picking up her bag, she approached the house thinking she should have a cross in one hand and a dagger in the other. Man, if she had Leeds's money, she'd live in something a little less dreary. Like a mausoleum.

One side of the double doors was opened before she got to the lion's head knocker. Leeds's butler, who was a hundred and eight if he was a day, bowed.

"Good evening, Miss Stroughton. May I inquire, did madam leave the keys in the car?"

Was his name Fletcher? Yeah, that was it. And Miss Leeds liked you to use his name. "No, Fletcher."

"Perhaps you will give them to me? In the event your car must be moved." When she frowned, he said quietly, "I'm afraid Miss Leeds is not doing well. If an ambulance must come . . ."

"I'm sorry to hear that. Is she ill or . . ." Claire let the sentence drift off as she handed over her keys.

"She's very weak. Please, come with me."

Fletcher walked with the kind of slow dignity you'd expect from a man sporting a formal British butler's uniform. And he fit in with the decor. The house was furnished in old-money style, with layer upon layer of art collected over generations choking the rooms. The priceless hodgepodge of museum-quality paintings and sculpture and furniture was from different periods, but it flowed together. Although what an upkeep. Dusting the stuff would be like cutting twenty acres of grass with a push mower—as soon as you were finished, you'd need to start again.

She and Fletcher took the massive, curving staircase up to the second floor and went down the hallway. On both sides, hanging on red silk walls, were portraits of various Leeds, their pale faces glowing against dark backgrounds, their two-dimensional eyes following you. The air smelled like lemon polish and old wood.

Down at the end, Fletcher knocked on a carved door. When there was a weak greeting, he opened the panel wide.

Miss Leeds was propped up in a bed the size of a house, looking as small as a child, as fragile as a sheet of paper. There was white lace everywhere, dripping from the canopy, hanging to the floor around the mattress, covering the windows. It was a wintry scene complete with icicles and snow banks, except it wasn't cold.

"Thank you for coming, Claire." Miss Leeds's voice was frail to the point of a whisper. "Forgive me for not being able to meet with you properly."

"That's quite all right." Claire came forward on tiptoe, afraid to make any noise or sudden movements. "How are you feeling?"

"Better than I did yesterday. Perhaps I have caught the flu."

"It has been going around, but I'm glad you're on the mend." Claire did not think it would be helpful to mention she'd had to go on antibiotics for something like that herself. "Still, I'll be quick and let you get back to resting."

"But you must stay for some tea. Won't you?"

Fletcher piped up. "Shall I get the tea?"

"Please, Claire. Join me for tea."

Hell. She wanted to get back.

Client is always right. Client is always right. "But of course."

"Good. Fletcher, do bring the tea and serve it when we're through with my papers." Miss Leeds smiled and closed her eyes. "Claire, you may sit beside me. Fletcher will bring you a chair."

Fletcher didn't look like he could handle bringing over a footstool, much less something she could sit in.

"That's okay," Claire said. "I'll get one—"

Without taking a breath, the butler easily hefted over an antique armchair that looked as if it weighed as much as a Buick.

Whoa. Bionic butler, evidently. "Ah . . . thank you."

"Madam will be comfortable in this."

Yeah, and maybe madam will drive it home if her car doesn't start.

As Fletcher left, Claire put her butt on the throne and glanced at her client. The old woman's eyes were still closed. "Miss Leeds . . . are you sure you don't want me to leave the will with you? You can review it at your leisure and I can come back to notarize your signature."

There was a long silence and she wondered if the woman had fallen asleep. Or, God forbid . . . "Miss Leeds?"

Pale lips barely moved. "Have you a gentleman caller yet?"

"Excuse—er, no."

"You are so lovely, you know." Watery eyes opened and Miss Leeds's head turned on the pillow. "I should like you to meet my son."

"I beg your pardon?" Miss Leeds had a *son*?

"I have shocked you." The smile that stretched thin skin was sad. "Yes. I am . . . a mother. It all happened long ago and in secret—both the deed and the birthing. We kept it all quiet. Father insisted and he was right to do so. That was why I never married. How could I?"

Holy . . . shit. Back then, whenever it was, women did not have children out of wedlock. The scandal would have been tremendous for a prominent family like the Leeds. And . . . well, that must be why Miss Leeds had never made any mention of a son in her will. She'd left the bulk of the estate to Fletcher because old mores died hard.

"My son will like you."

Okay, that was a total no-go. If the woman had had a baby when she was in her early twenties, the guy would be seventy by now. But more than that, the client might always be right, but there was no way in hell Claire was going to prostitute herself to keep business.

"Miss Leeds, I don't think—"

"You will meet him. And he will like you."

Claire assumed her most diplomatic voice, the one that was ultracalm and ultrareasonable. "I'm sure he's a wonderful man, but it would be a conflict of interest."

"You will meet . . . and he will like you."

Before Claire could try another approach, Fletcher came back pushing a large cart with enough silver on it to qualify as a Tiffany's display. "Shall I serve now, Miss Leeds?"

"After the papers, please." Miss Leeds reached out a veined hand, the nails of which were trimmed perfectly and polished pink. Maybe Fletcher had his beauty license, too. "Claire, will you read to me?"

The changes were not complicated and neither was Miss Leeds's approval—which made the trip feel utterly unnecessary. As that frail hand curled around Claire's Montblanc and drew a shaky approximation of "Eliza Merchant Castile Leeds" on the last line, Claire tried not to think of the four hours of work time she'd lost or the fact that she couldn't stand coddling people.

Claire notarized the signature, Fletcher signed as witness, and then the documents went back into the briefcase.

Miss Leeds coughed a little. "Thank you for driving all this way. I know it was an inconvenience, but I do so appreciate it."

Claire looked at the woman lying in the sea of frothy white lace.

This is a deathbed, she thought. And the Grim Reaper is standing close by. Tapping his foot and checking his watch.

It was hard not to feel like a heel. Man, she was a certified, cast-iron, career bitch, worrying about a couple of lost hours when it seemed as if Miss Leeds had so few of them left.

"It was my pleasure."

"Now the tea," Miss Leeds said.

Fletcher wheeled a brass cart over to the chair and poured what smelled like Earl Grey into a porcelain cup.

"Sugar, madam?" he asked.

"Yes, thanks." She hated tea, but the sugar hit would make swallowing it palatable. When Fletcher presented the stuff to her, she noticed there was only one cup. "You aren't having anything, Miss Leeds?"

"None for me, I'm afraid. Doctor's orders."

Claire took a sip. "What kind of Earl Grey is this? It tastes different than I've had before."

"Do you like it?"

"Actually, I do."

When she finished the cup, Miss Leeds closed her eyes with something that seemed oddly like relief and Fletcher took away the empty cup.

"Well, I think I'd better go, Miss Leeds."

"My son is going to like you," the old woman whispered. "He's waiting for you."

Claire blinked and called on all her tact. "I'm afraid I have to head back to the city. Perhaps I can meet him some other time?"

"He needs to meet you now."

Claire blinked again and heard her father's refrain in her head: *The client is always right.* "If it's important to you, I could . . ." Claire swallowed. "I, ah . . . I could . . ."

Miss Leeds smiled a little. "It will not be so bad for you. He is like his father. A lovely beast."

Claire rubbed her eyes. There were two Miss Leeds in the bed. Actually, there were two beds. So did that make four Miss Leeds? Or eight?

Miss Leeds looked at Claire with disarming clarity and a detachment that was discomforting. "You mustn't be afraid of him. He can be quite gentle if he's in the mood. I wouldn't try to run, though. He shall only catch you, after all."

"What—" Claire's mouth felt dry and fuzzy, and when she heard a noise to the left, it was as if the sound came from a vast distance.

Fletcher was taking the silver tray off the brass cart and putting it on a bureau. When he came back to the cart, he extended a hidden panel out at the foot of it so the thing became like a stretcher.

Claire felt her bones loosen, then collapse altogether. As she slid into the side of the chair, Fletcher picked her up and carried her to the cart, just as easily as he had brought over the heavy chair.

He was laying her flat when her vision started to slip. Desperately, she tried to hold on to consciousness as she was wheeled down the hall into an old-fashioned brass and glass elevator. The last thing she saw before she passed out was the butler pressing the button marked "B" for basement.

The lift lurched and she sank with it, falling into oblivion.

2

Claire rolled over in her bed, feeling velvet under her hands and smooth Egyptian cotton against her cheek. She moved her head up and down on the soft pillow, aware that her temples were pounding and she was vaguely nauseated.

What a strange dream . . . Miss Leeds and that butler. The tea. The cart. The elevator.

God, her head hurt, but what was that wonderful smell? Dark spices . . . like a fine men's cologne, only one that she'd never smelled before. As she breathed in deep, her body warmed in response and she ran her palm over the velvet duvet. It felt like skin—

Wait a minute. She didn't have velvet on her bed.

She opened her eyes . . . and stared into a candle. Which was on a nightstand that was not her own.

Panic roared in her chest, but lethargy prevailed in her body. She struggled to get her head up, and when she finally lifted it, her vision swam. Not that it really mattered. She couldn't see beyond the shallow pool of light that fell on the bed.

Vast, inky darkness surrounded her.

She heard an eerie shifting sound. Metal on metal. Moving around. Coming toward her.

She looked to the noise, her mouth opening, a scream rising in her throat only to get tangled on the back of her tongue.

There was a massive black shape at the foot of the bed. A huge . . . man.

Terror made her break out in a sweat and the shot of adrenaline cleared her head. She reached around for anything she could use as a weapon. The candle, with its heavy silver holder, was the only thing. She grabbed for it—

A hand clamped on her wrist.

Mindlessly, she tried to scramble back, her feet wadding up the velvet duvet, her body thrashing. It made no difference. The hold was iron.

And yet uninjuring.

A voice came through the dense darkness. "Please . . . I shall not hurt you."

The words were spoken on a long breath of sadness, and for a moment, Claire stopped fighting. Such sorrow. Such pervading loneliness. Such a beautiful male voice.

Wake up, Claire! What the hell was she doing? Sympathizing with the guy who had a death grip on her?

Baring her teeth, she went for his thumb, ready to bite her way free and then knee him where he'd feel it most. She didn't get a chance to. With a gentle surge, she was turned onto her stomach and her arms held carefully at the small of her back. She wrenched her head to the side so she could breathe and tried to buck free.

The man didn't hurt her. He didn't touch her inappropriately. He just held her loosely as she struggled, and when she finally exhausted herself, he let go immediately. While panting, she heard the chains being dragged into the darkness over to the left.

When her lungs stopped pumping wildly, she grunted, "You can't keep me here."

Silence. Not even breathing.

"You have to let me go."

Where the hell was she? Shit . . . that dream of Fletcher had been real. So she must be somewhere on the Leeds estate.

"*People will be looking for me.*"

This was a lie. It was a holiday weekend and most of her firm's lawyers were taking work to their summer homes, so there was no one to miss her if she didn't come into the office as she'd planned to. And if folks tried to reach her and got voice mail, they'd probably assume she'd finally gotten a life and was taking some time off for Labor Day.

"Where are you?" she demanded, her voice echoing. When there was no response she wondered if she hadn't been left alone.

She reached out for the candle and used the weak glow to look around. The wall behind the carved wooden headboard was made of the same pale gray stone as the front of the Leeds mansion, so that confirmed where she was. The bed she was on was draped in deep blue velvet and sat high off the floor. She was wearing a white robe and her underwear.

That was all she could ascertain.

Slipping off the edge of the mattress, her legs wobbled and she fell as her knees gave out. Wax spilled on her hand, burning her skin, and the stone floor bruised her ankle. She caught her breath and dragged herself up by the bed's duvet.

Her head was bad, aching and scrambled. Her stomach felt like it was filled with latex paint and thumbtacks. And panic made both of those happy problems worse.

She stuck her hand out and shuffled forward, keeping the candle as far in front of her as she could. When she made contact with something, she shrieked and jumped back—until she realized what the irregular, vertical pattern was.

Books. Leather-bound books.

She put the candle forward again and moved to the left, patting with her palm. More books. More . . . books. Books everywhere, organized by author. She was in the Dickens section, and going by the gold inlays on the spines, the damn things looked like first editions.

There was no dust on them, as if they were cleaned regularly. Or read.

Some countless yards later, she ran across a door. Angling the candle up and down, she tried to find a knob or handle, but there was nothing to mark the old wood except black iron hinges. To the right of it on the ground there was something the size of a bread box, but she couldn't guess what it was.

She straightened and pounded on the door.

"Miss Leeds! Fletcher!" She kept up the hollering for a while and threw in a good long scream, hoping to alarm someone. Nobody came.

Fear gave way to anger and she welcomed the aggression.

Scared but pissed off, she kept feeling her way around. Books. Just books. Floor to however high the ceiling was. Books, books, books . . .

Claire stopped and was suddenly relieved. "This is a dream. All this is just a dream."

She took a deep breath—

"In a manner of speaking, yes." The deep, resonant male voice sent her wheeling around, her back slapping against the stacks.

Show no fear, she thought. When you face off with your enemy, you show no fear.

"Let me out of this fucking room. *Right now.*"

"In three days' time."

"Excuse me?"

"You will be here with me for three days. And then Mother will set you free."

"Mother . . . ?" This was Miss Leeds's *son*?

Claire shook her head, pieces of the conversation she'd had with the woman skipping through her mind, landing on nothing rational.

"This is unlawful restraint—"

"And after three days, you will remember nothing. Neither where you went nor your time here. Nor me. Nothing will linger of the experience."

God . . . his voice was hypnotic. So sad. So smooth and low—

Chains dragged across the floor, the sound getting louder, reminding her that she needed to fear him. "Don't come near me."

"I'm sorry. I cannot wait."

She raced back for the door and beat against the wood, her jerky, frantic movements splashing wax everywhere. When the candle's flame went out, she dropped the silver holder and as it clattered away, she banged both fists against the solid panels.

The chains grew closer; he zeroed in on her. Terrified to the point of madness, Claire clawed at the door, her fingernails leaving long trails.

Two hands covered hers, stopping them. *Oh, God, he was right on her. Right behind her.*

"Let me go!" she yelled.

"I will not harm you," he said quietly, gently. "I will not hurt you. . . ." He kept speaking to her, word after word after word until she fell into a kind of trance.

Her body tingled as his scent filled her nose. He was the source of that dark, spicy smell, the delicious fragrance everything that was male and powerful and sexual. Her core grew swollen, heavy, wet . . .

Horrified by her reaction, she tried to jerk away. "Don't touch me."

"Be still." His voice was right in her ear. "I will not take much this first time and worry not. You will leave here with your virtue intact. I cannot lie with you."

She should not trust him. She should be terrified. Instead, his gentle hands and his quiet, deep voice and the sensual smell of him soothed her fears. Which was probably the thing that terrified her most.

He released her and one of his hands went to her hair. He pulled the pins out one by one until it fell down on her shoulders. "How lovely," he whispered.

She knew she should bolt. But she didn't actually want to get away from him. "It's dark. How do you know what it looks like . . ."

"I see you perfectly."

"I see nothing."

"It's better if you don't."

Was he ugly? Misshapened? Deformed? And if he was, would it really matter? She knew it wouldn't. She would take him however he was. Although, Jesus Christ . . . *why?*

"I am sorry to rush this," he said roughly. "I need just enough to calm myself."

She heard a hissing noise as her hair was moved to one side. Two sharp, blazing points sank into her neck, the pain a sweet rush. As her back arched and she gasped, his arms shot around her and locked her tight against what was an enormous male body.

He moaned and started sucking.

Her blood . . . he was . . . drinking her blood. And oh, God, it felt fantastic.

Claire, for the first time in her life, fainted.

When she woke up, she was in the bed, between the sheets, still wrapped in the robe. The pervading darkness made her whimper in a way she wouldn't have thought herself capable of, but there was nothing to ground her, no reality to grasp. She felt as if she were drowning in a dense, oily sea, her lungs stopped up with what she couldn't see through.

Anxiety tripped all kinds of wires in her head and she broke out in a cold sweat. She was going to go mad—

A candle flared next to her, illuminating the bedside table and the silver tray of food that was on it. A moment later another lit up on the other side of the huge bed. And so did another mounted high on the shelves beside the door. And another in what looked like a bathroom. And . . .

One by one they came on, lit by nobody. Which should have scared her, but she was too desperate to see to give a crap how the light came about.

The room was much larger than she'd expected, and the floor, walls, and ceiling were all made of that gray stone. The only major piece of furniture aside from the bed was a desk the size of a banquet table. Its smooth, glossy surface was covered with white papers and stacked high with black leather volumes. A thronelike chair was behind it, angled to the side as if someone had been sitting in it and had gotten up quickly.

Where was the man?

Her eyes went over to the one dark corner. And she knew he was there. Watching her. Waiting.

Claire remembered the feel of him pressing into her back and she put her hand to her neck. She felt . . . nothing. Well, not quite. There were two nearly imperceptible bumps. As if the biting had happened weeks and weeks ago.

"What did you do to me?" she demanded. Even though she knew. And oh, God . . . the implications were horrific.

"Forgive me." His lovely voice was strained. "I regret what I must take from an innocent. But I need to feed or I shall die and I have no choice. I am not permitted to leave my quarters."

Claire's vision took a little break and then came back with a checkerboard overlay—the kind of thing you got before you passed out. Holy . . . shit.

It was a long time before she could think straight and the cognitive vacuum was filled with visions from Hollywood: undead, white-skinned, evil . . . *vampire.*

Her body trembled badly enough to rattle her teeth and she curled up into herself, knees to chest. As she started rocking, she had the disassociative thought that she'd never been so terrified in her life.

This was a nightmare. Whether she was dreaming or not, this was a total nightmare.

"Am I infected?" she asked.

"Are you—do you mean, have I turned you into what I am? No. Not at all. No."

Fueled by the urge to flee, she shot off the bed and beelined in the direction of the door. She didn't make it far. The room swam in circles around her and she tripped over her own feet. Throwing her hand out, she caught herself against the books.

He caught her as well, so fast it was as if he'd dematerialized from where he'd been. His careful hands held her only as tightly as they had to. "You must eat."

She hung on to the shelf and noticed for no good reason that she was in front of a complete collection of George Eliot. Maybe that was why he talked like a Victorian. He'd been reading nineteenth-century books for however long he'd been in here.

"Please," that beautiful voice implored. "You must eat—"

"I have to go to the bathroom." She looked across the room at a marble enclave. "Tell me there is a toilet in there."

"Yes. You shall find there is no door, but I shall avert my eyes."

"You do that."

Claire broke free of him and lurched forward, too shell-shocked and weak and freaked out to care about privacy. And because if he'd wanted to take advantage of her he could have any number of times up until now. And because honor was in every timbre of his voice. If he said he wouldn't look, he wouldn't.

Except, Christ, she was an idiot. Why the hell should she have faith in someone she didn't know? And was *imprisoned* with?

Although maybe that was part of it. He was stuck in here, too, evidently.

Unless he was lying.

The bathroom was tiled in cream marble from floor to ceiling and there was an old-fashioned claw-foot tub and a pedestal sink. It wasn't until she flushed and went over to wash up that she realized there was no mirror.

She rinsed her face off and dried it with one of a stack of white towels. Then she cupped her hands under the rush of water and drank. Her stomach settled a little and she was willing to bet food would help even more, but she wasn't ingesting a thing she was offered. She'd done that once with a cup of tea and look where the hell she'd ended up.

Back out in the bedroom, she stared at the darkened corner. "I want to see your face. Now."

There was no additional risk in that. She already knew she was on the Leeds estate and she knew who he was—Miss Leeds's son. She had enough on them so that if they were going to kill her to keep her from making identification, they had plenty to go on already.

"You will show me your face. *Now.*"

There was a long silence. Then she heard the chains and he stepped into the light.

Claire gasped, her hand fluttering to her mouth. He was as beautiful as his voice, as beautiful as his scent, as beautiful as an angel . . . and he looked no older than thirty.

His six-foot-five frame was dressed in a red silk robe that

fell to the floor and was tied with an embroidered sash. His hair was as black as night and pulled off his face, falling down in vast waves to . . . God, probably the small of his back. And his face . . . The perfection of it was stunning, with his square jaw, thick lips, and straight nose the pinnacle of male magnificence.

She couldn't see his eyes, however. They were downcast, to the floor.

"My . . . God," she whispered. "You are unreal."

He shrank back into the shadows. "Please, eat. I will have to . . . come to you again. Soon."

Claire imagined him biting her . . . sucking at her neck . . . swallowing what was in her veins. And had to remind herself that it was a violation. And she was a prisoner against her will being used by . . . a monster.

She glanced down. Part of the chain that moved with him was still in the light. The thing was as thick as her wrist and she guessed that it was locked onto his ankle.

He was definitely a prisoner, too. "Why are you chained down here?"

"I am a danger to others. Now, eat. I beg of you."

"Who keeps you like this?"

There was only silence. Then, "The food. You must eat the food."

"Sorry. Not going to touch the stuff."

"It has not been tampered with."

"That's what I thought about your mother's Earl Grey."

The chains rattled as he came back out into the light.

Yes, they were locked on his ankle. The left one.

He walked across the room, staying as far away from her as possible and not looking at her. His stride was lithe and graceful as an animal's, his shoulders rolling as his legs carried him over the stone floor. The power in him was . . . frightening. And erotic. And sad.

He was like a gorgeous beast in a zoo.

He sat down where she had lain and reached out to the silver tray of food. Lifting the lid off the plate, he set it aside on the table and she smelled a wonderful blend of rosemary and lemon. He unrolled a linen napkin, took out a heavy silver fork, and sampled the lamb, the rice, and the green beans. Then he wiped his mouth with the damask folds, cleaned the fork off, and put the lid back on.

He rested his hands on his knees, keeping his head down. His hair was gorgeous, so thick and shiny, spilling over his shoulders, the curling ends brushing against the velvet duvet and his thighs. Actually, the locks were of two colors, a wine red and a black so dense it was close to blue.

She'd never seen that color combination before. At least not as it naturally grew out of someone's head. And she was damn sure his mother from hell wasn't sending a beautician down here every month to give him a foil job.

"We will wait," he said. "And you shall see the food is not tampered with."

She stared at him. Even though he was huge, he was so still and contained and modest, she wasn't scared of him. Of course, the logical part of her brain reminded her that she should be terrified. But then she thought of the way he'd subdued her without hurting her the first time she'd woken up. And the fact that he seemed frightened of her.

Except then she glanced at the chain and told herself to back up the brain train. That thing was on there for a reason.

"What is your name?" she asked.

His brows flicked down.

God, the light falling on his face turned it into something positively ethereal. And yet the thrusts of bone were all male, hard and uncompromising.

"Tell me."

"I don't have one," he said.

"What do you mean you don't have a name? What do people call you?"

"Fletcher does not call me anything. Mother used to call me Son. So I suppose that is my name. Son."

"Son."

His palms rubbed up and down on his thighs, the red silk of his robe moving with them.

"How long have you been down here?"

"What year is it?" When she told him, he said, "Fifty-six years."

She stopped breathing. "You're fifty-six?"

"No. I was brought down here when I was twelve."

"Dear Lord . . ." Okay, clearly they had different life expectancies. "Why were you put in this cell?"

"My nature began to assert itself. Mother said it was safer for everyone this way."

"You've been down here for all this time?" He must be going insane, she thought. She couldn't imagine being by herself for decades. No wonder he couldn't meet her eyes. He wasn't used to interacting with anyone. "Down here alone?"

"I have my books. And my illustrations. I am not alone. Besides, I am safe from the sun here."

Claire's voice hardened as she remembered nice, little old Miss Leeds drugging her and throwing her down in this cell with him.

"How often does she bring you women?"

"Once a year."

"What, as some kind of birthday present?"

"It is as long as I can go without my hunger becoming too strong. If I wait, I become . . . difficult to handle." His voice was impossibly small. Ashamed.

Claire could feel herself getting viciously angry, the flush blooming up the skin of her throat. Man, Miss Leeds had not been matchmaking with a kind heart as she'd talked about her son up in her bedroom. The woman had seen Claire as food and her son as an animal.

"When was the last time you saw your mother?"

"The day she put me down here."

God, to be twelve and imprisoned and left . . .

"Will you eat now?" he asked. "You can see I am unharmed."

Her stomach growled. "How long have I been here?"

"For dinner, only. So not long. There will be two breakfasts, one lunch, and one more dinner and then you will be free."

She glanced around and saw there were no clocks. So he'd adapted by telling time through meals. Jesus . . . Christ.

"Will you show me your eyes?" she asked, taking a step toward him. "Please."

He stood up, a towering force draped in red silk. "I will leave you to eat."

He walked by her, his head turned away, the chain dragging over the floor. When he got to the desk, he turned the chair around so it faced away from her and sat down. Picking up an artist's pencil, his hand paused over a piece of thick white paper. A moment later, the lead began stroking across the page. The sound it made was as soft as a child's breath.

Claire stared at him and made up her mind. Then she glanced over her shoulder at the food. She had to eat. If she was going to get them both out of here, she was going to need her strength.

3

Claire finished everything that was on the tray, and as she ate, the silence in the room was oddly unstrained considering the situation.

After she put her napkin down, she shifted her legs up onto the bed and leaned back against the pillows, tired, though not in a drugged way. As she glanced at the tray, she had an absurd thought that she couldn't remember when she'd last let herself actually finish a meal. She always dieted, leaving herself a little hungry. It helped keep up her aggression level, made her sharp, focused.

Now, she felt a little fuzzy. And . . . was she yawning?

"I won't remember this?" she asked his back.

His head shook, that mane of hair waving, nearly brushing the floor. The red and black combination was stunning.

"Why not?"

"I will take the memories from you before you leave."

"How?"

He shrugged. "I know not. I just . . . find them among your thoughts and bury them."

She pulled the duvet over her legs. She had a feeling that if she pressed him for more details, he would have none to give—as if he didn't understand himself or his nature all that well. Interesting. Miss Leeds was human as far as Claire could tell. So clearly the father had been . . .

Shit, was she actually taking this seriously?

Claire put her hand up to her neck and felt the faded bite mark. Yes . . . yes, she was. And though her brain cramped at the idea that vampires existed, she had irrefutable proof, didn't she.

Fletcher came to mind. He was something different, too, wasn't he. She didn't know what, but that odd strength coupled with his obvious age . . . Not right.

Silence stretched out, the minutes fluid, passing through the room, draining into infinity. Had an hour passed? Or half of one? Or three?

Strangely, she loved the sound of his pencil's soft strokes over the paper.

"What are you working on?" she asked.

He paused. "Why did you want to see my eyes?"

"Why wouldn't I? It will complete the picture of you."

He put the pencil down. As his hand came up to push his hair off his shoulder, it was shaking. "I need to . . . come to you, now."

The candles began to extinguish one by one.

Fear had her heart going like a bat out of hell. Fear and . . . oh, God, please let that rush not be partially about anticipation.

"Wait!" She sat up. "How do you know you won't . . . take too much?"

"I can sense your blood pressure and I am very careful. I couldn't bear to hurt you." He stood from the desk. More candles were extinguished.

"Please, not the whole darkness," she said when only the one on the bedside table was left. "I can't handle it."

"It will be better that way—"

"No! God, no . . . it really won't. You don't know what it feels like on my end. The darkness terrifies me."

"Then we shall do this in the light."

As he came to the bed, she heard the chains first; then his shadow emerged out of the blackness.

"Perhaps you would stand?" he said. "So I may do it from behind again? That way you wouldn't have to see me. It shall take a little longer this time."

Claire exhaled, her body heating, her blood running hot. She wanted to tease out the whys of her dangerous lack of self-preservation, but what did they matter? She was where she was. "I think . . . I think I want to see you."

He hesitated. "Are you sure? Because once I begin, it is difficult to stop in the middle. . . ."

God, they sounded like two solicitous Victorians talking about sex.

"I need to see."

He took a deep breath, as if he were nervous and girding himself to get through the anxiety. "Perhaps you would sit on the edge of the bed then? That way I may kneel before you."

Claire shifted so her legs were dangling off the mattress. He lowered a little, bending at the knees, then shook his head.

"No," he murmured. "I shall have to sit beside you."

He sat with his back to the candle, so his face was in darkness. "May I ask you to turn toward me?"

She changed her position and looked up. The light of the flame formed a halo around his head and she wished she could see his face. Craved the beauty in him.

"Michael," she whispered. "You should have been named Michael. After the archangel."

His hand came up and moved her hair back. Then it planted into the mattress as he leaned into her.

"I like that name," he said softly.

She felt his lips against her throat first, a light caress of skin brushing skin. Then his mouth drew back and she knew it was parting, revealing fangs. The bite happened quickly and decisively and she jumped, much more aware this time. The pain was greater, but so was the sweetness that followed.

Claire moaned as heat swept through her body and the pull of his sucking started, his mouth finding a rhythm. She wasn't exactly sure when she touched him. It just happened. Her palms went up to his shoulders.

He was the one who jerked now and as he pulled back, the light hit part of his face. He was breathing hard, his lips parted, the tips of his fangs just barely showing. He was hungry, but shocked.

She ran her hands down his arms. The muscles were thick and cut.

"I can't stop," he said in a distorted voice.

"I just . . . want to touch you."

"I can't stop."

"I know. And I want to touch you."

"Why?"

"I want to feel you." She couldn't believe it, but she tilted her head to the side, exposing her throat. "Take what you need. And I'll do the same."

This time he lunged at her, clamping a hand on the opposite side of her throat and biting her with power. Her body surged, her breasts making contact with the hard wall of his chest, his scent roaring. Gripping his heavy upper arms, she fell backward onto the pillows and he came with her.

Michael's body was now solidly on hers, the weight of him pushing her down on the mattress. He was blocking out the candlelight so she couldn't see anything clearly, though the glow behind him grounded her against infinity. Somehow it was okay, although for a dangerous reason: The darkness made the sensations of him at her neck all the more vivid, from the wet cup of his warm mouth to the tugging draw of his swallows to the sexual current between them.

God help her, she liked what he was doing to her.

Claire searched out and found his hair. With a groan of satisfaction, she tangled her hands in the silken thickness, balling up huge chunks of it, feeling her way to his scalp.

As he froze, she fell still and felt the trembling that went through him. She waited to see if he would continue and he did. When the drinking started up again, the room began to spin, but she didn't care. She had him to hold on to.

At least until he pulled back quickly and left her on the bed. Retreating into the dark corner, with his chains to mark his movement, he all but disappeared on her.

Claire sat up. When she felt wetness between her breasts, she looked down. Blood was running down her chest and getting absorbed by the white robe. She barked out a curse and scrambled to cover the puncture marks he'd made.

Instantly, Michael was in front of her, peeling her hands back. "I'm sorry, I didn't finish it properly. Wait, no, don't fight me. I need to finish it. Let me finish it so I can stop the bleeding."

He captured her hands in onc of his, moved her hair back, and put his mouth on her throat. His tongue came out and stroked over her skin. And stroked again. And again.

It wasn't long before she'd forgotten all about bleeding to death.

Michael let go of her hands and cradled her in his arms. With abandonment, she let her head fall back as he lapped at her and nuzzled her.

He slowed. Then stopped. "You should sleep now," he whispered.

"I'm not tired." Which was a lie.

She felt herself get repositioned against the pillow, the curtain of his hair falling forward as he made her comfortable.

When he would have pulled away, she took his hands. "Your eyes. You're going to show me. If you're going to do what you just did to me for the next two days, you owe me this."

After a long moment, he pushed his hair back and lifted his lids slowly. His irises were brilliant blue and bright as neon; in fact, they glowed. And around their outer edge, there was a black line. His lashes were thick and long.

His stare was hypnotic. Otherworldly. Extraordinary . . . just like the rest of him.

His head lowered. "Sleep. I shall probably come to you before breakfast."

"What about you? Do you sleep?"

"Yes." When she glanced at the other side of the bed, he murmured, "Not here tonight. Worry not."

"Then where?"

"Worry not."

He left suddenly, disappearing into the darkness. Left alone in the candlelight, she felt as though she were floating on the vast bed, at sea in what was both a luscious dream and a horrid nightmare.

4

Claire woke up when she heard the shower go on. Pushing herself off the pillows, she put her feet to the floor and decided to do some exploring while Michael was busy. Picking up the candle, she walked in the direction of the desk. Or at least where she thought the damn thing was.

Her shin found it first, banging into a stout leg. With a curse, she bent over and rubbed at what was no doubt going to be a hell of a bruise. Damn candles. Moving more carefully, she felt around for the chair he had sat in and lowered the mostly useless light at what he'd been working on.

"Oh, my God," she whispered.

It was a portrait of her. A stunningly deft and frankly sensual portrait of her staring straight out of the page.

Except he never looked at her. How did he know—

"Step away from that, please," Michael said from the bathroom.

"It's beautiful." She leaned farther over the table, taking in a wealth of different drawings, all of which looked very modern in execution. Which surprised her. "They're all beautiful."

There were forests and flowers that were distorted. Vistas of the Leedses' house and grounds that were surreal. Depictions of the rooms inside the mansion that were all a little off, but still visually arresting. That he was a modernist was a shock, given how formally he spoke and his old-fashioned manners—

With a chill, she looked back at the drawing of her. It was a classic portrait. With classic realism.

His other work wasn't a style, was it. The depictions were skewed because he hadn't seen what he was drawing in over fifty years. It was all from a memory that hadn't been refreshed for decades.

She picked up the portrait. It was lovingly executed, carefully rendered. A tribute to her.

"I wish you wouldn't look at any of that," he said, right into her ear.

She gasped and wheeled around. As her heart settled, she thought, damn, he smelled good. "Why don't you want me to see it?"

"It's private."

There was a pause as something occurred to her. "Did you draw the other women?"

"You should go back to bed."

"Did you?"

"No."

That was a relief. For reasons she didn't enjoy. "Why not?"

"They did not . . . please my eye."

Without thinking, she asked, "Were you with any of them? Did you have sex with them?"

He'd left the shower on and the raining water on marble filled the silence.

"Tell me."

"No."

"You said you won't have sex with me. Is it because you aren't . . . able to be with humans?"

"It is a matter of honor."

"So vampires . . . have sex? I mean, you can, right?" Okay, why was she going down this road? Shut up, Claire—

"I am capable of arousal. And I can . . . take myself to conclusion."

She had to close her eyes as she pictured him on the bed gloriously naked, his hair let loose all around him. She saw one of those long lean hands wrapped around himself, stroking up and down his shaft until he arched off the mattress and—

She heard him inhale sharply and he said, "Why does that entice you?"

Jesus, his senses were acute. And how could it not?

Although it wasn't as if he needed to know the ins and outs of her arousal. "Have you ever been with a woman?"

His lowered head went back and forth. "Most of them have been terrified of me and rightfully so. They have shrunk back from me. Especially as I . . . fed from them."

She tried to imagine what it would be like to only have contact with people who thought you were horrific. No wonder he was so self-contained and ashamed.

"Those who didn't find me . . . repugnant," he said, "those who got used to my presence, who would not have denied me . . . I found that I lacked the will. I did not find them comely."

"You have never kissed someone?"

"No. Now answer the question I asked. Why does the idea of me . . . relieving the ache arouse you?"

"Because I would like to . . ." *Watch.* "I think you must look beautiful when you do that. I think you . . . are beautiful."

He gasped.

When there was nothing but shower sounds for a long while, she said, "I'm sorry if I shocked you."

"You find me pleasing to your eye?"

"Yes."

"Truly?" he whispered.

"Yes."

"I am blessed." The chains rolled across the floor as he turned away and walked back to the bathroom.

"Michael?"

The metal links just kept going.

She went over to the bed and sat at the end of it, holding the candle with both her palms as he took his time. When the water was switched off and he finally came out from the bathroom, she said, "I'd like a shower, too."

"Avail yourself." The water came back on as if he'd willed it. "I assure you of your privacy."

She went into the bathroom and put the candle on the counter. The air was warm and moist from his shower, scented with milled soap and his dark spices. Dropping her robe and her underwear, she stepped under the spray, the water pouring over her body and soaking into her hair and cleansing her skin.

She was appalled by the lack of compassion he'd received over the last five decades. By the cruelty that his only companions were stolen for him, their rights violated so that he could survive. By his imprisonment that had persisted and would continue unless he was freed. By the fact that he didn't even know he was beautiful.

She hated that he had lived alone for all his life.

Getting out of the shower, she dried off, put the robe back on, and tucked her panties and her bra in the pocket.

When she was out in the bedroom, she said, "Michael, where are you?"

She went farther into the room. "Michael?"

"I am at the desk."

"Will you turn on some lights?"

Candles flared instantly.

"Thank you." She stared at him as he shuffled to hide what he'd been drawing. "I am taking you with me," she said.

His head lifted and for once so did his eyes. God, they were amazing the way they glowed. "I beg your pardon?"

"When Fletcher comes for me, I'm going to make it so you get out." Most likely by beaning the butler with the very candleholder in her hands. "I'm going to take care of him."

"No!" Michael jumped to his feet. "You must not interfere. You shall leave as you came, without violence."

"*The hell I will.* This is wrong. All of it. It's wrong for the women and for you and it's your mother's fault. Fletcher's, too."

And would that she could take things to their right and proper conclusion. That woman and her thug butler needed to be put behind bars; Claire didn't care how old they were. Unfortunately, turning them into the police because they'd kept a vampire chained in the basement wasn't exactly what you wanted to lead with when you were trying to have one of Caldwell's most prominent citizens arrested.

That would be one hell of a hard sell. So freeing him was the best course.

"I cannot let you resist," he said.

"Don't you want to get out of here?"

"They will hurt you." His eyes were grave. "I would rather be imprisoned herein for all my days than have you harmed."

She thought about Fletcher's uncanny strength given his age. And the fact that he and Miss Leeds had been stealing women for fifty years and getting away with it. If Claire disappeared because they killed her, it would be a pain to justify, but bodies could be dealt with. Sure, her assistant knew where she'd gone, but Miss Leeds and Fletcher were no doubt smooth enough to play dumb. Plus they had Claire's car keys and the signed will. They could get rid of the car and maintain Claire had come and left and whatever bad things had happened had nothing to do with them.

Man . . . she was surprised they'd picked her, for no other

reason than her personality was so assertive. Then again, she'd been pretty damn ladylike around Miss Leeds. And she was an acceptable target, she supposed: a single woman traveling alone on the last, rowdy weekend of the summer.

Clearly, they had an M.O. that had worked for five decades. And they were going to protect themselves. By force, according to Michael's fear.

She was going to need help getting him out. Maybe she could have him—no, he probably wasn't going to be the kind of backup she needed, given the head fuck that had been done on him. Damn . . . she was going to have to come back for him and she knew who to bring. She had friends in law enforcement, the kind who would be willing to put their badges in the drawer and leave their guns on their hips. The kind who could take care of a messy scene.

The kind who could take care of Fletcher while she took care of Michael.

She was coming back for him.

"No," Michael said. "You will not remember. You cannot come back."

A fresh wave of anger hit. That he could obviously read her mind didn't piss her off as much as the idea that he'd prevent her from helping him—even if it was because he wanted to protect her. "The hell I won't remember."

"I shall take your memories—"

"No, you won't." She put her hands on her hips. "Because you're going to swear on your honor, right here, right now, that you won't."

She knew she had him because she sensed there was nothing he would deny her. And she had absolute faith that if he promised he would leave her memories alone, he would.

"Swear to it." When he stayed quiet, she pushed her wet hair back. "This needs to stop. It isn't right on so many levels and this time your mother picked the wrong bitch to throw down here with you. You are getting out and I'm going to spring you."

The smile he gave her was wistful, just a little lift to his mouth. "You are a fighter."

"Yes. Always. And sometimes I'm a whole army. Now give me your word."

He looked around the room with yearning in his face, his eyes intent as if he were trying to see through the stone walls and the earth up to the sky that was so far away. "I have not known fresh air in . . . a long time."

"Let me help you. Give me your word."

His eyes shifted over to her. They were such kind, intelligent, warm eyes. The sort of eyes you would want in a lover.

Claire stopped herself because being his Good Samaritan did not include sleeping with him. Although . . . what a night that would be. His big body was no doubt capable of—

Stop it.

"Michael? Your word. Now."

He dropped his head. "I promise."

"What. What do you promise." The lawyer in her had to nail down the specifics.

"That I shall leave you intact."

"Not good enough. Intact could mean physically or mentally. Say to me, 'Claire, I will not take your memories of me or this experience from you.' "

"Claire . . . what a lovely name."

"Don't stall. And look at me as you say it."

After a moment, his eyes rose to hers and he didn't blink or look away. "Claire, I will not take your memories of me or what transpires from you."

"Good." She went over to the bed and lay on top of the velvet duvet. As she arranged the lapels of the robe, he sank down into the chair.

"You look exhausted," she said to his back. "Why don't you come lie down? This bed is more than big enough for the both of us."

He braced his arms against his thighs. "That would not be appropriate."

"Why?"

All the candles dimmed. "Sleep. I will come to you later."

"Michael? Michael?"

Abruptly, a wave of exhaustion came over her. As she blacked out, she had a fleeting thought that it was because he had willed it so.

Claire woke up in total darkness, with the sense that he was looming over her. She was in the bed, as if he'd tucked her between the sheets.

"Michael?" When he didn't say anything, she asked, "Is it time for you to . . . ?"

"Not yet."

He said no more and still did not move, so she whispered, "What is it?"

"Did you mean it?"

"About getting you out?"

"No. When you asked me if I would . . . lay beside you?'

"Yes."

She heard him take a deep breath. "Then may I . . . join you?"

"Yes."

She moved the sheets, making room as the mattress dipped low under the great weight of him. But instead of getting in, he stayed on top of the duvet.

"Aren't you cold?" she said. "Come inside."

The hesitation didn't surprise her. The fact that he lifted the blankets did. "I will retain my robe."

The bed moved as he shifted and the sound of the chains

chilled her, reminding her they were both trapped. But then she smelled dark spices and could only think of holding him. Easing herself over, she touched his arm. When he jerked then settled, she was aware she had decided to be with him.

"Have you had many lovers?" he asked.

So he knew what she wanted, too. And she had a feeling he had come to her because he was seeking it as well. Still, she wasn't sure how to answer the question without making him feel insecure.

"Have you?" he prompted.

"A few. Not many." She'd been much more interested in winning at the negotiation table than sex.

"Your first time, what was it like? Were you scared?"

"No."

"Oh."

"I wanted to get it over with. I was twenty-three. I started late."

"Is that late?" he murmured. "How old are you now?"

"Thirty-two."

"How many." Now, there was a masculine demand in his voice, an edge. And she liked the contrast with his essentially gentle disposition.

"Only three."

"Did they . . . please you?"

"Sometimes."

"When was the last time?" The words came fast and low.

He was jealous and it shouldn't have pleased her, but it did. She wanted him to feel possessive, because she wanted to have him.

"A year ago." He exhaled as if relieved, and in the silence that followed, she became curious. "And when was the last time you . . . relieved yourself?"

He cleared his throat and she was damn sure he was blushing. "In the shower."

"Just now?" she asked with surprise.

"It was hours ago. Or at least it feels that way." He coughed a little. "After I came to you—well, during the time that I came to you, I became . . . needful. To resist, I had to leave you and that is why I didn't finish you properly. I was afraid I would . . . touch you."

"What if I wanted that?"

"I will not have sex with you."

She sat up on her elbow. "Light a candle. I need to see your face while we talk like this."

Candles flared on both sides of the bed.

He was on his back, his lids closed, his red and black hair a great sea of waves over the white pillows.

"Why won't you look at me?" she asked. "Damn it, Michael. Look at me."

"I look at you all the time. When the lights are off, I watch you. I stare at you."

"So meet me in the eye now."

"I cannot."

"Why?"

"It hurts."

Claire ran her hand up his arm. The muscles underneath strained, his biceps thick and well defined, his triceps cut.

"It shouldn't hurt to look at a person," she said.

"It is too close for me."

She stayed silent for a moment. "Michael, I'm going to kiss you. Now." When she heard the demand in her voice she throttled back a little. She didn't want to force him. "That is, if it's okay with you? You can absolutely say no."

She could feel his body tremble, the subtle quakes transmitted through the mattress. "I want you to. Until I think I will suffocate from the wanting. But then you know that, don't you. You know that's why I came to you."

"Yes, I do."

He laughed a little. "That is why I am as needful of you

as I am. You see everything about me and you are unafraid. And you are the only one who has ever thought of getting me out."

She moved over to him and those burning blue eyes shifted to hers.

"Raise your head," she told him. When he did, she reached out and freed his hair from the leather tie. Splaying it out fully, she marveled at the glory and the weight and the incredible colors. Then she made eye contact and started to lower her mouth to his.

His lids pulled back, his stare bursting.

She stopped.

"Why are you frightened?" she asked, smoothing his widow's peak.

He shook his head impatiently. "Just kiss me."

"Tell me why."

"What if you don't like me?"

"I will. I do." To reassure him, she dipped her head down and pressed her lips to his softly; then she stroked over his mouth. God, he was velvet. And warmth. And anxious heat.

Especially as he groaned. The sound was all male and all about sex and her body responded by going loose between her legs.

To get his mouth parted, she licked at him, becoming lost in the sensation of soft on soft, breath on breath. When he opened up, she pressed inside, meeting the hard polish of his front teeth, then sinking in. She stroked his tongue and felt his chest rise sharply.

Worried that she'd gone too far, too fast, she pulled back. "Do you want to stop—"

The growl came out of nowhere. And he moved so fast, she couldn't track him.

The room spun as he flipped her over onto her back and then straddled her, a huge male animal who didn't frighten her in the slightest. He leaned down, the weight of his chest compressing hers, his legs bracketing her hips. He was breathing hard as he put their faces together, his eyes positively glowing.

"I need more," he demanded. "Do that more. Harder. *Now.*"

Claire recovered quickly and lifted her head off the pillow, fusing their mouths. He pushed back, forcing her down, deepening the contact. And he learned fast. In a slick penetration, his tongue shot into her mouth and she surged under him.

With his legs straddling her, she couldn't feel his erection. And she wanted that, needed that.

She yanked her mouth away from his. "Put yourself between my legs. Lie between my thighs."

He lifted up and looked down at their bodies; then he used his knee to part her and fused them together.

"Oh, God," Claire moaned as he gasped. His arousal was hot and hard through the thin layers of silk they wore. And he was massive.

"Tell me what to do," he said. "Tell me . . ."

She raised her knees up and tilted her pelvis, cradling him into her sex. "Rub yourself against me. Your hips. Move them."

He did until they were both panting and groaning and his head was buried in her neck. The silk was a conductor, an enhancement, hardly any barrier at all. And maybe because of their circumstances, because this was like a fantasy, Claire let herself go, giving herself permission for once just to feel. She didn't think of anything but the contours of his body against her own and the way his surging motion was absorbed by her core and the incredible smell of him and the heat of the sex.

When he pulled back, she was ready to have him inside. Especially as he said, "I want to see you."

"Then take off my robe."

As he reared up, he took her breath away. His hair spilled all around him in glorious waves that caught and magnified the candlelight. His face was too beautiful to be real. And at his hips, a hungry, proud length was straining behind red silk.

"You are a dream," she said.

His hands shook as they gripped the tie that was around her waist and slowly slid the two pieces apart. He took the lapels and pulled them back, revealing her breasts.

As he looked at her, she became aware that he was making a strange sound, like the deep purr of a cat.

"You are . . . resplendent," he said, his eyes wide with wonder and awe. "May I touch you?"

When she nodded, one of his long-fingered hands came out. He brushed the underside of one breast and then traveled up to the pink, tight crown. The instant he made contact with her nipple, she arched and closed her eyes. His touch was like a flame, weighing nothing and burning her.

"Kiss me," she said, reaching for his shoulders so she could pull him down to her breast. When he went for her mouth instead, she stopped him. "On my breasts this time. Kiss me on them. All over them. Take them into your mouth and roll the nipples with your tongue."

Michael eased himself down her body until he was eye level with one of her nipples. His expression was part animalistic lust, like he wanted to devour her, and part winsome, aching gratitude.

He nuzzled at her and then covered her with his lips. As she shuddered and linked her legs around the middle of his back, he sucked gently, learning her body, taking his time. Impatient, needing more, she threaded her hands through his hair and urged him on so he'd work her with power.

He didn't need much encouragement.

Sexually speaking, his natural inclination was to dominate. She might have started out as the teacher, but he was taking things from there, driving the sex, taking them both higher. He watched her as he suckled on her, his eyes greedy and hot, all male satisfaction as she writhed under him. And then he was kissing her again and his hands were grabbing on to her hips so he could rub his arousal into her.

They had reached the point of no return as far as she was concerned and she was about to say so when he pulled back.

His mouth was open, his fangs showing.

That was when she came.

She convulsed under his body, her thighs clamping around his hips, her core pressing upward, seeking more even as it released.

She was vaguely aware as his expression changed to one of shock. Which made sense because she was shouting something incoherent and digging her nails into him.

When she'd settled down, her eyes focused.

"Are you all right?" he asked.

"God . . . yes." Her voice was haggard.

"Are you sure? What happened?"

"You made me orgasm." He frowned as if he were trying to figure out whether that was a good thing. "It felt fabulous."

"Can you do that again?"

God, she couldn't wait. "With you? Absolutely."

His smile was guileless, nothing but a generous, kind lift to that amazing mouth of his. "I want you to do that again. You're beautiful when that happens."

"Then touch me between my legs," she whispered against his lips. "And I will."

Michael rolled off her while pressing kisses to her breasts as if he hated leaving them. Then he took his hand and moved it down over her stomach, pushing the robe completely aside.

She had a passing moment of worry. She had no idea how he'd react to her naked.

He tilted his head to one side as the silk fell off her body. "You have hair there."

"Don't you?"

He shook his head. "I like yours," he murmured, running his fingers back and forth ever so lightly. "It's so soft."

"There's something even softer."

"There is?"

She spread her legs and guided him where she wanted him to go. At the first surge of contact, she bit her lip and torqued—

Michael moaned. "You're . . . slick."

"I'm ready for you."

He took his hand up and stared at his fingers, then rubbed them together. "It's like silk." Before she could say another thing, he slipped them into his mouth. Closing his eyes, he sucked at what had touched her.

Which brought her right to the edge again. "Michael . . ."

And that was when breakfast arrived.

5

As the sound of a metal gate slamming shut ricocheted around the stone walls, the smell of bacon wafted over. Michael looked torn.

"Later," she said.

"You need to eat."

"Later."

"No, now. I am . . . very hungry for you. I will come to you when you are finished." With that, he went over for the tray, which had arrived in that bread box thing by the door. He brought the food over by the bed, then dissolved into the darkness.

As the sounds of the chains ceased, Claire pulled the robe around her. It was hard to imagine that she could be frustrated after the release he'd just given her. But she was. She wanted him inside of her.

Claire lifted the lid, looked at the food, and went cold. "This is lunch."

The bacon was in a quiche and there was a glass of wine as well as a fruit tart.

"You slept through breakfast and I didn't want you to eat cold food."

Jesus, she had only a day and a half left. Under normal circumstances that would be cause for celebration, assuming she was going to make it out alive so she could come back for him. But the fact that she had to leave him, even if she was returning to free him, made her anxious as hell.

"Michael, I'm going to get you out of here." When there was no answer, she leapt off the bed with an urgency grounded in her fear of the future. "Did you hear me?"

She started to walk in the direction of the black corner.

"Stop," he commanded.

"No." She grabbed the candleholder that was flickering on the bedside table and held it in front of herself as she marched straight across the room.

"Come no closer—"

As the light penetrated the dark corner, she gasped. Four lengths of chain hung from the wall with shackles on the ends, two about five feet up from the bottom, two right at floor level.

"What is this?" she hissed. "Michael . . . what do they do to you here?"

"It is where I must go when my rooms are cleaned. Or when my visitors come and depart. I must lock myself in and I am released later after Fletcher makes me sleep."

"He *drugs* you?" Although it wasn't like she didn't believe the butler was capable of that shit. "Have you ever tried to escape?"

"Enough. You will eat now."

"To hell with food. Answer me." Her sharp voice came from the desperation in her chest. She couldn't bear the idea of him suffering. "Have you tried to get out?"

"It was long ago. And only once. Never again."

"Why?"

He walked away from her, the chain on his ankle seething over the stone floor.

"Why, Michael?"

"I was punished."

Oh, God. "How."

"They tried to take something from me. In the end, I prevailed, but someone got hurt. So never more do I protest. Now, eat. I must come to you soon." He sat down in front of his drawings, picked up a pencil, and got to work. As quiet as he was, she knew he'd shut her out until she did what he'd asked.

He might be shy and modest, but he was not a pushover. That was for sure.

The only reason she went back to the bed and started to eat was because her mind was scheming and it was a way to pass the time. As she thought about freeing him, and worried about what had been done to him, she looked over at the dark corner, then around the room.

"Please turn on all the lights."

He did so immediately and the place was flooded with illumination.

Claire shifted her eyes back to the dark corner where the chains hung from the wall. She feared retribution for him. She really did. If she left, and they knew she was coming back . . .

She couldn't leave him here. It was too dangerous if they'd already tried to hurt him once.

Back to plan A. She was taking him with her.

As she put down the fork, she knew what she had to do. Michael would have to play a small role; she would take care of everything else. But he was coming with her. There was no way she would risk leaving him here.

She was wiping her mouth when she realized there was only one plate.

"Was this for both of us?" she asked, suddenly horrified. She'd finished a good half of the quiche.

"No. Just for you." He looked over his shoulder. "Please, don't stop. I want you to be full."

As she started in again with the food, he seemed to take a disproportionate happiness in her eating, practically glowing with satisfaction. And it was a strange, freeing joy to be encouraged like that. Accepted like that. So much of the dating scene in Manhattan was about staying sharp and keeping tight: being thin and in fashion while sitting across from a professional suit and tie. Keeping the conversation going through talk about Broadway plays and what was in the *Times* and who you knew. One-upping each other in a sophisticated way.

When Claire put the plate back on the tray, she was full. Satisfied. Relaxed in spite of the horrible situation. Sleep tugged at her like a child on a pant leg, wanting to embrace her.

She closed her eyes, and shortly thereafter all but one of the candles went out and she felt the bed moving.

Michael's voice was in her ear. "I need to take from you."

She offered her neck without reservation and urged him on top of her. With a groan, he sank his fangs into her throat and positioned himself as she'd taught him to—between her thighs, his erection pushing against her core. She shifted beneath him, loosened her robe, and he took to the invitation with greed. His hands traveled over her skin, working downward in strokes with his warm, male palm.

As he slipped his fingers between her legs, he nursed at her throat.

Her orgasms shattered her, the combination of the bite and the sexual power of him too much to bear and how glorious that was.

When he finally released her neck, he licked at her for some time and she wanted more. So did he. His mouth went to her breasts and she shamelessly pushed him lower, down the smooth skin of her stomach. She was delirious, blissed out, coasting on the heat between them.

She heard him gasp and knew he was looking at her core.

"You are delicate," he whispered. "And you glisten."

"Because of you."

"Where would a man . . . go?"

She couldn't believe he didn't have a clue, but then how would he? The kind of books he read couldn't have included female sexual anatomy.

She guided one of his fingers inside herself, arching as he penetrated her. "Here . . ." Her breath pumped harder. "Deep. In here."

He groaned and shut his eyes as if overwhelmed. In a very good way. "But you are small. You hold me so tightly now and yet I am much . . . larger where I am most male."

"Believe me, you would fit." She moved against his hand, pleasuring herself, wondering when the last time her inner harlot had come out.

Never.

He watched her body, her face, his eyes everywhere. His awe and fascination made it new for her, too.

"I find I want . . ." He cleared his throat. "I fear I have a . . . perversion."

"What is it?"

"I want to kiss you here," he said, running his thumb around her. "Because I want to swallow you."

"Then do it."

His eyes flared. "You would let me?"

"Oh, yes." She laid her knees wide, undulating her hips. "And it's not perverse."

His hands smoothed the insides of her thighs, holding her in place as his mouth dipped in for a kiss. He moaned into her flesh at the first contact of their lips, and his huge body shuddered, the bed magnifying the shimmying movement so that his erotic anticipation added to hers. He was slow at first, learning carefully, his eyes looking up over her mound and past her belly and breasts to her face. He was watching her to make sure he was doing it right.

And was he ever.

"Yes . . ." she said hoarsely. "God, yes, I love it."

He lifted his head and smiled at her; then he slipped his arms under her legs and lapped at her gently, slowly. At first. Soon, he was driving her hard, taking over until that purring sound he made became wild and cut through the darkness, the rhythmic pump paralleling the rush of her blood. There was no end to pleasure, no end to that swirling, darting tongue of his or his pliant lips or his hot breath against her or the orgasms she had.

When he finally lifted his head, she nearly wept.

She reached up and pulled him higher, ready to return the favor. Except, as she reached for the belt on his robe, he grabbed her hands.

"No."

She could see his erection. Thc silk outlined its thickness. "I want to—"

"*No.*" His voice shot through the room and he shied away from her, shied away from what they both needed.

"We don't have to . . . make love." When he said nothing, she murmured, "Michael, you must be aching by now."

"I will ease myself."

"Let me ease you."

"No!" He shook his head sharply. Then rubbed his face. "Forgive me my short temper."

Considering how sexed up he must be, it was perfectly reasonable. "Just help me understand why."

"You will try to negotiate the reason."

"Because I want to be with you. I want to make you feel good."

"That cannot be."

He started to get off the bed.

"Don't you do this," she snapped. "Don't shut me out."

As Michael froze, she sat up and wrapped her arms around him. "I swear I will go slowly. We can stop whenever you want."

"You will not . . . want what I have."

"Don't make up my mind for me. And if you're embarrassed, get rid of all the light."

After a moment, the room plunged into darkness.

She kissed his shoulder and eased him back to the pillows. Along the way, she found the tie to his robe and slipped it free.

His breath was coming in short bursts as she put her palms on his chest and stroked the pads of pectorals and his tight nipples. She went lower, on to his ribbed stomach, the muscles clenching under his smooth, hairless skin—

She ran into the head of his erection and they both gasped.

Dear . . . Lord. It hadn't dawned on her that it would be that long. But then . . . he was big all over.

Michael jerked and hissed as she gripped him with her hand. God, he was too thick for her to close her palm around, but she knew how to treat him right. She stroked him up and down and he moaned and worked his hips instinctually.

"I am . . ." He made an incoherent noise. "I am . . . so close. Already so close."

She eased off, sweeping down to the base of him and—

Claire froze. And he stopped breathing.

There was something wrong. An abnormal ridge that went down to his—

"Oh, Jesus . . . Michael."

He pushed her hand away.

"You needn't finish me," he rasped.

She threw herself on top of him to keep him from running. "They tried to castrate you."

Thank God they hadn't succeeded.

"Why? Why did they—"

His body trembled, but not from anything sexual this time. "Mother thought . . . it would help control me. But I couldn't let them do it. I hurt the doctor. Badly. That was when the chains came." He forced her off him and she heard the rustle of his robe going back on. "I am dangerous."

Claire's throat was so tight she could barely speak. "Michael—"

"But I would never hurt you."

"I know. I don't doubt that."

He was silent for a time. "I don't want you to see what I look like."

"I don't care about a scar. I only care that it's you. That is what matters." She reached her hand out through the darkness. When it found his shoulder, he jumped. "I want to keep going. I want my mouth on you, just like you wanted your mouth on me."

There was a long silence.

"I fear you," he whispered.

"Dear Lord, why?"

"Because I want you to . . . do what you said. I want . . . you."

"Then lie down again. Nothing that passes between us will ever be wrong. Come back to me."

She found his hands and tugged at them until he eased back into the pillows. Then she split the robe below the tie and took him into her hand. He was partially erect and he swelled against her palm, instantly hardening to stone. When she went down on him, the blunt tip of him parting her lips and filling her mouth, he called out her name and shoved into the mattress with his heels, his body going rigid.

He tried to pull her away. "I shall finish in your—"

"No, you won't. You're going to finish somewhere else."

She found a rhythm with her hand and sucked his head and felt him shake and sweat and . . .

And when he was wild and raw, she released him and crawled up his chest.

"Make love with me, Michael. Finish inside me."

He groaned. "You're so small—"

She straddled his hips, ready to join them, but then she hesitated as he went totally still. God, now she knew what decent men felt like, the disquiet before taking someone for their first time. She didn't want to force him into it. She was desperate for him but only if it really felt right on both sides.

"Michael?" she said softly. "Are you okay?"

He wasn't and the length of time it took him to say yes proved it.

"If you think I'm taking this too f—"

His arms shot around her. "What if I hurt you?"

"Is that your only concern?"

"Yes."

"You won't. I promise you." She stroked his chest. "I'm going to be fine."

"Then . . . please. *Take me.*"

Thank God . . . "Let's roll over. You'll like it better that way." Considering his dominant streak, she knew that he'd get into being in control. "If you're on top, you can drive the—"

Man, he moved fast. She was on her back in a split second. But she moved just as quick, reaching in between them and positioning him against her.

"Push with your hips, Michael." He did and . . . "Oh, *Christ.*"

"Oh . . ." he groaned.

She grabbed on to him and arched. He was huge inside of her and her thighs tightened up around his lower body as she adjusted.

"Do I pain you?" he grunted.

"You feel beautiful." She encouraged him into a rhythm of surges and withdrawals, a slow erotic dance she partnered perfectly. It was glorious, his body so heavy on top of her, his skin so hot, his muscles hard and fluid. "More, Michael. I'm not going to break. You can't hurt me."

He dug in and started to pound and suddenly she smelled something in the air, something coming off his body. The dark scent was his natural fragrance, only much, much stronger and with a different underlay that was all about sex. As he went wild on top of her, his hair tangling around them, his lips finding hers, his tongue in her mouth, she had a passing thought that nothing in her life would ever be the same. Something was transferring between them, a trade made and accepted—she just didn't know what she was getting or what exactly she was giving up.

It all felt right, though.

And then her body was lost, shooting over the edge, falling in a shower of stars. Dimly, she heard Michael roar and he seized up, jerking once and then again and then many more times.

When they finished, he laid on top of her, panting, and she ran her hands up his sweat-beaded shoulders.

She smiled, sated. Content. "Was that—"

He pushed off of her and leaped from the bed, the chains rattling fast over the floor. A moment later, the water came on in the shower.

After a good dose of numb shock wore off, Claire wrapped her body in blankets and curled into herself. Clearly, she'd read the wonder of them being together wrong. He was in a hurry to clean her off of him.

Then she heard the sobs.

Or what sounded like them.

Claire sat up slowly, trying to sift through the rush of the water and isolate what her ear had picked up on. She wasn't sure what she was hearing so she put on her robe and got out of bed, making her way to the bathroom by using the bookcases as a guide. When she was at the doorway, she hesitated with her hand on the smooth jamb.

"Michael?" she said softly.

He let out a shout of surprise, then barked, "Go back to bed."

"What happened?"

"I beg you. . . ." His voice broke.

"Michael, it's okay if you didn't like—"

"Leave me."

The hell she would. Stumbling forward, she put her hands out into the infinite darkness, moving toward the sound of the running water. When her palms hit the spray she stopped.

God, what if she had done some harm to him? Pushed this innocent recluse too far, too hard?

"Talk to me, Michael." When there was nothing but running water, she felt tears come to her own eyes. "I'm sorry I made us do that."

"I didn't know it would feel so . . ." He cleared his throat. "I am shattered. Apart in my skin. I shall never be whole again. It was so beautiful."

Claire sagged. At least he wasn't upset because he'd found it unappealing. "We need to lie down together."

"Whatever shall I do when you leave?"

"You're not staying here, remember?"

"But I am. I must. And you must go."

Fear shrunk her skin tight. "Not going to happen. That's not what we agreed to."

He shut off the shower, and as the water dripped, he took a deep breath of defeat. "You must be reasonable—"

"I am damned reasonable. I'm a lawyer. Reasoning's what I do." She reached out for him, but met only marble tile.

Turning blindly, hands in front of her, she searched for him and got tangled in the darkness as surely as if it were vines. She had a feeling he was deliberately staying away from her. "Will you quit ghosting around?"

He laughed a little. "You are so . . . assertive."

"I am."

The sound of a towel being worked over a body called her to the left, but the flapping moved as she went toward it. "Stop that."

Michael's voice came from behind her. "Were the men who loved you that way, too? Powerful and tenacious? As you were with me?"

"Can you dematerialize or something? How can you move so fast?"

"Tell me about the men who loved you. Were they as strong as you?"

She thought of Mick Rhodes, her childhood friend who was also a partner at WN&S. "Ah . . . one of them was. The others, no. And they didn't love me. Look, let's focus on the now, okay? Where are you?"

"Why were you intimate with them, then? If they didn't return your love?"

"I wasn't in love with them, either. It was just sex." In the silence that followed, an odd kind of chill set up shop in her spine. "Michael? Michael?"

"I'm afraid I feel rather foolish."

"How so?" she asked cautiously.

Somehow she knew when he left the bathroom; it was as if her body sensed his or something. She fumbled her way back out into the bigger space. "Michael?"

"I've behaved in a childish manner, haven't I?" His voice was calm and level now. Horribly so. "To have cried over something that was . . . quite normal for you."

"Oh, God, Michael, no." Normal? That hadn't been normal. Not at all. "I feel like crying right now myself because—"

"So you pity me, do you? You shouldn't. There is no crime in not feeling as I do—"

"Shut up. Right now." She wanted to point her forefinger at him, but wasn't exactly sure which direction to target. "I'm not into pity and I don't lie. Those other men are not you. They have nothing to do with us."

So they were an "us" now, were they? she thought.

"Michael, I know this is all so hard for you, and probably throwing in the sex on top of everything wasn't such a great idea. I can also understand why getting out of here is scary. But you're not alone. We're going to do this together."

She had no idea how it was going to work out or where they would go, but the commitment had been made. With their minds. With their bodies.

Well, wasn't she a romantic all of a sudden. All her life she had mocked the whole consummating a marriage thing. Sex, to her, was just sex. Now, though, she knew differently. She felt for no good reason that they were tied together. It made no sense, but the bond was there and the physical intimacy had been part of it.

His arms came around her from behind. "It does make sense. I feel the same."

She held on to his hands and leaned into him. "I don't know where we'll end up. But I'm going to take care of you."

His voice was low, his vow grave. "And I'm going to do the same for you."

They stayed that way, linked in the darkness, embracing. His body was warm against her back, and when he shifted closer, she felt his arousal. She moved her hips, rubbing against him.

"I want you," she said.

His exhaled breath shot into her ear. "You would be . . . ready again so soon?"

"Usually the guy is the one who needs to recover."

"Oh. Well, I think I could do that all night long. . . ."

And as it turned out, he could.

They made love so many times, the sex blurred together into one seamless erotic episode that lasted . . . God, hours and hours. Through the second dinner. Into the night.

Michael's body was capable of orgasm again about ten minutes after he came and he was driven to explore all the carnal joys of sex. He took her every way possible, and as he got more and more comfortable, that domination strain came out in him to a greater extent. No matter how he started them off, he always ended with her on the bottom, either face up or down. He liked to hold her in place with his weight, and sometimes with his hands, making her submit to him. Especially as he drank from her throat.

And she loved it, all of it. The way hc overpowered her, the feel of him thick inside of her, the clamped seal of his mouth on her throat. It wasn't until the penetrations became painful for her that she could bear to stop him and she was frustrated that she couldn't keep going. She wanted more of that sweet suffocation underneath his surging body, more of his power.

In some ways, although she hadn't known it until Michael, she'd felt like a man in a woman's body. Her attitude, her drive, her edge, all those warrior components of her personality, had never really fit the body she was in, and her interests had never been of the female variety, even when she was young.

But with Michael's massive body on her, his sex pushed deep into her, his hard muscles straining, she gave way and, in doing so, came together within herself. She was strong and weak and powerful and submissive; she was all the yins and yangs, just as everyone was. And the warmth she felt for him was transformative, changing the way she saw things: those happy, mothering women with baby food on their blouses who she'd never understood? Those men who still got a dopey expression on their faces when they talked about their wives—even after having been married for fifty years? Those people who had so many children their houses were demilitarized zones—and yet who couldn't wait for Christmas so they could spend time with their families?

Well, she got it now. Chaos and love went hand in hand and oh, the glorious grace of the world because of it.

The thought had her frowning. How would the outside treat him? How would he fare out of this prison? Where would he go during the day? What would he do?

Her penthouse apartment with all those windows was a no-go. She would have to buy them another place. A house. In Greenwich or somewhere close to the city. She would make him a bedroom in the cellar where he could stay.

Except . . . wasn't that just another cell? Wasn't she just trapping him in her own way? Because what she saw on the other side was him sequestered away, waiting for her to come to him. Didn't he deserve to experience life? On his own? Perhaps even with his own kind?

How would he find them?

Michael stirred against her naked body. As he kissed her collarbone, he said, "I wish you . . ."

"What?"

"I wish you fed as I do. I would like to give you something of myself."

"You have given me—"

"I shall treasure this night always."

She frowned. "There are going to be others."

"This was particularly special."

Well, of course it was. It had been his first time, Claire thought with a heated face. "I think it was, too."

That was when the final meal came. Breakfast.

Michael got up and brought the silver tray to her. As he set it down, the bedside candle flared, and in the soft light, she watched him run his fingertip over the silver fork's ornate handle.

It was close to breakout time, she thought. And he knew it, too.

Claire stood, took his hand, and led him into the bathroom. After she turned the shower on, she spoke in a hush.

"Tell me the procedure. What happens when he comes for the women?"

Michael seemed confused, but then got with the program. "After the meal, I go to the corner and secure myself. He checks through the hole in the door. The woman is on the bed, just as she came. He rolls the cart in, moves her onto it, and then departs. Later, I am drugged. He releases the chains. And it is done."

"What do the women look like?"

"I'm sorry?"

"Are they out of it? How aware are they? What's their affect?"

"They are still. Their eyes are open, but they seem unaware of their surroundings."

"So the food is drugged. That food is drugged." Which was fine. She could pull off the out-of-it thing with no problem. "How do you know when he's coming?"

"He arrives when I put the tray back out and secure myself."

She took a deep breath. "Here's what we're going to do. I want you to chain yourself up, but leave one of the wrist locks loose—"

"I cannot do that. There are sensors. I'm not sure how, but he knows. Last year one was loose because part of my sleeve got caught in it. He knew it and made me fix it before he came in."

Damn it. She was going to have to do this on her own, then. Her advantage would be the fact that Fletcher had to come over and pick her up.

Claire waited a little bit longer then shut off the water. After she flapped the towel around in the darkness, she led Michael back out to the bedroom.

She took the silver fork off the tray and put it in the pocket of her robe—then thought better of it. If she were Fletcher, she would count the silverware to make sure none of it would be used as a weapon.

Claire glanced over to the drawing table. Bingo.

She picked up the tray and carried it into the bathroom where she shoveled most of the food into the toilet and flushed. Then she headed back over to Michael. On the way past his table, she took one of his sharpest pencils and put it in her robe's pocket.

She stopped in front of him and held out the tray. "It's time."

His eyes lifted to hers and they shimmered for a reason other than their extraordinary color. Tears hovered at the base of his thick lashes.

She put the tray on the bedside table and wrapped her arms around him, but somehow he ended up holding her. "It's going to be okay. I'm going to take care of you."

As he looked down into her face, he whispered, "I love you."

"Oh, God . . . I love you—"

"And I will miss you forever."

One of his tears hit her cheek as she started to push free in a panic. But then he passed his hand before her face and all went blank.

6

Three weeks later . . .

Claire stared out of her office window at the painfully clear autumn sky. The sunlight was so bright and the air so dry that the hard edges of the skyscrapers were honed to something like optical knives, the buildings cutting into her sight, giving her a headache.

Man, she was tired.

"What the *hell* are you doing?"

She swiveled away from the view and looked across her desk. "Oh, Mick. It's you."

Mick Rhodes, former lover, partner in the firm, all-around good guy, took up the whole space between her doorjambs. "You're leaving?" When she just nodded, he shook his head. "You're not pulling out. You can't walk away. What the hell are—"

"I've lost the burn, Mick."

"Since when? Back at the end of August you were eating opposing counsel for lunch on the Technitron merger!"

"I'm not hungry anymore." Which was both a professional figurative and a literal truth. She hadn't had any appetite for the last week.

Mick yanked his red tie loose and shut the door behind himself. "So take a vacation. Take a month. But don't throw your whole career in the shitter over what is just a case of the momentary burnouts. So Technitron didn't go through. There'll be other deals."

Absently, she listened to the sound of the phone ringing on Martha's desk just out in the hall. And the talk of other attorneys as they hurried by her. And the bird-pecking sounds of a printer.

"I've always loved your name," she said softly. "Did I ever tell you that?"

Mick's eyes popped like she was nuts. Well, natch on that. She'd been feeling nuts ever since Labor Day weekend when instead of working, she'd slept for three days straight.

Truth was, she was worried that she was why the Technitron deal hadn't gone through. Ever since that lost weekend, she'd been fuzzy. Soft. Anxious and distracted.

"Claire, maybe you should talk with—"

She shook her head. "Except why do you use Mick? I've never known you as anything other than Mick. Michael is such a . . . beautiful name."

"Um, yeah. Listen, I really think you should talk with someone."

He was probably right. At night, she couldn't sleep because she was plagued by dreams and during the day she was preoccupied by a depression for which there was no basis. Sure, Technitron had fallen apart, and maybe some of it was her fault, but that just couldn't account for her prevailing listlessness or the ache in the center of her chest.

Martha knocked and put her head in. "Excuse me, your doctor's on line two and I thought you might want to know that old Miss Leeds died. Her butler left a message Tuesday that got lost in the system. I only found it now."

Miss Leeds.

Claire put her hand up to her head as a wave of disassociated hatred washed through her and her temples started to pound. "Ah, thanks, Martha. Mick, I'll talk to you later. I think Friday's my last day, by the way. I haven't totally decided."

"What? You can't take off that fast."

"I've drafted a list of my files and clients and the status of everything. I'll let the rest of you fight over them."

"Jesus Christ, Claire—"

"Shut the door on your way out. And Martha, please find out the where and when on Miss Leeds's funeral, please."

When she was alone, she picked up the phone. "This is Claire Stroughton."

"Please hold for Dr. Hughes."

Claire frowned and wondered what she needed to talk to the doctor about. The tests she'd had done yesterday weren't supposed to be back for several days—

"Hi, Claire." Emily Hughes was typically to the point. Which was why Claire liked her. "I know you're busy so I won't waste your time. You're pregnant. Which is why you've been feeling tired and nauseated."

Claire blinked. Then rolled her eyes. "No, I'm not."

"You're about three to four weeks along."

"Not possible."

"I know you're on the Pill. But the antibiotics you took at the end of August for that cold could have reduced its effectiveness—"

"It's not possible because I haven't had sex." Well, at least not in real life. Her dreams had been hot as hell lately and probably part of the reason why she was so exhausted. She kept waking up in the middle of the night, writhing, covered in sweat and wet between her legs. Try as she might she could never remember what her dream lover looked like, but God, he made her feel spectacular—at least until the end of the fantasies. They always parted at the end and she always woke up in tears.

"Claire, you can become pregnant without technically having sex."

"Okay, let me be more clear. I haven't been with a man in over a year. So I'm not pregnant. Your back room must have gotten my blood sample mixed up with someone else's. It is the only logical explanation. Because, trust me, I would have remembered having sex."

There was a long pause. "Would you mind coming down and giving another sample?"

"No problem. I'll stop by tomorrow."

When she hung up, Claire looked around her office and imagined herself taking down her diplomas from Harvard and Yale. She wasn't sure where she would go. Maybe upstate. Caldwell, for instance, was really nice. And it wasn't like she needed to work. She had plenty of money, and if she got bored she could put her shingle out and do a little legal work for private individuals. She was good at wills and anyone with half a brain could close a residential real estate deal.

Martha knocked and stuck her head in again. "Miss Leeds's funeral starts in a half hour, but it's private. There's a reception afterward at the estate, though, which you could make if you left now."

Did she really feel like driving all the way up to Caldwell? For a dead client who, for some reason, she hated now?

God, she had no clue why she absolutely despised poor, elderly, nutty Miss Leeds.

Martha pushed her sleek silver glasses up on her nose. "Claire . . . you look like hell. Don't go."

Except she couldn't not go. Even though her head throbbed to the beat of her heart and her stomach was rolling, there was no way she wasn't making the drive. *She had to get there.*

"Call for my car. I'm going to Caldwell."

Claire parked at the end of the Leedses' estate driveway, capping off a line of some fifty cars that stretched all the way up to the mansion. She didn't use the valets because she wasn't going to stay long and there was no reason to wait for someone to bring the Mercedes around.

Plus she needed a little fresh air.

And, as it turned out, a bottle of aspirin. The moment she stepped out of the sedan and looked up at the big stone house, her head screamed with pain. Sagging against the Mercedes's hard body, she took shallow breaths as dread washed through her.

Evil was in that house. There was evil in that house.

"Ma'am? You okay?"

It was one of the parking attendants. A young kid of about twenty or so, dressed in a white polo shirt that had MCCLANE'S PARKING on the breast in red thread.

"I'm fine." She carefully leaned in for her Birkin then shut her door. When she turned to smile at the guy, he was looking at her funny, like she was about to faint and he was praying she didn't on his watch.

"Ah, ma'am, I'm just getting this car right here." He nodded to the Lexus in front of her. "Do you want a ride up to the house in it?"

"Thanks, but I'll just walk up."

"Okay . . . if you're sure."

She went up the drive, eyes fixated on the gray stone house. She was shaking by the time she stepped up to the front door and lifted the knocker. Light-headed, weak, she felt as though she had the flu again; with hot and cold waves assaulting her body and her head pounding.

The door was opened by Fletcher.

Claire stumbled back in the face of the old man, her panic going out of control for absolutely no good reason.

Except abruptly she was rescued.

Her lawyer instincts, the ones that made her so good at confronting opposing counsel, the ones that made her a killer negotiator, the ones that had kicked in time after time when she couldn't afford to have her emotions show . . . her instincts clamped down on the out-of-the-blue panic and dread and calmed her instantly.

You never show weakness to your enemy. Ever.

Although why the hell an elderly butler would engender such a reaction, who the hell knew? Still, she was grateful because at least she didn't feel like she was going to pass out anymore. Once fogged, now she was clear.

Claire smiled coolly and extended her hand, the sounds of the wake inside bubbling in her ears.

"I'm sorry for your loss. And I brought the will." She patted her shoulder bag.

"Thank you, Miss Stroughton." Fletcher looked down, his drooping eyes even lower than usual. "I shall miss her."

"We can go over the will next week or do it after the wake. Whatever is best for you."

He nodded. "Tonight would be best. Thank you for your thoughtfulness."

"No problem." Claire flashed him her teeth and gripped the straps on her bag tightly. As she walked into the foyer, the fact that she wanted to use some of Hermes's best as a weapon against him was a shocker.

Claire joined the throng of people milling about between the dining room and the living room. She nodded to a number of folks, several of whom were CEOs of the companies the Leeds family had interests in and Claire's firm represented. Out of the rest of the hundred or so men and women, she guessed at least half were senior staff from various philanthropies. No doubt anticipating a huge payday.

As she bumped shoulders and declined passed hors d'oeuvres and tried to figure out why she was in battle mode when there was nothing to fight against, her eyes kept going over to the grand staircase. There was something about it . . . something . . . behind it.

Working her way through the crowd, she went over to the foot of the great, rising spread of steps. Putting her hand on the ornate balustrade, a voice came into her head, one that overrode all the noise of talk and her headache and her urge to kill Fletcher.

Behind the stairs. Go behind the stairs. Find the elevator.

Without stopping to wonder how she knew what was back there, she slipped around to the flank of the staircase and found her way into a little alcove . . .

Where there was an elevator. An old-fashioned brass and glass one.

Take it to the basement.

The voice was undeniable and she reached out to slide the filigreed gate wide. Just before she stepped in she looked up. There was a lightbulb mounted at the top.

If she used the lift, that thing was going to send a signal. And her instincts told her to hide her tracks. If Fletcher knew where she was going, she wouldn't be able to . . .

Well, shit, she didn't know what she was doing. The only thing that was clear was that she had to get down to the basement without him knowing.

Looking over her shoulder, she saw a door beneath the curving staircase and went over to it. There was a brass bolt lock at the top and she flipped it free before trying the handle.

Pay dirt.

On the other side, there was a set of rough stairs, lit by cloudy, ancient yellow lightbulbs. She glanced behind her. No one was paying any attention to her and more important, Fletcher was nowhere to be seen.

Slipping into the stairwell, she closed the door after her and descended, her heels making a clipping sound that echoed around her.

Damn, they were loud.

She paused and removed her pumps, slipping them into the Birkin. Making no noise now, she moved even faster, her instincts on high alert. God, the staircase went on forever, its stone walls and floor reminding her of an Egyptian pyramid, and she felt like she was halfway to China before she came to the first landing. And still there was farther to go.

As she went down, the temperature dropped, which was good. The cooler it got, the more focused she became until her headache was gone and her body was nothing but harnessed energy. She felt as if she were on a rescue mission, although damned if she knew who or what she was springing from the basement.

The stairs dumped out into a corridor made of the same stone as the rest of the house. Lights mounted in the ceiling glowed dimly, barely penetrating the darkness.

Did she go left or right? To the left, there was just more hallway. To the right . . . there was just more hallway.

Go to the right.

She went down about fifty yards, maybe seventy-five, her stockinged feet quiet, the only sounds the bumping of her bag on her ribs and the rustle of her clothes. She was about to lose hope and turn back when she found . . . a huge door. The thing was like what you'd expect to run across in a castle's dungeon, all studded with iron supports and with a sliding bar lock as thick as her thigh.

The moment she saw the thing, she started to weep uncontrollably.

Sobbing, she walked up to the stout oak panels. At about eye level, there was a peephole of some sort. She arched up onto her tiptoes and looked—

"You shouldn't be down here."

She wheeled around. Fletcher was standing right behind her, one of his arms discreetly behind his back.

Claire wiped her eyes. "I'm lost."

"Yes, you are."

She slipped one hand into her shoulder bag and another into her suit jacket pocket.

"Why did you come down here?" the butler asked, stepping nearer.

"I wasn't feeling well. When I found the door under the stairs, I wanted to get away from the crowd so I just wandered down here."

"Instead of going out to the gardens?"

"There were people there. A lot of them."

He wasn't buying it and Claire didn't care. She needed him to get just a little closer.

"Why didn't you go into one of the drawing rooms?"

When he got in range, she flipped her pump out of her bag and sent it skittering across the stone floor to the left. Fletcher pivoted to look at the sound and she took out the Mace that was on her key ring and put it to his eye level—so when he turned back and lifted up the hypodermic syringe he held in his palm, she nailed him right in the face.

With a howl, he dropped what he'd been going to use against her and shielded his eyes, stumbling backward until he banged into the far wall.

Mace was illegal in New York, of course. And thank God that was one law she'd been breaking for the last ten years.

Moving fast, Claire grabbed the needle, shoved it into the butler's upper arm, and pushed the plunger down hard. Fletcher squeaked then slumped into a heap on the stone floor.

She didn't know whether he was dead or tranquilized so she had no idea how much time she had. Running for the prison door, she broke two nails as she struggled to get the bar to slide free.

Urgency made her frantic, giving her the strength to move what felt like hundreds of pounds of iron up and back. When the barricade was out of the way, she gripped the toggle handle, wrenched it downward, and put her whole body into dragging the door open.

Candlelight. Books. A dark, lovely scent . . .

Her eyes shot across the space. To a man who was rising up in utter disbelief from a desk full of . . . drawings of her.

Claire's head swam, a screaming pain robbing her of sight. Her body sagged and then her knees gave out altogether, the stone floor no cushion whatsoever as she went down.

At once strong arms were around her, picking her up, carrying her over to . . . a bed with a velvet duvet and pillows as soft as a dove's wing.

She looked up at the man and tears poured from her eyes as she touched his face. God, his beautiful face was that of her dream lover, the one who had been keeping her up at night, the one she had been mourning during the day.

"How did you come back?" he asked.

"Who are you?"

He smiled. "My name is Michael."

The pain in her temples abruptly eased . . . and then the memories came to her, a rapid-fire collage of images and feelings and smells and tastes . . . all of Michael and her, together in this room.

Claire grabbed on to him and buried her face in his hair, sobbing at the near miss, at the fact that had Miss Leeds not died now, Claire might never have come back because she'd been determined to leave the firm.

And then she got pissed and shoved him back. "Why the hell did you do that! Why did you let me go!" She punched at his chest. "You let me go!"

"I'm sorry, my love—"

"Don't 'my love' me!" She was going to keep the tirade going when it occurred to her that the butler might only be temporarily incapacitated. She had no idea what had been in that syringe—and the bastard had that odd strength of his.

Claire hugged Michael tightly and forced herself to calm down. "Okay . . . all right . . . look, we're going to fight about this later. Right now, you're coming with me."

Although how was she going to get him out of the house? Hell, how was she going to get herself up and moving? The headache was gone but she felt dizzy—

Holy shit. She really *was* pregnant.

Claire looked at Michael. "I love you."

His face transformed, the stress leaving it, a love so deep and strong flooding into his handsome features that the angelic sight of him burned her eyes. "I am not worthy, but so grateful—"

"With all love and affection, shut up with that 'you're not worthy' crap. Now help me off this bed." She swayed a little as they stood up; then she looked at the shackle on his ankle. "We've got to get that thing off of you."

Michael stepped back and shook his head. "I can't go. I can't leave. They won't let me. Fletcher and Mother—"

"Your mother is dead," she said as gently as she could—considering she wanted to dig up that woman and kill her all over again.

Michael paled. Blinked a number of times.

"And Fletcher is out cold in the hall on the floor." When he didn't say anything, she took his hands in hers. "Michael, I want to help you with what you're feeling right now, but we don't have the time. We need to get you out of here. I need you to focus."

"I . . . where will I go?"

"You're coming to live with me. If you want. And even if you don't want that, you'll be free. To do what you wish."

His eyes bounced around the room, clinging to the bed and the books.

He was going to fight to stay, she thought. Which was a

product of his decades of isolation and abuse. She needed to shake him up somehow—

She took his palm and placed it on her belly. "Michael, while I was with you, we created something together. A baby. It's in me. Your child is in me. I need you to come with me. With . . . us."

He went dead pale. And then . . .

Well, the change in him would have been scary if she hadn't trusted him implicitly not to hurt her. He seemed to grow bigger even though his body stayed the same, his eyes narrowing, his face becoming a mask of male authority . . . and rank aggression.

"My baby? My child?"

She nodded even though she was worried now whether telling him was the right thing—

He grabbed on to her and pulled her in so tight her bones bent. As he buried his head in her hair, his voice dropped to a growl.

"Mine," he said. "You are *mine*. Always."

Claire laughed a little. So much for her worrying about him wanting to experience life without her. "Good. I guess we're engaged. Now move it. We need to get out of here."

"Are you well? First, tell me if you are well?"

"Fine as far as I know. I just found out."

"Are you sure?"

"I can do anything I want. I'm young and healthy." She put her hand on his face. "We need to go. We *really* need to go."

Michael nodded and released her. Walking calmly, he went over to where the chain around his ankle was anchored to the wall and pulled the goddamn thing out with a vicious yank. A whole hunk of masonry came with it, something about the size of a head, and Michael swung the ball into the wall, shattering it free.

Then he came back to her like it was all nothing doing.

"Jesus Christ! Why didn't you do that before?"

"I had nowhere to go. No better place to be." He looked at his books one last time; then he picked up the chain, coiled it around his arm, and gallantly put his arm around her. "Let us go."

They stepped through the door together. Fletcher was still down on the stone floor, but his eyes were open and blinking slowly.

"Shit," she said as Michael looked at the butler. After running a quick analysis in her head, she muttered, "Let's just leave him here."

After all, considering the man had abducted about fifty women and had unlawfully imprisoned his employer's son for half a century, it was unlikely he was going to try to come after them legally. And asking Michael to kill the guy was too horrific to contemplate. Probably because Michael would do that if she asked him to.

She tugged on her man's arm. "Come on. Let's go . . ." The wake upstairs was a complication. "Shit, there are about a hundred people in the house. How can we—"

Michael snapped to attention. "I know a way out. From when I was a boy. We go this way."

They'd gone about ten yards when she spun around. The needle. Her fingerprints were on the hypodermic needle. In the highly unlikely event Fletcher decided to come after her, it would be harder without that kind of evidence. And her shoe. She had to get her shoe.

Best to cover all tracks.

"Wait!" She ran back. Searched for the thing. Found it still sticking out of the man's arm. He looked up at her as she yanked it out and put it into her shoulder bag. His mouth was moving. Gaping, like a fish's.

After grabbing her shoe, she headed back for Michael, but her legs were like rubber.

"You are weak," he said, frowning.

"I'm fine—"

He scooped her up and started walking twice as fast as she could, his huge strides eating up the distance of the basement corridors. He moved quickly and decisively, which surprised her a little and reminded her that sweet-natured or not, he was a man, a man who had his woman in his arms. And God, he was strong. He was carrying her full weight in addition to however much that chain weighed and none of it seemed to slow him down in the slightest.

When he got to a sturdy door down at the far, far end of the basement's hallway, he leaned to the side and tried the handle. When it refused to budge, he took two steps back, punched his foot flat into the thing and busted it wide.

"Christ," she said. "You make the Terminator look like a two-year-old."

"What's a terminator?"

"Later."

Outside, the cool night air rushed at them and Michael faltered, his eyes peeling wide. He started to breathe heavily, like he was having a panic attack.

"Put me down," she said softly, knowing he was going to need a minute to get orientated.

He gently let her go and looked at the sky and the trees and the vast landscaped grounds of the house. Then he glanced up at the stone monolith he'd been trapped in for so long. She could imagine how lost he must feel, how his emotions must be boiling up, how conflicted he must be at leaving the claustrophobic comfort of his prison. But they had no time for him to acclimate.

"Michael, my car is at the end of the driveway. In the front of the house."

"I can do this," he whispered.

"Yes, you can."

She took his hand, which was clammy, and pulled him

forward. Without hesitation, he hiked up the chains and led her around the side of the vast house.

Her car was parked where she'd left it and they hustled across the lawn, staying close to a row of hedges. The grass was damp and springy under her stockinged feet and her lungs ate up the autumn's clean oxygen.

Please, God, let us get away in one piece.

When she was in range of the Mercedes, she hit the remote and the sedan's lights flashed.

"What kind of car is this?" Michael asked, stunned. "It looks like a spaceship." Then he looked at the others. "They all seem like—"

Now was *so* not the time for him to channel his inner *Car & Driver.* "Get in."

"Ma'am?"

Claire looked up. The parking attendant, the kid who'd seen her before, was coming down the driveway. He seemed confused, as if he couldn't figure out where she'd come from. Or maybe he was just surprised to see her with a huge man in a red silk robe with a length of chain wrapped around his arm.

"Just leaving," she said with a wave as she hissed at Michael, "Get in the damn car."

The kid rubbed at his spiky hair. "Ah . . ."

"Thanks for your help." Even though he hadn't given her any.

She was beyond relieved as she started the engine and pulled out of the spot—

Another Mercedes appeared right behind her, ready to put the drive to use, preventing her from putting them in reverse and doing a K-turn to get right out onto the street. She had no choice but to head up the ring—around in front of the house where the attendants were all lined up and people were milling around.

God*damn* it.

"Put your head down," she said to Michael as they approached the front door.

Please, oh, please, oh, please . . .

Just as she came up to the mansion, an elderly couple stepped forward to get into their car. With the Mercedes on her ass, and the pair's Cadillac blocking her way, she was trapped.

Sweat broke out between her breasts and under her arms and she tightened her hands on the wheel.

The front door opened wide and she fully expected to see the butler stumble out.

But it was just another elderly couple, ticket in hand as they approached an attendant.

Claire's eyes bounced to the car in front of her. The man was behind the wheel, but the woman was chatting with the kid who was holding her door open. *Move it, Grandma!* Of course the woman didn't. When she finally sat down, she fussed with her skirt and seemed to bitch to her husband a little, then turned back to the attendant.

One hundred and fifty-five million years later, the Cadillac's brake lights flashed and the sedan began to move at idle speed.

Heart pounding, hands straining, lungs frozen solid, Claire begged and pleaded with the universe to let them get away.

And then it happened.

The Cadillac went down the hill. And so did she. And then she turned onto the road behind the couple. And then she was going thirty-two miles an hour heading away from the Leeds estate.

As soon as she got a dotted line, she floored the accelerator and sucked the doors off the Cadillac.

Eyes on the road, she fumbled with her bag. She needed her phone. Where was her— She pulled it out and hit speed dial.

As it rang, she glanced at Michael. He was braced in the seat, arms out straight against the door on one side and the armrest on the other, legs crammed under the glove compartment. He was as white as paste and his eyes pinged around his skull.

"Put your seat belt on," she said. "It's to your right. Reach down and pull it across like I've done with mine."

He found the strap and yanked it around himself, then resumed his deer-in-headlights routine, bracing himself for an imminent impact that wasn't going to happen.

It dawned on her that he might well have never been in a car before.

"Michael, I can't slow down. I—"

"I'm fine."

"We're going—" Her call was answered, the man's hello an incredible relief. "Mick? Thank God. Listen, I'm coming to your house and I need some favors. Huge favors that I won't ever be able to rep—thank you. Oh, Jesus, thank you. About an hour. And I have someone with me." She hung up and looked across the seat. "This is going to be all right. We're going to a friend's house in Greenwich, Connecticut. We can stay there. He's going to help us. It's going to be okay."

At least she hoped it was going to be okay. She assumed the butler wouldn't come after them through legitimate channels, but as she drove through the night, she realized there were other ways to get someone. Ways that didn't involve the human legal system. Shit. There was no telling what kind of resources Fletcher had at his disposal, and if he had enough wherewithal to be successful at what he'd done for so long, he was smart.

Which meant he'd taken down her license plate. And he also knew where she lived, didn't he. Because . . . oh, God, she'd woken up in her bed at home after the three days with Michael. Fletcher had somehow gotten her back there.

Maybe he had some mind tricks at his disposal as well.

Maybe they should have killed him.

7

When Mick Rhodes's Federal mansion came into view an hour later, Claire wondered whether she was doing the right thing by getting her friend involved even tangentially.

After all, she was pulling into the guy's driveway with an escapee vampire who had a bad case of justifiable agoraphobia. Who was also carsick.

Michael was green around the gills as she put the Mercedes in park. "We're safe."

He swallowed hard. "And we're not moving. This is good."

The front lights came on and Mick walked out onto the porch.

Claire opened her door and got out as Michael did the same. "Mick is an old friend. We can trust him."

Michael sniffed the air. "And he was your lover, was he not?" he said softly. "He remembers you with a certain . . . need."

Jesus. "That was a long time ago."

"Indeed." Gone was the fear and the queasiness. Michael was dead serious. And staring at Mick like the other man was his enemy.

Vampires were evidently rather territorial of their mates.

Mick lifted his hand in greeting and called, "Glad you made it. And who's your friend?"

"He's going to help us, Michael," she said, going around to her man and taking his hand in hers. "Come on."

Michael's eyes shifted over to hers. "If he touches you inappropriately, I'm going to bite him. Just so we are clear." Michael glanced back at her friend. "I'm not an animal and I shall not behave as such. But you are mine and things will go better for him if he respects that."

Vampires were evidently *very* territorial of their mates. "He will. I swear it."

Mick shifted impatiently. "Are you two coming or going?"

"Coming," she muttered as she started to walk forward. When they got to the house, she said, "This is Michael."

"Nice to meet you, Michael."

Michael glanced at the palm that was offered. As he bowed slightly instead of putting his hand out, she wondered whether he didn't trust himself to touch Mick even in a polite way. "How do you do?" he said.

"I'm all right." Mick put his hand back in his pocket with a shrug, then frowned. "Chains . . . is that what you have on your arm?"

Claire took a deep breath. "I told you I needed big favors."

There was a moment's hesitation. Then Mick shook his head and indicated the open door. "Come on in, you two, and how about we start by ditching your iron, buddy. Unless you're wearing it as a fashion statement? I've got a hacksaw."

He glanced at Claire. "And maybe you'd like to tell me what the hell is going on here."

An hour later, Claire was drinking a cup of coffee in the library, looking over the rim at Michael, who was free of the chain and seemingly much more himself after the nausea of the car ride had fully faded. Dressed in his robe, he fit in perfectly here, she thought. With the formal, antique feel of the library, he seemed to have stepped out of a Victorian novel—maybe the very one he held in his hands. He was loving all of Mick's books, examining their spines, taking them out, leafing through them.

"Where did you find him?" Mick asked softly from behind her.

"It's a long story."

"He's . . . unusual, isn't he?"

Christ, you have no idea, she thought, taking another sip from her cup.

"Michael's unlike any man I've met."

"And he's why you're leaving the firm, isn't he?" When she didn't reply, her friend murmured, "So what do you need from me?"

"Somewhere to stay the night, for starters." She stared down into the coffee. "And I want to buy him a new identity. Birth certificate, social security number, credit history, tax payments, driver's license. I know you know people who can take care of this, Mick, and what I get for my money has to be impregnable. It has to stand up in court. Because we might end up there."

Which was going to be no fun at all.

"Shit . . . what kind of mess are you in?"

"No mess." It was far, far worse than a mess.

"Liar. You show up here with a man who's covered in iron links . . . talks like a Victorian but looks like he could cheerfully eat me alive . . . has hair down to his ass and is dressed in a red silk Hugh Hefner special. And who smells like a . . . well, he smells really good actually. What kind of cologne is that? I think I want some."

"You can't buy it. And Mick, frankly, the less you know the better." Because she was about to become a white-collar criminal. "I also want to use your computer. Oh, and we have to sleep in your basement."

Michael turned, frowned at the two of them standing so close together, and came across the room, putting his hand on her shoulder. Mick had the smarts to step back.

"So will you help us?" she asked Mick.

Mick rubbed his face. "Let me buy the identity for you. The man I know is really touchy and he won't accept a payment from anyone else but me. You can reimburse me somehow. And you're serious? You want to sleep in my basement? I mean, I've got six guest rooms in this ark and this is an old house. It's not nice down there."

"No, downstairs is better."

"We shall stay in a proper bed," Michael announced. "We shall stay upstairs."

She looked over her shoulder. "But—"

His hand squeezed gently. "I shall not have you sleeping in quarters unfit for a lady."

"Michael—"

"Perhaps you will show us to our room, kind sir?" Okay, clearly when her man decided something, that was that.

Mick frowned. "Ah . . . yeah. Sure, buddy—"

Michael wheeled toward one of the windows. And positively growled.

"Stay inside," he said. Then disappeared into thin air.

Mick barked out a curse, but she wasn't about to worry over her friend. Claire ran for the window and watched as Michael took form on the side lawn in the moonlight.

The butler was back. Fletcher was standing there like

something out of a nightmare, glowing like a ghost though his form was solid.

Her first thought was that he'd probably put some kind of GPS device on her car. It was the only explanation for how he could have found them. But then she realized he was not human. So God only knew what kind of shit he had at his disposal.

"Who is that?" Mick said from behind her. "Or . . . Christ, Claire, should the question be *what*?"

What happened next was gruesome and horrible and the only option. Michael and the butler faced off, and they fought to the death.

Fletcher's.

Claire couldn't watch, but Mick did and she tracked his face as he witnessed the carnage.

"Is Michael . . ."

"He's doing—" Mick winced. "Yeah, there's not going to be much left of that other guy to bury."

She knew it was over when Mick took a deep breath and rubbed his face. "Stay here. I'm going to go see about . . . your man?"

"Yes," she said. "He's mine."

Mick went around the corner to the front door, and she heard the men talking softly from the other side of the doorway.

"Claire?" Michael said without coming into the room. "I'm fine, but I shall go get cleaned up, shall I?"

It wasn't a question even though he'd posed it as one. She knew he was staying outside because he didn't want her to see him, but screw that.

She walked across the library and through the—

Okay, that was a lot of blood. But it didn't appear to be his because it was on his hands and his . . . mouth. As if he'd bitten Fletcher. A number of times.

"Oh, God."

Except then she looked into his eyes. They were grim and serious and resolute. As if he'd done what he'd had to and that was that. But there were shadows in them, as if he were afraid she'd think he was a monster.

She pulled herself together and walked over to him. "I'll help you wash."

After she bathed Michael, she got him some clothes. Which was a joke. Though Mick was a big guy, the only thing that fit her man even remotely was a pair of flannel pajama bottoms and a button-down shirt—and even still, it was all tight and showed a lot of ankle and wrist.

But he looked good, his hair damp and curling at the ends as it dried, its red and black colors coming to life.

Mick showed them into a lovely bedroom that mercifully had only two windows and thick drapes. Hopefully that would be enough protection.

Mick was the one who pulled the lined curtains into place.

"You need anything, you know where I sleep," he said. He hesitated at the door, then closed them in together.

Claire took a deep breath. "Michael—"

He cut her off. "You said you could do anything while you were with child, correct?"

When she nodded, he looked at the bed as if imagining them on it. "Even . . ."

She had to smile. "Yes, even that. But first, we need to talk—"

He was on her in a heartbeat, pressing her back against the door, his hands rough on either side of her waist.

"No talking," he growled. "First, I take you."

His mouth clamped onto hers, his tongue going deep, and then there was a tearing noise—her blouse being ripped open. *Oh, God, yes* . . . He kissed her until she was dizzy for a reason other than her pregnancy, and sometime in the middle of the rush, he picked her up and laid her out on the bed. With smooth coordination, like he'd been planning the moves, he pushed his pajama bottoms down, pulled her skirt up, bit through one side of her panties, and then—

He was inside.

Her body arched up against him and she held on hard as she gasped. She was extra tight because she was only partially ready for him, but the moment he drove into her, she caught up with him. He pumped heavy and strong, but with care as well, the antique bed groaning under the force of his body as he took her.

The glorious smell of him invaded her nose and she knew what this was about. This was him staking his claim to her in addition to loving her. This was a possession by something other than a human man and it was so totally fine by her.

Michael came with a great clenching of his body and a roar that broke through the silence in the house. Loud as it was, their host had to have heard it so it was a good thing she didn't care enough to be embarrassed as her own orgasm swept through her.

After it was over, they stayed locked together, intertwined, their breathing hard for precious moments.

And then he said, "Forgive me . . . my love." He pulled back and smoothed her cheek while gently kissing her lips. "I fear I am rather . . . territorial when it comes to you."

She laughed. "You be as territorial as you want. Coming from you, I like it."

"Claire . . . what do we do about the future?"

"I have it all planned out. I'm very good at strategy." She put her fingers through his long, luxurious hair, the red and black strands curling around her wrist and arm. "I'm going to fix it so your mother leaves you everything."

"How?"

"I redrafted her will every four months or so while she

was alive and I'm going to do it one last time downstairs in Mick's study tomorrow morning."

Yes, she was violating the professional code of ethics she'd sworn to when she'd taken her oath as an attorney. Yes, she could be disbarred. Yes, she was compromising her personal standards. But a great wrong had been done seemingly without remorse and sometimes to right something, you had to get your hands dirty. There were no more Leedses left, so there were no heirs to contest the will. And the philanthropies would be left in, so there would still be millions upon millions going to them.

The wrong she would commit was the right thing to do.

And the fact that Fletcher was dead? Just made it all easier.

"She owes you," Claire said. "Your mother . . . your mother needs to take care of her son and I'm going to make sure she does."

"You are my hero." The love shining in Michael's eyes was a benediction unlike any she'd ever seen.

"And you are my sun," she replied.

As they kissed again, she had the weirdest sense it was all going to work out, even though none of it made sense: a human woman who never thought she'd get married and have a family because she was too tough for that kind of thing. A male vampire who was both pliant and fierce—and who hadn't been out of a dungeon in fifty years.

But it was right. They were right for each other.

Although God only knew what the future had in store for them.

EPILOGUE

Nine years later . . .

Daddy! I'm coming for you!"

Claire looked over the moonlit lawns of the Leeds estate and watched her oldest child, Gabriella, go into full stealth mode. Her waist-length red and black hair was a shroud in the night, her coltish legs long for an eight-year-old. She moved quickly and silently to the stand of fruit trees in the back garden, going over the grass like her father did with fluidity and grace—as was the way with vampires.

Michael materialized behind his daughter and shouted, "Boo!"

Gabriella jumped about twelve feet into the air, but recovered quickly, landing on her feet and tearing after her father while giggling. She tackled him, and the two went down in the grass, fireflies hovering above the tickling fest as if they too were laughing.

"Mama, I'm finished," came a quiet voice from the left.

Claire put her hand out and felt her son's little palm slide into hers. "Thank you for cleaning your room."

"I'm sorry it got so messy."

She tugged Luke into her lap. At six years old, it was clear that he took after his father's side as well and not just on looks. Luke was going to grow up to be what Michael and Gabriella were. He had an aversion to the sun; he was a night owl; and his hearing and eyesight were abnormally acute. The real tip-off, though, were the adult-sized canines that had come in already. Well, that and the fact that Luke and Michael smelled exactly the same, like dark spices.

Claire kissed her son's forehead. "Have I told you I love you today?"

Luke hid his face in her neck, as was his nature. "Yes, Mama. At dinner when you told Daddy and Gabby, too."

"When else did I tell you?"

"At lunch." Her son's laughter was coming through in his voice, but he was trying to hide it.

"When else?" She gave his ribs a little squeeze to get him to loosen up.

Luke wriggled in her lap and gave up the fight. "At breakfast!"

The two of them laughed and she hugged her shy, gentle son close as Michael and Gabriella came racing up the lawn.

Claire looked at her husband and felt a wave of respect and love come over her. He was so amazing, so steady and strong in his quiet way, taking care of her and the children with tender kindness. He was also a ferocious lover and vicious protector—as a vandal had learned a couple of months ago.

She loved him even more than she had this morning, though less than she would tomorrow.

"Hi," she said to him, as Gabriella took Luke's hand and led him off to show him the fresh buds on the tea roses next to the gazebo.

"My love," Michael murmured, sitting down on the grass next to her and pulling her into his arms. "You are beautiful in this light."

"Thank you."

She had to smile, thinking that the beautiful stuff was because of him. As was the fact that she looked younger than she had when she'd met him and not just because she'd stopped working around the clock. The two of them had discovered through some kinky moments that he liked to be used for drinking and that his blood had a curious effect on her. It seemed to have halted her aging process—or at the very least slowed it down to such a degree that she hadn't aged at all in the last nine years. Had even regressed a little.

There were a lot of unanswered questions. Michael still had no idea who his father was or whether there were any other vampires on the planet. They were both worried about their children's futures and the isolation at the estate and the fact that kids needed friends their own age. And health care was an issue because how could they take the children to a human doctor?

Generally, though, things were better than imaginable. Claire managed the huge Leeds fortune. Michael homeschooled the children. Luke and Gabriella were thriving and healthy.

It was a good life. An odd life, but a good life.

And there was some news to share.

"You're a very good father, you know that?" Claire said, brushing back her man's hip-length hair.

Michael kissed her neck. "You're a very good mother. And a perfect wife. And a brilliant businesswoman. I don't know how you do it all."

"Time management is a wonderful thing." Claire put her husband's hand on her belly. "And I'm going to need to do a little more managing."

Michael froze. "Claire?"

She laughed. "You were very busy with me last month and it seems as if . . ."

He hugged her tight and trembled a little. She knew there

were moments when the abuse and imprisonment came back to him, and unfortunately it was typically when he got good news. All these years later, he still struggled with anything he viewed as lucky or miraculous. It made him feel, he said, as if he were in danger of waking up and having this new life of his be just a dream.

"Are you okay? Do you feel all right?" he asked, pulling back, eyes going over her.

"Fine. As always, I'm fine." The home births were not a walk in the park, but through Mick, who seemed to know someone who knew someone about all things, they'd found a midwife they could trust.

Michael rubbed her tummy. "You make me so happy. So proud."

"Right back at you."

He kissed her as he always did, lingering before he pulled away. Funny, after all their time together, he still hated to part their mouths.

"If it's a boy, I'd like to call him Matthew or Mark," she said.

"And a girl?"

"Michael can be a girl's name as well." Claire grinned. "And have I mentioned how much I like that name? Michael is a great name."

Her husband dipped his head. With their lips touching, he said softly, "It might have come up once before. Yes, if I do recall correctly, that is your favorite name."

"My very favorite."

Claire smiled as she was thoroughly kissed by the vampire she loved. While she wrapped her arms around her husband, she thought, yes, they definitely needed another Michael in the family.

BEYOND THE NIGHT

by

Susan Squires

1

Drew Carlowe fingered the heavy iron ring of keys in his breast pocket as he pushed into the Goose and Gander. Grim satisfaction suffused him. He was about to get his life back, along with a heaping portion of the cold revenge that had filled his dreams for so long.

It had been nearly fifteen years since he'd set foot in the little tavern. He was making a huge wager that no one would recognize The Maples' young groom Andy. He had a mature man's bulk of muscle from hard labor now, and his face had grown more angular, more lined with care. A scar ran across his cheek from a cutlass. It stood out whitely against the tan provided by the years at sea. His eyes looked much bluer, his hair much blonder with his new coloring. Young, guileless Andy Cooper, lover of horses and Sir Melaphont's daughter, was long gone.

The September evening was unseasonably hot and the tavern had all its doors and windows open, beaming light and raucous laughter into the darkness. It still smelled of yeasty ale and yesterday's cabbage and mutton special, as it always had. It was crowded with the working classes and a couple of gentleman farmers. The noise subsided at the entrance of a stranger.

He bore their scrutiny and stepped to the bar. "A pint of ale and a beefsteak," he ordered. He didn't ask for a private parlor. The little inn didn't have one. He'd have to eat his dinner in the taproom with everyone else. So be it. He was famished and the risk had to be faced sooner or later.

"Yes, milord," the owner said, eyeing the cut of his coat and the polish on his boots. Barton didn't recognize him. That was good. Drew would have known Barton anywhere. The long fringe around his head never had made up for the bald pate that shone above it.

"Just plain Mr. Carlowe," he corrected.

"Carlowe, is it?" old Mr. Henley wheezed, sidling up to him. "Rumor 'as it ye mean to buy Ashland."

"Signed the papers this afternoon." The keys against his heart felt like a triumph.

The attention of the room was riveted on him now. Barton slapped down a tankard of foaming ale in front of him. "Too bad," he muttered.

Drew frowned. He had expected them to be impressed. Ashland was second only to The Maples in grandeur hereabouts. It must be big news that it was purchased at last after standing empty for so many years. "I'll renovate of course." It had been half-ruined even when he was nineteen. "And I'll need a staff." That would be good for the neighborhood.

"Don't think nobody will work up at Ashland," old Mr. Henley observed, looking pointedly at his empty glass with a rheumy eye.

Did they know he was an imposter? Was that why no one would work for him? He'd studied carefully to remove all traces of the stable in his accent and avoid any lapse in his taste and style. "Why not?" he challenged.

"Th' place is 'aunted," Old Henley said, cackling.

Drew relaxed. Those rumors had been rampant even when he was a boy. "Every empty house has ghosts according to the locals." He motioned to Barton to give Henley a pint.

"This house 'as just got th' one," Barton said as he turned the spigot on the barrel. "A beautiful young woman."

"Perhaps I'll enjoy having a beautiful ghost." Drew grinned. He hadn't had a woman in a long time. Once he'd cashed out, he'd saved himself for Emily.

"Not when ye run screaming from th' 'ouse because th' ghost 'as sucked yer blood," a farmer guffawed. There were nods around the room and chuckles.

Drew smiled. "Vampires suck blood, not ghosts."

"I'll wager ye won't spend a full night in th' place," Barton said. He wasn't smiling.

A little game of "intimidate the stranger." Every village played it.

"I intend to go up there later tonight. Shall we stake a pint of beer then?"

Barton set a pint down in front of Old Henley. "Ye're on."

There were things he wanted to know that the house agent hadn't been able to tell him. What better place for information than the Goose and Gander? "I'm sure my ghost can't compete with Sir Melaphont's daughter for beauty. The agent, Bromley, was singing her praises." Actually the agent for Ashland didn't know Emily, which could be thought strange since he worked for Melaphont. Melaphont acted for the family that owned Ashland, since they lived in some obscure corner of world. The Carpathian Mountains, wasn't it?

Old Henley cackled. "Pretty much th' same, they are, I'd say."

That brought knowing chuckles along the length of the bar.

A thought occurred. He was shocked he hadn't thought of it before. "Is Miss Emily Melaphont married?"

"Not any more," Henley remarked, pulling on his ale.

"Is . . . is she resident here abouts?"

"Why, Mr. Carlowe? Lookin' for a 'eiress?" A man to his left smirked over his tankard.

"No need." Drew smiled. "Made my fortune in shipping." True. Technically. "Always good to have young ladies of birth in the neighborhood, though. Gentles the place."

Old Henley looked thoughtful. "She's still 'ere. Ain't never left."

His heart expanded. He had known she'd wait for him. The years away had been painful. But he couldn't come back until he could hold his head high. Until he could look her in the eye and ask her to come away with him, knowing he could provide for her in the fashion to which she was accustomed. It was a terrible risk he took now. But he was tired of living a half-life of regret, the victim of another man's spite. He didn't want to be a victim any more.

"Barton," he called then cursed himself. The man had never introduced himself. But no, it was all right. He might have heard the tapster's name from a customer. "Can you deliver supplies up there?" He'd have to make do for himself until he could find servants.

Barton looked uncertain.

"Surely someone has the courage to leave a package in the kitchen if they go in the bright light of day?" These superstitious villagers were far more annoying now than when he had been one of them. "I pay quite handsomely."

"I can get a boy to leave a box by th' door, I guess, though we're short'anded because of th' influenza." He motioned to a table where the serving girl was setting a sizzling beefsteak. "I'll send one up tomorrow, if ye're still 'ere."

Drew laughed and took his drink over to the table. "The devil himself won't keep me away."

Freya sat in the window seat, looking out through mullioned windows over what once were the formal gardens. They were overgrown with weeds and wildflowers now. The full moon rode low over the hot night. It was only nine o'clock. The darkness stretched ahead. Moles were making heaps. A fox trotted over the meadow beyond the gardens that stretched down to the cliffs and the sea. She saw well in the dark, of course, much better than humans. The fecund, salty scent of the sea hung in the still air. Not a breath was stirring, making one wonder how the cypress trees had been bent away from the cliff's edge. Freya caught herself. She didn't want to wonder anything. She wanted to sit, quietly, as she always did these days, not thinking, or feeling. They said time healed everything. What did they know about time?

She daubed the perspiration at the place between her breasts with a handkerchief. Even the diaphanous white gowns she wore seemed oppressive in this heat.

She heard the horse long before she saw it, of course. She stood, sighing. One of the young men from the village must have accepted a dare to stay in the house. She thought they had tired of that after the last one had wet himself as he scrambled for the door. He was so pathetic she hadn't even bothered to take blood from him. She hadn't been in need, having fed several nights earlier in Tintagel. That had been more than six months ago and she'd had peace and quiet since then. Or as much peace as her thoughts left her.

Tonight was a different matter. She did need blood. Perhaps it was as well that hubris and ignorance had sent this callow youth her way. She'd frighten him, take what she needed, and send him back to the village blubbering of ghosts with two drooling bites on his neck but otherwise none the worse for wear. That would keep others away.

She rose and turned into the room. The dust covers were still on the furniture. She hadn't bothered to remove them, though she'd been here a year. The only mark that she spent her days here was the bed, which was neatly made, and actually had clean sheets on it.

The horse did not pull up at the front portico but headed round for the stables. That was odd. Usually they left their horses tied near the doorway so they could be away quickly. She glided out the door and down the dusty hall. Dust was the worst of her situation. It made her sneeze. And spider-webs, of course. Hastening down the servants' stairway and out through the kitchens, she saw a light flicker on in the stable.

Well, the intruder was certainly bold. She stepped quietly across the yard and slid through the open stable door into the shadows.

The horse heard her if his owner did not. He sidled away, snorting, as the intruder tried to uncinch his girth. The prowler was a man, not a boy. All she could see was his silhouette, but no boy had shoulders like that, or thighs. How long it had been since she had had a man? The parasite that ran in her veins and made her what she was, her Companion, worshipped life. What surer urge to life than the sexual act? So she was easily aroused. That was her curse. She shut down those thoughts. She, of any of them, was not to be trusted with thoughts like that.

"Whoa, now, Darley," the intruder soothed, in a baritone that came from no callow youth. "What's wrong with you, boy?"

The horse quieted when she stilled herself. Animals always liked her. It was the energy she emanated. The man heaved the saddle off and turned into the light to lay it over the edge of a stall door. His breeches were close about his thighs and bulged in just the right place. Hmmmm. Interesting. His riding boots were made by the finest of bootmakers. He was in his shirtsleeves, his collar open in the heat. His sleeves were rolled up over strong forearms, and his shirt clung damply to his body. He had blond hair, tanned skin, and very, very blue eyes. He also had a scar along his left cheek, white against his tan. That might distract the simpler of those he met into thinking he was not handsome. Hunger itched along her veins as she saw the pulse throb in the damp skin at his throat. He was definitely no boy. The lines in his face were as hard and unforgiving as the scar. But his mouth was soft and full. Incongruous. Interesting even.

But she wasn't interested in men. Not any more. She couldn't be trusted around them. She jerked her eyes to his horse, as he pulled the bridle over its head. The creature was magnificent: big, well muscled, with a piercing eye and flaring nostrils. Just now the horse was sweating from the ride up from the village. It would take quite a rider to master this beast.

"Good thing you were fed in the village, boy. There's no hay in this molding old place." He led the horse into a stall. "You'll have to make do." He followed the horse in and took some handfuls of old straw to rub it down. She watched the muscles move in his back and arms. The fine linen of his shirt was made almost transparent by his perspiration. She remembered that smell now, the scent of a man sweating. The throb began between her legs. She mustn't let the beast within her rouse itself. But she couldn't stop watching him. He looked up once or twice and peered around. He sensed her presence. He would feel her vibrations. Most humans sensed it only as vitality, an aliveness that made her incredibly attractive. But he shook his head and chuckled at himself, apparently writing off his senses to the tales he must have heard about the place being haunted.

She glanced to a large valise that sat just outside the circle of light from the lamp. No intruder had ever brought a valise. An uneasy feeling settled on her.

Nonsense. He'd be running down the road, leaving his beautiful horse behind, just after he nodded off. She'd see to that. And she'd have quenched her hunger.

Perhaps she should wait and go to one of the surrounding villages for her blood. Perhaps it was a danger to engage in the sensuous act of feeding with this one. She daren't give in to the rising pressure between her legs.

He picked up the lantern and the valise and, with one glance behind him, strode out the door. He certainly didn't look afraid. She'd fix that.

She glided after him. Where did he plan to wait for her? Probably in the front drawing room in the main wing of the house. He'd sit up with his lantern, pretending to read, just to say he'd spent the night. A wager no doubt. Which she would insure he lost.

But he didn't go round to the front again. He went in through the kitchen door. She slid after him. Holding his lamp high, he found another and lighted it, and another. He rummaged around until he found the candles she had ordered—her supplies were brought from three villages over in Tremail, far enough away that the house's reputation was not a problem. He lit a candelabra full of candles. Not good. The kitchen was fairly bright now. He looked around, surprised. She drifted into the maw of the pantry where the light did not penetrate. The kitchen was the one room she kept tidy. No dust here. And her supplies were in evidence if he looked. He did, peering into cupboards. He found the flour, the vegetables, the smoked ham. He stood, and after thinking a moment, he walked to the great kitchen fireplace. She sighed.

He held out his hands and felt the heat. When he kicked at the banked coals the ashes fell away, revealing the last glow of the fire she had used to heat water for her tea.

"Well, well, well," he murmured. "Ghosts, have we? More likely trespassers."

That didn't seem to frighten him, either. He pumped water into two buckets. Pouring the buckets into the cauldron to heat, he stirred the coals into a blaze. Then he took a lantern and started off to explore the house.

He settled on a bedroom in the main block that overlooked the gardens in the back, just as hers did from the ruined side wing. She watched from the shadowed dressing room as he opened the windows wide and flung the Holland covers from the furniture. Dust hung in the air, and she had to hold her nose to prevent sneezes. The man was not here for one night, at least in his own mind. He was moving in. He hung two coats and several shirts in the wardrobe, and placed folded cravats and smalls in the highboy drawers. Breeches went in the bottom drawers. She had to retreat to the adjacent bedroom when he came in to rummage in the dressing room. What was the stupid creature looking for?

She heard him drag it out. A bathtub. This was not good. She slipped back into the dressing room. The door was left wide open. Not tidy, this man. He had the tub out in the middle of the old Turkey carpet in front of the fireplace. He took the candelabra and strode out into the hall. He was so . . . purposeful. Soon he was back with two huge buckets of water and some soap from her stores. He poured the steaming water into the bath and took off again. This time when he returned he had clean sheets tucked under one arm and two more buckets of water. He poured these into the bath as well and bent to remove his boots.

She could come back later when he was asleep and haunt his dreams. She was in danger if she stayed. Watching him would rouse everything she had worked to suppress.

He took off his shirt.

Oh, my. He was certainly strongly built. His shoulders were positively brawny. His biceps swelled as he worked at the buttons on his breeches. His chest was covered with curly blondish hair. His nipples were soft and browned, his belly ribbed with muscle. She should go. Was he as tanned all over as his upper body? He moved his breeches over his hips. She covered her mouth to prevent an appreciative sound escaping. No, he was not so tan all over. Though everywhere had seen some sun. The nest of hair around his man parts was dark gold. He was well endowed, and she had seen many men. No wonder his breeches bulged in such an interesting manner. But it wasn't just his male equipment that fascinated her. The hips were slim, the thighs flaring with muscle, the buttocks in profile. . . oh, dear, firm, round. Tight.

Just like she felt inside.

He stepped into the bath, easing himself down with a sigh. He just sat in the steam with his eyes closed for a while. She half thought he'd gone to sleep. She, on the other hand, might never sleep again. She was so wet between her legs she practically dripped. She could relieve the torture if she left now. Or perhaps not. She was going to remember that body for a long time. So why leave when it was no use?

He sat up at last and washed himself briskly. She thought she might faint as he soaped his hands and then scrubbed his body under the waterline. She knew exactly what he was doing. She closed her eyes.

Why was she here torturing herself? *You don't care about sex,* she told herself. It had always been a job to her, no more. *You turned vampires into Harriers, weapons the Council of Elders could use to protect your kind. And making Harriers meant teaching them the sexual arousal and suppression that increased their power. You never took pleasure in it. You did it because your father, the Eldest, demanded it.*

And now she didn't even do that any more. Her purpose was gone. Her job was gone.

The water sloshed. She opened her eyes. He was drying himself in that unconscious way men had, because they didn't know how arousing it was to see their silken skin, slick with water, rubbed down. He stepped out of the bath and turned.

Her eyes widened.

His back was crisscrossed by dozens of ugly white troughs and ridges of scar tissue. He had been whipped. Someone had treated this man very badly. He opened the wardrobe and took out a nightshirt, but thought better of it. He flung it on the bed. Instead, naked, he went to the writing desk and opened a box he had set there. It was a traveling writing case. He removed paper, an inkwell, and a quill, and began a letter. After a few lines, he paused, growled in dissatisfaction and crumpled up the paper, throwing it into the middle of the carpet. He was acting exactly like he lived here, not as though he was staying for one night, quaking, in a haunted house just to prove he could do it.

Unbelievable.

He couldn't live here. Her father owned this estate, though he hadn't come here in centuries. She had a right to the house. She wanted to be left alone. She wanted a small existence. She wanted peace. And here this oaf came and stabled his horse in her stables, and moved in and took a bath and now was sitting, naked, writing a letter, and making her throb the way she didn't want to throb at all any more.

Well, it wouldn't last for long. She drummed her fingers on her arm. She had only to wait until he retired. She'd get the blood she needed from him and she would then send him packing, ashamed of his fear. If that idiot landowner her father had entrusted to oversee the place had rented it out, he would soon find that tenants were hard to come by.

Drew set down the pen and sighed. How could a letter he had composed a thousand times in his mind suddenly become so difficult to write? What did one say to a woman with whom you were wildly in love, but hadn't seen in fifteen years? She wasn't married, but did that mean she still pined for him? Were their stolen moments together, made all the more piquant by her father's certain disapproval, enough to last so long? He hadn't even made love to her. A few kisses, some heated promises, the pain of lust restrained. Did they have more than that?

Of course they did. For her love he had endured pain and humiliation, near death. He'd almost died a dozen times.

And for her he had turned himself into Drew Carlowe, respectable and very rich with an educated accent and excellent taste. The perfect husband, if one didn't count the scars on his back, or on his soul. In coming home he risked everything. But he was no longer a feckless youth. They'd have a hard time holding him, if they realized who he was and turned him in.

Drew sanded the letter. It was the best he could do. Had Emily's father turned her against him? She must still love him. She must. The best revenge on her father was to have his daughter in spite of all. She was of age. Drew was rich. Tomorrow, he would pay a boy from the village to deliver the letter into her hands alone. They would meet. He would woo her all over again if necessary, until she agreed to run away with him. He'd let his new father-in-law know just who his daughter had married sooner or later. That would hurt Melaphont. And then he'd take care of her father in some particularly personal way. Not right away. It was hardly conducive to a happy marriage to have one's revenge on the bride's father. But he had vowed to see Sir Elias Melaphont suffer for the suffering he'd caused Drew and Emily. He would not be denied.

He decided to let the letter dry before he put it into the envelope he'd addressed. He rose, gathered up the sheets, and staggered to the bed, rubbing his neck.

He'd had the oddest feeling all night that he was being watched. But he'd searched the house, all except the ruined west wing, and no one could be staying there. He was alone here. The supplies in the kitchen and the banked fire must have been arranged by the agent as a welcome to his new home, or by Melaphont himself. He didn't like to think that. He didn't want to be beholden to that cur for anything. Whoever had left the supplies had been very thorough. The linen closet even held clean sheets. He was grateful for that.

It was too hot to put on the nightshirt. He piled the brocaded coverlet in the corner and put the sheets on the bed himself. He realized why the villagers thought the house was haunted. It had a kind of electric feeling, as though something important was about to happen. He grinned as he plumped the pillows. The beautiful young ghost was just wishful thinking. Though here in Cornwall the supernatural was always foremost in people's minds. Pixies and ghosts were as real to the locals as Jesus and his disciples. Perhaps the two concepts were not so different. He'd lost all belief in God a long time ago. Bible stories were just tales these days.

He turned back the sheets and blew out his candles. Without more ceremony he lay out on the bed, naked in the heat, and closed his eyes.

2

Did he have to sleep naked? The parasite in Freya's veins that made her what she was needed blood. It itched with anticipation. But the throbbing between her legs watching him all evening was unwelcome to say the least. She had banished sexuality the day she walked away from her duty to her kind, the day her only remaining sister died through her fault. Her father was angry. But she couldn't do it any more. She had always done everything her father asked her. He was so old, so overpowering in personality. She had been tired, sick, her mind tattered after that day that changed everything. It was her achievement, or her failure, that she had not gone home to Mirso. She had come to Ashland to heal, away from what she had been, not sure what she ever would be.

But she couldn't possibly heal if this naked man in her house aroused all the sexuality she wanted to suppress. She crept out of the dressing room as his breathing became regular. He lay across the bed, one hand behind his neck, his body casually displayed. She didn't want to take blood from him this way. The sensuality of it prodded her most womanly parts even now. But she needed blood, and he was here, and her resolve was weakened by hours of watching him.

She glanced to the desk. He'd written draft after draft of something. What would such a hardened man write that he cared so much about? Cocking an ear for the rhythm of his breathing, she moved to the desk. The moon shone in through the open windows, laying a channel of silver across the letter. It was as clear as day to her, who never saw the sun.

My dearest Emily, if I may still call you that, I have returned at last. I know I was unworthy of you then. But I was not a thief. And in these years away, I have made myself into a man of means, one you will not be ashamed to claim as an acquaintance. I hardly dare hope to be more than that. If you do not wish to see me, I shall never approach you, on that you have my word. But if you will allow me to visit you, just once more, I should be honored and grateful. Send word of your decision back with the bearer of this message to

Your humble servant,
Andrew Cooper, now Carlowe

That such an active, virile man, who wore a carapace against feeling in his features, could write such a letter was . . . surprising. She glanced to his form, spread out upon the bed. His muscles, quiescent now, still spoke of latent power. Men were usually so wrapped up in themselves, especially men who looked like that. Yet this letter was tentative, utterly without pretensions. He must love this woman very much. She was lucky to be loved so.

Freya had never loved, not in all her long centuries. It was not allowed in one who made Harriers. Sex, yes, almost constant sexual stimulation of the Aspirant to bring out his power, but not love. She sighed. Best get this over with before she collapsed in self-pity.

She glided toward the bed, stopping when she was some few feet away. He was really quite a lovely looking man. She resolved to take the blood she needed, a cup or perhaps two in total, but that was all. She drew her power. *Companion!* she called to the thing in her blood, and it responded, sending a feeling of throbbing life up her veins. A matching throb in her loins was almost painful. When her Companion sent her power, the urge to life and to the sexual act was made stronger still. But she could resist. She must resist. The familiar red film oozed down over her field of vision. Her eyes would be glowing red now with her power. Time to wake him. She would feel his fear, fuel it by compelling his consciousness all during the time she fed from him, and then release him without the suggestion she usually left in their minds to forget what she had done. That way he would be able to spread the tale of his experience. He would scurry out to the stables and gallop away from her house. She wagered he would not even stop to put on his breeches.

"Andrew," she called softly.

He was dreaming of Emily, her fine blond hair, the swell of her bosom under the crisp white lawn of her morning dress . . .

"Andrew," she called and smiled at him. She had an accent. Eastern European?

"Andrew." Louder this time, almost insistent, and he knew he was dreaming, but he didn't want to leave this dream and Emily.

"Andrew, wake up!"

He opened his eyes, irritated.

There, standing near his bed, was what had to be the ghost. She had red eyes that glowed in the darkness, translucent white skin, and hair black as midnight. An ethereal white dress wafted around her in the breeze that belatedly coursed in through the open window. If one could call it a dress. Two strips of diaphanous fabric hung from her shoulders and plunged to her waist, leaving her arms bare and a vee of white skin that revealed the swell of her breasts. The garment was bound by a jeweled girdle at her waist and fell in translucent layers to the floor. She was petite and beautiful. They hadn't lied about that. They hadn't lied about there being a ghost, either.

But he didn't believe in ghosts. There was enough memory and regret to haunt one without the need for ghosts. So it must be a trespasser got up to look like a ghost. Though how one achieved those red eyes, he didn't know.

He sat bolt upright. "You can leave off with whatever game you're . . ." He intended to get up and loom over her and send her screeching from the room. But he didn't move. Her eyes got even redder—almost carmine. They seemed to hold him. He couldn't speak, he couldn't move at all. He just sat, one leg stretched toward the floor, the other tucked up under him.

It was frightening, to be helpless like that. She moved closer. Her hair hung, unbound, over her shoulders and down her back. She wore no jewelry other than the girdle and needed none. Her features were fine, and her eyes, though red, were sad. She seemed to float as she moved toward him, but he could see her bare feet peep out from beneath the translucent dress that trailed on the floor. Now he caught her scent. Cinnamon, and underneath that something sweet. What was it? Ambergris. The combination made a heady perfume.

He realized that the electric feeling he had experienced all evening came from her. It was an expectant vibrancy. Had she been near all night?

She reached out one small hand and touched his shoulder. It was shocking—not shivering cold as a ghost's touch was supposed to be, but warm and terribly alive. She recoiled and jerked back her hand, as though she felt a shock, too. Her eyes faded a little. He squirmed, but then her eyes went redder again and all hope of movement was gone. She moved her hands over his chest and again the sensation shot straight to the core of him. Must she thumb his nipples? They peaked and tightened. The sensation found its destination and his loins grew heavy. He was getting aroused by a . . . a something who could hold him immobile while she touched him. The possibilities were frightening, and . . . exciting.

One hand moved over his hip, the other slid over his biceps, as all the while she stared into his eyes. She glanced down. He knew what she would see. He was fully erect—almost painfully so. He had been saving himself for Emily for months. He couldn't be held accountable for his reaction to being touched by a beautiful ghost or trespasser, or whatever she was, while he was naked. Maybe the reason he couldn't move was because somewhere deep inside he didn't *want* to move.

She pushed him gently backward, his head on the pillows that still smelled slightly musty. She made a very unghostly dent on the bed as she sat beside him. One hand cupped the nape of his neck under his hair, the other still moved over his bare chest. Her palm across his nipples made him feel like jam inside. The hand moved lower. Was she going to . . . ?

It brushed across his cock. He arched involuntarily. Lord, in a few moments she had him in such a state he was like to spill his seed right on his belly as though this were a wet dream when he was fourteen.

Maybe this *was* a wet dream. How else could he explain the red eyes? But his wet dreams had been the usual male expressions of his burgeoning strength and power, noticeably lacking in this one. Still, the very thought that she could do anything to him while he was in this state was exhilarating as well as horrifying. He must tell her that he was saving himself for Emily. He made several ineffective grunting sounds before she touched her finger to his lips.

"Shush now," she whispered in that very attractive accent, "I won't hurt you."

That was a very strange thing for a ghost to say, even a ghost in a dream.

Why was she trying to comfort him? She wanted to frighten him. But the pounding of his heart against her palm could not help but bring a morsel of remorse. All the pain she and her sisters had given Aspirants, all the torment of raising their capacity for arousal and then suppressing their release, had become too much for her at the end. She didn't think what they did was right. So the last thing she wanted was to feel the thumping of his heart in fear or see the very pronounced erection she had caused. He was definitely aroused.

As was she, if truth be told. She was unable to resist touching his body. How long since she had felt the warmth of a strong male form, its miracle of soft skin covering the hard muscle beneath? And this was a very attractive specimen. Actually it wasn't just that he was attractive. This man had written *that* letter. She trailed a hand across his hip again, so near the delightful erection she had just caressed so lightly . . .

She must *not* succumb to her desire. Under compulsion, any kind of sexual dalliance with him was nothing short of rape.

She'd just take his blood and let him go. He had to be frightened enough to keep others away. There was no way around that. But she didn't want him having some sort of apoplexy.

He was staring up at her as though he was the one who was hungry. But he wasn't of course, not for the same thing she needed. She turned his chin gently to the side, baring the big artery under his jaw. She felt his heart gallop a little irregularly as she leaned down, pressing her breasts against his chest. She kissed his neck, gently. His skin was salty from the heat, though the breeze had dried him. His smell, unique to each human male, filled her nostrils. His hips rose, his body arching as she murmured reassurances.

She let the power coursing through her veins run out her canines. She cradled his head in the crook of her arm and sank them carefully into the artery. He jerked against her, once. The twin circular wounds leaked sweet, copper-tasting life into her mouth, thick and satisfying. Her Companion practically purred. She let her canines retract and now there was only licking and sucking, making soothing sounds at him while she lapped. He did not relax as they sometimes did, though. Instead, his hips began to move against her in rhythm with her sucking. She could feel the hard rod of his erection pressing into her hip. How sexual this act was, for both the donor and the receiver of the blood, though normally she managed to control its effects. Not now. She fairly hummed with arousal.

The blood is the life, she thought. It had been so for millennia, tied as her kind was to humans in this most intimate of bonding. They lived one to a city, so that humans would not know vampires lived among them. It was a lonely existence. The only place her kind could congregate was Mirso Monastery, for most of them a last resort when ennui or the insanity of eternal life had made them unfit for the world. She and her sisters had been born at Mirso, and lived out their lives making Harriers there. She had never lived in the human world until now.

She raised her head when she had taken enough. He watched her steadily as she licked her lips. “Thank you,” she said, sitting up. “For your generosity.” Even though he had no choice.

His eyes were big, dark blue in the moonlight, but they were no longer afraid. They were . . . speculative. That was not good. Was he wondering if she was real? If he told people there was a real woman at Ashland who drank blood, they'd be up with torches to burn her out. He had to believe the place was haunted and there was nothing he could do about it except leave.

She rose. "You have been touched by the spirit world," she intoned, and let her Companion make her voice echo. "You will go from this place immediately."

She called for even more power from her Companion. The familiar whirling darkness started at her feet and began to rise up over her knees. He sat up now that she had released him. He was still erect. Two tiny rivulets of blood coursed down his neck. He stared in fascinated horror as the darkness engulfed her. His bedroom disappeared around her. One moment of familiar pain, and she popped into her own room. She hurried across the hall to look out the windows of a dank room whose ceiling was collapsed in one corner. It looked out to the stables. He was a brave man, and he wouldn't leave a horse like that behind.

What the bloody hell had happened here? Drew struggled to his feet, feeling light-headed. That was no doubt because his entire blood supply was currently engaged in the area of his loins. A woman had . . . Had what? Held him immobile while she drank his blood? Given him the most incredibly sensual experience of his life?

And let's get back to the "woman" part. What woman could do what that one did?

"There are no such things as ghosts," he murmured to himself. Ghosts weren't warm to the touch. Thinking about how warm she was, and what she had done with that touch, was definitely not redistributing his blood supply. And what ghost made a dent in the bed when she sat on it?

On the other hand, what human had red eyes and disappeared in a whirl of blackness?

His head ached so he couldn't think. He ran his hands through his hair. Wait! He strode to a mirror, fingering his neck. It was too damned dark in here to see. He crashed about looking for the candelabra. When he finally found it by nearly knocking it over, he felt for the flint and lit it, then took it over to the mirror on the dressing table, craning to see his neck.

Two tiny wounds drooled blood. "Christ Almighty!" he whispered. What *had* happened here? He held the candelabra high and looked around the room. A shiver starting down his back was ruthlessly suppressed. He went to the window. It was a sheer thirty feet to the ground. But there were some vines crawling halfway up the wall. Not enough. She hadn't got out that way. He whirled. Maybe she was hiding in the dressing room. Flinging open the door, he saw it contained only shelves for shoes, a headless mannequin that held coats for brushing, and a tangle of clothes hangers, just as it had when he'd come in to get the hip bath. She wasn't here now. He opened the door to the room beyond. The dust on the carpet was disturbed near the door. But no trail of footprints led to the hallway. She had not escaped this way either. He went back to the dressing room. Nothing said she had ever been here.

Except the faint perfume of cinnamon and ambergris that lingered in the air.

She had watched him from the dressing room.

Perhaps all evening. He had felt that strange electric energy all night.

As he bathed? She had ducked into the room adjoining as he got the bath, standing near the door. Had she watched as he wrote, naked, at the desk? As he slept?

It was intolerable. And strangely erotic. He had never experienced anything more sensual than that light touch on his naked body and the gentle sucking at his neck. Even now his cock was stubbornly erect.

He took the candelabra back into the bedroom and set it down. His eyes fell on the letter he had written to Emily. He steadied himself. That was why he was here. To find love again that would bring him revenge and heal the wounds he had suffered so long ago, deepened by bitterness until they had eaten away part of his soul.

He wasn't going to let some ghost, or some trespasser pretending to be a ghost, shake him from his resolve. She could order him to leave this house as much as she wanted. He had survived much worse than a little erotic haunting. He was not about to turn tail and run before he tried to claim what was his. Drew wouldn't miss the look on Melaphont's face when he finally recognized him for anything in the world.

He folded the letter and put it in its envelope. Tomorrow he would have this letter taken to Emily, and he'd know where he stood. She was no longer married, and she must remember their love. Now, if her father had not poisoned her against him, he had a chance. If the bastard had, well, then Drew would be sorry. And then he'd skip the part about Emily and take revenge on Sir Elias Melaphont in some more direct and forceful way.

He stalked to the bed, blew out the candles defiantly, and eased himself down in the bed. He did not need light to stave off what lurked in the dark.

That didn't mean that he would sleep.

Drew strode into the Goose and Gander rather later than he intended. He had fallen asleep after all, whether it was from loss of blood, or just the adrenaline subsiding, he wasn't sure. And he had dreamed, waking with another erection. The dreams had not been of Emily.

The whole thing seemed outlandish in the light of day, except that he had to tie his cravat rather carefully to cover up the twin wounds on his neck.

Still, he'd decided that it was a trespasser, not a ghost. Didn't some Portuguese friar practice an oriental version of Dr. Mesmer's animal magnetism to exert control over men without using magnets? Abbe Facia. That was the fellow's name. That was how she had controlled him. She must have used some trick of light to make her eyes glow like that. They'd looked just like animal eyes glowing when light shone on them at night, except red. And the wounds? A pair of tacks perhaps—he hadn't seen a knife. The whirling darkness was no doubt a swoon on his part from loss of blood. Well, he was going to search the place in earnest for her later and send her packing.

"Barton," Drew called. Old Henley was about the only one in the taproom at this hour. He was nursing an ale in the corner. The tapster stuck his bald pate out from a curtain that separated the kitchen from the taproom. He looked pale and drawn. The sheen of sweat on his brow caught the light.

"Didn't expect ta see ye here this mornin'. Did ye spend th' night?" Barton asked.

Drew had forgotten the wager. "Yes," he said in clipped tones.

"Did ye see th' ghost?" Henley wanted to know.

"I saw someone." He didn't care to go into detail. "I think I've got squatters up there."

Both Barton and Henley snorted. "Squatters doesn't suck blood," Henley remarked. "Did she suck yer blood?"

Drew felt himself coloring. He did *not* want to have this conversation. "Barton, do you have a boy who could take this note round to The Maples?"

"Jem took th' cart into Camelford for supplies," Barton apologized. "And Billy's come down with th' influenza. His ma says he's bad." Barton wiped his forehead with his handkerchief. His hand was a little shaky.

"Damn," Drew said under his breath. He didn't want take the note himself. Was he afraid of meeting Emily?

"I'll take it fer ye." Old Henley had somehow appeared at his shoulder and was peering at the envelope. He looked up at Drew with a strange expression on his face. Pity? Ah, he had seen it was addressed to Miss Emily Melaphont. That likely wasn't her name any more since Henley had intimated that she had once been married.

"I'll make it worth your while." Drew fished in his pocket. He didn't care if delivering notes to young widows wasn't respectable behavior.

"Save it. Ye can deliver it yerself. I'll show ye th' way. I'm goin' right by there."

No one "went right by" The Maples. It was four miles from the village and stood in its own impressive grounds. He hesitated. Still, Henley was already starting out the door.

"Don't ye want to collect yer pint?" Barton called.

"Later," Drew flung over his shoulder. Henley didn't give him any choice.

Drew had to pace his long strides to the older, shorter man's. The creature was still spry for all his years. Drew thought he would have to field a lot of questions. But Henley was silent. Drew's pulse raced. He might meet Emily face-to-face in a matter of moments. Henley turned off the road. Drew looked around, disoriented. They were heading up the hill to the church. It was a small affair, fifteenth century, its rough stone mellowed golden with age. His pulse quickened. Perhaps she was dressing the altar with flowers. Would she know him? They had been in love. How could she not? The expression on her face the instant she recognized him would tell everything. He and Henley crunched up the gravel path to the ancient wooden doors, carved with undecipherable pictures in bas relief. He was reaching for the great iron latch when Henley pulled him to one side.

"Around th' back, son."

He started off, eager. Then his steps slowed. The churchyard was back there. Was she putting flowers on a grave? Perhaps her husband's.

There was no one in the churchyard. A breeze leavened the heat up here. The grass between the graves still smelled of summer.

He knew then. His intestines knotted and threw a loop around his heart. He couldn't seem to breathe. Henley was pointing. He didn't have to. Drew walked slowly to the area fenced off with iron spikes topped with tiny fleur-de-lis. The Melaphonts were all buried there.

His eyes filled so he could hardly see the inscription on the stone.

Emily Margaret Melaphont Warner. 1788–1806. May she and her unborn babe find peace everlasting in Jesus' arms.

A year. She'd lived only a year after he'd been sentenced. She'd married so soon? Had Drew meant so little to her? She'd died while he was still on the prison hulk. All these years of longing for her had been so useless. She'd been pregnant, too. Who was this Warner fellow she'd loved? He felt cheated. All his dreams of making her love him again, of marrying under the nose of her father in spite for all he'd done to Drew, seemed foolish.

Drew felt Henley come up behind him. Anger surged up from his belly. "You said she wasn't married, that she was still here."

"Aye. Truth, when ye come ta think on it."

He didn't know what to ask. What difference would any of it make now? His throat was so full he thought he might choke.

"'Er father found 'er a 'usband before th' summer turned brown th' year ye left," Henley said philosophically. Drew saw out of the corner of his eye that Henley had taken out a pipe and was tamping down the tobacco in its bowl. "'E were a nice enough lad. Family was weavers, I think. 'Ad factories up ta Cumberland. Paid 'andsome for th' Melaphont name." Henley took an old flint striker from his pocket and lit the pipe, drawing on it to make it catch. "Melaphont made 'em live under 'is thumb up at Th' Maples while 'e put on th' new wing with Warner's money. Said she were poorly and 'e daren't let 'er go. But you know 'im. 'E just wanted control of th' both of 'em." Drew knew. Puffs of smoke curled into the air. "Warner went back to 'is people when she died."

Poor Emily. Sold off to provide a new wing for The Maples. It had always been a symbol of Melaphont pride. Wait. Through his haze he had let one fact slip by. "The year ye left." Henley knew who he was. He turned fierce eyes on the old man. "Don't think to spread my identity about. You'd find me a formidable foe." He hoped the threat did the trick. He wouldn't actually harm the old man.

"So ye slipped yer chains," Henley mused. "They can throw ye back inta prison if ye ain't served yer full time. Must 'ave wanted ta come back fair bad."

"I have a marker to redeem," Drew growled. "You wouldn't want to hold one of my markers, old man."

"No. Expect I wouldn't," Henley said. "'Ard to believe an old fool knows 'ow to 'old 'is tongue, Carlowe, but I do." He stabbed the air with the stem of his pipe. "Just ye 'ope ye don't get what ye think ye want right now. Bad business, that. Rots a man's soul."

Drew managed a sneer. It was a good defense against his hollow feeling. "I haven't got a soul, old man. Remember that." He turned and stumbled down the hill, hardly knowing where he was. Everything had changed. Emily was dead.

He collected Darley from in front of the tavern and galloped back toward Ashland, anger churning in his belly. All those years he'd dreamed, not knowing she was dead. Not fair. And now he'd have to find another way to exact his revenge on Melaphont. Because those years were Melaphont's fault.

So the first thing to do was to eject his beautiful squatter. He was going to be spending some time at Ashland while he evolved a new plan to take his revenge and carried it out. He had no desire to spend another sleepless night, or to lose any more blood.

3

Unbelievable! Carlowe hadn't run away last night and now after Freya was sure she was rid of him, he was back, banging around the house, poking in every room. No one could get a good day's sleep with that going on. He hadn't come into the ruined wing yet. But she had to keep a wary ear out.

The sounds subsided. This day had been difficult in many ways. When she thought he had gone, she should have been glad. But she found herself thinking about what had happened last night between them. It had kept her in a state of semiarousal all day.

Boot heels sounded on the servants' stairs. Thank goodness for her vampire hearing. Where was he going? Outside? She slipped over to the heavy draperies and pulled one out from the window just enough to see. The late afternoon light cut at her eyes and she squinted. She was very old, and could withstand some sunlight, but it certainly wasn't comfortable. Yes, there he was, in shirtsleeves and breeches, fists on his hips, looking up at the ruined wing, examining each set of windows. That was not good.

He started off at a run. Her window was the only one with draperies intact. Where could she go? This was ridiculous, on the run in her own house. She needed someplace she could darken to protect against the sunlight.

Footsteps thudded in the hall. He was counting doorways. No time to think! She called her power and imagined the room across the hall. The familiar moment of pain washed over her.

Drew pushed into the room. It was dark. Only the channel of light made by the open door revealed the features of the room. He didn't have to wonder whether it was hers. He could smell her marvelous scent and feel the electric energy hanging around him as if she had disappeared into thin air a moment ago. And actually, in view of her performance last night, that might just be what had happened.

He was being ridiculous.

He stared around the room. The furniture was still shrouded in Holland covers. But the bed was freshly made, the sheets crisp. Ashes stood in the fireplace. And there had definitely been a path where the dust had been disturbed in the carpets in the hall outside. There was no dust on the carpets here. And no leaks apparently. Someone could live here.

He pulled open the drawers of the highboy, and stood, transfixed. These were like no woman's underthings he had seen before. And he had seen his share. No chemises, no stockings. There were only filmy, lacy . . . somethings that would hardly cover anything. His loins tightened. He couldn't help but remember the sensuous feeling he had experienced last night when she had . . .

He strode to the wardrobe and swept open the doors. Dresses, if one could call them that, like she had worn last night, all sheer layers, and all white. A traveling cloak of black wool lined with white satin and edged with ermine, delicate slippers, and even little heeled, white leather boots. There could be no doubt to whom the room belonged.

But she wasn't here. How could he throw her out if he couldn't find her? Rage boiled up inside him, because he couldn't find his lovely trespasser, because Emily was dead and he was fourteen years too late to mourn and because all his dreams of getting back the eager and optimistic boy he had been by claiming her were dashed.

It was all Melaphont's fault. The bastard had taken Drew's innocence, his love, his very life from him. Drew pulled the clothes from the wardrobe and flung them around the room. He snatched drawers from the highboy and dashed them against the bedposts until they splintered and strewed their contents across the carpet. He wanted to stop. But he couldn't. He wanted destruction more. He pulled the pocketknife from his breeches pocket, flipped it open, and slashed the pillows on the bed. Feathers floated everywhere, uncontrolled, just as he was. The coil of hatred in his belly controlled him. He threw himself on the mattress, stabbing it over and over until he was left gasping as feathers floated to the floor around him like drifting snow.

His shoulders sagged. How could he lose control like that? Emptiness ate at him. He turned and lay in the ruined bed, dry-eyed and exhausted. The room was dark, its heavy draperies totally shut out the light. The open door cast little light into the room any more as the windows in the hallway dimmed with sunset.

He felt the hum of energy at the edge of his consciousness.

He sat up. How long had she been here?

"You can come out now." Had she seen his reckless display? But no one emerged from the dressing room. He pushed off the bed and flung open the dressing room door, but there was no one there.

His anger deserted him. He felt . . . helpless. He couldn't find the beautiful trespasser, though he was now sure she was somewhere in the house. The evening stretched ahead. His stomach rumbled and he realized he hadn't eaten since mid-morning. He stalked down to the kitchen. If she appeared later tonight, he wanted to have all his wits about him.

What was she going to do? Freya paced the stable. The horse looked at her with interest. She'd used every way she knew to frighten her unwelcome houseguest last night, and he wasn't frightened enough to leave. He had just shown how deranged he was. When the draperies in the room across the hall proved too tattered to keep out the sunlight, she'd crept back to the dressing room and watched the destruction. She couldn't have anyone living in her house, let alone a madman. Why was he so angry? His actions wouldn't frighten away a real ghost, so he obviously didn't believe she was supernatural.

She didn't want to hurt him. What other way was left to her? Reason, perhaps. But with a madman?

She had no other choice. She peered out the stable door. Lights flickered in the kitchen. He was probably getting dinner. She slid out into the evening. If she were going to try reason, she'd need to open the priest's hole where her father kept a copy of the deed.

She'd wait for him here, in his room. She laid the fragile roll of paper on the desk and began to pace impatiently. It was some minutes before she noticed the shreds of paper on the floor. She paused, peering down. The envelope from last night. She could still see parts of the address. She picked up a corner. It had still had the letter inside it when he ripped it up.

Oh. That's why he was angry. His ladylove had rejected

him. Well, that meant he wasn't precisely a madman, and her reasonable approach might actually work. It also meant he might be just as glad to leave this place.

She heard him coming up the hall. She didn't bother to transport herself out of his way this time. He threw open the door, holding his candelabra high. He seemed distracted. It was a moment before he saw her.

"You," he accused. "You have no right to be here, and don't tell me you're a ghost."

"Very well," she said. "I am not a ghost."

He looked satisfied. "I thought not. You must tell me sometime how you achieved your effects." His gaze swept over her and noticed the fragment of envelope in her hand. He strode forward and snatched it from her. "Leave my things alone."

"I'm sorry your suit did not prosper, but you should not take it out on me."

The anger, the hurt in his eyes were palpable. "The lady has been dead for fourteen years. So my suit was unlikely to prosper. Now get out of my house, whoever you are."

"*Your* house. This is my house." The insolence of the man!

His eyes narrowed. "I bought this house yesterday."

She practically gasped. "I beg pardon, but since I was not selling it, you could not have."

He went to the desk and opened his writing case. He noticed her scroll. "What's this?" he snapped, taking it up.

"Be careful, brute. It is very fragile." She took it, and carefully pulled the ribbon. The scroll unfurled a little. "It is the deed granting the property to my . . . ancestor." She'd almost said her father, and since it was made out in 1564 that would seem a lie.

"Let me see that," he barked. He set the candelabra down on the desk and Freya smoothed out the scroll. The spidery, ornate writing sloped across the parchment. The *s*'s looked like *f*'s and continued below the line. But it was clearly readable. His eyes darted back and forth across the lines, then lingered on the seal of the young queen.

"And you are a descendent of this Rubius Rozonczy?"

"Yes." If he ripped up the scroll before her eyes, she had no other proof. Her entire ploy depended on him having honor. A man with a scar like that across his cheek. Was she the one insane?

"How do I know that?"

"I have the deed." That didn't really prove her identity, but then what could?

"There could have been an intervening sale that was quite legitimate."

"There was not." A thought occurred to her. "From whom did you buy it?"

He must have had the same thought she did, for his brow darkened. He could look quite fierce with those lowering golden brows and that scar that stood out so whitely against his cheek. "Bromley. He acted as agent for the owner."

"Isn't he Sir Melaphont's agent, too?"

He nodded and chewed his lip. "And Melaphont was the caretaker of the property while the owner was away in—"

"In the Carpathian Mountains," she finished for him. "Transylvania to be exact. Sir Melaphont probably needed money, and thought my family would never know of his perfidy."

"Bromley would have to have been in on it," he mused.

"I am sure he was well compensated."

Carlowe's face fell. His shoulders sagged, just as though the air had been let out of him, like one of those hot air balloons people were always careering about in these days. "Melaphont wins again."

"Did you pay much money for this place?"

"It isn't the money," he said, his voice dull. "I've plenty of that."

"With my deed, and the receipt for the property, could not your law help you? I'm sure you could persuade Bromley to testify against him."

He combed his fingers through his hair. "That would take years."

"I suppose you could call him out," she offered. "Is that not what one does these days?" Especially if one was a man interested in honor. And this one had honor. He hadn't destroyed her scroll. And he didn't seem to question her right to the place.

"That would draw a bit too much attention to myself." His mouth was wry.

Ahhhh. He had something to hide.

"Besides, that would be a quick death. Much too good for him." His eyes went harder than she had ever seen a human male's expression. Only her father could look more implacable. "But I *will* have my revenge on him, for everything he's done. I'll find a way." His eyes took on a gleam. "Perhaps I could take a page from your book and haunt him. Bedlam would be a fitting end for him." He glanced up at her. "I suppose I owe you an apology for ripping up your room."

She shrugged. "You thought it was your room, and I an intruder."

He nodded then sucked in a resolute breath. "I shall relocate to the tavern immediately."

All she had wanted was to have him out of her house, and now when he was going, she found she did not want him to leave at all. There was a familiar full feeling of arousal in her woman's parts. That was almost expected. But it wasn't her physical attraction to him that filled her with regret. Something about this man was incredibly appealing. He was a mystery, hard with his need for revenge, tentative in his feeling for his dead love, honorable, damaged in some complex way that went deeper than the scars on his back.

This was not in her plan. She was resolved to have no contact with the world, no painful engagement with anyone, until she knew who she was and what she wanted.

"Don't go tonight," she found herself saying. It was almost shocking. But she realized that what she wanted was to know this man better. "It's getting late. In fact, you might as well stay here while you plan your revenge. I promise not to bother you. I sleep during the day."

He looked doubtful.

"The tavern is noisy, I'll wager. The curious will poke you with questions."

He pressed his lips together and she knew she had him. "Very well," he said, his voice tight. Was he thinking of last night, dreading that it might happen again, or that it might not? Because that was what she was doing—dreading both possibilities at once. She was insane for allowing temptation inside her very doors. Or maybe she was mad to refuse temptation.

She smiled. It was the first time she'd smiled in . . . in a year. It made her mouth feel strange. "I'll get fresh sheets and make up another room for myself."

"You'll need some help," he growled to her surprise and opened the door for her.

Freya chose a bedroom down the hall from his with red brocade draperies that would hold out the sunlight nicely. They had stripped the Holland covers off the furniture, and were making up the bed. They said nothing, perhaps because this feeling of electric attraction between them was almost stifling in its intensity. Could she be thinking of having sex with a man who had lost his love today? But she was. Imagining him naked, aroused, plunging inside her, consumed her thoughts. How could all the restraint she had managed in the last year be cast aside so . . . easily? She was shameless. Despicable. Worse, he might be giving way to imagination, too. The smoldering looks he was sending her from across the bed were not something she could mistake. To take her mind off her very vivid imaginings and to remind him why he should not be interested in having sex with her, she said, "I did not say I was sorry for your loss earlier. I am." That would dampen things.

He froze in the middle of putting a pillow into its case. "Ahhhh. Yes. Thank you." He shook the pillow down into place and threw it on the bed. Then he paused. "You know, I was nineteen and she seventeen when we shared a few kisses and told each other how much in love we were. But *are* you at that age? In love? I mean"—here he turned to face her—"what does one that young know of love? I still don't know what love is. But I'm not sure that was it. Perhaps I was in love with the idea of being in love with her. That idea kept me alive when her father had me charged with horse stealing. He passed sentence himself, supervised the lashing and condemned me to be transported to the prison colony at New South Wales."

That was how he had gotten those horrible scars. No wonder he hated Sir Melaphont.

"There was no ship available, since so many criminals were being transported. So I was sent to a prison hulk in Portsmouth." He must have seen her look of puzzlement. "They pack six hundred prisoners on a dismasted ship and float it in the harbor. Foul conditions. I nearly died of fever there, while my back healed."

"How could Sir Melaphont do such a thing?"

"Because he is a magistrate, and I was a bastard groom in his stables who dared to love his daughter."

"But you did not stay transported, and you do not talk or dress like a groom."

"The transport ship foundered in a storm. I made it to an island." He pulled the sheets up and tucked in the blanket as he talked. "I was rescued by free traders of the sea."

"Pirates?" She'd only read about pirates. What a romantic life he had lived.

"Yes. And they took me on. I was a strong lad. I learned the sea." They pulled up the brocaded coverlet together. "Did you know that pirates elect their captain?"

"You were a pirate captain." She believed it. It gave him that very dangerous feeling.

"I prefer to say I made my fortune in shipping." He smiled a very attractive smile—almost a boyish grin. It was the first time she had seen it, and it was . . . dazzling. "We did well. I sold out. I'd learned mathematics in order to navigate, so I knew I was not stupid. I hired tutors to teach me the skills of a gentleman. Much easier than mathematics. Voilà, Drew Carlowe."

He called himself Drew. Lovely.

He stood, surveying his work, but she knew from the way he frowned that he wasn't seeing the bed. "I may have cared for Emily only for the revenge winning her would have wreaked on her father. Not something to be proud of. I would have made her a damnable husband if that was the reason I wanted to marry her." He sighed. "I'd make a damnable husband to any woman, I suspect."

"Some women don't want husbands," she whispered.

He looked up and his eyes were alight. Now she'd done it. They raked her body. "Why do you wear clothes like that?"

What did he mean? "I've always worn clothes like this."

He came round to her side of the bed. He was stalking her, almost like the pictures she had seen of panthers, all powerful grace, deadly. "Those clothes say you know of sensual things. Most women would never dare wear them."

"I am not most women." *That* was true. She was not even human.

He took her upper arms in his hands, and immediately the sexual part of her began to throb with the beat of her heart. She was already wet between her legs. He just stared at her. "I don't know what you are." Oh, dear. His teeth were gritted, as against some pain. "And I don't care."

That was better.

"What is your name?"

"Why do you care about my name?"

"Because I generally do not make love to women whose name I do not know." He laughed. It sounded on the edge of hysteria. "As a matter of fact, lately, I do not make love to women at all."

"That's not healthy," she whispered. Wasn't that true for her, as well?

The muscle in his jaw clenched. "Don't play with me. I won't force myself on you."

"You needn't. I'm of age." Oh, yes. Centuries of it. "And I am not inexperienced." Sex was the one thing she knew how to do. She'd done it almost constantly before this last year, as she and her sisters made Harriers for her father. She insinuated herself against his body and was pleased to feel the hard erection at his groin. She ran her hands lightly over the front of his breeches and felt him take a ragged breath. She was going to do this, consequences be damned. Not because it was her job, but because she wanted to do it. She was going to give this man, who had known pain and hardship in his life, a glimpse of ecstasy.

She pulled at the end of his cravat. The knot unraveled and she stripped it from around his neck. There were the two bites she'd left from yesterday, already healing. He was strong, this one. She opened the button at his collar. He was undoing the buttons at his waistcoat. She pulled the shirt out of his breeches and worked at the buttons at his cuffs. So many buttons . . . He pulled it over his head. Ah, yes. The light dusting of hair, the tanned nipples, peaking now in anticipation. She rubbed her hands over his pectoral muscles.

All those years of hard work at sea had left him . . . impressive. He was pulling at the buttons on his breeches. She pushed him back against the bed, and he let her.

"Let me pull off your boots." She was stronger than he was, though she couldn't let him know that. They slid off as though they were loose.

He didn't seem to notice, but pushed his breeches over his hips as she stripped off his stockings. His erection, freed, hung between them. She stood and let the tip rub against her belly as she moved her hands over his shoulders. The ridges of his scars almost broke her heart.

Surprise replaced the lust in his eyes, followed immediately by chagrin. He reached for his shirt. "I forgot myself. I . . . have scars which would be distasteful to a lady."

"I saw them last night." She took the shirt gently and tossed it on the floor.

"You're sure," he said doubtfully.

She nodded, suppressing a smile, and pulled his neck down. Heat flashed back into his eyes. She thought his kiss would be fierce with the need she felt in him. But he brushed his lips across her forehead, down her temples. Tiny kisses he placed on her cheeks, even as he slipped her dress from her shoulders. She pressed her breasts to his bare body, her own breath coming harder, and he found her lips. She licked his with the tip of her tongue. She felt his surprise and then he opened her mouth and deepened the kiss, probing her with his tongue. How she loved kissing. She had never kissed the Aspirants. In some ways it was more intimate even than intercourse. Kissing him was some signal that this was different than all that mechanical arousal she had engaged in to train the Aspirants and develop their power.

She slipped the clasp of her girdle, and it fell with a metallic jingle to the carpet. Her dress floated after it. It was just their naked bodies, hers wet and soft, his hard. His arms slid around her, even as his kisses made her almost dizzy with desire.

He stiffened when her palms caressed the ridges on his back. She didn't stop, just continued kissing him while she rubbed her hands down over his buttocks and cupped them, pressing his groin against her, rubbing herself against his erection.

"What do you call your man part?" she asked. She had not been out of Mirso in so long and she didn't want to seem strange.

He drew away, smiling, puzzled. "My . . . my cock, I suppose. It's a good Saxon word."

"Then may I say, Drew Carlowe, that I would like to pay special attention to your cock for the next few hours."

My God, Drew thought, the woman might not be a ghost, but she was certainly a witch. Special attention for a few hours? He might just die.

"Only if I may pay special attention to you," he murmured, sweeping her up into his arms. The accent was incredibly sensual, along with everything else about this woman. He laid her on the bed. Her petite form was perfect; her breasts peaked with delicate, dusky-colored nipples. And her skin was the most translucent, creamy perfection he had ever seen, almost as though it had never seen the sun. Her scent was erotic, cinnamon and ambergris mixed with a woman's musk. And the vibrancy he always felt around her seemed to find the life force inside him and pluck it like a string, so he vibrated in sympathy. He crawled up after her and laid himself beside her. He was almost painfully erect, his cock straining against her hip.

"We will go slowly," she whispered as she turned into him. Her tongue snaked out and licked his nipple. "So that you have the maximum amount of pleasure." Her hand cupped his balls and lifted, gently massaging the stones inside across each other. He groaned. It slid up along his cock, softly, her thumb finding the drop of clear fluid at the opening and smoothing it across the head. He bent to her throat, which she bared to him. He kissed down the delicate column to the notch where her pulse beat and licked there. She was running one finger down the big vein in his erection, lightly. He wanted to scream the sensation was so acute. He buried his head in her breasts and found her nipple with his lips. He suckled, gently, and she arched to present him easier access.

"Oh, Drew," she moaned. "You have the hidden talents."

"You haven't seen the half of them." He slid his hand down to cup her mound. She was wet and ready. "I want you shrieking many times tonight."

She opened her eyes, surprised. "I thought the Englishman, he wanted only to spill his seed without caring for the woman's pleasure."

"What Englishmen do you know? That is not the way to entice a woman to your bed more than once."

She gave a throaty chuckle. "You are most practical, Drew Carlowe." He slipped his finger inside her then drew her slickness over the nub that gave a woman pleasure. She hissed and clasped his cock firmly. She didn't rub it, thank God, or he wouldn't have been able to hold out. He rubbed her, though, even as he kissed her thoroughly. It was only moments before she was rocking against his hand and giving small yips of satisfaction as she coiled tighter and tighter. And then unwound, wailing.

"Oh, dear man. You are very skilled," she breathed when it was done.

"You were ready." But he was proud she thought him skilled.

"I was ready last night. I have been ready all day. It has been torture." She raised herself on one elbow. "But I promised close attention to your cock and I have been shirking." She pushed him onto his back gently and stroked his hip. "Now, we are going to play a game."

A game? He could feel his eyes widen. Her hand strayed to his cock.

"Do not look at me so. You will like this game." She was right if it had anything to do with continuing exactly what she was doing to him now. He was having trouble getting his breath. "The game is that I play with your cock, and you try not to come." She looked up at him. "You say 'come'? Ejaculate."

" 'Come' is fine," he gasped.

"This will increase your pleasure. And if you think you cannot hold it, tell me."

He jerked a nod. "Yes. Yes."

She stroked him, her thumb pressing on the head as it slid up off the underside. He sucked in a breath. She scooted down. He was taken by surprise when he felt her tongue follow the trail her thumb had laid. "Where did you learn that?"

"Shhhhh. Go within yourself. You feel the sensation, savor it." She licked again. "Held in the suspension of endless pleasure. You find your center, and you just . . . stay there."

Would he disappoint her? Already the sensation was so intense he thought he might come. "What if I can't?"

"You can." She left off with his cock in the nick of time and kissed his inner thigh. "We will rest periodically, and you will make me come, and then we will begin again. A virile man can remain hard for hours with practice. And you are a very virile man."

How did she know these things? But he didn't have time to wonder, because now she was lying between his legs with her arms over his thighs. She pulled up his cock and her tongue swabbed along its length and flicked over the vein that fed it and she sucked very gently on the tip before she took the whole into her mouth and he felt the head rub against her throat. He thought he might die of sensation. He arched his hips up against her, groaning. She pulled away just in time, leaving him gasping. All the feeling in his body seemed to have pooled in his genitals. They had never been so hard, so needing.

She stroked his body with her hands, making comforting, soothing sounds while he caught his breath. And then she began again. Off and on, and off again just as he was about to explode. It seemed she knew a man's body, *his* body, so thoroughly that she was in complete command of it. She hadn't learned that in a brothel. Brothels held women who went mechanically through the motions of pleasure without taking any pleasure in it themselves, or really caring about their partner's pleasure. Not this woman. She was perfectly attuned to him, as though they were connected somehow. Perhaps she was a courtesan, trained in some subtle way . . . Or perhaps their connection was even more elemental.

God, she was starting again.

He really *was* quite virile, this Drew Carlowe, she thought with satisfaction. Her reassurance to him had turned out to be true. It was good to put her talents to giving pleasure, not training men to be Harriers. The difference between work and pleasure. And she knew for certain she had been giving him pleasure for more than an hour. He was trying very hard. She could feel him focusing inward, finding his center. She had not yet had to help him hold himself with a little compulsion, but she could when it was necessary. He was a determined man. It was time for a longer respite, and that meant she would get another orgasm. She liked orgasms. It was one of the few benefits of slaving away to make Harriers at her father's command.

She waited for the moment when he was just beginning to slide over his brink and pulled away. She wormed her way up toward his chest, kissing him lightly as she went, inhaling the scent of him. His cock was red and throbbing, lying swollen along his belly. He was covered with a light sheen of sweat, courtesy more of her efforts than the hot night.

He gathered her into his arms. "You are a witch," he murmured, "a witch who deserves pleasure in return." She expected him to want to plunge his cock inside her. She'd definitely have to hold him with a little compulsion if he did that.

He surprised her by simply holding her in his embrace, his cock hard and pulsing against her thigh. His hands moved over her body. The remains of calluses said he had once labored. A chink in the armor of the man he had created. She didn't mind. It occurred to her that he had made himself into what he was out of sheer determination, something she was unable to do. She didn't know who she was, apart from the maker of Harriers her father wanted her to be.

He raised her chin from where she burrowed into his shoulder and kissed her with such slow tenderness it made tears spring to her eyes. It was . . . generous. In all the sex she had engaged in over the years, no one had ever shown her tenderness. She had been a tutor and a demanding one, no more. He worked her mouth open gently, and probed her thoroughly, all the time his hands moved over her, now rubbing her shoulders, now cupping her buttocks. The throb between her legs began to be almost painful. She had come quickly and very forcefully the first time—almost as soon as he began rubbing her. She had been too long without release. But this time he seemed determined to draw out her experience. She smiled into his mouth. Very well.

She let him control the pace. That was new for her. Always before it was she who controlled, whether the Aspirant was the one receiving stimulation or it was her turn. It might be a matter of trust, this deciding to let him control. He suckled at each breast attentively. She wanted his cock thrusting inside her so badly she almost wanted to scream. But she did not. Why did she trust this man? Perhaps because he had written that letter. Perhaps because he had not seized her deed. He rolled her onto her back. But again he surprised her. He slid down between her legs, and she realized that he was going to reciprocate by using his mouth. The very thought made her squirm in anticipation. Who would have thought an Englishman knew how to do that?

But he did. He opened her carefully and lapped across her moist tissues. How glad she was that she had bathed, earlier. He began to tease her point of pleasure with his tongue. She squirmed against him, and tangled her fingers in his hair. He brought her slowly but relentlessly toward climax. He began to hum some sailors' tune. The vibrations nearly sent her wild. His hands slid up to her breasts, and fondled her nipples as he began to suck in earnest.

The orgasm, when it struck, was savage. It took her and shook her and made her roll her head convulsively from side to side as she shrieked and strained her hips toward his mouth. It broke over her, wave after wave of it, until her hips jerked away of their own accord and she collapsed into a pool of sensation that subsided only slowly.

He crawled up beside her, wiping his mouth. She opened one eye and saw that he looked very satisfied with himself. She smiled. He should. She wasn't certain she had ever experienced an orgasm like that in all the many thousand thousands in her life. Was it because he was tender? Was it because she trusted him enough for some strange reason to open herself to the full impact of it? What he had done to her was more than just to give her pleasure. He had showed her an emotional closeness she had never known.

That thought brought tears. It felt like a gigantic knot of tension had been released inside her, one that had been building over centuries. He must have felt her crying against his chest, for he rocked her, soothing. No one had ever done that for her. She wanted to give him something in return. She raised her head and smiled at him. It was time. She would love keeping him at the edge of insanity. The sexual act would be an act of giving, not demanding performance. She sat up and pushed him gently to his back. Then she straddled him. She wanted to feel him filling her. And now that she was sated, she could be attentive to just how long he could stand the strokes inside her. How long could he hold his release tonight? She was going to find out.

It was the wee hours of the morning. But Drew wasn't tired. The hours of making love to this woman seemed to fill him with energy rather than drain him. He had brought her to release several times now. And he had held his in abeyance. That should have been onerous. But it wasn't. Even now she was caressing his cock as she sucked at one of his nipples. She was so skilled, the sensation so intense, he seemed to find some core of stamina that allowed him to appreciate the pleasure she gave him for what it was in the moment, not the orgasm it would bring. Several times he had felt that constriction in his testicles that came with lust unreleased. She seemed to sense it. Perhaps his balls tightened. Always she would massage them gently until the aching passed. Once or twice when he was on the brink of orgasm, her eyes seemed to glow red again. He was so centered in the moment he could not focus on the questions that raised. She would whisper, "Find your center," and he would regain control again.

He had never felt closer to a woman. She was so generous, so attentive. He was only glad he could return the favor. She rolled on to her back, her breasts flattening, and opened her knees to invite him in. He hung on his elbows above her, positioned his cock.

"Fill me. Please," she whispered.

He sheathed himself in her wet warmth. She bit her lip in pleasure. He began to stroke in and out, slowly. He could do this. He went inside himself again, trying to get lost in the rhythm.

Until she changed it. She wanted it faster now. "I'm not sure I can hold it," he panted.

"Now is the time to stop trying," she breathed.

He blinked. Now? Then he grinned. He repositioned himself so that his cock touched her on that spot that women liked the most, just in front of the entrance to her womb proper, and pumped in and out a few times to stimulate it. That made her open her eyes. They slapped together in delicious counterpoint. His loins were so tight, his genitals so heavy and sensitive, he thought he might burst. But he had to wait a little longer. Surely a woman as sensual as she was could reach ecstasy just once more tonight. He grabbed her buttocks as he knelt upright, his knees wide. She wrapped her legs around him. He plunged into her harder and harder, as if he could never get enough of her. He felt her begin to contract around him, and he let go.

The explosion was like nothing he had ever felt. His seed pulsed into her, on and on, stripping him of all his fluids. His vision contracted to a single point of light. He could hear himself grunting from somewhere far away, a bass counterpoint to her shrieks.

They both collapsed, finally, nothing left of themselves to share. He cradled her against his body. This most sexual of experiences had felt almost . . . spiritual. He'd started tonight as one kind of person—alone, inviolate, sure of his purpose. And he'd ended as someone else, a man who needed someone else.

He'd never needed Emily, except as revenge on her father. He'd never even known her. He'd certainly never loved her. He knew that now. But this woman, with whom he'd shared only a few words, he knew with every fiber of his being.

He just didn't know any facts about her. And now that he was not buried in the sensation of the moment, there were definitely questions.

Well, he'd have to remedy that.

4

She snuggled against him. They had been drowsing together for a while, but he knew she was awake. He had been wondering where to start with his questions. His preoccupation with his mission to find Emily, the incredible sexual attraction they'd felt—all had distracted him and made his denial of those questions easy. But he could no longer ignore them. He would come round to red eyes and disappearing and the wounds at his neck. He was not frightened of her, not after tonight. But he could not dismiss them as mere tricks. He would start his questions with what had happened to him. What he really wanted was to know if she had experienced it, too. "I've never felt anything like that."

She stretched and pressed her breasts against him. He thought she'd stripped every drop of semen from his body, yet still he felt a stirring in his loins.

"Good," she said, her mouth softening into a smile.

"What . . . what was that?"

"The closeness we felt?"

We. He nodded, brushing his lips across her hair. She had felt it, too.

"It is the teaching of the Tantra. It comes from the Hindu, though Buddhists and Jains practice also."

"They teach sex?" You could study sex? Apparently. She must have.

"Well, more it is the meditation that they teach. They believe the physical is an expression of the divine. And physical acts can bring you closer to God. Like sex, if you do it correctly."

"You do it correctly," he murmured, holding her close. Had she done this thing with others? To distract himself from that thought, he asked, "Will you tell me your name now?"

She looked conscious, as though she didn't realize she had never revealed even this much of herself to him. "Freya. My name is Freya."

After the Norse goddess of fertility and plenty. That was appropriate. "Freya." He savored it. "Well, Freya, why do you live here alone, without even removing the Holland covers from the furniture and make the villagers think you are a ghost?"

She stiffened and he thought she would push away from him. Then he felt her soften. Maybe it was resignation. Her voice was small, and she did not look at him. "I am a bad person, Drew. I have done bad things. My father required them of me and of my sisters but we did not protest. One sister went mad from doing them. And I never even thought to refuse. I had never been away from my father's . . . house until he sent my remaining sister and me to England. We were doing this thing, and it was dangerous, and it had perhaps eaten at her mind, as well. I told her she must quit. But she wouldn't. And . . . and then I couldn't do it any more. So I stopped. And that meant I didn't support her. She . . . died." She took a shuddering breath.

Her sister had died. Perhaps she had as many scars as he did. He waited for her to go on, just holding her.

"But my job, evil as it was, it was all I knew," she said at last. "If I was not that, who was I? But I knew if I went home

I wouldn't have the strength to stand against my father when he wanted me to pick up where I left off. So I did not go home. I came here."

He wouldn't ask her what she did. She was not ready yet to tell him. Not that he thought whatever it was would be evil. He knew she wasn't evil on some deep level he couldn't explain. "And the ghost act was to keep people away."

She nodded. "I needed time to think. And these English, they are so strict with all their rules for what a woman must not do, and how she must be attended always by servants, and receive callers and live just so and I could not stand this. So I lived outside their censure."

"What were you thinking about?" he asked softly, moving a strand of her midnight hair away from her forehead.

"Who I was."

He could understand that. He'd defined himself as a bastard, a servant in Melaphont's stable, a lover of Emily, a prisoner, a pirate, and now a gentleman. He wasn't sure he was any of those, not really. He nodded, and waited.

"I look back on all those months." Her voice was pensive. "I was half-alive. Not thinking, though that was what I came here to do. Not feeling." The silence stretched.

"Does that mean you know who you are now?"

She chuckled. "No. I am more confused than ever. I know only that I was not living."

"Well, that's something."

"Yes." She looked up at him and smiled.

He could not help but swell a bit with pride. He might not be alone in the sensation of joining tonight. But if there was any way forward together there were other things he must know.

"So tell me about the red eyes and the disappearing." He didn't dare mention the wounds at his neck.

"Must you ruin all with your questions?" she snapped, pushing away from him and sitting up. "Can you not just live in the moment?" She looked around, as though she realized where she was for the first time. She got out of bed, gloriously naked, and pulled the heavy draperies closed. "It will be light soon. I must move my things from the other room."

"I'll help," he said. But he felt bleak inside. The bond he'd felt to her had snapped.

He got hold of himself. He couldn't dally with a woman anyway. The revenge he'd desired for fifteen years had to be planned all over again. Melaphont must be his focus, not this tiny woman who had ravished his soul as well as his body tonight. She had secrets she would not share. He had no time to pry them from her. Where was his determination now? He forced himself to think about revenge. Money. Money was what Melaphont cared about. That and his house. Then those things were what he would lose.

By the time she had finished moving her things, it was daylight. She was getting sleepy. The room was over warm, but she couldn't open the draperies to catch a breeze. Drew was sweating and pale. She could not make him suffer here. "Go to your room and get some sleep." She managed a smile.

He examined her face, nodded once. And he left.

She felt bereft. She had trusted him last night with her fragile psyche as well as her body. And she had felt almost . . . reborn. Until he had ruined everything with questions that reminded her what a gulf there really was between them. They were not even the same species, no matter how close they had felt. She lived forever and he but a blink of time. The feeling of being joined spiritually was only the effect of the Tantric exercise she had always made the Aspirants practice. It wasn't real closeness, and certainly not anything else she might name. She had just been surprised by his tenderness.

She could never even tell him she was vampire. It was strictly against the Rules established by her father and the

Council of Elders. Even if it wasn't, she couldn't trust him enough for *that.* He would be appalled, as humans always were.

She slept fitfully until nightfall. No light leaked from his doorway as she went to the kitchen. She heated water for a bath. A roast chicken he must have prepared sat, untouched, on the cutting board with some greens she did not recognize. The English always overcooked their vegetables. She ate standing. The night was hot again. Thunder sounded in the distance. Lightning threw the kitchen into periodic bright relief. She bathed, sorry the soap washed his scent from her body, then dressed and wandered to the front of the house. But there were no lights on in that wing. Where was he? Perhaps the stables.

His horse had his nose stuffed in the manger, and the barn was filled with contented grinding. The creature didn't seem to mind the storm outside as long as he had his oats and hay. There were several bales piled neatly at the end of the barn aisle, and his stall was clean and filled with fresh straw. The place smelled of hay, and saddle soap and oil from the freshly cleaned tack. But there was no sign of Drew. At least she knew he wasn't far. He wouldn't go anywhere without his horse. She realized she'd been worried he might have left.

She wouldn't want that.

She headed back to the house. The skies let loose in pelting rain. Drops bounced off the gravel and flapped in sheets across the stable yard. She was soaked to the skin instantly. Breaking into a run, she made it to the kitchen.

His room. It was the only place left. Had he been sitting there in the dark? She, who had wanted nothing more than to be alone for the last year, without thinking or feeling, was now atwitter to know what he was doing and what he felt. She changed into a wrapper and laid her gown out to dry. Then she stalked purposefully to his room.

"Drew Carlowe," she called, rapping softly.

A hoarse voice said, "Go away."

Was he that angry with her? "I . . . I want to talk to you." He didn't know how much it cost her to say that.

"You c-can't come in." He sounded strange—not like himself at all. "I'm . . . b-busy."

She tried the door. It was locked. "Are you . . . well?" She didn't have the faintest idea what sick people sounded like. She had grown up among vampires and they were never sick.

"I . . . I might have a t-touch of the influenza." He was trying to sound casual. But she could hear the lie in that. Pursing her lips, she twisted the knob until the lock creaked and broke. She pushed her way in.

He was huddled in the dark in a chair in front of the empty fireplace with a blanket round his shoulders. He sounded strange because he was shivering uncontrollably.

"Go away. You m-might catch it."

Not possible of course. Her Companion killed all disease. She was immortal, for God's sake, to all intents and purposes. She hurried over to him, frowning. "I won't catch it. You must have a doctor." One got a doctor for a human who was sick.

"No n-need," he managed.

She ignored him and put a palm on his forehead. He was incredibly hot. "How long have you been like this?" Had she weakened him with a night of sex?

"It got bad t-this afternoon. I'll be all right."

"Let's get you into bed." She pulled him up.

"I'm all right." But he had to turn away, as a dry, hacking cough took him. She could have carried him bodily, but she didn't want to frighten him with her strength.

"Don't be childish." She practically dragged him to the bed and pushed him up into it.

He was already in his stocking feet. She began to undress him.

"I'm perfectly c-capable," he protested. But he made no move to help her. That frightened her more than anything else. His flesh, wherever she touched it, was burning hot. When she had him naked and tucked under the sheets, she drew up the comforter to quiet his shaking. It didn't help.

"I'm going to get a doctor."

He gave a breathless chuckle. "No one will c-come up here at night."

He was right. Her stupid ghost impersonation had insured that.

"I don't need a doctor. Besides, I expect he's b-busy. I think Barton h-had it yesterday at the tavern. A good p-place to spread it." He dissolved into the cough again.

She came up and stood over him, frowning. "Can you die from this?"

"Only the frail die. I'll just be a little unc-comfortable for a few days. You'd b-better keep your distance, though."

"I told you. I can't get it from you. So," she said briskly, "I'm the perfect sickroom attendant." She drew up a chair. Actually, she felt rather helpless. What could she do but watch him shake with fever?

That's what she did over the next hours. He didn't complain but the racking cough and the shaking seemed to exhaust him. Finally he subsided into a restless sleep. She lit a single candle and pulled over a book he must have been reading. It was a story about a man named Faustus. She could barely concentrate on the words. Was this what it was like to be human, prey to every sickness, every wound? Her only consolation was that it was only uncomfortable. He wasn't in any real danger.

He broke out in a sweat halfway through the night. That was a good sign, wasn't it? She peeled off the comforter and found the bedclothes soaked. So she went down to the kitchen and brought up several pitchers of water and cloths.

When she returned he appeared to be awake. His eyes

were slitted, but they were open. Still, he was nearly insensible. She pulled back the sheet and poured her water in the room's washbasin. The thunderstorm appeared to have broken the unseasonable hot spell. She opened the windows to the night air, which now held the hint of autumn September should bring. Then she wetted a cloth and wiped him down.

"Better?" she asked when she was done.

He roused himself. "Thank you," he murmured. "You are kind."

She touched his forehead to push back his soaked hair and he flinched. "What's wrong?" This man had undergone torture. What could make him flinch?

He tried to smile. "Headache." He squinted against the dim candlelight. "I feel like I've been put on the rack. Hell, my hair hurts."

"What does this mean?" she asked, alarmed.

"It means I have influenza." His eyes closed. "It will pass soon."

It didn't. She added blankets when he was shaking, and left him naked to the air as he broke into a sweat. She tried to cool him by wiping him down with a damp cloth periodically, but always he was hot to the touch. Morning came and she closed the draperies against the sun. But the fever wouldn't let him go. He had periods of insensibility. You couldn't call it sleep. He refused all food though she made him drink water. He must replace the sweat he was losing. He roused himself to use the chamber pot, though infrequently.

In the late afternoon he opened his eyes.

"How are you?"

He seemed to consider. Then his eyes opened wide. "Damn!" he whispered. "Darley." He struggled up on one elbow and pulled at the covers. She pushed him back down.

"I'll feed him. Only tell me what to give him."

He sighed. "Two flakes of hay and two scoops of oats."

She turned to the door.

"And water."

"Of course." She smiled. "I'll be back shortly."

By the second night, she had begun to worry. He had said a few days. Surely a few days included time on the mend, as well. So shouldn't he be getting better? He seemed to be getting worse. She had to steady him to use the chamber pot at all. His lips were cracked and dry, his eyes glazed and overbright. He still flinched at her touch. And always he was hot.

She laid him back in the bed near morning.

"You're good to me," he murmured. There was a softness in his eyes behind the fever.

"Anyone would help you."

He shook his head ever so slightly. "You're a generous person."

"No one has ever called me that."

"Then they didn't know you . . ." He closed his eyes.

That startled her. Perhaps no one *did* know her. She had been an anonymous extension of her father at Mirso Monastery. She had the benefit of his position. He was the Eldest, after all. No one dared give her offense. But no one thought of her as anything but his daughter, either. She had always depended on him. He knew everything, having lived so long. And he always told her what to do.

But here she was on her own. And she didn't know what to do for Drew.

A doctor would know. She'd get a doctor up here today, no matter that Drew said he didn't need one, if it were the last thing she did.

The village street was deserted, though it was still an hour to sunset. Freya had bundled up in her hooded cape, with gloves and half-boots to protect her from the sun. Still its stinging needles reached her, even through the lined wool.

She lifted the hood and squinted around. Where was she going to find the doctor? Actually, where was everybody?

A sign creaked back and forth in the wind rising on the threat of sunset. GOOSE AND GANDER it said. A tavern. Drew thought he had caught this influenza there.

She pushed in through the doors, grateful for the refuge from the sun, and slipped back her hood. The tavern was deserted except for one old man in the corner. Well, that was more people than she had seen anywhere else.

He studied her over an empty glass.

"Excuse me, sir," she said. "Can you tell me where I might find a doctor?"

He rose and went to pull another pint for himself. "I expect he's up to The Maples."

Freya was fascinated with very old humans. After all, her kind stopped aging at maturity. She had never seen an old person until she left Mirso last year. The wrinkles, the rheumy eyes, the joints she could actually hear creaking and cracking, all held a dreadful attraction. What would it be like to feel death approach as your body failed? This was the fate that waited for Drew.

"Which way is this Maples? I need the doctor quickly."

"Yer foreign, ain't ye?" he asked, without answering her question.

Freya went wary. These English were quite provincial. They did not take easily to anything strange. "I am from Transylvania." He would never know where that was, or what it might mean.

"That would be where th' Carpathian Mountains are, I'd 'azard. Would ye like a pint? It's on th' 'ouse at th' moment, since Barton's dead."

She shook her head. Wait! Drew said he caught this influenza from Barton. She sucked in a breath. "Was this Barton old like you?"

The old man shook his head, sighing. "'Earty as a 'orse one day, stiff as a board th' next. Fever took 'im."

Freya felt her heart contract. Drew was wrong. He could die from this sickness. "Please, I *must* have a doctor."

"Someone got th' influenza? This is a bad bout, certain." He sat back down. "'Alf the county's down with it."

How could he be so calm? "Yes, yes," she said, sitting across from him, leaning forward. She *must* make him understand the urgency. "Mr. Drew Carlowe has this influenza."

"I thought so. Yer th' ghost, ain't ye?"

She went still. Then she mustered a laugh. "Do not be nonsensical." She touched his hand. The skin was paper-thin. "Quite corporeal, I assure you."

His pale blue eyes were quizzical. "Then ye've been playing ghost. Naughty girl."

She sighed. Maybe the truth would make him tell her how to get this doctor. She nodded. "I wanted to be alone and in England this is impossible for a woman. I frightened people away."

"Th' bites?"

Oh, dear. "Some were more stubborn than others. I pricked them with a knife point."

He pressed his mouth together and nodded. "Th' disappearing?"

"People see what they want to see. And I wore a white dress that seemed to float."

"Red eyes?"

She shrugged and tried to look confused. "Did they say I had red eyes?"

He sipped his ale. "Must 'ave been a shock when Carlowe bought th' place."

"Yes, especially since I own it."

"Ahhh, th' absent landlord. Or 'is daughter. Guess Melaphont got a little overanxious."

"He is a greedy man, this Melaphont." She frowned. "And he has been very bad to Mr. Carlowe." She was going to take care of Melaphont for Drew, after Drew was well again. She'd start by making him give Drew's money back for the house. After that . . .

"He's about to get his due, I expect."

She couldn't spend any more time here. "Please, please tell me how to get to this Maples."

"I doubt th' quack'll come. Melaphont's an important man around 'ere." She glared at him. He sighed. "Th' road turns up into the 'ills three miles past Ashland. It's marked."

"Thank you, thank you, sir." She rose. "What is your name, if I may ask?"

" 'Enlcy."

"Mr. Enley, I hope you do not catch this influenza. I would not wish you to die."

He looked surprised. "Thankee, young lady. I would not wish it, either."

She curtsied in the English fashion and rushed from the room, pulling up her hood, then hurried behind the tavern, drew her power. She must get to The Maples.

The dusk was settling in as she materialized in the wood at the edge of the road to The Maples. She threw back her hood, freed of the itching pain of the sun at last. The doctor had to come, though it was growing dark, even though he thought Ashland was haunted. She could not compel him because she needed his medical judgment and under compulsion there could be no judgment or creativity. She would just tell him it was she who haunted it, as she had told Henley. He *had* to come. She stepped out onto the road.

The Maples turned out to be even larger than Ashland, with twenty chimneys poking up from a late-sixteenth-century façade of stark gray stone. It stood across a man-made lake, lights blazing from every window, a solid vision of wealth and power. On one side, a new wing rose, half complete. Its style did not match the rest of the house. Melaphont had no taste. She hurried over a bridge that crossed a stream that fed the lake and crunched up a wide gravel drive to the portico. Up shallow steps, she took the great knocker and banged on the door.

A very severe man with a mouth that turned down opened the door. He said nothing, but stared at her in disapproval.

A woman alone could not be either wealthy or of good character in England. "I must see the doctor," she panted.

"He is engaged with Sir Melaphont." The man began to shut the door.

"But there is someone who needs his help!" she pleaded, stopping the door with one delicate hand. She did not wait for another refusal, but pushed past him.

"See here!" he protested.

Twin staircases wound up from the far end of the immense foyer. She couldn't search this entire pile looking for the doctor. She drew her power even as she whirled on the majordomo. The world went red. "Take me to the doctor. Now."

His gaze became vague. He nodded and moved off toward the stairs. She followed. In the broad hallway of the first floor a young man paced. He affected a curl of dark hair that he let hang across a pale brow, but there the likeness to a portrait of Lord Byron she had seen in books stopped. His face was pudgy and petulant.

"Grimshaw!" The boy started forward. "The damned doctor won't let me see my father."

Grimshaw said nothing of course, because he was under Freya's compulsion. He just opened the door and ushered her inside.

"Grimshaw! I say—"

The door shut in the young man's face. The bedroom was huge. A portly man stood with his back toward her, his hand on the wrist of an immense figure only dwarfed by the great, curtained bed in which it lay. The figure emitted wet, gasping sounds and the room smelled of blood. A basin of it sat on the table by the bed. What was this? The doctor turned at her entrance.

“I said no visitors, Grimshaw.” The doctor glowered.

Freya willed Grimshaw out of the room. He closed the door behind himself. The younger Melaphont could be heard protesting in the hall.

“Who are you?” the doctor said. He was an austere older man with luxuriant mustachios and iron-gray hair swept back from an intelligent forehead.

“Never mind that. Mr. Drew Carlowe needs your help. He is at Ashland.”

“The new owner? It’s influenza, I assume.”

She nodded. Her glance darted to the figure in the bed. This was Drew’s nemesis. He was immensely fat, his jowls dripping down over the collar of his nightshirt. His face looked like it was melting. Still, there were cruel lines about his mouth. She could believe he had lied about Drew and punished him unjustly. Now he was like pale yellow dough, still, his eyes closed. The doctor laid his patient’s hand back on the coverlet.

“And I would come if I thought it would do any good, young lady,” the doctor was saying. “But there’s really no use. Oh, I bleed them, because one must do something. But there is really nothing to be done but make them as comfortable as you can and let the disease run its course.”

Freya was stunned. “You . . . you cannot help him?”

The doctor looked at her with sympathy in his eyes. He shook his head.

Freya felt tears of frustration well up. Her throat closed. These humans were at the mercy of some silly disease that wasted one away with fever? And the doctor only bled them. This would weaken them for their fight with the illness. She if anyone knew that the blood was the essence of life. One did not drain it lightly. This whole effort had been useless, and she had left Drew alone. The doctor turned back to his patient. A dreadful gurgling sounded then silence.

Freya was stunned. "He is dead?" It could happen, just like that?

"I'm afraid so," the doctor said. "He was my most important patient, too."

Freya did not wait to hear more, but pushed out of the room, past the petulant son, and out into the night.

5

Freya hadn't slept for days. She'd insisted Drew take broth as she held him in her lap. He had to keep up his strength. Supplies had mysteriously arrived the day after she'd gone to the village, in spite of the fact that she had made no order in Tintagel, where she got her own victuals. The delivery had included a salve which she put on Drew's lips to keep them from cracking, and some apple vinegar she used in the water in which she bathed him. It seemed to cool the intensity of his fever.

If he were vampire he would live forever, barring some bizarre accident of decapitation, or murder by the same means. They wouldn't be a different species any more. Could they become even closer? He would be even more easily aroused than he was as a human, have even more stamina. The prospect would have given her shudders of anticipation if she could feel anything but anxiety.

If she had made him vampire before this happened she might have prevented all this. She couldn't do it now. He was too weak to survive the ravages of ingesting her Companion. It was a difficult transition, until the immunity she gave with her blood could take hold.

But there were so many reasons she couldn't make him vampire, then or now. It was against the Rules of her kind, for one thing. And for another he would never agree to be made a monster like she was. That's what she would be in his eyes if he knew what she was. Vampire. The very word struck fear into the hearts of humans. Yet another reason she couldn't tell him. A gulf had opened between them. Why did she struggle so vainly against it?

In the wee hours of the fourth day, his breathing grew wet and labored. It sounded only too familiar. She brought pillows from other bedrooms and propped him up. That seemed to make his breathing easier. His eyes opened and, as always during these past days, he thanked her. This time he only whispered it before he drifted away.

She sat on the side of his bed and took his hand. "Don't die," she ordered to his closed eyes, as though it was in his power to decide. "Don't die." This time it was a plea. What should she do? What *could* she do? Nothing. Nothing but wait.

Hours passed. The sun rose. Her kind always felt the exact position of the sun. She sat, listening to Drew's breathing. She was so sorry she had pushed him away when he wanted to know about her. Not that she could tell him she was vampire. But he had trusted her with his story, with his pain, and she had not returned his confidences in full measure.

She turned her head. She had neglected to close the heavy drapes on one of the windows. The sky was reddening over the tangled gardens that looked east. She rose to twitch them shut, then sat heavily in a chair.

She woke with a start. How long had she slept? Hours. She jerked upright and went to Drew. His breathing was definitely easier. She placed a hand on his pale forehead. It felt . . . cool.

She sucked in a breath. He opened his eyes. They were clear. Exhausted but clear.

"Welcome back," she whispered.

Drew reclined on the divan in the drawing room. The windows were thrown open to the dusk. Freya put down a tray with tea and preserved fruit and scones. He watched her as from a distance. Everything seemed distant these days. Influenza had left him weak and strangely lethargic in his mind. He lived in the moment, as Freya would say. Hell, he was just glad he *had* moments.

"Is this not a pleasant room?" Freya asked, as she poured and handed him a cup. "I must say living here is much easier with an army of servants."

"An army?" He smiled. How could one not smile when one looked at beautiful Freya?

"Well, six. Mr. Enley sent two granddaughters to set the house to rights and a cousin as cook, and a nephew to take care of the stables. And the two young men—are they his family? No, I think not. They are beginning to cut back the overgrown gardens."

"I *thought* the house felt more alive," he murmured. He didn't correct her about Henley's name. "I seem to be keeping backward hours, sleeping all the day."

She blushed. "You keep my hours. I . . . I have a sensitivity to light."

Well, at least she was saying something about herself. He had not pressed her further about what she was. Such considerations seemed far away. Or was he afraid to drive her away?

"I noticed," he remarked. "Why has Henley had a change of heart? He was a proponent of the 'ghost who drinks blood' theory. I shouldn't think he'd send his relatives to serve here."

"I told him I was not a ghost when I went to the village."

"You went to the village?" He found himself mildly curious. That was a new sensation. It must come with leaving his bed for the first time.

"I tried to find you a doctor."

"That was good of you." How she had exerted herself to care for him. He would never have asked it. In fact, he had never been so dependent upon anyone as he had been on her in the last days. She who had never wanted a houseguest, especially a needy one, had been exceedingly generous and tender. She hadn't even allowed the new servants to relieve her. "I expect the doctor was busy and couldn't come."

She turned her eyes away as though concealing something. "He said he could do nothing but bleed you in any case, and I knew that would do more harm than good."

He nodded and sipped his tea. Old Henley didn't seem the type to just accept a strange woman with an Eastern European accent showing up. But he must have. He had sent half his extended family to help out. "Do you need money to pay the servants? I shall write a letter to my banker in London."

"I have no need of your money, Drew. I pay them in gold." She sounded haughty. Then she screwed up her face and shook her head. "I am sorry. A foolish arrogance, when I use my father's money and live in my father's house. He left gold in . . . storage here, against need." She sat abruptly back in her chair. "I suppose I will never be independent of him."

Drew was not independent himself. He'd been dependent physically on Freya. He wasn't independent of her psychologically, either. He couldn't imagine waking and not seeing her calm, almost black eyes rise from her book.

He'd forgotten all about his obsession with Melaphont.

The thought was like a cutlass tearing the shroud of distance that enveloped him. What was he doing, lolling here and thinking of Freya when Melaphont no doubt strode around his precious house, directing the building of his new wing with his chest puffed out? Did the villain ever think of the boy he had wrongly ruined? No. But he would.

Drew set down his teacup too bluntly. It sloshed tea onto the table. "It's time to get back to my purpose. I've an idea how to make Elias Melaphont regret the day he sentenced me."

"Had you thought that by ruining him, you would also ruin his son?"

Drew blinked. "He has a son?" He set his lips. "Then maybe that is the way to get to him." He threw off his blanket and pushed himself off the divan. His legs were so cursed weak. He sat down again abruptly.

"You mustn't worry about Sir Melaphont now," Freya soothed. "Have you overtired yourself? I'll help you to your room."

"Damn it, Freya," he fumed. "I can't lie here when that worm is up there gloating."

Freya went still. It was as though she was gathering her courage. "He isn't gloating."

Drew frowned. "How do you know?"

"He is dead. Of the influenza. I saw him die."

Drew felt as though he'd been punched in the gut. "Don't make jokes about this, Freya."

She raised her brows. She was right. She didn't joke.

"The bloody man went and *died* before I could give him back his own?" Drew heard his own voice crack. Not fair! Not fair in a long line of things that were not fair. "Then I'll have my revenge on his son."

"No you won't, Drew, not when you think about it. That poor creature has suffered enough, with that man for a father."

The air went out of him, along with something else. It was as if the energy he'd expended in that flash of vengeful rage had used up whatever he had left. He looked away. "You're right." His life stretched ahead, without purpose. He took in the heavy wood furniture in the Tudor style that littered the room, now gleaming with wax instead of dust. Why was he here? It wasn't his house. It had no meaning now that Melaphont was dead. It had only been a means to an end, like Emily.

He staggered out the salon door toward the stairs. Freya moved to help him but he pushed her hand away. "Leave me alone," he growled, and pulled himself up the stairs by the banister.

Freya sat in her room on the window seat, looking out over the night garden. Things had not changed much after all. Oh, the gardens were being slowly pruned into shape. And the dust covers were gone. She was no longer alone in the house. But the distance from herself she had felt for over a year had come back to nest in her heart, as though it had never left.

It had been two days since she'd seen the horrified look on Drew's face when he heard his nemesis was dead. Last night he'd tried to leave. She'd stopped him, of course. He was too weak to travel and he knew it. But his eyes were dead. He didn't see any reason to go on, now that the vengeance he'd been planning for so long was useless. It was only a matter of time until he went. She didn't want him to go this way, drifting and half-alive like she was.

For a week or two she had felt . . . connected again, interested in living.

It was because of Drew Carlowe. Her tragedy was that she . . . cared for him. The way she had never cared for anyone in her long, long life. Vampires did not fall in love. That's what her father always told her. Especially not with humans who lived for only a flicker of time. Not long enough to love, he said. And Drew would be horrified if he knew what she was. So he would never know. So there could be nothing between them but that lie.

But if she cared for him, she couldn't let him suffer. How to prevent the emptiness from consuming him? She remembered the feeling of wholeness their sexual union had produced. Maybe she *could* bring him back from the brink. The very thought of leaving herself open to his rejection was alarming. But she had to try.

She rose from the window seat and drifted through the dark room to the doorway. Light leaked from behind the closed room of his door. She turned the knob. The lock was still broken. He sat at his desk, just as she had seen him that other night, writing a letter. Only this time he wasn't naked. He looked up. The pain in his eyes was startling. He quickly masked it with indifference.

"I . . ." He was casting about for a lie. His shoulders slumped. He was deciding to tell her the truth. "I was just writing you a letter."

"Perhaps you should say your message in person."

He looked away. "It was mostly 'thank you.' "

"Was it?" He had lied again. That had her curiosity up.

He nodded. He wasn't going to tell her what it really said. She noted that there were several crumpled drafts around the carpet. Whatever it was, apparently it was not easy to say. Dread suffused her. *You have to try,* she reminded herself.

She stood behind him and rubbed his shoulders, kneading the knotted muscles there. It wasn't just the shock of attraction that shot through her. Something deeper flashed inside her that she'd never felt with a man before. It warmed her heart as well as her loins. His shoulders relaxed and he rolled his head, giving a satisfied growl. She ran her hands under his shirt collar to the silken skin on the nape of his neck.

Then he was standing. He had her by the shoulders. "I'm so weak," he whispered, angry.

"I . . . I am sorry. I shouldn't have . . . You've been sick. I know that."

"I *mean* I'm weak to want you so." He took her in his arms and kissed her fiercely as she turned up her mouth to his. Kisses were so intimate. "I shouldn't give in," he said, between kisses. "You don't even care enough to tell me what you are." He was panting now. He dragged her to the bed by one arm. "But I want you, Freya, just once more."

She ripped his shirt getting it off him. He popped buttons on his breeches as she unbuckled her girdle and let her dress drop in a pool at her feet. Naked, he picked her up and laid her on the bed. He was already erect. The lingering effects of influenza were not enough to cool his ardor, apparently. She stroked his cock as she sidled up beside him. One of his hands covered her breast as he held her to him and kissed her thoroughly. Her breasts felt swollen and tender. When he bent to suckle, she arched up into his mouth, moaning.

"Forgive me, my love, but I must feel you around me right now."

She opened to him, nothing loath. She wanted him to plunge himself inside her, pry open her most secret parts and fill them with his strong cock. She wanted to be demanded of, not to demand. They took the simplest of positions, and somehow the most satisfying. She would not ask him to control himself. He had been sick, and probably had little stamina. And if they did not achieve the closeness of the first time, well, that was as it may be.

Wait. What had he called her?

He hung above her, and his eyes were hungry. "My love." It was a figure of speech, no more. He wanted her skills at sex, and she would give them to him, as long as his strength held.

Drew lay back and drew Freya down with him to cradle her in his arms. Not bad for an invalid. He'd brought her to ecstasy three times, and even come twice himself. Now he should be lethargic, but he was consumed by a strange energy, vibrating in sympathy with her energy, as she lolled against his chest, her curtain of hair covering her face. It didn't matter that they hadn't played her Tantric games. He felt just as close to her as he had the first time they made love all night. That's what it was. Making love. It wasn't just sex. Just sex was what he'd had with every other woman.

The letter he'd written her told her that he loved her, though he knew she didn't love him in return. She didn't even trust him enough to tell him what she was. And she was something all right. He remembered her lifting him bodily into bed when he was fainting as he tried to use the chamber pot. She carried him as if he was a child. No ordinary woman could do that. He had told Henley that first night in the tavern that vampires drank blood, not ghosts. Perhaps that was what she was. It was an ugly word. His stomach churned. His head said vampires didn't exist. His heart said it didn't matter to him what she was. She had not hurt him. On the contrary. She had cared for him and set him free in a way he had never imagined possible.

He wouldn't burden her with his presence. A partner who lingered on after he was no longer wanted was annoying. His eyes filled. He lay there, thinking about the emptiness ahead. His revenge on Melaphont was thwarted. But that didn't matter any more. In the last days, Melaphont had seemed to shrink in importance. Drew had been consumed by his past, but now his eyes were on the future, a future without Freya in it.

He was a coward. He couldn't face a future like that. All his resolve to go washed out of him. She didn't love him. He would be rejected. But he had to try.

"Freya?"

She lifted her head. Her great dark eyes were soft. She smiled an inquiry, waiting.

He swallowed once. His mouth had gone dry. "Marry me."

Her eyes widened in shock. "What?" It was a frightened whisper.

He was at least as frightened as she was. "I love you. I haven't the courage to leave you. I know you don't love me. But if . . . if you let me stay, I could . . . I could take care of everything for you. You wouldn't have to deal with the servants, or . . ." He tried to think of how he could make himself useful to her.

"I can't." Her voice broke.

There it was. He gathered her into his arms. He wouldn't let her know that something inside him had just shattered. "It's all right. I knew it was a long shot. Had to try, though."

He felt the convulsion of a sob shake her. He stroked her hair. "Don't cry. I won't importune you. You could never love a man like me." He tried a laugh. "And I told you I'd make a damnable husband."

"I *do* love you, you stupid man," she choked.

"You . . . you what?"

"I love you." She jerked her head up, apparently angry. "I love you past all sense."

"My God." His heart swelled. He frowned. "Then why won't you marry me? That is the customary thing when two people love each other."

She sat up, her lovely breasts hanging above him. She set her lips. "I am going to tell you what I am sworn not to tell anyone, so that you may know why I cannot marry you." She took a breath and let it out. "I am vampire." She watched for his reaction.

He swallowed carefully. He'd guessed. But to have it confirmed was . . . horrifying. He hoped it didn't show on his face. He had to get past the word itself to Freya. He needed to buy time. "So you did drink my blood that first night."

She nodded.

"Tell me about it. Being vampire, I mean."

She looked wary. "Well. I have a parasite in my blood. We call it our Companion. It gives us certain . . . qualities."

"The sensitivity to sunlight." He could start there. That wasn't so bad.

"Strength. Heightened senses."

He could deal with that. "Red eyes?"

She chewed her lips. "This thing in our blood has power we can use. The red eyes happen when we call the power."

"And what does the power do?"

She gave a tiny shrug. "I can . . . influence minds." Her voice was small.

And he had though she was a proponent of "animal magnetism," like Dr. Mesmer.

"And if I draw enough power, the field collapses in on itself in a whirl of darkness and I pop out into another place."

"I . . . guess I . . . saw that once."

She nodded. "And if I die, the parasite dies with me. It has a keen urge to life. So it rebuilds its host. Forever."

Drew closed his mouth to prevent his jaw from dropping. "Immortal?" he managed.

"Unless I am decapitated." She looked down at her hands. "I am very old."

"How old?"

"Nine hundred years, or thereabouts. So you see why I couldn't marry you."

"I'd get old. And you wouldn't." He shook his head. "You must think me a baby, naïve, uninteresting."

She reached out for his hands. "No, no. You make me see that I have not been living at all. You . . . you showed me how to make love."

"*I* showed you? You're the most skilled practitioner of the art of love I can imagine."

She straightened her shoulders. "That's because sex was

my job. It wasn't love." She must have seen his shocked expression. "The Companion gives us a heightened sexuality. By using our sexuality, increasing it, we can increase our power as well. My job was to use Tantric teachings to train selected men of our kind to increase their power. They became Harriers, the weapons my father sent against those who threatened our kind by making other vampires." She looked down at her hands. "He used them against those who threatened his power, too."

He had to go slowly here. There was so much. "Your father made you have sex with these apprentices?"

"I wanted to serve our kind. It was a kind of sexual torture in some ways, this training. But I did it to them, for the greater good. But then he sent my sister and me to kill one we had made. I came to understand that what we were doing was wrong." She stared out the open window directly across from the bed into the night. "I realize now that she had gone a little insane with the power we had over the Aspirants. She liked the torture. It was dangerous, the training. And when I wouldn't help her with it, it killed her."

"So it wasn't your fault she died."

"Oh yes it was. I knew it could happen. But she had to be stopped. I carry the guilt of stopping her." She turned back to him. "So never think I knew love. I didn't even know tenderness and sex could exist together until I met you."

She hadn't known love in more ways than one. What father could do that to his daughter?

"But," she said, making her tone light. "You see why marrying me would be a bad idea. One can't marry a vampire who lives forever."

A little thought darted through his brain. He pushed it down. He sat up and put his arms across his knees. "What about the blood?"

She looked down. "I need about a cup every fortnight or so. That must seem horrible to you. But I don't kill anyone.

And I can erase their memory, or supplant it with some better one; that they had wonderful sex, for instance, or that they are handsome."

So far, so good. He could live with that. "And do they become vampires?" If they did, he might already be one.

She gave a weary chuckle. "Of course not, else the world would be littered with vampires. No, our kind survives in a delicate balance with humans. It is strictly forbidden to make a human vampire."

"And how does one do that?" He made his voice as neutral as he could.

"Well, you have to get some of my blood in your system somehow—an open wound, for instance." She tried on a smile. It came out lopsided. "I've been very careful, though. You're not infected. You'd know because you get sick immediately, and you'd die without infusions of a vampire's blood for the first three days, to give you immunity to the effects of the parasite on the human system."

"So, let me get this straight. Strength. Heightened senses. Heightened sexuality. The ability to compel others. You can disappear, and you're immortal. And the blood. Anything else I should know about?"

She raised her brows. "That is all, I think."

"And you love me. And you believe I love you."

She nodded slowly.

He took a breath. In for a penny in for a pound. He couldn't imagine life without her. And if she stayed with him and left him human, the differences between them would drive them apart. "So why not make me vampire?"

She hugged herself, covering her breasts. "I told you, it is forbidden."

"We're not talking about making hundreds here. Just one."

"If you covet eternity, let me tell you, it is a terrible burden, not a benefit."

It was as though she had slapped him. But he forged ahead. “Do you really think that of me?”

She shook her head, but she was growing more agitated by the moment.

“It would be easier with two facing eternity together.”

“You don’t understand.” She was almost pleading with him. “When love dies you’d be left a vampire. Did I mention it is impossible for us to commit suicide? The Companion’s urge to life doesn’t allow that kind of escape.”

“And what if the love doesn’t die, Freya? If I’m not vampire, our differences will stand between us. It might be better if we parted now.”

“I know,” she whispered. Her eyes were big with pain.

She was giving up. Tears rose to her eyes.

It was up to him, then. He reached out and took her shoulders. “Be bold, Freya. Seize what we might make of this. Take back your life from your father, and all these rules you’ve been forced to live by. Let’s carve our own place, make our own rules.” He couldn’t keep the pleading out of his voice.

Drew felt a hum of life against his spine. There was a new energy in the room, more powerful by far than Freya’s. They both turned. A whirling blackness, darker than the dim room, spun in the corner. Drew set his jaw. This could be bad.

6

Freya knew exactly what the whirling blackness was and who the vampire about to appear would most likely be. In some ways she had been waiting for this moment for over a year. She grabbed for Drew's shirt, which lay across the end of the bed, and pulled it over her head, her thoughts colliding. First Drew's outrageous proposal, which was everything she wanted but shouldn't have. She couldn't take him up on his offer, of course. Drew didn't know what life would be like as a vampire. Then came his accusation that she had ceded who she was to her father and to the Rules. And now . . . this.

Her father materialized in the dim room. She tried to still the thumping of her heart and see him through Drew's eyes. He would hardly look as dangerous as he was. He had a great paunch under the plain brown wool of his habit. His beard was white, his eyes piercing blue. If anything, he looked like the pictures human children had of St. Nicolas. But he was no kindly elf. He was the Eldest. He ruled Mirso Monastery, the final refuge for vampires sick with the boredom and repetition of eternity. She had lived there her entire life before this last year. Actually, all she had ever seen were the tortured vampire souls who took refuge there and the Aspirants she trained to be Harriers. Were there vampires who lived full lives out in the world and never needed Mirso? The thought had never occurred to her.

Her father's hard eyes swept the room. Drew scrambled out of the bed and stood beside her, naked. He put his arm around her shoulders for support. "Who are you?" he barked.

Her father didn't deign to answer Drew. "Well, Freya, have you tired of your little rebellion?"

It annoyed her that he didn't even acknowledge Drew. "He is known these days as Rubius Rozonczy," she said to Drew. "Father, this is Andrew Carlowe."

"It is time to return to Mirso, Freya. We have need of a new Harrier, and now you alone are able to produce one."

She had been trying to prepare for this moment for a year. "I cannot do that any more. Did you not read my letter?"

"Your petty preferences are not at issue," he said sternly. "You are a trainer of Harriers."

"No, Father." She wished her voice did not sound pleading. "The training is painful for them. And the endless arousal and suppression . . ." She broke off in confusion. In the end it had been torture for her as much as for them. "Sexual intercourse should be an act of trust and pleasure between two people. It . . . it shouldn't be like that."

"It is your calling, Freya. Vampire kind needs a Harrier." He glanced to Drew. "If you wish, you can bring your plaything with you. Use him for pleasure, if you need a respite."

She felt Drew stiffen. "He isn't an amusement, Father. I love him, and I'm not coming back to Mirso." There. She'd said it. Her mouth went dry. He was so much more powerful than she was, he could take her back by force. They both knew it.

Her father narrowed his eyes. "You are my daughter. I am the Eldest. You will obey."

"She's not doing anything she doesn't want to do." Freya started at Drew's intensity. He moved in front of her, as though that could protect her. "God, man, what kind of father makes his daughter engage in sex like it was a job? Fathers are supposed to love and protect their offspring."

"You know nothing, human." Her father's eyes roved over Drew's naked body. "Are you the reason my wayward daughter has grown disobedient? I can remedy that problem." His eyes went the deepest crimson. He stalked toward the two.

Odin and Loki, but he was going to kill Drew. He would, without a thought. Freya felt panic sweep through her. She was no match for him. He was the Eldest. Still, she called for power. *Companion!* The surge up her veins snapped the world into red.

"Father, no!" she shouted.

But he kept coming. *Companion, more!* She thought about pressing him back. He hesitated, looking over at her. Did he feel her push?

"You can't stand against me, child. You know that." His voice was a boom, amplified by his power. He reached out and grabbed for Drew's shoulder.

Drew struggled in her father's iron grip. He couldn't escape. Her father would just twist his head off. She had seen him do it. All would be over in an instant. Irrevocable.

"No!" she shouted. Her father had both Drew's shoulders. *Companion, more! As much as you have ever given.*

The world went white. That was shocking. Where was the red? What was happening? Her veins throbbed with power. Her father put both hands on Drew's head as Drew tried to twist away. A glow spread out from her like a white corona. She thought about pushing at her father. She even thrust her hands out. They glowed white, too. She knew that glow.

Her father jerked back, taking Drew with him. He turned his crimson eyes on her. They widened and he gasped.

"Let him go, Father." Her voice was like the wind, a whooshing sound she did not recognize.

Her father turned to her, seeming to forget Drew entirely. Drew slumped to his knees. "You . . . you are a Harrier, daughter. I have never seen such power."

The corona of light contracted and the room went back to dim. Freya was left gasping. How had this happened? She had seen the corona of power on other Harriers and knew what it could do. She had trained a hundred Harriers over the years. But how had she become one? "I . . . I guess all the time I was training Aspirants, I was also training me."

"Excellent." Her father actually rubbed his hands. "Now we won't even have to wait through the training of another Aspirant for our Harrier."

She was as powerful as her father. How odd. And that changed everything. "Don't think I'm going to be your emotionless instrument of revenge, Father. I'm staying here with Drew, and now I am almost certain there is nothing you can do about it."

He snorted in derision. "Humans are not worth the abandonment of your true purpose, Freya. What can they understand of the scope of our existence? They do not even live long enough to become wise."

In some ways that was the best thing he could have said. All became clear to Freya in that moment. "There is a wisdom of the heart that you have lost, Father. Or maybe you never had it." Tears sprang to her eyes. She looked past her father to where Drew was struggling to stand. "Drew is already wiser than you are, for all your age. I only hope I can learn from him."

Her father looked back to Drew. Did he see the softness in Drew's eyes? Would he recognize it for what it was? Freya was fairly certain it was love.

When her father snapped his head back to her, he said, "Remember the Rules, Freya." She smiled. He recognized the look, all right. And he knew what she intended. She did intend it, though she couldn't name the moment she had decided.

Drew was standing now, his feet apart. Lord, but he was magnificent. "A father has to let his daughter go, Rubius. Even if she makes mistakes. Your mistake was that you never learned that." Freya was proud of him.

And wonder of wonders, she saw her father look away. Was he ashamed? He took a breath and let it out of his massive chest. Maybe the fact that he recognized the look in Drew's eyes meant something. "You must have loved someone, Father, or been loved."

He didn't acknowledge anything. He looked at her. "Had it occurred to you that I might want you by me because I missed you as well as needed you? If you want to see me, you will know where to find me. I'll find another way to make Harriers."

The whirl of blackness engulfed him in mere seconds, much faster than she had ever been able to muster. He was . . . gone.

She turned to Drew. "Are you all right?"

He nodded, and ran his hand through his hair, half laughing. "You have one scary father, my love." He shot a glance her way. "How do you feel?"

The smile that welled up in her brought a threat of tears with it. "Good." She shrugged, trying to make light of the fullness she felt inside. "Maybe . . . whole."

His eyes widened in memory. "You . . . you were quite amazing."

"I amazed myself. That was a demonstration of a Harrier's powers, in case you're interested."

"I love a young lady whom I can truly call accomplished."

But did he? "Having second thoughts now that you know who I really am and have seen my very scary father?"

"I always knew who you really were, if you did not. And

I think your father loves you in his very frightening way." He stepped in to her. They stood a handbreadth apart, not touching, the surface tension of attraction and hesitance in perfect balance. "And no, no second thoughts. You should have asked if I'm afraid."

"Are you?"

"Oh, yes. But you'll be there, won't you?"

Warmth suffused her. She reached up and slipped one hand around his neck under the curls at his nape. "I will, Drew Carlowe. And do you want this?"

"I do, Freya Rozonczy."

She smiled and felt the tears spill over and course down her cheeks. That was not her last name. To her knowledge she had no last name. But it was fitting she acknowledge that, for all his faults, she was her father's daughter. And she was her own person, too, for the first time. Drew led her back to the bed, climbed up and pulled her up beside him. He lay back, his strong body even now calling to the core of her. She asked for power, enough to run out her fangs. Her eyes would be glowing faintly red. She let him see the teeth extend. He must have no illusions. "There is no going back."

He pulled her close and kissed her, running his tongue over her fangs. "Then let us go forward." She felt his erection rising against her thigh. She throbbed in response.

He turned his head toward her and raised his chin, exposing the artery in his neck. But she wanted this to be special, sacred even. She reached down and caressed his cock. He was fully aroused now. So was she. She kissed her way from the pulse in his throat to the place directly under his jaw. "Not yet," she whispered. Her breasts rubbed against his chest hair. He rolled her to her back. She spread her knees. She wanted him to impale her, plunge himself inside. He positioned his cock and she pulled his buttocks into her. The sweet sensation of being filled possessed her. He moved in and out with controlled intensity. Sensation built and she did not want to stop it, prolong it, or deviate from its inevitable course. She turned the tables after a while and rolled him on his back. She straddled his hips and rocked up and down, back and forth. He groaned. She bit her lips, licking them. The saliva would keep the wounds from healing immediately, but there wasn't much time.

He bared his throat again.

She took a breath. She was about to baptize her newfound self by an act her father would find repugnant but that she was sure was very right. Drew's trust as he exposed himself to her would not go unreturned. She bit down, gently, rocking against his cock. He moaned, but she didn't think it was from the slight pain of the twin wounds she had inflicted. He was hard and needing inside her. The copper tang of thick life filled her mouth. She could feel the blood on her lips mingle with his. For better or worse, it was done. She sucked lightly, caressing his shoulder as he thrust inside her. She could feel his release building. Her own was moments away. The sweet sensation of sucking at him even as they raced toward orgasm in some complex and most intimate exchange of fluids, body to body, soul to soul, enveloped her. Her world thrust outward, blood and semen and her own wild juices mingling in chaotic abandon as Drew exploded inside her. They slumped together, Drew crushing her to his chest. She felt her lips heal as though the cuts there had never been.

"The blood is the life, my love," she said.

"For both of us," he whispered.

MIDNIGHT KISS GOODBYE

by

Dianna Love

This story is dedicated to my mother-in-law Jane O'Hern who gave me my first romance novel many years ago, and my hero as well when I married her only child.

My deep appreciation goes to Sherrilyn Kenyon for her friendship and endless support. I want to thank Caren Johnson for placing this story and Monique Patterson for being a fabulous editor. Thanks also to Maureen Hardegree who as an early reader gave me great feedback. Thanks so much to all those who have supported my writing, to name a few—James and Terri Love, Jim and Mary Buckham, Walt and Cindy Lumpkin, Gail and Dave Akins, Bart and Hope Williams, Bill Gayton, Joanne and Hank Shaw, Mae Nunn, Annie Oortman, Darlene Buchholz, Donna Browning, Debby Giusti, Jacqui Sue Ping, the RBLs, GRW members and all of you—the READERS—who allow me to write these stories. Please visit my website at www.AuthorDiannaLove.com and I love to hear from readers at dianna@authordiannalove.com.

Most of all, thanks to my incredible husband and hero, Karl Snell, who makes it possible for me to pursue my dreams.

1

Where are you, Ekkbar? Show yourself so I can send you back to the flames of hell that birthed you.

Trey McCree raised his head and visually swept the room filled with Goth partiers out for some early action on the night after Halloween. He telepathically listened to snippets of conversation from the partygoers' private thoughts as well.

Hey, loosen up, babe. . . . I want a man tonight. . . . What a loser. . . .

When the woman he followed moved again, Trey pushed ahead through the tangled mass of patrons decked out in sinister black outfits, bloodred accessories, and silver studs pierced through some interesting places. Most of the clientele visited in cozy corners on several levels, but that still left a packed dance floor of writhing bodies. Unconcerned over blending in with nose rings and scary hair, Trey had donned black jeans, a matching long-sleeved turtleneck, and a leather jacket.

He was here for one reason.

The Black Fairy nightclub in a renovated midtown Atlanta warehouse near a historical cemetery had piqued the interest of a woman he was *not* letting out of his sight—Sasha Armand.

Not with Ekkbar visiting this millennium.

Calf-high black boots pranced twenty feet away, a silver cross-and-skull zipper pull at her boot cuff flicking with each sexy step. The liquid movement of Sasha's derriere swayed erotically in time with the pulsing music, reminding Trey of why he couldn't stay in Atlanta beyond this week. Temptation was easier resisted from a distance.

Sasha was better off without him anyhow, *if* she'd stay out of trouble, dammit.

A wave of dark energy rippled through the room. Trey's skin pricked with warning. He slowed, immediately on alert. He surveyed the crowd for Ekkbar, but the eight-hundred-year-old servant of a Kujoo warlord melded with the jumble of noise before Trey could detect him.

Ekkbar had almost exposed himself. He was a dimwit, but a lethal one to an unprotected human like Sasha.

As a strong empathic, Trey avoided crowds until learning how to filter telepathic noise to prevent sensory overload. He now closed the gateway to his mind within a blink, watching.

That flash of metaphysical energy had either been Ekkbar catching Sasha's hunter scent or another otherworldly entity who *could* recognize Trey's physical signature as a Belador warrior. There was no way the magician had picked up on his presence. Unlike the Hindu warlord's elite Kujoo soldiers, Ekkbar didn't possess combat powers necessary to detect a Belador. But he *was* a magician who could hurt a human woman.

Sasha paused across the room, swiveling her head left. Blue, green, and pink lights shimmered along the straight black hair pouring across her shoulders and back. She narrowed her eyes at something and then blinked. A thick ruffle of lashes kissed her cheek before she continued on.

Trey had kissed that same cheek when she wore tattered jeans and a ponytail that fit with her girl-next-door smile. Maybe if she'd kissed him like just *any* girl next door they might not have ended up in his bed having explosive sex, or on his back porch at midnight with her homemade whip cream, or . . . damn, he'd never forget the night at the lake with water cascading over her moon-kissed body when he lifted her high in the air.

He'd come close to reconsidering his future as a Belador right then. But he hadn't and couldn't change the past now.

Careful not to let her catch sight of him, Trey moved forward again, breathing the bitter smell of incense mixed with hot skin damp from dancing. He had to figure out what to do about Ekkbar without creating a disaster. Since accepting his destiny, Trey had been warned against ever engaging the warlord cursed to live beneath Mount Meru. A river of blood had been spilled once centuries ago when Beladors faced off against the Kujoo. Since then both had upheld an unwritten truce.

If he disturbed the fragile peace between the two, he'd open the gates to a war like none before.

Leave it to a woman to ruin a two-week sabbatical from his contract work with VIPER—Vigilant International Protectors Elite Regiment—where he defended this world against supernatural predators. Gathering intel on Sasha had been a major pain in the butt since he'd been forced to use conventional methods. Any other time, he'd just read a person's thoughts, but he'd never been able to read Sasha's mind and had no idea why not since he refused to ask other Beladors. No warrior ever admitted a deficiency to another one.

Tapping her phone line worked, but the only inkling Trey had gotten into this fiasco had been when Sasha left a message on her home phone for her sister that she was out working and hoped to locate Ekkbar at the Black Fairy tonight.

A tall blond female in an outfit that would bring the devil himself to heel stepped in front of Trey, blocking his path. She eyed him like a new soul to devour. His gaze danced over the very revealing red and black lace jumpsuit sending his mind to search her thoughts out of natural curiosity.

No words. Just erotic images of what she envisioned doing . . . to him . . . naked . . . tied to a bed.

He snapped his mind shut, smiled politely, and sidestepped her, then glanced ahead to make sure Sasha remained in sight.

When had she morphed her business from researching family ancestries to becoming a private eye? Who had hired her to find a creature that should still be living beneath a mountain?

A roar on the dance floor drew his attention. When he turned back to track Sasha the crowd had swallowed her. He stretched up, searching. No Sasha. His palms dampened, something he rarely experienced during an op, but those missions didn't involve a defenseless woman facing a monster.

Heart pounding sharply with each thump of the music's concussive base, Trey rushed forward, parting the sea of macabre costumes. He reached the far side of the wide room just as a pair of thigh-high boots with a dangly zipper pull headed through a hallway then out the rear door. He could move fast as light when necessary, but not in public without good cause. At the back exit, he caught the bouncer monitoring activity distracted and blitzed past in a rush of air.

Outside, Trey stepped onto an empty back street and took a breath of fresh air, enjoying the brisk late October chill. He caught a familiar tap of footsteps clipping along the sidewalk in the direction of the cemetery.

Next to woods where rapes had occurred in the past.

Where the hell was Sasha going?

Moving cautiously now, he tuned his senses to his surroundings. Survival in his unusual line of work depended on always being prepared. A half-block down, Trey stopped next to the cemetery, trying to pick up the sound of her steps again. He felt another body taut with animosity move into his zone, the area ten feet away. Trey spun around, hands flowing together into a bladelike move that would take off a man's head.

He stopped barely a half-inch short of Sasha's lithe neck.

"What are *you* doing here?" Her blue-black painted mouth pursed with irritation and all he could think about was testing her lipstick to determine if it would smear.

"How ya doin', Sasha?" He pulled his hands away and straightened to his full height. From what he could see, she was doing exceptionally well in the black vest split open ten inches wide down the center of her front and laced with leather. A link of chain swung from the tip of one breast to the other.

Trey forced his tongue to remain inside his mouth and not slide along his lips.

"I'm fine. Now, what are you doing here?"

"Checking out the Black Fairy." He flipped his palms up in a "what else" motion. "What a surprise finding you here. Thought you hung up your spikes years ago."

Her eyebrows flinched in a self-conscious frown.

Oops. That might have sounded like a reference to her turning thirty in a few months, but she had nothing to worry about based on that bunch of hardtails inside the nightclub giving her the once-over. Trey should have sent an air slap across a few heads, but the petulant act would have caused a disturbance confirming his presence.

"Thought what I did was of *no* interest to you. And there was a time you wouldn't have been caught dead in a place like this, so why the sudden curiosity?" Egyptian-shaped hazel eyes boldly outlined with an artist's touch sparked with challenge.

"To tell you the truth, I was looking for someone." He hoped the coy answer would keep her talking and buy him time to find out who sent her to hunt for Ekkbar.

"So was I until *you* spooked him."

"Me?" There was no way Ekkbar could have detected him, but Trey couldn't very well admit that. "Who you looking for?"

"No one you'd know."

"So how could I have spooked him?"

"You look clean cut for this place. The glasses are new, but they won't camouflage what you are. You stand out like you're a cop. Or a Fed." She snapped her fingers. One of her perfect eyebrows lifted in a sarcastic arch. "Oh, but that's right. You *do* work for the FBI or CIA or do something for national defense you couldn't explain or then you'd have to kill me, right?"

Not a conversation he wanted to be sucked into right now. The glasses were made of an optic material not found in standard eyeglass outlets. Rather than improve his vision, they protected his power that was directly related to his eyesight.

"You were searching for a felon?" Trey asked.

Sasha's brow puckered with a look that said she should have kept her mouth shut.

He held a mask of blank emotions in place rather than grin at her slip. "What are you doing down here this late at night hunting for someone afraid of law enforcement, huh?"

"I'm working, so how about not interfering."

Now he was getting close. "What sort of work?"

She drew a deep breath that brought her leather outfit to life, then exhaled an aggravated huff. "What makes you think you're entitled to know anything about me or my life?"

"Look, I'm just worried about you."

She laughed, deep and scoffing. "That's good." Sasha shook her head with a flip of disbelief. Hair the color of sin washed over her shoulder and brushed the smooth body Trey had spent many a night dreaming of freeing from clothes . . . again.

"It's true, Sasha."

She stilled, her eyes slanting up at him, all business. "You lost the chance to worry about me a long time ago, so don't start now. You have your life just the way you want it and I have mine, which doesn't allow room for past mistakes."

He had a life, not necessarily the way he wanted it, but that was his fault, not hers.

Trey felt several predators draw close. He spun to stand in front of Sasha and cursed his carelessness. A trio of twenty-somethings with matching jackets, matching dagger-and-blood tattoos, and matching cocky attitudes. Gang-bangers. He should have been paying attention to more than Sasha.

"Why don't you boys move on down the road, huh?" Trey assessed the one holding a gun, the leader. Stringy blond hair raked his thick shoulders and heavy rings on each finger of one hand like a modified brass knuckle—a big question mark.

"Start walking into the cemetery, quietly," the leader ordered, his acne-riddled face devoid of any emotion.

Trey entered the leader's mind and heard, *I'm going to enjoy making you watch me hump yo' bitch.*

This night only got better by the minute. Trey growled under his breath. He couldn't use his supernatural powers to hurt these guys. The Belador code required he only use force equal to what he was dealt.

Sasha stepped up beside Trey and he shoved her back.

"You need my help," she whispered sharply.

"No, I don't," Trey answered softly. "If you get in the way, you'll get someone killed."

"Do I have a choice in *who* gets killed?" she muttered.

"You gonna make me use this?" the stringy blond asked, waving the gun. Pretty confident pointing a weapon at someone unarmed.

"If your plan was to piss them off, it worked beautifully," Sasha grumbled. "Either give them money or let me help."

"No." Trey rolled his eyes. Didn't she realize he had enough to deal with without her jumping into the fray? He loved her tomboy side that thankfully kept her from freaking out in a crisis, but now wasn't the time to play tough girl. Trey couldn't explain that money was not their ultimate goal—she was. He had no way to know for sure what this fool might do, so he turned to a limited power he rarely used. Willing his energy toward the shooter's gun hand, Trey paralyzed the trigger finger then forced the assailant's wrist to quiver, but he wouldn't be able to hold the connection long.

Speed and agility were stronger gifts than his kinetic ability.

The leader stared at his vibrating hand, his fingers in an obvious struggle to fight the sudden involuntary shaking. Both his sidekicks backed away with worried looks. His hand shook harder.

"Screw this." The blond grabbed the wrist of his gun hand, trying to steady it as he backtracked, beady eyes locked on Trey. His two cohorts hustled in reverse with him. When they got a good fifty feet away, the trio turned and ran down the street, disappearing into woods bordering the cemetery.

Trey released his breath and turned to Sasha.

She stood with a hand on her hip. "Would have been smarter to give them the money. Since when did your wallet matter that much to you?"

He wouldn't have batted an eye over the cash or the credit cards, but he'd mangle bodies to keep her safe.

Trey shrugged. "Just punks. Had a gun, but no nerve."

"Is that what they taught you at Quantico?"

Quantico didn't train agents like him. Trey said nothing rather than lie to her yet again.

She shook her head, fanning a black curtain of hair over skin now pebbled with a chill. "Been interesting catching up, but I've got to run."

"Are you driving home?"

"No. I still live in the family house here in midtown. See you." She stepped away.

Slipping off his leather jacket, Trey fell into step alongside her. "I'll walk you home." He started to drape the coat over her shoulders when Sasha ground out an unladylike noise of discontent then stopped and wheeled to face him.

"Look, Trey. I'm a big girl, all grown up and capable of taking care of myself."

He wanted to go back to when she hadn't been so grown up and make things right with her, take the sting of hurt from her voice when she spoke to him. Instead he leveled her with a stare he used on new Belador trainees when called to do his time as an instructor.

"I am walking you home, Sasha. So we can stand here until you're ready or keep moving in that direction. Your choice."

She held his stare for ten seconds and then made a *pfft* sound of annoyance. She stalked off, contradicting her dismissal by asking, "Why are you back in Atlanta?"

Trey dropped the jacket over her shoulders and ignored the evil glare she tossed his way.

"Taking a break." He wished he had more time to hang around. If his last op hadn't run so long, he'd have been back here in September like normal. Until tonight, he'd thought the sporadic trips home each year to check up on her were torture.

Not even. Standing this close to Sasha again and not being able to touch her was shredding his insides.

The familiar dainty smell of her perfume spun away the years and the lost time. He wanted to hold her close once more and feel that connection he'd never had with another woman.

"How long are you here, Trey?"

Had that been interest in her voice?

"Two weeks . . . well, one more week."

"So you've been here for a week *already?*" Her question had been more statement, rife with disillusionment.

Trey would like to tell her how he'd seen her every time he visited even though she never saw him, but refrained from digging a hole he could drive a truck into. He gave another shot at finding out what she was up to. "Why are you hunting for people? You start working with the police department?"

"Hardly." She walked in silence for a few minutes. "I'm a private investigator."

"Hm. So who did I scare off? A husband playing around?"

"Not exactly. Just a nobody," she murmured then turned to the right down a sparsely lit street Trey could navigate blind. Scattered leaves shed during a breezy autumn covered the sidewalks he once strolled along with Sasha's hand in his—before he'd had to make the hardest choice of his life. He'd always admired the classic homes built here in another era, most of which were in restored condition now.

At the steps to the two-story Victorian home Sasha once told him had been in her family for three generations, she stopped and turned to him, her boot heel scuffing against the concrete with finality. Porch lights dusted a subtle glow over the swing where he'd told her goodbye.

His throat tightened at the painful memory.

She lifted a hand he thought was going to touch his chest, the desire for her to do so stabbing him deep. But Sasha drew her fingers up and away instead, fingering a lock of hair she twisted just like she used to do when she was nervous. His fingers twitched, missing the feel of her soft hair.

"I do hope life has turned out well for you, Trey, and appreciate your help tonight with those guys, but please don't come back. Okay?" Her eyes slipped away from his, then back, filled with an uneasy glimmer that said more than her words.

He would love to know what she was really thinking, but had developed migraines trying to reach into Sasha's mind in the past. That problem alone had sealed their fate to travel different paths. He could never trust his heart to any woman he couldn't hear the truth from. It was too unpredictable.

"Do me a favor, Sasha, and don't go out alone again to track strange men. Like you said, money isn't that important."

Her dark eyebrows drew together in disbelief. "I won't stay in business long if I'm not willing to take a few risks and go out after dark, now will I?"

"You don't know what you're hunting."

"Yes, I do. A man with information."

A man? Trey wanted to shake her. Ekkbar was not a man, nor did he possess any human qualities like compassion. He would do more than hurt Sasha for hunting him. He would steal her soul. But she wouldn't believe Trey if he told her.

"You aren't trained to deal with these . . . situations."

"You have no idea what I am or am not trained for. I excelled at Tae Kwon Do, for your information."

"I just—"

"Good night, Trey." Sasha flipped off his coat and tossed it at him, then turned and climbed the stone steps without a look back. She stuck a key into the ornate brass lock, opened the leaded-glass door, and disappeared inside the dark house.

He had his work cut out for him if he was going to find Ekkbar before she did and keep her safe as well.

Sasha held her breath until she got inside her home, then slumped next to the door away from the oval glass center. Cool plaster touching her back did nothing to ease the heat firing through her body and roaming across her skin.

That was close. If Trey hadn't annoyed her at the last minute, she might have embarrassed herself by asking for a kiss . . . or just taking one. She leaned around and peeked at him walking away. His coat was slung over broad shoulders that seemed to droop.

Did he regret breaking up? Was he wishing she wanted to see him again? She did.

He paused under the streetlight on the corner, the amber beam of light outlining six-foot-three of pure sensuous male she missed seeing next to her when she woke up. Maybe he was considering coming back and pulling her into his arms to ask for a second chance and . . . he strolled off.

She swung back around. *I'm pathetic.* When was she going to truly accept that he was gone and not coming back?

Damn him for blowing her search tonight.

Damn him for questioning her ability.

And damn Trey's lopsided smile and his searing green eyes for still sending her heart into fits. She wished he'd kept his coat on. The last thing she needed filling her head before bed was the clean male scent she remembered vividly from the days of wearing his discarded T-shirts after hours of making love. How could he just pop in tonight and start chatting like nothing had ever happened between them? Like he hadn't spent nineteen incredible months with her, then just walked away two days before she turned twenty-one without offering anything that would help her make sense of his actions.

Actually, he *had* suggested, "You'll find someone better."

She'd tried. Boy, had she tried and tried and tried to fill the gaping hole he'd left in her life and her heart. But just because she still wanted to jump his bones didn't mean he could dance back into her life and start giving her orders.

Leave it to a man to screw up a simple plan.

Sasha straightened up and patted herself mentally for showing a strong front. Who was Trey to question her abilities and act as if she couldn't take care of herself. As if she hadn't been doing a damn good job for the past nine years.

Striding up to an Empire classical table in the foyer where three Ping-Pong sized balls of aqua glass sat in the center of the light brown marble, she passed her hand over the smooth surface. The globes flew into the air. She flipped her hand palm up a few inches beneath them, then wiggled her fingers. The floating orbs glowed and spun in circular patterns—her personal version of stress-relief.

Trey thought she wasn't cut out for PI work, huh? Well, he was wrong. She had more than a few tricks up her sleeve. Sasha waved her free hand, kinetically locking the front door and turning off the outside lights. She then headed for the kitchen where a light spilled from the open doorway.

"Where were you tonight?" Her sister, Rowan, sat at their butcher block table with a mug of tea that smelled like Rowan's personal blend of raspberry and mint.

"At the Black Fairy looking for Ekkbar." Sasha gently lowered her glass balls to the tabletop. She plopped down, hooking a handful of hair behind her ear.

"You shouldn't have gone searching for Ekkbar without me." Rowan leaned back gracefully, looking like any other attractive mid-thirties woman in the historic neighborhood.

Except her sister's face exposed a fragility Sasha had never seen before.

"You're in no condition to help me. I'd be more worried about something happening to you." Sasha took in Rowan's gaunt cheeks and shadowed eyes. Her sister was losing the battle.

"Your powers aren't stable yet," Rowan said in that older sister tone reminiscent of when she'd told Sasha she was too young for makeup at nine years old.

"I've been practicing. In fact, I think I'm pretty solid, getting better every day."

"Really?" Rowan smiled indulgently. "Then why were all the clocks off downstairs this morning?"

What? Sasha thought back to last night. Could she have misdirected her power when she'd been too tired to physically walk through the house to turn off lights? The all-knowing hike of Rowan's eyebrow confirmed she was busted. *Well, hell.*

"Must have screwed up something," Sasha admitted, thankful nothing worse had happened.

"You can't just wave your hand, sweetie. You have to focus your thoughts. That's why Ek—er, that's what I've been trying to teach you."

Sasha cringed when her sister didn't finish the sentence with *That's why Ekkbar slipped past you in the cemetery.*

"I'm working on it." Sasha had practiced daily before Rowan became sick, making her wonder if the witchcraft had caused her sister's bizarre behavior. Their coven refused to help, believing Rowan must have brought this on herself by performing magic for the dark side. Her sister would never do that.

Sasha didn't have years to practice if she hoped to save Rowan. She started to ask for more details when Rowan's head snapped back. The spoon her sister had been holding slipped from her fingers and clattered against the floor.

Oh no. "Rowan . . . hey, sis . . ." Sasha tensed with fear.

Her sister's head rolled forward, eyes no longer hazel but a bright orange color. In deference to what happened the last time Rowan's madness struck, Sasha stood and backed up a step.

Rowan moved so fast Sasha had no chance to escape before her sister had her by the throat. "Don't . . ." Sasha squeezed out, gripping her sister's thin wrists now strong as steel.

"Find Ekkbar or you die, witch," Rowan threatened in a high-pitched voice that sent chills skating up Sasha's spine.

"Rowan . . . please . . . it's me . . . Sasha," she croaked.

Her sister's eyes shifted between crazed and confused. "Stop . . . killing me . . ." she whispered in a frail voice.

Prying desperately at Rowan's fingers, Sasha struggled to breathe. Her vision clouded. The world turned gray.

Rowan's fingers loosened at the same moment her eyes cleared, mortified. "Oh no, I'm so sorry."

Released, Sasha staggered backward. Rowan fell into a heap at her feet, crying, finally free of whatever had held her mind prisoner. Wheezing for air, Sasha massaged her aching throat. *Dear God, how am I going to help her if she kills me?*

Anger and hurt jumbled her emotions, even though she didn't believe for a minute Rowan would intentionally harm her if she weren't possessed. Sasha squatted and grasped her sister's arms, helping her stand.

"I'm so sorry I hurt you." Tears flooded Rowan's eyes.

"I know, honey," Sasha assured her, feeling bad for her sister in spite of what had just happened. Normally, Rowan was not a threat when she slept. She seemed worse after sleeping, but lost her appetite and strength when she didn't rest—a vicious battle either way. "Why don't you lay down for a bit?"

When they reached the bedroom at the top of the stairs,

Sasha helped her sister into bed, then handed her a set of headphones. Rowan believed soothing music helped, but Sasha was beginning to wonder if the music sounded like the soundtrack from *The Exorcist* in her sister's mind.

Once Rowan was asleep, Sasha headed back downstairs to continue her Internet research on demonic possession, since their coven had barred anyone from helping them. With their brother, Tarq, off on some trip where he couldn't be reached, Sasha was flying solo.

Not even Trey can help me. She paused at the bottom landing of the staircase, wishing she could go back nine years.

She wanted one more time to feel him deep inside her and wake up together. Give her that and Sasha would let him return to his precious bachelorhood and secretive work without a word. *I've got more to worry about than how much I want him back.*

Curing Rowan came first.

By then, Trey would be gone for another decade. Sasha sighed. Better that he leave rather than have Trey as a distraction. If she didn't stay focused on keeping herself cloaked the way Rowan taught her, Sasha would expose herself to Ekkbar before she was ready. The manservant couldn't be trusted. After she'd helped the little bastard open a portal between his world and hers, he'd slipped through and scurried away from the cemetery in a blur of pungent mist.

He wouldn't go far, not after negotiating through dreams for a chance to live here and now . . . as a red-blooded human male with full sexual ability again. And she'd felt an energy pass through the nightclub that was evil. Had to be Ekkbar, lying in wait. He probably thought he could trap her with his ancient Hindu magic and make her *his* servant.

He was a fool to underestimate a tenth-generation witch.

When Sasha did drop her protective cloak, she'd have Ekkbar cornered and ready to pay up for having been brought forward in time from Mount Meru.

He *would* cure her sister's madness.

"Ekkkkkkbaaarrrr!" thundered through the stone-and-myst world below Mount Meru.

Batuk's voice raced from the great hall, fingering out along pathways and tunnels in search of his manservant.

The warlord's muscles tightened hard with the need to kill, his perpetual frame of mind since being cursed to live beneath this mountain with his soldiers and their families. He should never have trusted *Ravana* who had offered Batuk and his people everlasting life if he swore fealty to the Hindu demon god.

Gripping the two smooth green serpents carved of malachite stone that served as chair arms on his throne, Batuk roared in frustration. The serpents came to life, hissing. Flames licked off the tips of their forked tongues.

Rock walls in the towering great hall glowed bright red like a dormant ember breathed to life, then settled back into their normal molten purple state that left the air cold as a winter freeze. Serving wenches scurried from the room. Soldiers lounging with concubines merely lifted a respectful glance his way then returned to their activity, having earned a respite from training.

Batuk glowered and slouched against his throne. There'd been a time when he'd lived a flesh-and-blood life as a revered Kujoo warlord, one his foes feared and women worshipped. When he'd loved one woman above all others . . . the reason he'd lifted a sword against the Beladors. What sin had he committed to end up in a place worse than *Fene* where the damned were sent upon death? None, as far as he was concerned.

He'd only warred against the Beladors to regain what was

rightfully his. That *and* he'd trusted Ekkbar's assessment of *Ravana's* offer.

Where was his manservant? The spindly magician had sworn he was close to finding a way out of their demise or Batuk would never have given permission for the fool to experiment with a new incantation. Ekkbar's last attempt infested their underworld home with lost souls screaming in pain nonstop until he'd concocted a way to remove them. Exterminating rodents from an infested dung pile would have been easier. The stench the damned left behind hung in the air for decades.

If the idiot had blundered again, Batuk would . . . what? He'd already neutered the loathsome blight on his existence.

A ball of smoke rolled into the room, parting the fine *nihar*—a pungent-smelling veil of myst floating chest high—and stopped in front of Batuk.

Ekkbar appeared on his knees, head bent and hands in supplication.

Batuk almost laughed. No God listened to the prayers of the damned. "Where have you been, knave? I've called you for hours." His fingernails sharpened and curved into steel claws with the desire to rip out a throat. Ekkbar's.

"My lord, my lord," Ekkbar began in his echoing manner, his voice humble. "I've just awakened from being hurt unmercifully, *most* unmercifully."

Batuk flipped a braided strand of hair from his face, waiting for the eunuch to lift his milky-yellow gaze. Only Batuk and his elite Kujoo soldiers had double pupils, each surrounded by a ring of deep gold—to mark them as cursed.

What? Did Ravana think they'd forget? Wasn't like any of them could stray from this forsaken pit.

Ekkbar's brows puckered with feigned distress. He lied with the expertise of Ravana some days. But unlike the demon god who was safe from repercussions, his manservant was not.

"My lord, my lord, I see you do not believe me, but I speak the truth." Ekkbar crossed his delicate arms in front of his naked bony chest in a child's attempt at indignation. Torchlight danced across his shiny head wrapped with a cloth bandage. "I had just found a way to leave this—"

"What?" Batuk sat forward, not believing his ears. Could the fool really deliver his people from this hellhole?

"As I was saying"—Ekkbar adjusted his position, jade-green silk pants reflecting off the polished stone floor—"I believe I've found a way to leave, but—"

"Show me now!" Batuk bellowed.

Ekkbar frowned. His eyes shifted toward the heaven none of them would ever see, then back to Batuk. "My lord, my *lord*, if you'll allow me to finish, I might be able to explain *all*."

"Careful not to take that tone, lest you pay the price."

"What more would you take from a man who can no longer bed a woman?" he groused.

"Do you risk finding out by raising my ire?"

Ekkbar muttered something, pouting about ungrateful warlords and all he'd done.

Batuk fantasized putting them both out of their miseries by killing the irritation, but none of his people could die as long as they lived beneath Mount Meru, a curse in itself since no one aged beyond the point at which they'd arrived.

But they *could* feel the pain of his sword.

Batuk sighed heavily. "Finish your tale, magician."

Ekkbar straightened his scrawny back and began anew. "I found a connection, yes a connection to the outside world. A witch heard my chants and communicated with me. I explained my, er, our, yes *our* dire dilemma and pleaded for her help, swearing you would repay her handsomely. She agreed to help me open a portal through which we could travel to her world. As I was experimenting—with all intentions of contacting Your Highness once I could ensure success—I was attacked in a most unkind manner. Most unkind. When I awoke the path had disappeared."

"Who did this?" Batuk shouted, vibrating with the need to crush a skull. Who would have ruined their chance to escape?

"I, uh, believe it was one of your elite soldiers." Ekkbar touched his bandaged head in a wasted effort to incur pity.

"*What*?" Batuk's elite would lay down their lives for their warlord and the people he protected. "*Who*?" The walls glowed again at his roar. Heat churned the *nihar* into steam.

"Vyan. I found his shield in the room when I awoke." Ekkbar began wringing his hands. "My lord, he must come back."

"No."

Ekkbar's dull skin paled to a mottled gray. "Wh-what? Vyan is possessed with a fierce need for revenge. He rages over the loss of his wife and family at the hands of Beladors. He will go after the Belador leader, he *will*. You know what that will mean!" Ekkbar trembled, eyes turning pure white.

"Yes. It means if he *is* successful, Vyan will have found a way out for all of us and not just himself as you were obviously trying to do."

"Not true, not true! I merely planned to test the pathway before inviting your wrath for failure." Translucent gold tears spilled from Ekkbar's eyes. "What about the curse? If we start a war again, we will be sent to Fene for a thousand years."

Batuk could not see much difference in where they lived now with the exception of eternal fires and becoming sex slaves to Fene's perverted creatures. However, he'd rather slice off his *own* manhood than submit to those beings.

"Vyan is one of my best strategists. He has a plan, no

doubt. If he is successful in killing the Belador leader Brina, we will be liberated. Ravana swore if we were lured into battle and produced the head of the army's leader, he would return us aboveground and force the Celtic goddess Macha to prove her honor by sending the Beladors to their fate beneath Mount Meru for breaking the truce."

Ekkbar's thin lips gaped open. "I don't understand."

"You said a witch called to you." Batuk stared off into the distance, calculating.

"Not exactly," Ekkbar murmured.

"That proves *we* did not incur this problem. You told me the last time you dreamed of the outside world the Beladors now inhabit all continents. Vyan will find a clever way to provoke one into battle and draw out their leader. If he is successful, we will finally breathe air into our lungs again, breed children, prosper and live as a powerful civilization again." Batuk lowered his glare to his manservant. "And if Vyan fails, I will tell Ravana how you tricked my soldier since he burdened me with you. The demon god would no doubt show his displeasure for the mistake of allowing you to live."

Batuk leaned back, feeling a sense of calm he hadn't enjoyed in centuries.

Once they were freed from this curse, Batuk owed his fealty to no one but his people. He would unleash terror on the new world like it had never seen before.

2

Trey parked his 1974 Bronco at the curb in front of Sasha's house. His plan had holes—like relying on her cooperation—but it was the best he could come up with this quick. He climbed out and bounded up the porch steps to knock on her door.

The faint sound of approaching footsteps inside reached his ears just before the door yawned open. Sasha wore a faded T-shirt that looked suspiciously like one he used to own and a scowl. Her eyes were puffy with exhaustion and her hair tousled as if she hadn't slept well.

But damn what a vision for first thing in the morning.

"I wake you up?" he asked, forcing himself back on task.

"No, I just haven't showered. Why are you here?" she grumbled then ran her fingers through her hair.

"I want to hire you."

"Hire me for what?" she snapped.

"To find someone."

"I'm booked." She tried to close the door, but Trey blocked it with his hand. "Can't we talk for a minute?"

"Like I said, I'm booked, which means I'm too busy for a new case." Her gaze broke from his, flitting around as if she searched for a thought. "Got a ton of paperwork to do today."

He doubted that was the reason. She probably needed to sleep during the day since her client had likely informed her that Ekkbar preferred to move at nighttime. Trey wanted her client's name first . . . and head next.

"Come on, Sasha. I need some help."

"No." She smiled in an evil way that let him know she enjoyed the chance to use that word. He deserved the rejection, but guilt wouldn't deter him from his plan. Trey stepped forward, his foot now also blocking the door's path. When he leaned his head down, she bent her neck backward to face him. She smelled the way he always thought of her—soft and flowery with a touch of wildness that kept him on his toes.

"I just want to talk for a minute," he pressed, hoping he hadn't completely destroyed everything between them.

"Should have tried in the last nine years."

Trey stifled a flinch, wishing on one of his trips home he could have repaired the damage his leaving had caused. What would he have said? "Sorry, Sasha, but I've committed my life to fighting unnatural beings." Better to suffer in silence than to expose her to his world. Besides, he'd cut off his arm before he broke her heart a second time and he was leaving again.

"I'm asking as a friend for a few minutes," Trey implored. He'd camp out on her porch if she still refused him after hearing his full proposal. He needed her help to keep her safe.

"Fine," she huffed then took a step forward, forcing him to retreat. She closed the door and shuffled over to the swing that held too many visions of times past.

But he couldn't be choosy right now.

Trey sat down on the worn oak slats. Like memory cells springing to life, his body reacted with Sasha so close, shifting his heartbeat into high gear. What he wouldn't give to hold her in his arms and taste her lips just once more.

"So what can I possibly do that your secret hoo-doo agency can't?" she wanted to know.

He'd anticipated that question. "I need to find an informant for a personal objective. Can't involve my agency."

"Why not use a better established PI firm? I'm just getting started in this business." She toed the wood porch floor, giving the swing a little shove. The gentle movement fanned loose hairs across her face.

He fought the urge to reach over and brush them back. Instead, he answered, "I trust *you*."

She stopped moving the swing. Her eyes narrowed.

Trey didn't need telepathic powers to figure out she sure as hell didn't trust him after he'd broken up with her.

Sasha shot up from the swing. "Trust is such an overrated commodity," she said with the snippiness of a woman wronged. "Good luck finding your person." She stormed to the door.

"Suit yourself, but I'll pay well to find Ekkbar."

Sasha paused, her hand on the doorknob. "*Who?*"

"A Hindu guy goes by the name Ekkbar. Supposed to be in Atlanta this week. Been told he has information I need."

She swung around. "What information? Who told you?"

"Can't tell you all of that," he dodged, hoping to stoke the interest simmering in her whiskey-gold eyes.

"You and your secrets," she muttered then glanced away, inhaling a deep breath. When she cut her eyes back at him, she was clearly in a dilemma. "How are we supposed to find him if you aren't going to share information?"

We? He had her. "I'll share everything I can. He's rumored to be around Piedmont Park this evening."

"Really?" She clamped her lips shut as if realizing her enthusiasm was a mistake. "Why not go find him without me?"

"It will be easier to blend in and snoop around if we team up. A couple isn't as quick to make as a single tail."

She tapped a sexy royal purple fingernail against the door, thinking, then drew a deep breath. "Okay, but only for a week. If we don't find him after that, I'm free from the contract."

"Fair enough. I'll pick you up at five." Trey expected to locate Ekkbar and send him back beneath Mount Meru by tomorrow. In the meantime, his bogus PI contract would keep Sasha close enough to protect from the magician's clutches.

The only other problem was keeping her out of Trey's hands.

Ekkbar peered into a pool of water hidden beneath Mount Meru he'd located the first week he'd lived there. He waved his hand through the air, swirling the *nihar.* When the mist cleared, he chanted in his native Hindu language, words spoken only by past sorcerers.

He had to locate Batuk's miserable soldier Vyan. The filthy dog had ruined Ekkbar's plans, destroyed his chance to escape. Now everything hinged on the elite soldier's success. But how could Vyan possibly defeat a Belador or even the pair of witches with his meager powers? Ekkbar had to devise some way to help the wretched interloper. But first, he had to find him.

Black water began moving, spinning the pool gently. Ekkbar extended his neck forward two feet until he could stare down into the whirling water.

An image formed of buildings and metal chariots Ekkbar had seen before when he gazed into the future. Vyan probably hid in fear. The soldier came into view, huddled inside a dark room, just as Ekkbar expected. Rays of sunlight striking Vyan's face from the slats he peered through faded away as the sun plunged behind trees, shrouding the land in darkness.

Vyan stood. He wore strange clothes, no longer dressed

in a warrior's mantle of tanned skins. Batuk had been right about Vyan's craftiness. The soldier looked similar to others in the twenty-first millennium. Even his shoulder-length hair and two small braids alongside his face were of that era.

Vyan hooked his sword in place.

Ekkbar scowled at the warrior's stupidity as Vyan covered the sword with a long coat.

"The fool is wasting his time if he thinks a sword will kill a Belador." Ekkbar extended an arm out from his body to his head, rubbing the slick surface in worry. He was doomed if the warrior's best plan depended on a blade.

When Vyan reached inside his pocket and withdrew a multicolored stone, Ekkbar gasped, cursing the thieving warrior, then leaned forward to confirm he was correct.

Batuk's elite soldier held the weapon that could ensure success, *if* Vyan did not destroy the world by carelessly wielding the Ngak stone's magic.

Trey parked his Bronco along the curb on Tenth Street then circled the truck. The short leather skirt Sasha had on would never allow her to make that step down with modesty.

She opened her door. "How can you be sure Ekkbar is here?"

Trey caught her around the waist and lowered her slowly between him and the truck. His gaze dove to the plunging neckline of her violet and black lace top that showcased a cleavage he'd like to dip his tongue into.

Wonder if she still liked having her nipples . . .

"Trey, did you hear me?"

Barely. Blood roared through his ears from the image his last thought had conjured.

"My resource is pretty dependable," he answered, closing the door and taking her hand. Both of his intel hits came early this morning from nightstalkers—vagrants who had died during natural disasters such as violent storms or deep freezes, then lived as tortured souls in the half-world between life and death. Nothing new entered a territory without their notice, but all they could do was inform.

Unfortunately, nightstalkers held no allegiance to either side of life and possessed no moral code. They relayed information in exchange for a handshake with a supernatural being. The longer the handshake, the longer they could remain as a solid body—much desired over a vaporous form since they could down a bottle of wine as a lifelike ghoul.

"You know what this guy looks like?"

Glad for the change of subject, Trey nodded. "Yes. Short guy, about five feet tall, frail-looking, bald with a big hook nose, and . . . odd eyes."

"What are you going to do when you find him?"

Trey would love to know why *she* wanted to find Ekkbar.

"I just want to ask him a few questions." Unless the cursed Hindu got near Sasha, at which time Trey would dispense the bastard into a million pieces. "We've got to behave naturally and not look like undercover agents," he pointed out as they reached a stadium on his right where he'd played a few football games. He stepped into Piedmont Park, guiding them to the concrete route that wound throughout the park he and Sasha used to jog along.

His conscious questioned the real motive for bringing Sasha here.

Okay, so he wanted to spend a little time with her tonight. Where was the harm in talking? He'd missed that as much as everything else about her.

"I wish it was summer," Sasha mused, drawing Trey from his thoughts.

He smiled as they reached the bridge where she always admired thick clusters of yellow flowers during the summer. A middle-aged man in a newsboy cap yanked his beagle's leash to keep the dog out of a bed of pansies. Trey kept an eye on their surroundings, though few people were out this close to midnight.

"Haven't been here in a while," she murmured after they crossed the bridge and neared the stone and brick overpass decorated with ceramic tiles and halfhearted graffiti attempts. Had he unconsciously routed them to where he stole his first kiss from Sasha?

Maybe.

Probably. But that didn't give him license to do so again.

So stop thinking about how hot she looks in leather and lace. He grabbed at a new topic. "How's your family?"

"Same dysfunctional group you knew, except now I don't have to deal with them on a daily basis. Rowan lives with me."

"I'll have to say hello when I take you home."

Sasha caught herself before shouting *no* at Trey. She could just imagine Rowan flying at his throat, trying to kill him. "She's a little under the weather right now."

"Sorry to hear that."

Her eyes inadvertently shifted to his mouth. The same mouth that could be hard one minute and soft the next. Trey was making her nuts. How could he be so indifferent to her after she'd pulled out all the stops to dress for him? Couldn't he pay a little attention and flirt? Her ego could use the boost. He was all business. She would be too if she could stop thinking about how she had only one night with Trey and wanted to enjoy some of it. Was that too much to ask?

One night because of Ekkbar. That slimy worm must have seen her with Trey last night and was playing with her. He was better socialized than she'd expected.

Trey stopped near the crossing beneath the old Park Drive Bridge overpass. The same spot where they'd shared a first kiss. Every intelligent brain cell she had said to turn around and walk away, far away from Trey.

But all the nerves in her body were doing a great job of

convincing her she could weather a kiss without losing her heart again. She was an adult this time, one who should be capable of convincing a man to kiss her—or more—then go on with her life.

She wouldn't mind a rousing night of "or more," but the chances of that were probably as good as convincing him to stay after the end of this week. Trey seemed to be reconnoitering the area, not paying her any attention. She could fix that.

Sasha stretched her arms above her head and took a deep, deep breath, turning so her top shimmered in the ambient light. She wiggled her leather-sheathed bottom.

Trey's eyes whipped to hers. His gaze rippled with heat as it trailed every curve below her neck.

So he *wasn't* as indifferent as he acted. Good start. When he sliced a suspicious glance back at her face, she offered her innocent expression and grimaced as if the move caused pain.

"Are you okay?" His brows cinched together.

"I've got a kink, down low," she said, then drew another breath and exhaled, twisting to arch her back. "Could you . . . rub it?"

His Adam's apple floated up and down with a swallow. "Rub *what*?"

Sasha should feel guilty and not encouraged. "My back. I sit at the computer too long every day." She turned around.

Nothing happened at first. She remained with her back to him, unwilling to quit now. He grasped her gently at the waist with both hands and started working his thumbs slowly up each side of her spine. His touch sent streaks of heat across her sensitive skin. She wanted to moan over the incredible feel of his hands, wanted more than that. When his fingers reached her shoulders, she turned, her chest a breath from his.

"My brother used to hug me and crack my back. Think

you could do that?" She poured on the innocence and held a straight face. Tough act to pull off when she wanted his hands between her legs.

Trey wrapped her in a hug that sent her thoughts tumbling back to when she'd turned to him for escape from a family plagued with problems, for comfort and . . . for love. He slowly lifted her up against him. When her hip met his, she felt solid proof he was still just as affected by touching her as she was by his hands.

Oh yes, very affected.

He groaned into her hair. Hot breath raked her skin.

She folded her arms around his neck and kissed his throat, then ran her tongue along the bottom edge of his ear.

He shuddered and turned his face to hers, pausing for a fleeting second before his mouth captured her waiting lips, the kiss powerful and filled with longing that melted her heart.

No one else had ever made her feel anything close to this cared for in all these years. She'd grown out of her tomboy looks in her mid twenties, but Trey had always found her attractive. Where other women had been intimidated by his stature, she'd enjoyed a male that made her feel feminine.

His mouth stoked the simmering heat she'd thought never to feel blaze up again, until now. She wanted this man, craved him like a drug. Long fingers of one hand drove up into her hair, holding her as if he thought she'd stop. No way. She wanted him here, now, anywhere. His mouth demanded more, caressing her tongue with his. He reached up, grazing a finger across her hard nipples through the sheer material.

Her thighs tightened in reaction, damp and ready for him.

Why had she never felt this way about another man?

His hand cupped her bottom and raised her up. In a move as natural as breathing, Sasha's legs wrapped around his waist, wishing she could unzip him so he could drive inside her.

Trey growled with the contact as though he couldn't believe what they were doing. She locked her legs tighter and rubbed against the thick bulge from his hard shaft.

She smiled, happier than she'd been in forever. "Trey, I want—" A force jerked her backward.

Her muddled mind fought past the sensuous fog. What the devil was happening? Another yank broke the kiss.

"Something's got me," she blurted out. Her eyes met Trey's. The fury rocking through his gaze took her breath.

He lunged for her and wrapped an arm around her waist, drawing her back to his chest in an iron grip. Feet planted wide, Trey shoved his other arm up, palm out.

Wind lashed the park, tearing at her hair. Sasha followed Trey's gaze to see what he stared at with murder in his eyes.

Standing high above them on one end of the Park Drive Bridge overpass was the silhouetted shape of a man. Red lightning bolts sparked everywhere, highlighting the trees towering above each side of him and outlining his body, which was well over six and a half feet tall.

This guy was larger than Trey and just as deadly looking. His shoulder-length hair and long jacket whipped back and forth in the rogue wind that had come out of nowhere. The rest of his body remained rigid as a statue, one arm extended with a rock that glowed with multicolors in his open palm.

That couldn't be Ekkbar. Trey's description of the spindly magician had matched Rowan's from her dreams.

The crazy guy held the stone high and called out, "She is mine, Belador. Owed for a blood debt."

A stronger force wrenched her body hard. She shrieked and clutched Trey, terrified of losing her grip. How was he holding them back against a magician's power? Trey's massive build vibrated with strain.

With no time to question what was going on, Sasha searched for a way to help. Birds fluttered between the trees on each side of their attacker, back lit by the red aura. Sasha concentrated and started chanting, "Hearken elements, thy power I seek . . ." Her voice blurred with the loud roar of the wind.

A sharp crack rent the air. Then another.

She stared in horror as two trees crashed down, barely missing the strange guy.

The magnetic pull disengaged.

"Hold on." Trey yanked her tight then raced away.

Sasha clung to him, her heart banging her ribs. She opened her eyes to see if the lunatic was pursuing them, but no human could have followed at the speed Trey was traveling. Before she took three breaths, he'd shoved her inside the Bronco, cranked the engine, and tore away from the parking spot.

Sasha didn't loosen her death grip on the door until they'd passed the Carter Center, shocked as she studied the profile of a man she'd thought she knew at one time. But the feral look in his eyes tonight was one as foreign to her as watching him battle an unworldly being.

"Um, Trey," she started carefully. "Want to talk?" Did he think he could just drive her home after *that* and not explain?

His neck muscles pulsed, pumped as tight as his fingers gripping the steering wheel. "Yeah, I do."

She held her breath, wondering how she could possibly believe any explanation for what just happened. And maybe he'd been so caught up in the metaphysical battle he hadn't noticed the trees falling.

"Sasha, what exactly *are* you and why is a cursed Hindu warrior trying to take you from me?"

3

Trey ground his molars then eased up before they turned into powder. What the hell had happened back in Piedmont Park? The stoplight he barreled the Bronco toward changed to amber. He shoved an annoyed glare at the swinging lamp that switched right back to green before he reached the empty intersection and spun the truck left. Adrenaline surged so hard through his tight body he could wrench the steering wheel off the column.

He took a breath and glanced at Sasha.

She stared openmouthed at him in a stupor then recovered to yell, "*Me*? What are *you*?"

Touché. His fury subsided. He'd been so shocked at her dropping two trees he'd overlooked exposing his own abilities.

But he could not share much about Beladors outside his own kind and only to protect the tribe. The one exception was telling his mate, which Sasha would never be. Aside from the telepathy issue, he'd still never risk linking her life to his, a condition of taking a mate. And mating to anyone with powers was a major no-no that was rarely allowed.

Trey wiped a hand over his face, buying a minute to formulate an answer then went with a stock line that VIPER's PR department doled out for government bureaucrats.

"I'm trained to deal with . . . *unusual* situations. That's why I can't talk about what I do. Our agency's identity and operation are tightly protected secrets." Not bad. That was a reasonable answer without giving up anything significant.

"If you think I'm going to accept a blanket statement written by someone who deals with damage control for your troops, you're crazy."

"Sasha, I can't—"

"Don't you Sasha me! I just watched you battle something from another world. What was *he*? And what did he mean about being owed for past blood debts?"

Trey swung the Bronco onto her street, parked along the curb several car lengths from her house, and cut the engine. Tension battled for space in the sudden silence. He turned to her, expecting a woman close to hysteria.

Sasha had swung around to face him and leaned back against the door, arms crossed with a you-better-have-answers look in her eyes. Forever his tough girl.

"He's a Hindu warrior who lived eight hundred years ago," Trey answered. "I'm wondering why he's here and thinking he must have come in Ekkbar's place. As for the blood debt, I wouldn't want to speculate." He knew the story, but preferred to wait until he contacted Brina, who led the Belador warriors and answered to the Celtic goddess Macha. Bottom line—his Belador ancestors had murdered families of the Kujoo in an attempt to enslave the race, forcing future generations to make amends for past sins. How the hell was he going to keep Sasha safe from this demon and not draw the Beladors into a war?

"Wait, you *know* who Ekkbar is?" Sasha asked.

Trey leaned an elbow on the door panel and supported his forehead with his fingers. "Yeah, and you do, too. Time to start explaining, but first tell me how you dropped two trees."

"I didn't hit him," she protested and shrugged sheepishly. "I was *trying* to send the birds down to break his focus so we could get away." She stared off in thought. "Must have used the wrong inflection. But I had the words right. Or maybe I—"

"Sasha, what—are—you?" he repeated.

She sagged against the door. Her arms relaxed. One hand lifted to her hair, twirling a length round and round a finger. She answered in a soft voice. "I'm a . . . witch."

He wanted to laugh it off as a joke, didn't want to believe she'd kept *that* from him all this time. The embarrassed glance she sent him said she'd been serious. She'd never told him.

Who am I to quibble? He'd never told her about being a Belador. "Since when?" he asked.

"My whole life. My sister and I are tenth-generation witches. My twin brother, Tarq, is a warlock." She dropped her hand to her lap, tapping her fingers on one another.

"What about your parents? What are they?"

"Just plain dysfunctional." A wry grin touched her lips. "They aren't our biological parents. Rowan tried to tell me they weren't when I was a child, but I wouldn't believe her. When she moved in with me, I finally understood that she was a witch . . . and I was, too. Together, we found out our adoptive parents had inherited us from some distant cousin, but the records are vague. The house was given to our adoptive parents through a legal network that's been impossible to break through. That's why I started researching ancestries—trying to uncover mine—but my parents covered their tracks well."

"So you never realized you were a witch?" he said, still amazed at her admission.

"I should have since my ear drove me crazy sometimes."

"What do you mean?"

"After Rowan convinced me about being a witch, she explained that our ear burns as a signal when an unknown witch is nearby. The stronger the sensation, the stronger the witch."

"Why did trees come down instead of the birds?" he asked.

Her lips drew up to one side in a chagrined expression and she sighed. "Rowan is better than I am, but I'm learning."

Trey lost his smile, reality just sinking in. "So you don't have *control* of your powers?" She could have dropped a building on the two of them while his mind was lost to everything except wanting her. Naked and hot.

"Don't look at me that way. I'm not dangerous, just a half-bubble off sometimes," she groused. "Back to the original topic. What do you know about Ekkbar?"

"Uh-uh. You were looking for him first. Why?"

Her smooth brow puckered in thought. "How did you know I was looking for him first?"

Damn. He'd screwed up. "I just know."

"That will so not work right now."

Might as well tell her. He'd have to at some point if they were going to catch this guy. "I had your phones tapped and heard you telling your sister you were going to find Ekkbar."

"You *what*?" Sasha's jaw dropped. She jumped out of the truck. Trey was right behind, trying to catch her. Leaves blasted away from the sidewalk, taking refuge in the gutter.

"Sasha, wait a minute."

She rushed up the steps to her porch, shouting, "You *tapped* my phones? I know exactly what you are—a snoop. Go away."

He snagged her an arm's length from the door and wrapped her up from behind, her back to his front. She struggled, elbows digging into his side. "Stop it and let me explain."

"There's no explanation for spying on me, you bat dropping."

"Bat dropping?" He started laughing. "You don't boil lizard tongues and eyeballs in a big cauldron out back, do you?"

That was the wrong thing to say. She jabbed him with a hard elbow, banging his ribs.

Trey lifted her off the floor until she quit kicking. "I'm sorry for tapping your phones, but I saw you leave the cemetery alone at night a couple days ago. I was worried about you."

"Why would it matter to you after nine years?" she snarled.

Trey lost his smile. He didn't want to tell her about all the other times, but he owed her more than a lame reason.

He dropped his lips close to her ear. "Because I care."

She stilled. Her heart pounded under his fingers.

The porch light blinked on and the front door opened. Rowan stood before them in a flowing bloodred house gown and robe.

Trey spoke on his cell phone and paced across Sasha's living room while keeping an eye on her and Rowan, both curled up on the sofa. Rowan looked more exhausted than possessed, but Trey kept close watch of her in case she changed.

"Give me Findley," Trey said, asking for his VIPER field contact in Virginia. If the rest of that bunch escaped, every supernatural asset at VIPER, be it Belador or not, would have to fight the Kujoo army. Until then, one warrior did not warrant a team assignment from VIPER. The coalition of unusual beings functioned as a paranormal intelligence and defense force. Agents were deployed whenever a supernatural threat against the United States and other countries committed to peace arose, but Trey could handle Vyan with backup.

What a mess this close to November second.

When Findley came on the line, Trey explained the problem in general terms.

"Why can't you get a Belador, McCree?" Findley said.

"Nobody available," Trey lied. He could call in an army of Beladors, but felt certain that would play into the Hindu warrior's hand to put his whole tribe at risk. Trey's agreement with VIPER did not supersede his oath as a Belador. He wouldn't trust a covert agency full of supernatural beings with the fact that his tribe could be destroyed by this Hindu race.

"I'll have to check around and get back to you."

"I need an agent now." Finding Brina might have spared Trey this call, but she'd ignored his first telepathic message—prickly leader that she was—and he was fighting the clock. If he had to battle this warrior, he wanted to do so before tomorrow at midnight. On November second, All Souls' Day, Belador warriors suffered a loss of powers between midnight and dawn. The Hindu had to know this, which was why Trey needed backup to protect the women while he went hunting for Vyan.

"You can't just call in for an agent without getting this approved as a VIPER mission," Findley countered.

"Don't play red tape games with me. If we don't contain this and other warriors escape, authorization to send an agent into the field will be the least of your problems."

"I don't have anyone in your area," Findley hedged.

"I just want some damn backup."

"Fine. I'll send you Lucien."

"Lucien?" Trey started in a low voice full of menace. "I tell you we could be talking Armageddon if this gets out of control and you give me a new guy with an attitude?" He could all but see Findley bow up. Trey didn't give a rat's ass. He'd heard the scuttle on Lucien.

"You're just a contractor."

Trey stopped pacing. "One trying to save your ass along with the rest of this world so don't take that tone with me," he warned. Most agents around VIPER had the survival skills to back off when Trey was pissed, like now.

After a slight hesitation, Findley said, "He's all I can get to you quick and he can only stay three days."

Seventy-two hours? No problem. Trey intended to deal with this Hindu in the next twenty-four hours. "Send him. I'll call if I need anything else." He hung up and dropped the phone into his pocket then turned to Sasha and her sister.

"Can you keep Sasha safe?" Rowan asked without preamble.

"Yes," Trey answered swiftly, though he hadn't figured out how to protect her and keep his tribe out of a war. The thought of letting either down kinked his insides.

"I can protect myself." Sasha jumped up from the sofa.

"In that case, I'll stay here and out of the way unless you need me," Rowan told Trey.

"That would make it easier for me to keep an eye on both of you," Trey said. What triggered Rowan's madness, and was she getting worse as Sasha suspected? That must be why the warrior wanted Sasha rather than Rowan, the stronger witch.

"Hey, I *am* in the room," Sasha snapped at both of them.

Rowan stood, her cardinal-red silk gown and robe swirling around her body. "I know you're here, sweetie. You're getting better at handling your powers all the time and *will* be powerful one day, but you're no match for this Hindu warrior right now." She hugged Sasha, wished them good night, and swept from the room with a soft, "Nice to see you back, Trey."

"You still haven't explained everything," Sasha said to Trey and crossed the room to face him. "I've told you everything, including my deal with Ekkbar. *Your* turn."

He'd dodged Findley, but Sasha was another story. He didn't like lying to her, but was limited in what he could disclose. "I can't tell you everything about me."

She shook her head, the disappointment on her face too similar to the day he'd left her sitting on the porch. That cut deeper than he'd have thought.

When she started to walk away, Trey grabbed her arm gently, drawing her to him so that he could whisper in her ear. "I was born under a star, chosen at birth to . . . to receive powers upon adulthood if I accepted my destiny, which I did. But I've taken an oath that includes not sharing anything about this group, my tribe. It's not that I don't trust you with the information. Not even my dad knows as much as you do at this moment and I trust him with my life."

Sasha leaned back to face him. Her eyes lost all anger and softened. His heartbeats punctuated the wait while she studied his face, then gave a little nod and lifted a hand to brush a lock of hair from his forehead. The sweet gesture soothed the sharp edge of his nerves. She whispered, "I understand."

One look into her eyes and he could tell she *did* understand. She'd always accepted him as he was, not trying to change him. No other woman had ever reached so far inside Trey the way Sasha had. If only they could be together, but now there were more hurdles than the telepathy. Brina was difficult on a good day. Fat chance she'd approve a match with a witch.

"When will backup arrive?" Sasha asked.

"Probably not before dawn."

"You didn't finish what you started in the park." Sasha

lifted toward him and Trey gave up the battle not to kiss her. He cupped her chin and lowered his head. Her arms entwined his neck, her lips meeting his. Before he knew it, she was in his arms, shifting her hips erotically against him. The heat that had flamed between them threatened to incinerate him from the inside out. Desire raged through every nerve in his body, fanning a hot ember of want so strong he shook with need.

He'd never stopped wanting this woman, but after hurting her once by walking away, he couldn't allow this to get out of hand then disappear again.

She broke away from his mouth and whispered, "Don't leave me tonight." With two fingers to his lips, she silenced him when he started to speak. "I know you're leaving Atlanta—and me—when this is over. I'll let you go, but I need you now. I *want* you now." Her amber eyes flared with determination.

He wavered on the threshold of a decision he might regret for many years . . . no matter which choice he made.

She licked her lips and mouthed the word "please."

He closed his eyes and tried to convince himself to back away. He really did. Instead, when Trey opened his eyes, he captured her lips. Pleasure burst in his chest. She wanted him. Would understand when he had to leave again.

How could he back away after that?

When he scooped a hand under her bottom, Sasha's legs came up around his waist. She reached down and stroked his raging erection. He hissed at the contact, sure his growl shook the rafters. Not a wise move with her sister upstairs. The one who went into anti-Christ mode with no warning. Blood keened in his ears.

"My room," Sasha breathed between kisses.

"What about Rowan?"

"Sleeps with headphones on . . . music helps."

"What about Tarq?"

"On a sabbatical somewhere. Trey, you're not moving."

His feet heard her and strode to the rear of the house. When he carried her into the dark bedroom, her lips never left his as she waved a hand. Flames danced on candles arranged on a silver tray resting upon her dresser and soft rock music began to play. Trey shut the door with his foot, then crossed the room to her four-poster bed where he lowered her to the deep blue satin coverlet. Of all the places he'd made love to her indoors and outdoors, he'd never touched her in this room.

Trey paused and smoothed a hand over her cheek. "I don't deserve this—or you—and the last thing I want to do is hurt you . . . again."

"I know. Stop worrying. I mean it when I say I'm okay with this and you leaving." Sasha rose up, unsnapped his pants, then unzipped the fly. She reached inside to grasp him then took him into her mouth.

Trey sucked in a breath and croaked out a muttered curse at how close she came to sending him into oblivion. "Not yet, baby, or this won't be the long drawn-out affair I have in mind." He eased her back, shaking his head at her wicked grin, then shed his clothes with ruthless efficiency. Leaning a knee down beside her, he lifted the edge of her lacy top and worked it up the slender arms Sasha stretched above her head.

"I'm so ready," she breathed out, but he was taking his sweet time.

No bra. Just pure woman. His woman.

When he had the filmy material at her shoulders he stopped, leaving her eyes covered and her arms bound, vulnerable. She purred in anticipation. Trey lowered his mouth to her breast, licking the tip then the soft underside with his tongue. Sweet.

Sasha shivered and sucked in sharply.

He slowly peeled off her snug pants, kissing the inside of

her legs, which tasted salty where the warm scent of leather lingered on her thighs. So fitting for his wild woman who could be like buttery leather—tough and soft at the same time. He went back for the sliver of black underwear, lightly scraping his finger across the tight silk material shielding her folds.

She quivered. Her fingers locked around the downy pillow beneath her head. Her chest curved up with the motion.

Oh yeah, baby.

Trey stretched out alongside her and grazed his fingers beneath the underside of her other breast, barely caressing the skin, gliding along the curves . . . near the beading tip, but not touching it. Her back arched, feet digging in, toes curling, but she hadn't cried uncle yet. He grinned, enjoying every sweet minute of taking her closer to the edge.

She shoved her breasts higher toward his hand each time he came close to her nipple.

Then he'd move just out of reach.

Sasha's urgent moans grew into a warning growl. He smiled.

Trey raised his body over hers then lowered his lips, sneaking his tongue beneath the edge of lace to explore the smooth skin along her collarbone and kiss her neck.

She shifted her legs up and captured his penis between her thighs, rubbing gently. He clenched the sheets and mattress, clawing for control, then dipped down, licking circles around a nipple before taking the pearled tip into his mouth. She released him and bowed up tight, crying out, fingers strangling the pillow. He'd grin if holding back wasn't killing him. Trey spread his fingers wide to coax her taut body back down to the bed then gently massaged farther south.

Firm feminine muscles quivered, anticipating what she could not see. He caressed her hips, her navel, the insides of her legs and dipped his finger under the wisp of panties . . . only to slide them off side to side.

"Trey, you're killing me." She wiggled her bottom, obviously trying to encourage him to move things along.

He did grin at her now. "You'll die happy."

"I'm tempted to use magic to get you where I want you," she warned through the lace covering her face.

His hand stilled. "Don't. You might drop the ceiling."

She muttered something then snapped her fingers. A package appeared in her hand and she flicked it blindly at him. A wrapped condom hit him in the chest. "I stand corrected. Starting to have a whole new appreciation for this side of you."

"You wait until I show you what I *can* do. I have a few tricks . . . can hold my own . . . arrogant men . . ."

He sheathed himself and chuckled over her rant then sent a finger down between her legs. That silenced her.

Sasha lost any coherent thought and focused on what he would do next. Tiny flickers of light seeped through the lace covering her eyes. He was the only man she'd ever trust to put her in a vulnerable position. His hands held real magic. He teased her close to an orgasm. She tensed, ready, but his finger slid away taking her breath and leaving her mindless. He dipped a finger inside her, driving a sharp rush of pleasure through her womb, increasing the pace until every muscle in her body had stretched tight, reaching for release.

He stopped just short again and she whimpered. His finger withdrew and moved over the sensitive skin in tantalizingly slow motion, touching her long enough to leave her shaking before fading away and returning, each time driving her closer to the brink of insanity.

All her focus arrowed to the spot he refused to linger on until she tensed for the mind-blowing orgasm only to have it skitter away before she could take ownership. He plunged a finger inside her. She clenched. He pushed two inside.

"You're so wet and hot," he murmured between kisses to her breast. He pulled out of her again, his wet finger touching her other breast and tenderly destroying the last vestige of sanity she possessed.

"I want you inside me *now*, Trey."

"Not yet. I've missed a spot."

"You'll . . . get to it . . . later," she tried to assure him, but talking was beyond her when his fingertip brushed her wet folds, teasing with serious intent. She arched, reaching for that pleasure she was ready to beg for . . . reaching . . . then he massaged her G-spot . . . kinetically.

The powerful release broke her bounds with this world. She cried out and lost contact with the bed. Her body hummed, the sensuous delight rolling on and on. Pleasure rushed through her on a tidal wave. Time stilled. She floated, boneless and free of all worries until strong hands drew her down, gently pressing her back to the cool sheets.

Sasha panted, catching her breath, and opened her eyes to see Trey's face above her. The lacy top had been eighty-sixed at some point. In fact, nothing touched her but his rock-hard body. She took a deep breath, enjoying his musky scent.

He leaned down, kissed her lips, and whispered, "Why didn't you do that before when we made love?"

"What?"

"Levitate."

It took her a minute to realize he thought she'd held back when they were together before. "That's never happened before."

His gaze relaxed then shifted to a possessive look.

He cared. Sasha's heart pulsed, happy to see the truth in his face. He had to know they were bound to each other like no two other people had ever been.

If not, she'd enlighten him . . . later.

Without another word, Trey leaned down, his penis prodding her slick opening. She opened to him and he eased inside, filling her. How could he move like a rocket at the park one minute and be so incredibly patient the next? He stroked deep into her and unimportant issues faded away.

Sasha locked her legs around his back and Trey held her to him then sat upright. He kissed her, his tongue lazily dueling with hers until the kiss turned hot and serious. He scooped his arms under her knees, his hands supporting her back as he lifted her up slowly then slid her down his shaft with the same excruciatingly measured pace. She lost track of everything around her, swept up in a world that belonged only to them.

Sasha held his face in her hands, reveling in the feel of his mouth on hers and him buried inside her where he belonged. Her orgasm was building again, wicking all her thoughts to the man who held her close. He leaned back, which shoved him deeper on his next drive and she gasped with the pleasure.

He murmured something she didn't understand and could feel his fingers stroke her nipples even though his hands were on his back. Lovemaking reached new highs with kinetic ability.

The sensation torturing her breasts moved lower, targeting the tiny nub that controlled her immediate world. His rhythm turned urgent just as he kinetically fingered *the* spot.

Stars zinged through her vision in the turbulent wake of coming again. Had Trey not held her close to him she'd have shot to the ceiling, but his arms clenched tightly when he growled her name with his release right behind her.

The familiar fragrance of their lovemaking cloaked the air and washed away all those years she'd missed him. She slumped against him. He lowered them both to the bed on their sides, stretching his body and tossing one huge leg over her.

Tracing a fingernail across his lips, she wanted to say, *I love you*, but whispered, "I've missed you," instead.

Trey brushed a long strand of hair over her shoulder, his verdant gaze filled with love she'd never expected to see again. "I've missed you, too. You'll never know how much."

"So why did you leave me?"

He glanced away, just like he used to do when he'd gather his thoughts before speaking, then sad eyes met hers. "After I got over the shock of finding out there was a reason for all my odd behavior and that my abilities were needed to protect others, I accepted the responsibility that came with my destiny . . . as a Belador. That's the tribe I belong to. I had little choice but to accept my destiny since the other option was to end up an enemy of our tribe and possibly go insane from my undeveloped powers. I wouldn't subject you to that life."

He'd cared enough to walk away to keep her safe, but she sensed something more. She'd felt his love in all the silent ways a man showed a woman, but knew in her heart he held back something he wouldn't talk about.

"Was that the only reason, Trey?" Sasha asked, recalling the day he came to tell her good-bye. He'd stared into her eyes for a long time as if trying to discern something.

"I can deal with the truth, no matter what it is," she assured him.

He touched her cheek, indecision playing through his frown. "There is something else, but I don't want you to take it personally." When she nodded her encouragement, he took a breath and continued. "I realized as a . . . *child* that I could read minds; then later on as a Belador I learned how to communicate telepathically."

His face had flinched when he'd said "child." What had happened then? "Tell me about the first time."

"It was with my mother." Trey's fingers drifted through her hair. His eyes seemed unfocused and distant as he strived to recall a memory. "I always told her I loved her when I headed out to school or when she put me to bed. She'd answer back automatically with a 'love you too,' but she never looked me in the eyes when she said it. I was in third grade when I came home to find her and my dad arguing. Her suitcase was sitting by the door. When she lifted it to walk out, I panicked and begged her to stay. I asked her why she was leaving."

Sasha had never seen the hurt Trey had surely carried all these years behind the jovial mask he showed the world, but she witnessed it now in full force.

He lifted a handful of Sasha's hair to his nose and inhaled, then let the fine strands sift through his fingers and spill across her chest. "My mother didn't speak, but I could hear her thoughts as if she'd shouted them. I heard 'Why? Because I was a stupid teenager who married that truck-driving oaf and got knocked up with you. Giving birth to an ox would have been easier. You were one big mistake I should have aborted.' "

Sasha sucked a breath in horror that any mother could say such a thing. But she hadn't. Trey's mother had lied to his face. Memories of times with Trey raced across Sasha's mind. Times in the past when he'd look at her as if he questioned what she said, but never openly challenged anything she'd said to him. How many times had he struggled to accept whatever she said at face value rather than hurt her feelings?

"You've never been able to read my thoughts, have you?"

"No," he admitted. "But you deserved a normal life without the danger my world presents. One without being at risk."

Sasha wanted to argue. Trey would always protect her, but she wouldn't force the issue tonight after he'd shared a part of him she doubted anyone had ever been privy to. Instead, she tossed logic at him. "Normal? *What* was normal about my life back then? I had a closet-alcoholic father and a mother who couldn't leave the house for fear aliens would steal her human eggs. She never seemed to notice inanimate objects moving around the house with autonomy." Sasha relaxed. "Of course, even I excused it as my weird imagination or ghosts."

A smile tilted the corners of Trey's mouth. "Your family was pretty odd, but tonight you saw the kind of 'things' I deal with on a daily basis. I don't want you around that."

"I have powers, too. I can cloak myself. I can—"

That drew a scowl. "And if you don't stop using those powers until you're proficient you're going to get injured or killed. What if you'd unleashed a *legion* of warriors like him?"

"Ekkbar controlled who came through his end of the portal."

"Precisely the reason you should stop playing around with magic until you get a certified witch license."

In a swift movement, she rolled from his arms and hovered above him. He flipped to his back, her body stretched above the length of his, her black hair curtaining each side of her face. She clenched her fists. "I'm not that bad."

"Baby, come down," Trey said quietly as though he didn't want to frighten her.

"Why?" She'd had enough of everyone patronizing her.

"I didn't mean to insult you. I just can't live with the thought of anything harming you and felt like a heel for leaving you. I constantly worry about you. That's why I've spent every free minute for the past nine years coming back to Atlanta to make sure you're okay. Now I'm more concerned than ever."

Well, hell. Her heart was melting and she'd never get the fickle organ back to a normal shape again.

Sasha wanted to lash out at him for tapping her phones and following her, for leaving her, but couldn't. This was the Trey she knew, the one who had always stood between her and harm. She might not care for his tactics, but he'd acted out of concern, not with a malicious intent.

He opened his arms. She sighed then drifted down to settle along the length of his torso, propping her chin on her hands lapped over each other on his chest.

He *had* come back, had always been near.

She hadn't intentionally lied to him earlier, but she'd lied all the same when she agreed to let him go. Sasha was not allowing him to walk away from her again. Not if the *only* reason he had for breaking up was his job and supernatural abilities. She realized now that he loved her but feared hurting her too much to admit his feelings then leave again.

What about this telepathy issue? She didn't have an answer yet, but would think of some way to get past it . . . she hoped.

All she had to do first was figure out how to cure her sister's madness and send the crazy warrior back to where he belonged before he kidnapped her or killed Trey.

4

Trey finished showering late the next morning, annoyed no one from VIPER had shown and Brina still ignored his telepathic messages. He'd stepped from the bedroom in search of Sasha when the slap of the back door closing drew his attention. He swung around and strode to the rear porch where he found her in the yard tossing bread over the small patio and what little grass sprouted in the shady area.

"What are you doing out here, Sasha?"

"Duuhh. Feeding the birds."

"That's not what I mean. We agreed you would stay inside."

"Nope. We agreed I would stay home. This is part of my home." She continued moving around the small backyard filled with an eclectic array of potted plants and outdoor metal sculptures. An oak tree with branches too thick to reach around fanned wide across a third of the space.

God knew, he loved this woman, but if he bound himself to her she'd be linked to his fate if he screwed up. Stirring up a war between the Beladors and the Kujoo probably qualified as a serious screwup with Macha.

The Celtic goddess held all power over the Beladors.

Trey scanned the area for any threat, then sauntered down to where Sasha stood next to a cleaned-off potting table. Leaves and branches crackled beneath his heavy steps. The smoky aroma of a fireplace in use swirled through the crisp air, rolling a sense of déjà vu over him when he'd spent a weekend in a mountain cabin with her. Seemed all the memories he held dear were wrapped around Sasha.

When she tossed the last pieces to the greedy flock of pecking birds, he picked her up and sat her on the table.

"Trey!"

"Yes?" He ran his hands up her legs, bunching her skirt as he searched for . . . oh, man. No panties. Instant hard-on.

"What are you doing?" she hissed, glancing around.

Thick bushes boarded each end of the potting table.

"Shh, no one can see what I'm doing unless they look over my shoulder and you'll figure it out in a minute." He kissed her into silence then moved his lips to the sweet skin behind her ear. He parted her legs, running his hands up to caress her. He'd hardly teased her and slid a finger inside her damp and hot opening when she came so fast he barely had time to cover her mouth with his and protect her moment.

What woman would ever feel this passionate in his arms again? None.

Sasha slumped against him and muttered, "I know what you're doing. Wiping me out physically so I won't go anywhere today."

He laughed. "Is it working?" Trey held her close, savoring these stolen minutes of contentment for later when his world returned to an endless string of lonely nights.

"Yes. At this rate, I won't be able to reach the front porch unassisted." She started rising off the table.

"Trey! He's got me again!" She dug her nails into him.

He drew her to his chest as he swung around to face the threat. "I'm going to kill the bastard."

No! You can't, wicked through his thoughts with a sharp bite. Brina had finally shown up.

Why not, Brina?

Oh, I don't know—the end of civilization as you know it.

Got no time for this right now. Trey snapped his mind shut and focused on saving Sasha who was being dragged away from him, stretching his arms to the limits. Something she'd told him last night popped in his mind. "Cloak yourself now!"

She stared at him for a second then closed her eyes. The minute her cloaking took effect, she dropped into his arms. Trey made three strides to reach the back door where he set her on her feet and waited until she was steady. "Go inside, keep up your cloaking, and don't come near the doors or the windows."

She nodded, backing away until she bumped into her sister whose arms went around her. "I have her," Rowan called out.

Trey swung around to find the Hindu warrior standing twenty feet above the ground in the oak tree. "Who are you and what do you want?"

"I am Vyan of Batuk's first guard. I am here for the witch to save my race. She will break the curse. Beladors killed my family, my woman. This is only fair."

"No." Trey knew some of the ancient history, how his Belador ancestors had murdered and pillaged. A part of him could sympathize with the Hindu warriors pain and what it would be like to lose the woman he loved. But this guy was out of his mind if he thought he could have Sasha as payback or that Trey would allow him to use her to release the Kujoo warriors.

"I will take her," Vyan taunted.

"Try it and you'll die."

"I would welcome death after eight hundred years beneath a mountain. Give me the woman, Belador. She *sent* for me."

"She sent for Ekkbar, not you. What'd you do, kill him?"

Vyan shook his head, his mouth curving in a wry smile. "You know no one can die beneath Mount Meru."

He's baiting you, Trey.

I realize that, Brina. Let me kill him in a fair fight and be done with this. If the others had a way out they'd be here.

Doesn't work that way with the gods. If you battle him without being physically attacked first, you start a war. The truce will be broken.

He started the war, Trey argued hotly. *Not me.*

Sasha called him up, Brina snapped back at him so loud his head felt as though she'd slugged him, which was a good trick since she was literally thousands of miles away on a mystic island in the Irish Sea. *Sasha opened the portal so she's the one who should send him back*, Brina pointed out.

That's not going to happen. He's not getting near her.

Men will be the downfall of Beladors, always wanting to fight.

Why the hell make us warriors if you didn't intend for us to battle?

Do! Not! Curse!

Something sharp cuffed his ear.

Vyan lifted his hand which held a glowing rock. "She will come to me willingly, Belador." The back door swung open of its own accord, exposing Sasha huddled against her sister, terrified.

Fury lashed every protective gene in Trey's body to a fever pitch. He snapped his mind shut, unwilling to debate further with Brina. She was not here facing this demon and not helping. He took a step forward, bent at the knees, and leaped up to the branch two sword lengths from Vyan. The oak's mighty limb creaked under their combined weights.

Trey entered Vyan's mind for an insight to this man's intentions only to find raging emotions—aggression and anguish.

As if he realized what Trey was about, Vyan smiled, his gaze sinister. Double-black pupils floated in each of his swirling gold irises. "I will enjoy touching her, Belador."

Trey's discipline snapped. He lunged forward, but came up empty when the warrior disappeared. Momentum sent him one more step into thin air. He landed on the ground, searching for Vyan.

He's gone, Trey. Brina could never be locked out of his mind for long.

Where? Tell me the location of his hideout.

No. Our tribe's survival depends on not warring. I cannot interfere. I merely sent him away so you could cool off, but that is all I can do. You do realize what tonight is, don't you?

Yes. Trey rolled his eyes and headed for the porch. Every Belador across the world would lay low during the one day of the year they were most vulnerable to be killed. But he did not have that option with Vyan clearly after Sasha.

Do not sacrifice your tribe for one woman, Brina ordered.

Trey stepped up on the porch where he could see Sasha. She stood with her shoulders back, proud, trying so hard to show him a strong front. Impressive, if her face hadn't lost all color. He considered his options, but only one thing mattered to him right now—keeping Sasha safe.

I took an oath, Brina, Trey replied. *Honor above all else. Those four words have ruled my life. I'm trying to protect our tribe and Sasha, but I will not allow that demon to take her.*

I took an oath as well, Brina countered. *I will also do whatever it takes to protect my tribe . . . even if that means turning my back on you. There is no honor in sacrificing an entire race for one woman.*

That's your perspective. I have mine. He waited for her to snap at him, but she'd withdrawn without another word. Not an encouraging sign. He'd hoped Brina would show up with a solution, to give him a dragon to slay. Not to leave him even more guilt-ridden. Was he being selfish to protect Sasha?

"He's gone." Trey stepped inside the house and reached for Sasha, who rushed to his open arms. She trembled. He hugged her tight and whispered, "I'm not going to let anything happen to you." She nodded against his chin. Damn that Hindu. He'd scared a woman who wanted to take on a gang the other night.

Trey walked Sasha to the kitchen where pots and pans clattered. Rowan was starting to cook. He appreciated her effort to settle things down for Sasha by the simple activity of preparing breakfast. A knock rapped at the front door.

"That's for you," Rowan said to Trey. "Bring him to the dining room. I've prepared an early lunch for four."

Trey opened the front door to a dark-haired Hispanic guy standing several feet back. Most people wouldn't realize that the body shielded by a black turtleneck, black nylon jacket, and black cargo pants was close to Trey's build. The color suited the agent's dark gaze, wavy black hair, and brooding attitude.

"You Lucien Solis?" Trey asked, not extending his hand. *So this is the son of a bitch nobody wanted to work with.*

"Yep, but you got the wrong species. My mother wasn't a female dog." Trey hadn't even felt Lucien enter his mind and instinctively went into Lucien's mind where he heard, *Damn, Findley. Wasting my time on this when I should be—*

Should be where, Lucien? Trey asked, interrupting.

Silence. Black eyes flashed irritation just before Trey felt an impenetrable wall slam into place between their minds. Impressive and interesting, but not something he had time to investigate right now.

"Just so we're clear," Trey said, "I don't like Findley, either. If you don't want to be a part of this, then go."

Lucien shrugged. "I'll stay . . . for a while."

"In that case, Rowan has lunch ready. I'll catch you up while we eat."

Trey followed the aroma of warm bread and vegetable soup to the dining room where Rowan paused from pouring coffee and did a double take on Lucien who answered her curious glance with a scowl. *Wonder what that had been all about.* He didn't care enough to find out right now so he settled down next to Sasha and began reviewing the situation for everyone. By the time they had finished eating, he'd filled in Lucien on what they knew to this point, including Rowan's illness though she still had not shown signs of madness. Could Sasha be exaggerating?

Lucien hadn't said a word, which worried Trey. The guy could be a liability.

When Sasha started to stack dishes, Rowan said, "Please sit down. I'll take care of all this." She lifted her hands, palms up, and whispered words. The table cleared instantly.

Lucien's sharp gaze narrowed slightly, but still he said nothing. Rowan's eyes met his, hers sparkling with delight in the face of his dark mood. Trey caught her utterly feminine assessment of the agent. He'd have to warn both women later in private about being careful around Lucien.

"I'm wondering why Vyan has not tried to breach the house," Trey said, wanting to move ahead.

"Maybe because I placed a protective spell over the house when I moved in," Rowan offered.

"If that's the case, the women should be safe here, but I don't want to take any chances in case he's only waiting for an opportune time," Trey said. "I'm going out scouting tonight. Lucien will watch the house and can reach me if anything comes up." *If* Lucien would communicate with him.

"Where are you from, Lucien?" Rowan interjected.

"Spain." Lucien's terse answer didn't invite further conversation.

Trey kept his mind blocked from telepathy and leaned back to study Lucien while Rowan pressed her questions. He wondered if the rumors he'd heard were true, that Findley had been told to put Lucien in the field without a probationary time.

"Where do you call home now?" Rowan asked, clearly unaffected by Lucien's curt attitude.

"Wherever I sleep for the night." Lucien crossed his arms in a you're-wasting-your-time pose.

Sasha spiked an angry glare at Lucien, and Trey almost chuckled out loud. Atta girl. Maybe he should get rid of this guy. Why hadn't the council, specifically Sen, blocked Lucien's fieldwork until the coalition had time to assess him?

When this was over, Trey would ask Sen what was up. An immortal who appeared when he deemed an issue worthy of his time, Sen had insinuated himself into an unofficial liaison capacity with the VIPER coalition. He presided over a governing council created of different beings whose job it was to keep an eye on all the supernatural assets and their actions.

Rowan stood, her pink ankle-length dress loose on her. She'd lost weight. "Sasha, you want to help me refill coffees?"

"Sure." Sasha scooted her chair back.

"What, you're not going to blink your eyes and refill the cups?" Lucien asked with a sarcastic edge.

Trey checked Rowan to see if she was insulted. If so, he'd have to deal with Lucien's smart mouth before he kicked him out. Trey was beginning to think the guy had a thing against witches.

Rowan gave Lucien an amused look as she circled the table to the doorway directly behind him. "Not this time."

Having scooted from the other side, Sasha had just

reached the same spot behind Lucien when Rowan's body went rigid.

"Oh no. Rowan, don't . . ." Sasha pleaded.

"Sasha, what's wrong?" Trey was rising from his chair when Rowan literally flew at her sister, grabbing her by the throat and pinning Sasha to the wall. Trey reached them in a lunge and gripped his hands around Rowan's slender wrists and hands, which had turned into two cast-iron clamps at the moment.

"Don't . . . hurt . . . her," Sasha squeaked, face flushed deep red.

"Let her go, Rowan, or I *will* hurt you!" Trey yelled.

Rowan laughed and swung unholy eyes at him that burned bright as the setting sun. "You can't stop me."

"Oh, but *I* can, witch," Lucien said from behind her. "That is, if you aren't afraid of me . . . *witch*."

Rowan released Sasha and knocked Trey aside when she spun in midair. She rose another two feet higher, her dress fluttering as she locked in Lucien as her next target.

Trey grabbed Sasha up and wrapped her trembling body within his arms.

"Do you dare to taunt me?" she asked in a voice that sounded as dangerous as it did insane. Trey hoped Rowan would calm down and regain her sanity before he was forced to use his powers on her. Sasha might never forgive him for that.

5

A witch?" Lucien laughed. "You don't scare me."

Trey cursed Lucien's arrogance and stupidity. On the other hand, Rowan's strength had been amazing. Maybe she'd teach the new guy a lesson.

"Come on, witch," Lucien prodded. "What have you got?"

Rowan howled and lunged at Lucien whose face turned fierce. He shot a hand up as if to stop her with the simple gesture.

"Don't hurt her!" Sasha yelled at him, but Lucien's full attention was on Rowan who slammed to a halt as soon as her abdomen came into contact with his open palm. He held her suspended above his shoulders at arm's length, his unbending gaze slammed against her crazy one.

Energy charged through the room, slapping walls. The air whipped around Lucien. His lips moved with silent words.

Rowan's hands flew to her head. Her body quaked, rocking against Lucien's hold. She cried out, "Help me, help me, help me, please. It hurts."

Mouth in a hard line, Lucien seemed to debate something

then scowled. He raised his other hand and grasped her shoulder. At the contact, his body jerked and his jaw muscles flexed, lips curled back over clenched teeth. Sparks rippled across the top of Rowan, pooling at her abdomen, then wicking down Lucien's arms and along his body. The energy spun, engulfing him in a bright glow.

Trey couldn't believe Lucien was drawing whatever was inside Rowan into his body. What the hell *was* Lucien? Trey prepared for whatever might happen once Lucien released her.

The muscles covering Lucien's body pumped once, thickening his size to double before he murmured something strange and eased back into his normal shape. When everything stilled, Rowan went limp. Lucien caught her to his chest as she fell from her levitated position; then he lifted her into his arms.

"Rowan!" Sasha pulled against Trey, but he held her back.

Lucien was breathing hard. His gaze zeroed in on Trey. "Don't worry. I'm not going to attack anyone here."

"What did you just do?" Trey asked.

Shifting Rowan's rag doll body in his arms, Lucien said, "I purged the force holding her . . . temporarily. She's not mad, but someone has control over her when her guard is down. I'm thinking her mind's being poisoned while she's asleep since Sasha told us Rowan is tired and sleeps a lot. That's probably when the possession is woven into her subconscious. My bet is Ekkbar caused the insanity to use his ability to cure her as a trade for opening the portal. Why else would he be so sure he could cure her?"

"Good point. Shouldn't we wake her?" Trey asked.

"No. She needs rest to fight the madness. If she weren't so strong, she'd have killed someone by now." Lucien turned his attention to Sasha. "Where should I take her?"

"I'll show you." Sasha tugged away from Trey. "I'm okay, really."

At the top of the stairs, Sasha led Lucien to Rowan's room above hers, but her sister preferred lavender and cinnamon red to Sasha's Goth colors.

Sasha remained at the door as Lucien laid Rowan on the velour bed cover. Rowan roused, grasping his arms as he lifted up. When her fingers tightened on him, Sasha held her breath.

"You know what happened to me, don't you?" Rowan whispered in an exhausted breath.

"Yes."

"How did you make it stop?"

"I pulled the negative energy away from you."

"But you don't like witches. In fact, I felt an intense hatred—"

"I keep personal opinions to myself when I'm on a job."

He *hated* witches? Sasha took a step forward, ready to put him in his place even if he *had* just saved Rowan.

Rowan stared up at him with that same curious look she'd had earlier, pausing Sasha in mid-step when she said, "Well, this witch considers you a friend and welcomes you back into her home anytime you wish to visit or need a place to stay. Thank you." She offered him a weak smile.

"Rest for a while" was all he said in reply.

The man was sexy as hell, but scary too. Sasha debated what she should do when he remained caught in place. He didn't move until Rowan's eyes drifted close, then he gently pried her fingers from his arms and placed her hands alongside her body.

Had Sasha not been watching for any hint of threat from him she might have missed when he brushed a wisp of hair from Rowan's face in an almost intimate gesture.

He may not like witches in general, but Lucien didn't seem

to be a threat to Rowan so Sasha breathed a sigh of relief and backed away into the hall. When he stepped through the doorway and passed her in a fast stride, she fell into step behind him. A million questions bounced through her thoughts. None she was foolish enough to ask a man who had dealt with Rowan's madness so easily *and* wasn't fond of witches.

At the bottom of the stairs, Trey stood with his jacket on, clearly waiting on her to return. "I'm heading out," he announced. "I'll be back in a few hours."

"I'll go with you." Sasha raced past Lucien to Trey.

Lucien strolled past them, exiting through the front door and closing it behind him.

Trey kissed her forehead. "Stay with your sister until I return. You're the only reason I'd risk a battle. I hope to find him and come up with another way to solve this." When she nodded, he stepped through the front door.

"I have to trust you to protect Sasha and Rowan," Trey told Lucien, who stood at the edge of the porch, his face turned up to overcast skies.

"I don't harm defenseless women." Lucien swung around, arms crossed. "Not even witches."

Time to go while Trey had optimum use of his power. At midnight he'd begin to weaken until the point of total vulnerability at the first rays of daylight tomorrow morning. His powers would fade in and out like a bad radio signal.

"Rowan isn't entirely defenseless while she's possessed," Trey pointed out, just so they were clear.

Lucien shrugged. "I'm not worried."

That still hadn't been a straight answer so Trey told Lucien, "Just know that I won't let a breath pass without coming after you if anything happens to either of those women."

"Sooner you go, sooner you'll be back," Lucien quipped.

Trey sighed with the weight of responsibility balanced on his shoulders, but he'd been taught that his fate was set the day he drew his first breath and had little control. He had to repay past sins committed by others. The end of the civil war between Beladors and the Kujoo had come on this same night eight hundred years ago. Their goddess Macha had cut a deal with the Hindu god Shiva to end the blood shed by her wiping out male Beladors and only allowing future generations to thrive if they upheld an oath of honor. Shiva in turn sent the Kujoo to live beneath Mount Meru because they had spit in his face by swearing allegiance to Ravana, a demon god Shiva believed he'd killed.

Now Trey faced breaking the truce.

"I'll be back by midnight if I don't find him," Trey said, then strode to his Bronco where he traded his glasses for a set of goggles with the same unbreakable lenses. He climbed in and drove away, ready for the confrontation.

The sun had dropped out of sight hours before by the time Trey returned to the house having found no Vyan, no nightstalkers, and no other supernatural entity.

Something was definitely going down tonight.

When Trey stepped back on Sasha's porch, Lucien pushed the front door open. "Any luck?"

"No."

"Why do I get the feeling midnight means something significant to you?"

"It does, but I don't want to discuss it." Thunder pounded the heavens. Cool air filled with a dangerous scent washed across Trey's skin in advance of the storm building. "I won't be here long," he told Lucien, then walked away to find Sasha curled up on the sofa staring at the blaze in the fireplace. The warm room smelled cozy and inviting after racing through the cold downtown streets.

Trey wanted to stay, but time wouldn't let him.

Sasha jumped up when she saw him and dashed into his open arms, hugging him close. "What happened?"

"Nothing. I haven't found him yet." He hoped that came out as encouraging rather than the bad news it was.

She turned her face up to his for the kiss he needed, too. Trey broke the kiss and touched his forehead to hers, willing to do whatever it took to keep her safe from harm. Even take on the gods who might interpret his actions as starting a war.

"I've got to go back out . . . for a while."

Lightning crackled outside and flashed against the windows. A boom followed close behind.

"I've waited a long time for you to come back." She sounded angry, but he knew it was her way to hide her fear.

"I'm going to do everything within my power to come back tonight," he whispered. "No matter what, please forgive me."

A tear snaked along her cheek. She swatted it away. "I already did. I love you."

He opened his mouth to tell her he loved her, too, but thunder echoed through the still air, making him rethink his words. How could he say he loved her then never return?

"There's been no other woman to equal you," he finally said, his voice rough from the knot in his throat. "Stay here and be safe until . . . this is over." His watch beeped. Midnight.

Trey kissed her for all the yesterdays they missed out on and all the lost tomorrows. He deepened the embrace, silently giving his heart to her. An easy gift since she'd owned it from the day they'd first met.

He set her away from him, wishing things had worked out differently, but his destiny was set a long time ago. Turning, he took a step on the longest journey he'd ever faced, one that would likely lead to his death. He stopped to speak with Lucien.

"If I *don't* make it back, take Sasha and Rowan to a VIPER safe house." Trey cringed inside at the thought of his free-spirited Sasha locked away in an underground vault, but she'd be safe until the war ended if he failed tonight.

Lucien gave a terse nod of agreement.

"I'll contact you telepathically . . . if I can't come back." An aching tremor shook through Trey's body, reminding him it was time to go. He strode to his Bronco. When he reached the door, *I'm waiting, Belador,* whispered past his ear.

Where? Trey asked and stuck the key in the ignition.

Your ride will bring you to me.

The truck engine cranked without Trey touching the key. The gearshift moved into place and the Bronco accelerated.

"Why won't you wake up, Rowan?" Sasha sat on the edge of the bed, holding her sister's hand. She could not lose Trey or Rowan when both had just come back into her life.

Lucien strode into the room and placed the palm of his hand over Rowan's forehead. "Something holds her unconscious."

"What can I do?"

"Nothing. In fact, it's probably best that you stay away until we see what state she'll be in when she awakes."

"I'm not leaving her alone." Sasha crossed her arms.

"Go downstairs and rest. I'll stay with her."

Sasha tapped her foot, debating the merits of leaving her sister in the care of a man who Rowan believed hated witches.

"*I* never said I hated witches," he said with a sexy smile.

"You never said you didn't."

"Point taken, but your sister is safe with me."

His gentle assurance swayed Sasha's decision to relinquish guard over her sister. "Please call me if she needs me."

Downstairs, Sasha paced the house from one end to the other. She stalked off to her bedroom where she dropped to the bed and laid back. Sleep would be impossible tonight, but she'd conserve her strength in case her powers were needed.

Sasha.

She scanned the room. Was that Trey? He sounded far away.

Sasha, I need to tell you something.

She sat up quickly and glanced around. Was he reaching her telepathically? If so, shouldn't she hear it *inside* her head and not whispering through the room? "Trey, is that you?"

Yes. I'm hurt. I just wanted to say good-bye before I die.

Her heart jumped in her chest. She didn't waste another second debating telepathic properties and ran to her closet to change into nylon pants and a sweatshirt. She yanked her hair into a ponytail and donned boots then paused. Could she trust Rowan to a man Trey clearly did not trust? But Rowan did trust Lucien and Sasha put a lot of stock in her sister's intuitive ability. She prayed she was making the right decision then realized she didn't know where she was going.

"Trey, where are you?" she whispered.

Lying on the steps where we first encountered Vyan.

Piedmont Park. Her throat constricted at the image of Trey dying. She cloaked herself and slipped from the house, then let her Subaru roll down to the street before cranking the engine.

When she reached Piedmont Park fat raindrops pelted the windshield, but she couldn't waste a minute hunting an umbrella.

Sasha raced against sheets of water, sloshing through puddles in the park. She crossed the footbridge over the lake and wrenched to a stop when invisible hands grabbed her arms, lifting her a couple inches off the ground. She began to float forward until she saw Trey facing the Hindu warrior. She opened her mouth to shout but the words vanished from her mind.

Where was that Kujoo warrior hiding? The park was empty. Weariness bled through Trey's soaked body. His muscles ached with the astronomical pull that ruled a Belador's life from controlling a warrior's powers to when the females were fertile.

"I'm waiting for you, Belador."

Trey swiveled around to find Vyan standing at the top of the steps, his long jacket billowing in the wind. A sword the length of Trey's arm hung at Vyan's side.

"Too much blood has been shed in the past by both of our ancestors," Trey started, wishing he had a better argument. "Beladors today are repaying the debt in this lifetime. I have no other way to make up for the sins my ancestors committed."

"Oh, but you do. You have the witch."

"Sasha had nothing to do with the wars between our people."

"A witch is the key to freeing my people." Vyan reached into his pocket and produced the stone. The rock glowed and lightning bolts spiked around them. "Words will not end this conflict. Only one of us will leave victoriously from here."

"Then fight me like a true warrior." Trey opened his arms wide. "I've brought no weapons. Have you no honor?"

Vyan scowled and moved as fast as a flash of light to stand ten feet from Trey. "Do not question my honor. Unlike *your* people, I never raped and murdered innocent women and children."

"Neither have I. Leave Sasha out of this and I'll give you what you want."

"She will not go with you, Belador." Vyan turned to his left. "Is that not true, witch?"

Trey twisted to his right. Sasha moved toward where they stood, her boots not touching the ground. Her eyes were unfocused as if she didn't recognize him. Water ran down her pasty complexion and plastered her hair to her shoulders and face. Her soaked sweatshirt clung to her trembling body.

No. "Stay back, Sasha."

"Yes," she answered like a zombie before dropping down to stand on the grass. "I will stay with Vyan."

Trey cut his eyes at the Hindu warrior who was obviously using the stone to control her, *and* going to die painfully if he didn't let her go. He had to get that damn rock.

Vyan turned back to Trey. "You see? I may take her as my own unless Batuk chooses her as his new queen. A witch might better survive the demands of a mighty warrior than the women he's had in the past."

Trey's heartbeat pounded into high gear. Not a smart move when it would only deplete his strength faster, but his control slipped farther away with every poisoned word from Vyan's lips. Trey struggled to hold back in order to prevent a war.

"Watch, Belador. She wants me," Vyan taunted then turned to Sasha who was still twenty feet away. He lifted the rock from his pocket. She began walking toward the Hindu, who raised his sword, pointing it at Sasha's abdomen. "Better yet, watch as she walks into the sword and dies without me striking her. Then I will take her sister, the stronger witch who Ekkbar controls."

When Sasha continued to move toward the sword, Trey lost the ability to think rationally. He lunged at Vyan who shoved the rock into his pocket and blocked Trey with a swing of his thick forearm. Trey stumbled, caught his balance, and shook his head, relieved to see her stop walking. He'd never wanted Sasha to see him in combat, because of what he turned into. But she wasn't cognizant of anything at the moment and his powers were dwindling with each tick of the clock.

Vyan sprinted forward. When Trey would have hit him with a full body slam, the Hindu flipped up in the air, legs churning as he spun over Trey who swung to see the fighter land surefooted. Cramps hit Trey in his midsection. He gritted his teeth against the pain and roared, calling forth his warrior form.

Bones cracked, lengthening. Muscles flexed and pumped, growing his thick body even larger. His hands curved, fingers expanding into thick digits as hard as tempered steel, the sharp tips flashing with electricity.

Vyan shouted in his native tongue. Lightning struck around them, bursting craters the size of a sink in the ground. He tossed off his jacket and wielded his sword. Sparks crackled along the razor edge. He came at Trey, who spun, deflecting the sword. But the Hindu was quick and strong. He swung the weapon with blinding speed.

Trey charged forward. Vyan sliced the air with the sword, turning it flat as he brought the blade shoulder high . . . to take off a man's head. Shoving a hand up, Trey caught the brunt of the attack with his steel fingers. The blade skipped off and sliced him across the chest.

The cut was not deep enough to damage muscle, but his increased heart rate pumped blood furiously through the wound.

"Noooo!" He turned at Sasha's scream. Her eyes were clear and terrified. She struggled to move her legs as if her feet had been anchored to the ground.

"Get out of here, Sasha!"

"She can't."

Trey wheeled back around to the grinning warrior and lost any compassion he might have felt at one time for this man's losses.

"Aid him and I will make his death very slow and painful," Vyan warned her then turned to Trey. "And if you make a move toward her, she goes up in flames."

Thunder vibrated the ground beneath Trey's boots. Pain stabbed his thighs and neck. He was running out of time. Trey fisted his hands, the tips digging into his palms. He stretched his neck and rocked his shoulders back and forth, pumping his forearms. A guttural noise clawed up the inside of his chest and burst out, firing the air around him into a hot blast.

Vyan came at him, slicing that wicked blade with deft efficiency. He turned the blade sideways at the last minute and slammed Trey in the head, knocking him ten feet in the air, bouncing his head on the concrete. The goggles flew from his eyes, yanked away by an unseen force. He rolled face-first into a puddle of water. Mud splattered his eyes. Muscles kinked in his arms. His body began shrinking back to his normal size.

Death crooned to him, offering a quick end to the pain racking his muscles. His chest burned from the gash. Every breath became harder to draw.

Sasha screamed, "*Don't you dare die!*"

Trey shook his head and opened his eyes to the rain that washed his vision clear. He shoved himself up to his knees, wet hair slapping his face when he lifted his eyes to the Hindu warrior.

"Rise, Belador. I will not kill a man on his knees."

Trey clenched his teeth to contain the scream of pain that shot up his legs as he struggled to his feet. His gaze wavered to where Sasha stood with arms wrapped around her middle, shivering, her beautiful face contorted in agony, crying. He could not fail her.

He took a rasping breath and turned toward Vyan, drawing on what minimal power he had left to attack. But when he stepped forward, his legs almost buckled.

Vyan reacted swiftly, lifting the sword high in an arc intended to strike Trey in the center of his head and split his upper body in half.

The sword began the long descent with Trey powerless to stop the inevitable. Inches from his skull, Vyan went flying backward, landing against a tree and hitting the ground.

Trey stared in shock. What the hell had happened?

Then he felt the presence of another supernatural, more than one. Out of the black sheets of rain slashing through the park, three images took shape. Two men and a female.

The men were Beladors he'd fought beside before—Tzader Burke and Quinn Vladimir. The woman stood an easy six feet tall . . . and was an Alterant, a mix of Belador and some other species.

"What are you three doing here?" he croaked out.

"Helping you," Quinn replied, smoothing the water off the top of his blond hair slicked back into a ponytail. Decked out in a sleek black and silver tuxedo, his lean form belonged on a runway somewhere. But the international stock trader had probably come to the park from some shindig in downtown Atlanta. The spectacles covering his eyes had undoubtedly been crafted somewhere like Switzerland, one of a kind.

"Not tonight, Quinn." Trey gasped for air with each breath, his mind foggy. He wanted to go to Sasha, who stood wide-eyed and unharmed so far, but he wouldn't take the risk of her being burned alive. He shot a look at where the warrior had been tossed. Vyan didn't move, which meant nothing. The guy was probably playing possum to assess the new arrivals.

Trey frowned at the trio. "Don't tell me you forgot what tonight is, Tzader."

"Not likely." Tzader couldn't be more different from Quinn if he tried, with his black hair curling and thick on top, buzz cut on the sides. His coffee-brown skin glistened with energy and menace. Twelve-inch knives clipped to each hip would gut anything, living or otherwise. Close inspection of the serrated edges revealed fanged teeth. Not as tall as Trey or Quinn, Tzader's sleeveless shirt stretched to contain a body wrapped in two hundred and twenty-five pounds of badass muscle.

"I'm Evalle Kincaid," the brunette Amazon purred as "ee-val." "Unlike the three of you purebreds, my energy is not bleeding out right now. And unlike you, Trey, these two have conserved their powers and energy since midnight. So we need to get busy before your buddy over there regains consciousness." Her designer glasses rested against a pert nose and high cheeks. Her vision must be extremely sensitive for her to shield her eyes behind dark shades at night in a storm.

"No!" Trey argued and paid for the effort with a dagger of pain to his lung. Were they demented? "This isn't a sanctioned battle and I'm not risking all of your lives." Linking with Beladors increased their powers exponentially, but if one died in battle while linked, they all did.

"We all took an oath," Quinn interjected. "What kind of honor would we have if we didn't back you up? And Evalle is right. We need to get to it."

"You can't do this. The penalty will be high." He could only hope Macha would penalize him alone and spare the tribe.

"You don't have a say," Evalle said in a tone that indicated she was bored with the conversation. "When Brina says it's on, it's on. Like I said, the sooner the . . ." She angled her head toward the tree where Vyan had landed and muttered, "Too late, he's rousing. Let's link now."

Brina sent them? Trey couldn't believe it.

Why not, Trey? Brina sounded peeved.

I thought you wouldn't back this battle.

I told you, I protect my tribe. Even hardheaded warriors like you. I'll worry about Macha as soon as you kick this fool's butt back to that giant rock he climbed out from under.

The trio spread out, and Trey began to feel their energy flood his feeble body. He drew one breath, then another, standing taller with each infusion from the linking.

Vyan strolled toward him as if he were unconcerned about the new developments. He pointed a finger at his jacket on the ground and it flew to him. When he had the coat on, he lifted the stone from his coat pocket.

Trey cursed at not thinking to grab the stone.

"You would not have held the stone long, for it chooses its master," Vyan said, obviously snagging Trey's thoughts. He lifted the multicolored rock and murmured foreign words. "Your combined power will not match mine, Beladors." He spit out the last word as if the tribe's name seared his tongue.

The trio moved in, but Trey held up his hand. "I'll fight him alone."

"Let's help your odds," Evalle suggested. All the lights in the park and surrounding areas went out. Trey blinked, not believing his sharp vision.

You have my vision, Evalle said in Trey's mind. *The Kujoo can see too, but not with the high-definition optics you now have.*

Thanks, Trey sent back, then closed his mind to everything but confronting Vyan.

Vyan came at him, his blade sizzling with electricity along the edge. Trey dodged the first strike, spinning away and searching for a weapon. The thought had barely escaped his mind when he held Tzader's two knives.

The blades actually snarled, fangs extended, when Trey lifted them to brace against Vyan's next strike. The warrior fought with one hand wielding his sword and the other holding the stone that radiated spears of multicolored lights. Bolts of lightning sliced the air around them. Trey blocked charge after charge from Vyan with the knives until he saw a chance to knock the stone loose.

Trey threw one knife, aiming for Vyan's wrist, which supported the stone. The knife bounced away before it reached him. Vyan smiled and pointed the stone at Trey's other hand. His second knife flew out of his palm.

Tzader whistled and both weapons returned to his side.

"Take mine," came an order from behind Trey. He turned to find Lucien who produced a sword from thin air and sent it spinning end over end. Trey caught the weapon; that felt too light to be any good. He glanced at Lucien, who stood next to Sasha. Rowan was beside him wearing a yellow slicker, not looking anything like a witch.

Lucien crossed his arms, grinning. "You two go ahead. I just came to watch."

Which goddess of fate had it in for Trey to stick him with Lucien and his twisted sense of humor? And Rowan who could go airborne and out of control at any minute?

"Bring in a legion of warriors, Belador," Vyan said, waving the stone. "Nothing can stop me with this. When I am done with this one," he called out, pointing at Trey, "I will call forth Ravana who will dispense with the rest of you next."

"Bring it on," Tzader shot back.

Sasha couldn't believe what she was witnessing. She swiped a clump of wet hair from her face and turned to Rowan. "Can you do anything to help Trey?"

Rowan shook her head, water flicking from the hood of her slicker. "I could make it worse."

Sasha didn't think that was possible. Her heart raced at every move Trey and Vyan made. She had to help Trey somehow. Vyan had warned her not to, but how could he know who sent Trey help with this group present? And where had all these beings come from?

Metal clanged as Vyan attacked and Trey battled back. Trey fought with both hands on his sword, but Vyan didn't even seem winded . . . because of that stone, Sasha realized. He could be beat without the rock. She felt sure of it.

Trey battled Vyan to the edge of the pond that ran beneath the footbridge in the south end of the park. Vyan stumbled once, but bounced up on the balls of his feet as if he just hadn't been paying attention. Trey and Vyan's strikes echoed through the air until Trey missed his step and Vyan's blade sliced so close to his neck Sasha felt light-headed with fear.

Trey roared and shoved up, swinging that sword like a major leaguer with an aluminum baseball bat, driving Vyan backward to the pond.

Sasha saw her chance and began to chant, "Earth, wind, and rain, hear me well. . . ."

Vyan's coat lengthened, dragging the ground as he backed toward a quickly forming mud hole. He stepped on the tail of the coat, arms flailing to keep his balance, but his momentum threw him backward. The stone flew from his hand to the pond, boiling the water as it sank. Within seconds the glow from beneath the surface extinguished.

Five bolts of lightning struck the ground between her and Trey, exploding dirt from the hole it created. Howling preceded a wispy form that rose from the earth and hovered until the smoke cleared, leaving a dark man with Middle Eastern facial structure similar to Vyan's. But this male's eyes were a molten gold with red irises. He bared pointed teeth that dripped blood from the tips. His short hair started growing into lengths that thickened and took the form of serpents, hissing and striking the air around his head.

"Ravana, I have lost the stone," Vyan cried out, scrambling to his feet.

"Do not despair." Ravana pointed his hands at empty spots, and everywhere he directed, a mangle of arms, legs, and battered heads took shape as creatures Sasha had never seen. "They come from Fene and fear nothing since they live in hell's armpit."

Twenty creatures shrieked to life, their heads scabbed and rotting, their skin as dark as roasted meat. Sasha tried not to breathe in the wave of noxious stench clogging the air. Rags hung from the creatures' bodies, but that's where the disparity stopped. Muscles wrapped their torsos and limbs with sinewy tissue that gleamed like bands of woven metals. They crouched, pawing the ground as if waiting to be released.

A beautiful auburn-haired woman appeared next as a hologram with eyes so green they'd compete with an emerald struck by the sun. Her translucent skin was covered with a mint-green robe that sparkled when she moved, but she never completely took shape.

"Hi, Brina," Evalle said to the hologram, then muttered, "It's definitely on, now." The gleam in her smile that curved below the dark shades on the Amazon raised the hair on Sasha's arms, which was saying something at this point tonight. She wouldn't want to face this woman in a dark alley. The tall female stomped her boots and silver razor-sharp tips shot from around the soles. She shook her hands once, the water slinging away, and sharp points erupted from the smooth skin of her palm. Spiked cartilage raised along the back of her hands and up her arms to her shoulders.

"Beladors, unite and defend," Brina shouted in a voice so strong Sasha wondered if the woman was truly just an image.

"'Bout time." Tzader spun the knives in his hands as fast as a fan blade on high.

"I should say so," Quinn drawled, clearly tired of inactivity. He reached both hands inside his jacket and withdrew four triangular discs with daggers at each corner and a woven Celtic design in the center.

Sasha's ears were burning. What witch besides Rowan was present? This burning was hotter than anything she'd experienced before. She glanced at Rowan who rubbed her ear and searched the crowd with narrowed eyes.

"Destroy the Beladors, demons." Ravana waved his hands, which must have been the sign to attack.

"Why aren't you helping Trey?" Sasha demanded of Lucien.

"I gave him a sword." Lucien shrugged.

Sasha dismissed him and her burning ear. At this point, what did it matter if another witch was present?

The shrieking demons leaped into action. Tzader dove headfirst into the fray, taking out two with knives he wielded with blinding speed. Sasha never saw the cuts, but arms and heads rolled away, turning her stomach.

Trey and Vyan were back at it, but now it was a fair fight with no help from that blasted stone. Shouts, screams, and unearthly howls carpeted the air. Bodies hitting the ground and each other, splashing blood-soaked mud everywhere. The stench of death permeated each suffocating breath Sasha drew. Her ears felt as though they were on fire.

Her gaze tracked to Trey just as he turned to cover Evalle's back while she fought hand to hand against three demons, slashing off one's head with a kick of her boot. Vyan swung his blade in a wide arc toward Trey's head.

Sasha screamed at the top of her lungs for Trey to watch out. He spun toward her, Vyan's blade barely missing him.

"Behind you!" Sasha yelled.

Trey whirled around fast and knocked Vyan to the ground, pinning Vyan with the sword at his throat.

Ravana bellowed, "Kill him and you will face me, Belador! Demons, cease!"

All fighting slowed. The trio of Belador fighters backed up to one another, weapons ready to continue. The creatures slobbered blood, dropping down to all fours and pawing the ground again.

"You any better a warrior than him, Ravana?" Trey chided.

Ravana took a step forward.

"E-nough!" The booming voice that rocked the park bounced from earth to the heavens and back. A man stepped from thin air and Sasha's jaw dropped at the striking vision. Men shouldn't be beautiful. Shimmering mahogany hair hung to his shoulders. He brushed his hand over his head in an impatient gesture and his hair flew back into a ponytail, a leather tie holding it in place. Smooth olive-toned skin covered his cut body and the sharp-angled face. The scar slashing his forehead only added to his mystique. Mediterranean-blue eyes were Asian shaped. He had to stand close to six-foot-six and strode into the midst of the war zone as though he owned this planet.

"Hey, Sen. How's it hangin'?" Tzader called to the new arrival.

Sen glowered at him then swept his gaze over the battlefield. "You are *all* at fault for warring among civilians." His glare dared anyone to challenge him. He wore a leather vest, chain belt with skull engravings, and snug jeans that suggested he was hanging just fine to answer Tzader's lewd question. He shoved both hands to the heavens, flexing those rockin' biceps, his face hard and his voice terse when he spoke, yet undecipherable. The rainstorm continued, but the water fell away from where they congregated. He'd thrown an invisible canopy over them.

"Anyone so much as twitches a muscle and I'll dust you," Sen warned and sharpened his gaze at the grumbling demons. "You think Fene is bad? Just piss me off any more than I am now."

"The Beladors broke the truce," Ravana charged.

Sasha leaned forward, ready to take on that lying bastard, but Lucien moved an arm to bar, his eyes locked on the field.

"Kill me now, for I have nothing left to live for," Vyan ordered Trey. "I failed my people and deserve to die."

Trey stared down into the tortured eyes of a man who had lost his woman and his family. "No. There's been enough bloodshed." He turned to the man who had just arrived. "Good to see you, Sen, but this is not a VIPER issue, yet."

"It is when a war breaks out in this world," Sen answered.

"The Beladors broke the truce," Ravana yelled again.

"The Kujoo lured the Beladors into a battle and tricked them," Brina shouted back from her hologram state.

"You will solve this now or I'll call for a tribunal," Sen ordered, clearly in no mood to hear anyone's gripes.

Trey sighed. That would really turn this into a FUBAR situation. If the Celtic and Hindu entities that ruled the Beladors and Kujoo respectively did not resolve this issue, a tribunal made up of three entities unrelated to the problem would be called upon for a decision. That was the only way all these powerful gods and goddesses had managed not to destroy one another or the planet over the past millenniums.

"Call forth your rulers," Sen ordered.

Brina opened her arms and bowed her head. "Goddess Macha, please grace us with your presence."

A swoosh noise drew everyone's gaze up to where a giant swan glided down from the heavens to land gently at the site. Red hair flowed in waves to the waist of the elegant woman sitting upon the bird's back. Her iridescent gown glowed, illuminating the canopied area when she descended from the kneeling swan.

The Celtic goddess Macha had arrived.

All eyes turned to Ravana, who did nothing.

"Call your ruler, Ravana," Sen said in a tone not to be mistaken as a mere suggestion.

"No. You have no say over me or the Kujoo people," Ravana scoffed. "If you want to end this, punish the Beladors by sending them to live beneath Mount Meru and I will ensure that my people uphold the truce from now on."

Trey shook his head. Ravana obviously didn't know Sen.

Sen snarled and morphed into another form, one ten feet tall with a curved neck and bony face that popped further out of shape when he bared a mouth full of sharp teeth. Hair covered his shoulders and the back of his hands that turned into claws, but the lower half of his body remained human.

Trey had heard of his beast-state, but never witnessed it. He glanced at Sasha. The admiring gaze she'd cast at Sen earlier was gone. She shrank back in horror.

Evalle, on the other hand, smiled and said, "Cool."

And that's exactly why men will never understand women.

"Shiva, please bless us with your presence," Macha called out in a melodic voice.

Ravana stared in horror as a low rumble rolled across the earth and the ground trembled. Light speared through the canopy from different angles, the origins far out in the universe. When all the points met in one spot, a slender man in a white silk tunic, flowing pants, and bronze sandals appeared. Gleaming black hair fell neatly to his neck. His eyes were small like black beans, but filled with a thousand years of understanding and no apparent malice.

"Hello, Shiva," Macha greeted him, bowing her head. "It's good to see you again."

Sen relaxed, his body returning to the one Trey had heard women idolized.

"Hello, Macha," Shiva said. "I wish our meeting was under different circumstances. A break in the truce saddens me."

"I agree, but what are we to do?"

Shiva turned to Ravana. "I thought *you* died many years ago? How is it you are here now?"

"The Beladors broke the truce," Ravana repeated, his voice pitching high. "I rule the Kujoo and demand justice."

"You avoid my question, which perplexes me. I would know if a god such as yourself still lived," Shiva pointed out.

"A god? Wait a minute," Sasha called out.

Trey groaned. He couldn't walk away from Vyan, because the bastard might attack. The members of his tribe were still linked with him and would die if he made a mistake.

"Sasha, please don't interfere," Trey warned quickly before Macha took offense and vaporized her.

"But he's *not* a god. Trey, my ears were burning. I just realized he has to be a witch, a powerful one."

A collective gasp sucked through the group. Trey raced to think of what to say. Sasha had insulted an entity.

"Goddess, do you think—" Brina started, only to be silenced by a lift of Macha's hand.

"All entities, show your true form now," Macha called out, an order no entity could deny.

Ravana shrieked, "Nooo, nooo, noooooo," then wavered and bent double. His clothes spun in a fiery blur of red. When he stood upright again, he was no longer Ravana, but a woman who would be gorgeous if not for the sinister shape of her eyes.

"I should have known this was your dirty work, Moran," Macha said, her voiced no longer sweet. "How could you do this to your own people?"

Moran lifted off the ground, sneering at Macha. "Your tribe still broke the truce. What say ye to that?"

"I would ask that Shiva pass judgment with compassion for a tribe that has upheld the peace for eight hundred years and will continue to do so," Macha answered, her attention on the Hindu god.

Shiva tilted his head, a thoughtful expression on his calm face. "Your warrior spared a Kujoo life when he could have taken it. I am inclined to allow the truce to continue."

"The Beladors must be sanctioned," the witch Moran ordered.

Shiva and Macha stared at each other; a silent communication flowed between them until Shiva nodded and turned to Moran. "No, the Beladors will not be sanctioned, but *you* will be for impersonating another entity."

"You wouldn't dare." Moran lifted higher away.

"Oh yes," Macha answered. "We'll call the tribunal if need be. Our only dilemma is just what you deserve."

The crater unearthed by the lightning bolts yawned open

and vapor escaped, arching high over their heads and settling in the center of the area.

"I should choose," the vapor whispered in an eerie voice.

"So you did die, Ravana," Shiva said, identifying the vapor.

"Yes, I demand the witch as my slave in Fene for one year."

Moran gasped. "You cannot—"

"I accept that decision," Macha interjected.

"As do I," Shiva agreed.

Moran spun around, but her hair yanked toward the vapor. She screamed in pain, clawing to break free, begging for mercy. The vapor grew, drawing her closer until she was wrapped in a swirling cloud of red smoke. In the blink of an eye the entire mass was snatched back into the crater.

Shiva turned to the demons remaining and said, "Go. Now."

The demons scrambled to the hole and disappeared one by one. As soon as the last one vanished, the crater filled with earth, returning to its original state.

"What about him?" Trey asked, indicating Vyan.

"He has suffered enough and came to save his people," Shiva replied. "I will not release the others from Mount Meru, but he may remain if he swears not to attack you again."

Trey backed away and allowed Vyan to stand. What would this warrior do now in a world where he's an outcast and unfamiliar? There was one place Vyan could thrive if he would truly keep the peace. And in spite of all that had transpired, Trey knew he would be just as tortured if Sasha were killed.

When Vyan retrieved his sword and slid it into the sheath at his side, Trey said, "I understand the depth of your pain and feel for your loss, but as I told you to begin with, I'm part of a Belador tribe that is sworn to protect the innocent, not ravage them. If you can put aside your hate, I might be able to get you into a group called VIPER where your abilities would be welcomed. A place where you could belong."

Vyan's hard gaze shifted to one of defeat and exhaustion. "I want nothing to do with you, Belador. I will not attack you, but neither am I ready to join you, either."

Trey nodded, understanding Vyan's reluctance. "When you change your mind, find a nightstalker and tell them you're looking for VIPER and me. Someone will find you and bring you to me." That was the best he could do for Vyan at the moment.

Vyan stepped toward the pond and Trey tensed. The warrior was going for the stone.

"No, Vyan," Shiva said, stopping the warrior. "Now that the Ngak stone has been released from the hold of Mount Meru, it will choose its next master. It has already done so."

Vyan nodded then faced Trey. "Do not place great value on seeing me again, Belador." He turned to Sen. "Release me from this invisible tent. I wish to breathe untainted air."

Sen arched an annoyed eyebrow at the warrior then turned to Shiva and Macha. "I will rescript the minds of all civilians in this area to remember nothing more than a bad thunderstorm and return the park to its original state before leaving if you require nothing further of me."

Shiva and Macha nodded their assent.

The canopy cleared, as did the heavens. Clouds drifted lazily past a full moon. The park lights blinked on. Trey held himself in check when he wanted to go to Sasha and comfort his little kick-butt warrior. She'd saved everyone by exposing the Celtic witch Moran. But first he had to try to fix one more thing.

He approached Macha. "I wish to ask you something."

"You should be on your knees thanking me, Belador, not asking for more," Macha snapped at him. "You're fortunate not to have unleashed a legion of Kujoo soldiers or to have condemned the Belador tribe to a future beneath Mount Meru."

"I'm sorry for the risk I placed us all under, but I did so only with the belief that my actions were honorable." He lowered his head in respect, but he needed to ask about Rowan.

"That is the only reason I am not sanctioning you. As for Rowan, I have no authority over the magician Ekkbar."

"I have removed the magician's hold on the witch," Shiva interjected.

Relieved, Trey turned to Shiva. "Thank you." Shiva nodded, then placed his palms together in prayer and vanished.

Macha returned to the swan and settled on its back. She placed her palms flat, fingertips touching, and disappeared.

"Go in peace, Beladors." Brina's hologram disintegrated.

Trey dragged a hand through his wet hair and turned to Sasha, who ran to him. He bundled her into his arms and hugged her, taking a deep breath of joy. She'd survived. His gaze swept the terrain. No Vyan. No Sen.

Lucien and the three Beladors strolled up to him. Trey pulled Sasha to his side, loathe to let her out of his reach.

"I've got to work tonight, so I'm bugging out." Evalle's toned arms were covered in soft skin again. Her boots no more threat than a swift kick to the family jewels of the wrong man.

"Thanks, Evalle," Trey said then turned to the whole group. "I couldn't have done this without all of you."

"True," Tzader agreed. "Remember that next time you step into deep sh—uh, pardon me, Sasha. Deep trouble." He grinned.

"I dare say, you're going to be a hurting pup as soon as we pull apart the link," Quinn added. "I plan to spend the rest of this evening in the lap of luxury, or the lap of a luxurious woman willing to soothe the aches I anticipate as soon as we unlink. Shall we?" Quinn said to Tzader and Evalle.

The trio walked away, dispersing into the darkness. Trey groaned with the release of the linking, his body feeling like a Mack truck had run over him—twice. But he'd begin to heal soon and could make it home unassisted.

"Vyan tricked me," Sasha said quickly. "I thought it was you calling me telepathically, saying you were dying. But now I realize that couldn't have happened."

Trey cupped her head to his chest. "Don't worry about it, baby. I'm just glad you're safe."

"Thank you, Trey," Rowan said and hugged them both before stepping away.

Trey took in Rowan's skin and eyes that were robust, healthy.

"Thanks for watching over the women," Trey told Lucien whose answer was a frown. He chuckled at the touchy guy.

"I've got things to do." Clearly bored, Lucian walked away before Trey could extend his hand to shake.

Trey wouldn't hold it against him after all that Lucien had done to help with Rowan. He'd find out what Lucien was, but not now.

Rowan ran a couple of steps to catch Lucien's arm. He stopped and glared down at her. She smiled back, saying, "My offer is always open. Come back if you ever need to or want to. You'll be welcomed as a friend."

He studied her for a brief moment, then cupped her chin and kissed her just long enough to draw an earthy sigh from Rowan.

"I'll keep that in mind, witch." Lucien turned and sauntered away.

Rowan spun around, a smile in place. "I saw Trey's truck earlier. I'll meet you two there." She walked away.

"Where does this leave us?" Sasha asked Trey, stepping in front of him with a look of challenge in her eyes and hands on her hips.

He had to tell her the truth so she would understand why they couldn't be together. And that meant all the truth.

"Sasha, you mean more to me than you'll ever know, but—"

"I understand why you don't trust what you can't hear in someone's mind." Sasha took his hand in hers. "Believe me, in your shoes I'd never trust another living soul. But you're not me and I need you to trust me. I don't know how to make telepathy work, but I believe we can make *us* work."

He wanted to, more than she could imagine. "That's not the only problem or I would just accept what you said."

"No, I couldn't live with you always wondering," Sasha rushed on. "And I know you're thinking that you'll disappoint me when you question something I say. Shoot, I'll question you sometimes, too, but that doesn't mean I don't trust you. Besides, you can hear me if you listen real close."

"How, Sasha?"

She lifted his hand and placed it over her heart. "You hear love with your heart, not your mind. I can't read your thoughts, either, but I hear your love in every word you speak, every time you touch me, every kiss we share."

Damn. He'd never considered that she couldn't read his mind, either. She was taking as big a risk as him, more so if he could take her as a mate because she didn't know what she would be signing on for if they joined as one for life.

"I love you, Sasha." The words leaped out without thought, but now that he'd said them Trey would not take them back.

"I know you do. I love you, too, so let's stop spending our life apart."

"If I take a mate," he began and cleared his throat, "my mate and any children from the union would be subject to any repercussions I'd suffer from a bad decision."

"I don't understand." Sasha scrunched her forehead.

"Basically, if I break my oath—honor above all else—and

take an action Macha considers dishonorable any mate will face the same fate she decrees for me."

"Oh, is that all?" Sasha smiled. "You're the most honorable man I know. If she sends you away it means I go, too? That seals the deal for me. I trust you completely to make the right choices, so I'm in."

Which was exactly why that condition had been attached to all Belador unions. No warrior, male or female, would risk a mate by making a careless decision.

"The final decision is not in my hands," Trey added. "Beladors normally mate with humans, not another supernatural. We carry a gene from our ancestors that could turn into an evil spawn if two Beladors mate. The woman in the hologram was Brina, the warrior queen who leads our tribe. She answers only to Macha. We'd have to get her permission and she can be—" *Difficult, irritating, impossible to find . . .*

I can also send you to live in Antarctica, Brina snapped.

Sorry, Brina.

"*She's* the leader of the Beladors?" Sasha asked. "Wow, she's so totally awesome and beautiful."

I like this girl, Brina piped up.

Brina, would you approve of Sasha as my mate? Trey asked before he couldn't find her again.

Sasha proved she is honorable and worthy of a Belador. Now you must prove you are worthy of her. I welcome her into our tribe. She'll at least assure you won't start another war. So marry her with my blessing.

Thank you, Brina, and thanks for tonight. I'm going to do my best to not disappoint you for helping me.

You'd better not disappoint me. A spot on his forehead tingled briefly—a Brina touch of affection. Then she was gone.

"Uh, Sasha, we got approval already."

"What? Did you two just talk? I'll have to think on how I feel about that."

Trey's stomach fell through the floor. "So you've changed your mind?"

"About what?"

"Marrying me."

"You haven't asked. Now that I think about it, I may make you wait for my answer as payback for nine years of misery."

He pulled her into his arms and kissed this woman who believed in him without question. Fate had thrown him a curve ball at twenty-one when he accepted his destiny. If he'd known then he would end up with Sasha, he'd have been a lot happier about it.

Trey broke the kiss. "I'm asking you tonight and you're answering me immediately."

"You think?" She grinned, full of mischief.

"I know. Give me five minutes with you in bed and you'll be willing to agree to anything."

"That would be taking advantage of me, which may fall under the heading of dishonorable."

He turned serious. "There is no dishonor in loving a woman as much as I love you."

Sasha's mirth softened and her eyes glistened. "I believe you." She lifted up on her toes and kissed him, her lips hotter than fire. When she slid her hand down to rub an erection that might never go away with her always close, Trey groaned and kinetically turned off the lights near them. Sasha obviously intended to take just as much advantage of him as he wanted her to. He willed her sweatshirt to split open down the middle and fall away, then dipped his head to prepare her for their negotiations.

Batuk's bellow shook the foundation of Mount Meru, his fury beyond all that Ekkbar had ever witnessed. Serving wenches scattered. His soldiers shuffled from the great hall.

The walls glowed fiery red. Flames spewed from crevices and loose boulders crashed against each other.

"M-master, please listen. All is not lost." Ekkbar's knees chattered against each other. When his master turned burning eyes on him, the magician shrank away.

"I will not tolerate another lie from your poisonous mouth, knave!" Batuk reared up from his throne, chest expanding convulsively with each angry breath he drew. The tips of his fingers sparked, sharpening into claws.

"I do not lie, Master," Ekkbar whispered, his throat too dry to produce a full sound. "P-please hear me out. Hear me, please." He swallowed and rubbed a hand over his head. Sweat streamed into his eyes. Batuk's rant had steamed the *nihar*, threatening to boil the underworld inhabitants.

"Give me one reason I should not spend the rest of eternity in this dung pit slicing a strip off your skinny hide daily and making you fry it for my meal."

"B-because Vyan is still in the other world. Alive."

"I care not that he has survived when the rest of us are still imprisoned."

"Vyan can—" Ekkbar swallowed again, hoping he was not about to seal his grisly fate. "He can search for another to open the portal on his side." At the tiny spark of interest in Batuk's eyes, Ekkbar rushed ahead. "'Tis true, 'tis true. I can guide him through dreams, just as I did the witch."

Batuk bared his teeth and snapped his fingers. A razor-edged dagger appeared in the palm of his hand.

Ekkbar cringed at his stupid blunder. *Don't mention the witch again,* ever. "But this time, Vyan will be on the other side to assure success. We can do this, Master."

Batuk growled low in his throat, panting. He stared off into nothing, thinking. The temperature slowly lowered until he dropped his gaze to Ekkbar. "You have one more chance."

EPILOGUE

Trey leaned against a giant oak at the side of the wide clearing, arms crossed and impatient as he waited for the strike of midnight. The two months Brina had made him wait to marry wouldn't have been a big deal if he hadn't spent half that time away from Sasha on VIPER missions.

Beladors, VIPER teammates, and the Wiccan side of his new family milled around. A full moon smiled down at its reflection in the lake surrounded by a fortress of Blue Ridge Mountains.

"I'm sorry you couldn't invite your father, Trey, but we'll have a lovely ceremony with him, too." Rowan glided toward him so smoothly he had to check to see that her sequined shoes actually touched the ground beneath the tail of her garnet gown.

"I know." It hurt not to bring his father here, but Trey lived in two worlds sometimes and keeping his father in the normal one protected the only parent who had ever really loved him. And his dad was crazy about Sasha, always had been. He spent almost as much time now with Sasha as Trey did.

"Who all came from VIPER?" Rowan asked casually, but Trey knew who she was looking for.

"I invited Lucien, too, but I never heard a word from him."

"That doesn't surprise you, does it?"

"No. Just thought I'd let you know."

She smiled. "Thanks. I think I'll see him again. I like that Sasha wanted you in all black and everyone else in red."

He smiled, willing to have worn any color Sasha wanted, so long as she spent the rest of her life with him.

"Who sent the fairies?" Rowan asked. "Sasha loves them."

"Lucien." The dog. Trey glanced at the tiny sprites fluttering around the tall wedding cake, lighting the layers with their blinking glows. "Wish I'd had a resource for them."

"Lucien?" Rowan's eyes melted with adoration.

Trey appreciated anything that made Sasha happy, just not from that guy.

The fairies began to hum, their voices rising into a hauntingly beautiful melody.

"Excuse me, that's my cue." Trey stepped into the center of the opening.

From the shadows of the woods, Sasha appeared in a sprinkle of light where fairies fluttered around her. She wore short black boots with stiletto heels and a strapless dress of sheer material draped in alternating red and black layers. Trey had gifted her with the silver-and-black Belador pendant. The triangular icon crafted with their Celtic design hung from a silver choker.

Her lips were painted a deep red, so dark they were almost black. The silky rush of black hair fanned her shoulders.

Trey hadn't thought he could love her any more than he already did, but he'd never forget her walking toward him at this minute. The attendants circled them when Sasha reached him. She held a bouquet of black roses and red baby's breath that Rowan had conjured up for her.

Trey leaned down to kiss his future mate and the love of his life. The roses in the bouquet sighed. When a hologram spun into vision, he turned his left wrist up where the shape of a star glowed beneath his skin; then he took Sasha's right wrist and pressed it to his. By the end of the ceremony, they would be linked for life.

Shooting stars exploded in the cloudless sky, showering the clearing with a dazzling light.

Trey whispered in Sasha's ear, "*Those* are from me."

Her beaming smile outshined the light display that continued as Brina began the ceremony. No telepathy reached him tonight. His tribe had refrained from doing so as a consideration for his future wife, reaffirming for him the value of listening with his heart.

He squeezed her fingers. When Sasha smiled up at him, he accepted his destiny knowing she would always be at his side.